MARYSUE
RUCCI
BOOKS

ALSO BY MEGAN MIRANDA

The Last to Vanish

Such a Quiet Place

The Girl from Widow Hills

The Last House Guest

The Perfect Stranger

All the Missing Girls

BOOKS FOR YOUNG ADULTS

Come Find Me

Fragments of the Lost

The Safest Lies

Soulprint

Vengeance

Hysteria

Fracture

THE ONLY SURVIVORS

A Novel

MEGAN MIRANDA

MARYSUE
RUCCI
BOOKS

New York London Toronto
Sydney New Delhi

Marysue Rucci Books/Scribner
An Imprint of Simon & Schuster, Inc.
1230 Avenue of the Americas
New York, NY 10020

First Marysue Rucci Books/Scribner hardcover edition April 2023

For information about special discounts for bulk purchases, please contact Simon & Schuster Special Sales at 1-866-506-1949 or business@simonandschuster.com.

The Simon & Schuster Speakers Bureau can bring authors to your live event. For more information or to book an event, contact the Simon & Schuster Speakers Bureau at 1-866-248-3049 or visit our website at www.simonspeakers.com.

Manufactured in the United States of America

1 3 5 7 9 10 8 6 4 2

Library of Congress Cataloging-in-Publication Data has been applied for.

ISBN 978-1-6680-1041-9
ISBN 978-1-6680-1043-3 (ebook)

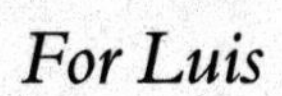
For Luis

THE ONLY SURVIVORS

PROLOGUE

There were things I had done to avoid this reunion.

I'd made a list. Made a plan. Justified it by reminding myself that these were not really my friends, and ten years was long enough.

This yearly trip wasn't helping anyone. This *promise*. We had been too young when we'd agreed to come together for the anniversary, as a way to keep one another safe. It had been a misguided impulse, an overreaction. A panicked grasp for control, when we all surely knew better by then.

I'd begun the process of disentangling myself six months earlier, in the hope of becoming invisible, unreachable. Three simple steps, seen through to the end:

I'd changed my number when I switched carriers, transferring most of my contacts, while deleting those I'd hoped to leave behind. A clean slate.

And when the group email from Amaya arrived in January, I marked it as junk, deleted it immediately. Unopened, unread, so I could claim ignorance. Though the details bolded in the subject line were already seared in my mind: *May 7th—Be there!*

Instead, I'd planned to stay at Russ's for the weekend, the final step of evasion. I needed to move forward. I was twenty-eight, with a steady job and a semi-serious boyfriend who cooked breakfast on Sundays and owned reasonably decent sheets.

But on Sunday morning, my phone chimed as I was finishing up my omelet and Russ was at the counter, back turned, refilling his coffee. There was a flash of light on the display of my cell, faceup on the table. A North Carolina number not in my contacts, a message in all caps: *DID YOU HEAR?*

My fork hovered over the plate.

"Who's that?" Russ asked as he sat back down across from me, hands circling the mug. He must've seen it in my expression, the blood draining, my shoulders tightening.

It had to be Amaya. She was the one who reached out with the details each year. She cared for us deeply, as a collective. She cared about everything deeply.

"Just spam," I said, dropping the fork to the plate, pressing my hands to my knees under the table, to keep them still. I fought the urge to turn the phone facedown.

It didn't have to be a lie. It could've been a wrong number, instead of Amaya tracking me down, making sure I knew that today was the arrival date. As if she knew I was sitting at my boyfriend's kitchen table hundreds of miles away at this very moment, with no intention of hitting the road.

But just in case, when I thought Russ wasn't watching, I would delete the message. Block the number. As if it had never happened.

We took the plates to the counter, and I waited for him to turn his back, for the water to run, before picking up my cell.

But by then a second message had come through. A link to an article. No, not an article—an obituary.

Ian Tayler, twenty-eight

I sank into the nearest chair. Read the notice of his unexpected death, words swimming.

Beloved son, brother, uncle, and friend. Donations to be made to the Ridgefield Recovery Center, in lieu of flowers.

They had used an older picture—when his face was boyishly full, blond hair just long enough to catch a breeze, tan skin and brown eyes and a smile I wasn't sure I'd seen in over a decade. So different from the last time we'd been together, one year ago, at our meeting place in the Outer Banks.

His face had been gaunter then, his hair cropped short. He seemed beset by a fidget he couldn't shake. *Until next year*, he'd said, one arm hooked awkwardly around my neck in half a hug.

We didn't like to stand too close anymore, because all I could picture as we lingered in those moments was the same thing I was seeing now: a flash of his brown eyes, large and wide, mouth open in a frozen scream as he faced the river—

I pressed my fist to my teeth, let out one single gasp, hoped it was muffled under the sound of running water.

Then, a second shock: the obituary was three months old, and I hadn't known.

Out of contact. Unreachable.

Shouldn't I have felt it somehow? That bond, connecting us all across time and distance? *Ian, I'm sorry*—

I left the room. Left Russ at the sink. Made a new plan: stop by home for the right clothes; email work with a family emergency; start driving.

It had been a mistake to believe I could just disappear. That I could forget any of this—the memories, the pact. That I could leave it—and them—behind for good.

On my way, I responded, my hands still trembling.

I shouldn't have tried to fight it. There was a gravity to this ritual week, to the past, to them. The only survivors. There were nine of us, at the start.

Their names were a drumbeat in my head, our lives perpetually bound. Amaya, Clara, Grace. Oliver, Joshua, Ian. Hollis and Brody. Me. A miracle, it seemed, that there were any of us at all.

In truth, they represented the facet of my life I wanted most to forget. An exorcism of my past that I couldn't quite complete. But, like Amaya, I did care, and deeply so. Because we had all made that promise: Then and always, we would see each other through this week. Keep our borders close, keep our secrets closer. One moment, pulling the rest of us back together, year after year.

Only now we were seven.

SUNDAY

CHAPTER 1

Our house, like most things, came down to luck.

Luck that the property had managed to withstand two hurricanes in the last decade, perched on a set of pilings at the edge of the dunes, protected only by aluminum storm shutters and cedar shake siding that had faded over the years to a weather-worn gray.

Luck that there was space for all of us within its five bedrooms, with balconies that connected via wraparound porches and precarious wooden steps over three stories.

Luck that the beachfront rental belonged to Oliver's family, and, that first year, after Clara's funeral, when we were panicked and desperate and made that pact, Oliver had said: *I know a place.*

The house was tucked away from the activity of town, at the far edge of a dead-end road. It was close enough to see the neighbors down the stretch of sand—especially in the dark, with the windows lit up, beacons in the night—but still private enough to feel removed. A peace of mind in both regards.

It was the perfect haven for us, the lucky ones: survivors of the crash, and then of the raging river, the unrelenting storm.

Oliver called it The Shallows, a name that felt like a promise. A place of safety, and retreat, isolated from the rest of the world, and surrounded on all sides by the endless deep. We came here the first time out of convenience, but we kept coming back because returning here year after year removed the necessity of decisions, the burden of plans. And because it was hundreds of miles from the site of the accident, protected from the undertow of the past.

• • •

I drove five hours to the coast, and then over a series of bridges to the southern barrier islands, passing the time in a state of steady dread, trying to distract myself with a variety of podcasts I couldn't focus on, before finally giving over to the silence.

The turnoff appeared before I was ready for it, a cluster of uncoordinated mailboxes before a faded street sign, bent from the wind and sun-scorched white at the center.

The house was at the end of the unpaved road, the parking area out front a semicircle of rocks and weeds, with a fine coating of sand that I'd felt under the wheels for the last ten miles. On the drive in, the land progressively narrowed between the ocean and the sound, and the dunes crept closer to the road, sand swirling across the pavement in gusty spirals. From a distance, the sand formed a sort of haze, suspended like fog in the atmosphere, encroaching from the sea. Without regular maintenance, I imagined, all of this would be swept away; every sign of humanity wiped clean, in a steady assault of nature.

The geography was constantly shifting out here. In the marshlands, water seeped onto the grassy edges of the road. After a storm, islands could have become peninsulas, or vice versa. And the dunes were always moving, growing—like everything in sight was waiting to be consumed.

But somehow this house remained.

There were four cars in a row out front, the last being Amaya's rust-colored sedan, with a collection of decals lining the rear windshield. It was already late afternoon—I assumed I was the last to arrive. Not everyone lived within driving distance anymore.

I pulled into the spot beside a familiar dark Honda, jarred by the car seat visible in the back, by how much could change in a year.

When I stepped outside, the air tasted like salt, like something from my nightmares. Sometimes, alone, in the dark of night, I'd wake from a dream still tasting the river, storm water, a gritty soil in the back of my throat. But other times I'd wake to the scent of saltwater air instead, like I wasn't sure which was the nightmare—then or now.

I breathed slowly, staring up at the house. The raised porch, multiple gables, windows reflecting the sun and sky. The structure was dated but objectively beautiful, I knew, in the way it rose unobtrusively from the landscape, like driftwood from the beach, positioned with care to welcome the forces of nature, instead of fighting against them.

A set of wide wooden steps led up to the front door, where we'd taken that single photo our first year—the eight of us crammed together, sitting shoulder to shoulder, knees pressing into the body in front of us, like proof: *We're still here.*

I straightened my spine, steeling myself. On a list of things that could set my nerves on edge, this would be near the top. Not quite as high as driving on curving dark roads, or being lost. But arriving late to this house, with this group: high.

They weren't bad people. They were just bad people for me.

A shadow passed the living room window, and I imagined them all together, sitting around that taupe sectional couch, waiting for me.

And then, before I could stop the image: I saw them running, funneling out the front door, a massive wave rising up behind the house, sky darkening, shadow expanding. The chaos of panic, and wondering who I would save first—

It was a habit I couldn't shake, the question always on my mind. In a room full of people, a bus full of strangers: *Who do you save?* A thought experiment playing out in real time. A horror interlude in the monotony of my daily life.

I grabbed my luggage, slammed the trunk of my car.

The first day was always the hardest.

• • •

The front door squeaked as I pushed it open, hinges rusted from the saltwater air and time. One step inside, and my memory sharpened: whitewashed, wood-paneled walls and an open floor plan, so I could see straight through the house, entrance to exit—first the living room, then the long table of the dining room and the kitchen beyond, the areas partitioned by furniture alone, and finally the back windows and the sliding door to the deck. But when I closed the front door behind me—loud enough to draw attention, to make sure they knew I was here—Brody was the only one I saw.

"There she is," he said, standing from the fridge, as if there were someone else in the room with us. He twisted the top off his beer while he walked halfway across the space, dimple forming as he smiled. He had the same shaggy haircut as always, a brown mop he was constantly pushing back from his face. He'd been the athlete of our group, one half of class-couple Brody and Hollis, and he still carried the confidence of someone used to being widely known in school.

"Here," I said, like I was a student calling out her attendance, and he laughed. From his greeting, it sounded like they'd been waiting. Unlike Brody, I was more accustomed to being overlooked, so I had gotten into the habit of going out of my way to make my presence known.

I set my luggage beside the couch and took him in. Every year, our first greetings were both familiar and jarring. He dressed the same—casually, in gym shorts and a T-shirt and slip-on sandals. But there was a car seat in the back of his car; he was a *dad*. An entire identity that had changed in a moment.

"The drive okay?" Brody appeared at ease no matter where he was or whom he was with. He picked up a conversation with me as if no time had passed since we'd seen each other last.

"Yes, but sorry I'm late."

He took a long drink, shook his head, brushed a rogue wave of hair from his eyes. "You're not even the last one." Then he nodded toward the back of the kitchen. "We're outside, after you get settled."

"I'll be out in a few," I said, grateful for the time to orient myself first.

Reasons to save Brody: he was a new father; people would miss him.

He smiled, standing at the back door, taking me in. I was wearing the first jeans and T-shirt I had managed to pull from my drawer, and pieces of dark blond hair had fallen from my haphazard ponytail during the drive. I felt self-conscious, exposed. "You look good, Cass," he said, as if he could read my insecurity. He left the sliding door ajar as he exited, in an offering, or an oversight.

In the silence that followed, I could hear the waves, the cry of a seagull. Out back, there was a wooden walkway through the dunes, patchy seagrass mixed in with the sand, and then—water, sea breeze, infinity.

Grace always said there was something healing about the ocean, but then, she was someone who believed in the mind's ability to right itself, and in nature's ability to do the same. She worked as a trauma therapist now, which I thought was reason enough to save her, even if she saw the rest of us as works in progress. Grace must've managed to convince herself that the enemy was not *water* but the lack of lights on a winding mountain road. A deer, caught in the blinding glare of headlights; a series of bad decisions in an approaching storm.

But I found nothing healing about this place.

Maybe it was the bridges I had to take to get here, cutting me off from the rest of my life, cutting us all off together. The single road in, and the way the light shimmered off the pavement, like water. The sea visible on both sides, and this sensation that something was closing in.

Maybe it would feel this way no matter where we were, as long as we were together. Maybe everything we touched together turned to ash.

• • •

My room—the room I had stayed in since that very first year—was one of three on the second floor. The door was open at the end of the hall, welcoming me. Inside, there were two queen beds with matching aqua-colored comforters, dark wooden furniture, and an antique, out-of-place mirror. Amaya's luggage was at the foot of the bed that had always been hers, nearer the entrance.

I almost didn't see her. It was the breeze I noticed first: the glass doors to the balcony cracked open, and the silhouette through the gauzy curtains—a person facing the dunes, the ocean.

"Hey," I said quietly, swinging the doors fully open. But I made her jump all the same. Her curly brown hair was up in her signature high ponytail, and it appeared shorter than the year before. There were hollows under her hazel eyes when she turned to face me, as if she'd traveled through the night, or been haunted by the drive in, same as me.

"Oh," she said, like she was surprised to see me here at all. She seemed even smaller than I remembered, drowning in loose joggers and an oversize sweatshirt, hands tucked inside the sleeves. The weather in the Outer Banks in early May was unpredictable. It could be sixty degrees with a crisp ocean breeze, or it could be closer to eighty with a strong sun and thick with humidity.

"Didn't mean to scare you," I said, dropping my luggage beside the bed closer to the window, in the room we always shared. Creatures of habit, all of us. The comfort of routines lingered from our school years, assigned positions and predicted places. The rooms were almost dormitory-style, with identical layouts: two beds and similar furniture in each. Only the color scheme varied, so we called the rooms by their colors: Grace and Hollis in the yellow room; Brody and Joshua in the navy room. The main bedroom on the first floor always belonged to Oliver.

Amaya leaned back against the wooden rail, fidgeting with the set of silver rings she always wore. Her nails were painted a chipping, stormy blue. "You made it," she said, as if to let me know she'd been waiting. We didn't hug. We never did, not until the end, when it was a relief. A release. "I was starting to worry."

She always seemed to have a sixth sense, like she knew I'd been sitting at Russ's kitchen table that morning with every intention of staying put, knew enough to text me—knew what it would take to get me to come.

I wondered what she'd been thinking while I'd made excuses to Russ, *So sorry, message from my boss. Last-minute business trip*—and waved off his offer to take me to an airport, the lies slipping so easily off my tongue.

"I didn't know," I said, and at her continued stare, I added, "About Ian." The loss was too fresh, impossible to process. I felt myself wanting to look for him, desperate, as always, to account for him—to check his room, or listen for his footsteps overhead; to hear his laughter from somewhere out back.

She scrunched up her nose as she looked to the side. "I had to hear the details from Josh."

Amaya, like me, like most of the survivors, had moved away from town in the years after the accident. Though her choice of location now was unsettling.

Joshua was the only one who still lived and worked in the town where we'd all grown up, who would've heard about Ian directly through the local rumor mill.

"I thought he was doing better," I said, my eyes burning, the act of discussion suddenly making it real. But the truth was, I had no reason to know how Ian had been doing at all.

Amaya blinked at me slowly. "Is everyone else here?" she asked, pivoting the conversation, sparing me the awkwardness.

"Brody said they're out back," I said, and she nodded. "Come on," I added. "Don't make me go out there alone."

"I'll be right down. I just need a minute," she said, turning back to the balcony.

She looked so small standing there, framed by the dunes, the ocean stretching out into the distance, the wind blowing her hair. A shudder rolled through me—I couldn't help picturing Clara on a different precipice, needing something, too.

But then Amaya looked over her shoulder, the faintest smile. "It's good to see you, Cassidy."

"You too," I said.

Long ago, she had once led us all to safety. I tried to find the shadow of that person in the one now standing before me.

Reasons to save Amaya: I wasn't sure she could make it on her own.

• • •

Stepping out the back door of The Shallows was always a trick of perspective. The dunes blocked the view of the beach from the lower level, but you could still catch a glimpse of the horizon beyond. It was easy to imagine you were alone out here, just sand and sea and sky. But the steps to the side led down to an enclosed patio with a hot tub, a patch of loose stones surrounding Adirondack chairs, and a fire pit in the center: a hub of hidden activity.

I saw them from above, sitting in a semicircle, the cadence of their voices carrying upward, but impossible to decipher.

As I descended the steps, only Joshua seemed to notice. I felt his eyes tracking me from the other side of the fire pit.

"Cassidy Bent," Joshua said, in the way he always did. No *Nice to see you* or *How was the drive* or *Grab a seat.* Just my name; just like that, an echo across time.

He never seemed glad to see me, for reasons I couldn't quite understand. Not from our interactions before the accident (nonexistent) or after (minimal). Eventually, I had stopped trying to figure it out. He was all sharp edges, sharp gaze, sharp comments. A pale scar across the ridge of his cheekbone. Khaki shorts and a striped polo, hair slicked back with gel. There were three crushed cans of beer under his chair, and he grinned when he saw me looking.

Reasons to save Joshua: nothing came to mind.

Brody gestured for me to join them, just as the woman beside him twisted in her chair, long dark hair falling over her shoulder as she did.

"Hey, Cassidy," Grace said, smile stretching wider, a complete contrast to Joshua's greeting. She had the rare ability of putting others at ease, myself included. She wore a maxi dress under a jean jacket, had a softness to her features and a way of moving that felt deliberate, fitting of her name. Everything about Grace felt designed to draw you closer, draw you in. "Did you see Amaya in there?" she asked, brushing her hair behind her shoulders.

"She's on her way," I said, slipping into the seat on the other side of Grace. I felt Joshua's gaze on me, and became hyperaware of every move: how to cross a leg, where to put my arms. My jeans weren't right for the beach, and my hair was at that awkward in-between length—I busied myself by undoing the hair tie now, running my hands through the shoulder-length pieces.

In the quiet that followed, I thought I caught an exchange of glances between the three of them. It made me think I'd interrupted something. But whatever they were discussing, they didn't pick up with it again.

Brody tipped his head back, cupped his hands around his mouth, and called, "Amaya, come on down!"

Grace gave him a tight-lipped look. Then: "Let her be." Grace spoke with an air of wisdom, or authority, how I imagined all therapists must, as if she had some extra insight that the rest of us didn't.

Then she leaned closer to me, two freshly manicured hands on my arm. "Oh, I love your necklace," she said. Grace operated in a series of compliments and optimism, and could disarm you so easily, so readily. A skill she probably used in her job, with patients.

Now she reached a hand to my neck, goose bumps rising along my arms as she slipped the chain into her palm, leaning closer, sliding the interlocking circles between her fingers, so they sounded like music.

"Thanks," I said, waiting for her to drop the chain. For all the things Grace believed in, personal space didn't seem to be one of them. Russ had gotten the necklace for my birthday last month, said he thought of me as soon as he saw it. At the center of the interlocking circles was the letter *C*, but it was something you noticed only if you were looking for it, in a way that felt like a secret, or a surprise.

Now it served as a connection to my real life. I slid the charm along the chain, suddenly transported back to my apartment when Russ handed me that box, his face at first guarded and unsure, before I felt his expression mirroring the joy in my own. *I love it*, I'd said as he helped clasp it around my neck—and I did. It was a reminder of the person I had become away from this group of people. The person I would return to again, in six more days.

Seconds later, footsteps echoed from the deck above, louder and more deliberate than Amaya's. And then a crisp voice called over the rail, "I see you all made yourselves at home."

"Well, well, the King is finally here," Joshua said, with half a smile.

Oliver King, who always seemed ready to command a room, strode down the steps, looking like he'd just come from a meeting or a business lunch, in slacks and trendy sneakers and a blazer that must've been perfectly tailored to his lean frame. He was Korean American and had lived down the street from me all through high school, a proximity that made us feel closer than we actually were.

"Glad someone managed to find the way inside this time," Oliver joked.

In past years, we had hovered outside or on the beach, until Oliver arrived with the key code for the unit, which apparently either changed each year or none of us had bothered to ask him before, or remember.

Reasons to save Oliver: this house, for starters.

"The door was open when I got here," Brody said with a shrug.

Josh handed Oliver a fresh can of beer across the fire pit, and it looked out of place in his hands. But he cracked it open, frowned before taking a sip, then wiped his hand across his mouth, in a way I couldn't imagine him doing around others.

Last I heard, Oliver was living in New York, managing some prestigious hedge fund. Maybe he was used to people waiting for him now. But he still, always, made time for this. All of us did.

It's why I believed that, for all our differences, for however disconnected our lives were ten years later, we all cared more for each other than we'd admit, face-to-face.

We hadn't missed a year, not even in 2020, when most of the restaurants were shut down and we were advised to stay put. Not even last year, when Brody's girlfriend was nine months pregnant and she'd begged him not to come. She'd gone into labor the very last day, and when he left—a rare moment of elation, kissing each of us on the cheek—I'd felt something shift, thinking maybe this was the end. That new beginnings and the promise of the future were releasing us. But now Brody was back, car seat in tow, like nothing at all had changed. The only person missing was—

"Someone's on the beach," Amaya called from the top of the steps. She had her hands on the wooden rail, though she wouldn't be able to see clearly from there.

"It's a beach," Josh said, not even looking her way. "People do tend to use it."

"Hollis is out there," Grace answered, ignoring Josh, waving Amaya down. "She spent about three seconds inside, unpacking. Just long enough to change for a workout."

"Is that all of us, then?" Oliver asked, taking us in slowly, one by one. I wondered if he did a mental tally, as I did—of who to save. I wondered where I'd fit into his list.

Amaya perched on the arm of the last open seat, looking around the circle. Each of us taking stock of the rest.

"All present and accounted for," Brody said, crossing his feet on the ledge of the fire pit.

I flinched in my chair. No one mentioned Ian, and it felt like a gut punch. How quickly we could each be forgotten: here one moment and then *poof*, gone, brutal and efficient. But then, wasn't this just like us. I couldn't remember the last time someone mentioned Clara either—not even Grace, and they had been best friends. We did not mention the dead, as if it were yet another layer of the pact of which I was unaware. Another tool of our survival.

Grace checked a message on her phone, while Josh bounced a single knee, the silence stretching.

Finally, Oliver cleared his throat. "Did anyone happen to pick up food?"

Josh let out a bark of laughter. "No, Mr. King, we did not prepare the house for your arrival." He rolled his eyes. "Speaking of, though. I took the upstairs room."

Grace's head whipped in his direction at the same time as Amaya's.

"The fuck you did," Amaya said, with more force than I'd heard her muster in years.

Josh and Amaya stared at each other wordlessly, and I remembered that they were bound in other ways, not just from these yearly trips—but through Amaya's family, and Josh's position in their law firm.

"To be honest," Grace cut in, attempting to temper whatever came next, "I was hoping we could use the upstairs space for work. I still have patients to see this week, virtual appointments set up—"

"The upstairs space?" I heard myself repeating, cutting her off. For the first time, everyone looked at me. "You mean *Ian's room*. Let's call it what it is."

His name reverberated through the group with a jolt. There was a prolonged stretch of silence before Josh raised one shoulder in a conceding shrug.

"Fine," Josh said. "I took *Ian's room*, seeing as he wasn't going to be needing it anymore."

"Are you *kidding* me?" Amaya said. I wasn't sure if she was referring to the fact that he'd taken the room, or that he was being so crass about it now. "You can't just take whatever you want."

"What should we do instead, Amaya?" Josh said. "Should we draw for it?"

Brody let out a low groan of frustration.

The first day was always like this. Like no one actually wanted to be here, and we bumped up against one another in sharp edges and passive aggressions. *Survivors' guilt*, Grace would say. But for every face here, there was another missing, a reality we had to come to terms with each time. Eventually we'd settle into it, into one another, and Grace would convince us that *See, we needed to do this. We needed one another.*

"Stop," Grace said, hands held out to pacify us. "Let's talk this out. And, Josh, *please.*"

"What?" Josh said, turning on Grace now too. "We're a dying breed. If we can't joke about that, who can?"

"Josh, come on," Oliver said, finally interjecting.

"Oh, that's right," Josh said, the corner of his mouth raised. "Your place, your rules, I forgot."

How quickly everything could turn. How quickly *we* could turn things.

Grace had her eyes closed, like she was meditating, or repeating some mantra to herself. "Are you going to say *anything*, Brody?" As if even her facade had finally cracked, and she was desperate to know that everyone was on her side.

Oliver caught my eye over the group, and I wondered, again, if he was weighing his options, as I was.

Quick, who do you save? *Amaya. Grace. Brody. Oliver.*

I stood from the chair. Turned away. Pushed through the back gate, heading toward the dunes.

It's a trick question, of course. The answer was always: yourself.

CHAPTER 2

I couldn't remember how to breathe around them.

I was usually able to navigate any of them, one-on-one—carefully, with precision. But in the group, I lost my bearings. There was too much history, too much I didn't understand—about them, about the people they used to be. We had been classmates and neighbors; couples and friends; strangers. But lines had shifted. Relationships had crumbled. New allegiances had been forged.

And there were too many memories tied to The Shallows. Eight years of secrets locked away inside those rooms.

Hollis had the right idea, getting out. Getting space. The house used to feel bigger.

The beach was fairly private. Not close enough to any tourist areas, it was frequented only by those who owned or rented along this strip of road. A dozen or so homes, with a pier at the end, stretching into the sea. I listened to my steps echo over the wood planks of the long path rising through the dunes, leading me to the set of steps that ended directly on the sand.

Hollis stood across from the steps, just before the rising tide, in black leggings and a matching tank. She remained unnaturally still. I was used to seeing her always, always on the move. Not like this haunting image, staring out at the ocean, like she might step into it.

She had always been striking, but now, motionless and framed against the sea, her white-blond hair in the halo of sunlight gave her the aura of something otherworldly, slightly unreal.

I almost called out to her. But then I realized she was balanced on one foot, and must've been in the middle of a yoga routine—practicing something, even in her stillness. There was a phone strapped to her upper arm. She probably had earbuds in.

I wasn't surprised she was tuning us out. Hollis had a tendency to disappear further into herself, putting her focus into miles run, goals achieved. She was a personal trainer—a lifestyle as much as a career.

Reasons to save Hollis: I thought, if it came to it, she could help save all the rest.

I rolled up my jeans and slipped my shoes off at the base of the steps before veering right, down the expanse of beach. Away from her.

The wind whipped off the water, a sharp contrast to the hot sand under my bare feet.

The first time we stepped out here, that very first year, Grace had looked toward the ocean and said, in her positive way, *It's impossible to feel trapped here*.

I wished I could see it through her eyes—that I could stay firmly grounded in the present, feel only the idyllic beauty of where we stood. But for me, anywhere can feel like a trap.

The bridges like a series of passageways closing behind you; the people we were stranded with. As if the roar of the waves would drown out the memory of the screams. As if the ebb and flow wouldn't make us think of the rain, and the rising water, and the bone-deep fear.

As if we wouldn't remember back further, to the nauseating, winding road, the swerve before the plunge; the crackle of moments that divided the before and the after.

The night was so dark here too.

A mistake. That's what the school kept saying. A mistake that the vans had detoured from the highway. A mistake that they'd told us we couldn't bring our phones on the trip. A mistake that the drivers hadn't checked in with the administration about the traffic or the change in plans.

Another mistake that we weren't together on the one-year anniversary. Though I had kept my distance, Clara had gone to the tribute at the school: a prolonged moment of silence in the courtyard, followed by twelve haunting chimes of the chapel bell—and that was the last she was seen by anyone.

Later, Clara had texted us in the middle of the night: *I'm going back.*

And then she'd done it. Driven that same route into the Tennessee mountains, taken that same detour to the Stone River Gorge, left her car abandoned on the side of the road, with a half-empty bottle of vodka in the passenger seat. Presumably, there, she'd walked to the edge—drawn by the roar of the river, the pull of it—and jumped. None of us had received her message until the next morning, when it was too late.

I'd had my fill of funerals by then. Couldn't stand the thought of one more, couldn't face the reality of losing yet another classmate—especially after all we'd been through. But Amaya asked us all to meet in the parking lot behind the school on the night after the funeral, and we each agreed. As if we needed to prove to one another that the rest of us were still here.

When we saw each other that night, the eight of us gravitating toward one another in the dim glow of a streetlamp, I suddenly felt that the real mistake was not in the lead-up to the accident but that we had somehow survived it. Without Clara, it was easier to believe that we were never meant to escape the river—that, somehow, it was still coming for us.

It was Amaya's idea: *We shouldn't be alone again.*

The pact was such an easy thing to agree to.

I used to think this was the way to save us too. That we needed to be vigilant, on high alert—or it could still come for us after all this time.

But more recently, I had started to believe that the thing we thought was saving us from the past might've been binding us to it instead.

I worried that Ian had been doing *fine* until he got that email from Amaya, reminding him.

I believed that there had to be a way out of this, for all of us.

A shock of cold water crept up around my ankles, and I jumped. I stepped farther out of reach of the encroaching tide, footsteps washing away in my wake.

The beach was dotted with only a few people: a little girl and presumably her mother building a sand castle; a man heading my way from the opposite direction, fishing pole resting on his shoulder.

I heard the next wave coming and sidestepped the surge. Ahead of me, a tangle of seaweed lingered in the froth, and at the edge, something black protruded from the sand. It looked like it might be a wallet, or—

Another wave crept over the mass, dislodging the object, and as the water receded, I saw it more clearly. I splashed into the cold surf, scooping it up before it was swept out again: it was a phone.

The screen was cracked, and the edges were coated in a cold, wet sand, and there was salt water streaked across the screen. It was out of a case, probably dead. A small miracle it had survived the pull of the tide and washed back up onshore.

I turned in a circle, looking for its potential owner.

"Excuse me," I called to the woman and child building the sand castle. The woman looked up, one hand on the brim of her straw hat, the other holding a small plastic shovel. The little girl, in a long-sleeved purple bathing suit, didn't look up from her digging. "Did you lose a phone?" I asked.

The woman pursed her mouth, then reached into her striped beach bag before pulling out a phone inside a sparkly case. "Nope," she said, the sun reflecting off the glitter.

The only other person in sight was the man heading my way from the pier—maybe he was looking for this.

I strode in his direction with purpose, noticed the bottoms of his khaki shorts were wet, and imagined him caught in a wave, losing his phone. As soon as I was close enough to be heard, I called, "Looking for this?" I extended the phone in my hand his way.

"What?" he called, or I thought he called. Sound moved oddly out here. Some voices carried; others were swept up under the wind and lost.

"Did you lose this?" I tried again.

His steps slowed, and he moved the fishing pole from one side of his body to the other. He was younger than I'd thought from the distance—with baggy clothes and wind-tangled hair sticking up in sections—but he was probably in his thirties, if that. His bright eyes stood out, sparkling, against a deep tan.

"Nah," he said. "I know better than to bring a phone out to the beach."

I looked up and down the stretch of sand, searching for another possibility. "Is there a lost and found around here?" I asked, hoping to hand off the responsibility to him. He seemed like he was local to this place.

He laughed, running his free hand back through his hair, smoothing out the pieces—though they shot up again immediately. "Definitely not."

"I don't know anyone here," I added. "I'm just visiting."

By his bemused expression, I assumed that must've been readily apparent. "Look," he said with a sigh, "chances are it didn't even come from someone on this beach." He gestured to the Atlantic, stretching out before us. "We get a lot of debris down here. Once got pieces of a shipwreck from the Bahamas, you know."

It seemed unlikely that this phone would be carried in on the surf from across the sea, but he stepped away, raising his hands, absolving himself. "Take care now," he said. Then he veered toward the nearest set of wooden steps, but instead of taking the path back to the house, he cut straight through a gap in the dunes, like he knew a shortcut.

I scanned the stretch of homes across the beach; this phone probably belonged to someone staying at one. I started heading back toward our path. When I thought about it, at least this would give me something else to focus on later, an excuse to get out of that house again. Knocking on doors, looking for the phone's owner. If it hadn't been in the water for too long, it's possible I could get it to restart, track the owner down with the information it contained.

By the time I approached the steps on the beach leading to our place, Hollis was no longer in sight. I walked the wooden path toward the house, past the engraved sign at the gate that read *The Shallows*.

I felt myself slow as I entered the enclosed patio, trying to place the feeling of *wrong* that washed over me. I listened closely: the waves, the gulls.

It was the silence. There were seven of us staying in that house, and right now, there wasn't a single sign of life.

I climbed the steps to the deck and entered through the sliding back door, into the kitchen. The inside was dim compared to the bright May sun, and as my eyes adjusted, I could make out a few discarded bottles and cans on the countertops. The downstairs appeared deserted, but I could hear the creak of footsteps from the floor overhead.

"Hello?" I called.

No one answered. I walked toward the stairs near the front door, where I could see through the living room windows. There was a new black Jeep wedged in behind my car—Oliver's rental, I was guessing—but there was an empty spot at the other end of the parking area, where Amaya's rust-colored car used to be. And then: a pitter-patter of feet coming down the steps. I backed away as Hollis came into view, swooping her blond hair over one shoulder. "Finally," she said. "I thought I had been abandoned."

Neither of us acknowledged that we hadn't seen each other in a year. Honestly, I thought that in some ways she was most like me: here against her better judgment, but here all the same. Her hair fell in a curtain around her face, bangs to the top of her eyes, so exact that I imagined her trimming it every morning, a vision of efficiency. The only jewelry I ever noticed her wearing was a single diamond stud nose ring. Now her blue eyes flitted around the room, like even they couldn't keep still.

It was then I saw the note on the coffee table. One of the folded take-out menus with dark writing over top: *AT HIGH TIDE*.

I picked it up, held it out to Hollis. "Mystery solved." High Tide was a restaurant on the sound side of the island, the closest eat-in place, which we had frequented over the years. It was conveniently within walking distance.

"Oh, thank god, I'm famished, actually," Hollis said. She had changed from her yoga gear into a bright-colored top, shorts, and sandals that showed off her long legs, toned from years of marathon training. Hollis always looked like she had stepped straight out of her wellness-focused Instagram account. "You coming?" she asked.

"Give me a minute to get changed, and I'll walk over with you."

I took the lost phone upstairs with me to the aqua bedroom, then brought it straight out to the balcony. The wind blew into the room, sheer curtains billowing behind me. Outside, the shade was beginning to stretch, so I left the phone on the corner of the wooden railing, where the sun would continue to hit as it moved across the sky. Sand and grit traced the path of the crack through the screen, but I had seen things survive worse.

Back inside, I peeled off my jeans, stiff and wet at the cuffs, and traded them for the casual skirt that had miraculously made it into my luggage. There was no dress code for the restaurant, but I hadn't had much time to pack, and my bag was mostly full of workout clothes and a few T-shirts.

I took a quick glance in the antique mirror, then searched for my brush, before realizing I must've forgotten to pack it. I checked the surfaces for something of Amaya's I could use—I didn't think she'd mind—but there was no sign she had begun to unpack. I spun around, taking in the room. I didn't see any of Amaya's things. Not even the bag that had been beside her bed earlier.

Maybe she'd moved her things to the room upstairs, in an attempt to convince Joshua to trade. But their last interaction had unsettled me. She'd been so tense, so forceful. I stepped into the hall, then took the narrow stairwell across from our room up to the top floor.

I could hear a noise coming from the room before I reached the landing.

There was no door to enter the room up here, just a stairwell leading straight into a loft space with slanted ceilings, a queen bed low to the ground under a set of dormer windows.

I could think of this only as Ian's space. It was impossible to be up here without picturing his lean frame, hunched over, sitting on the edge of the bed. The way his face would change as I climbed the last step, like he knew it would be me.

The room was empty, but there was a balcony door leading to the upper deck area, a single square of overlook that connected to the lower levels by a steeper set of steps that I assumed must've been added after the initial build. I couldn't imagine they had passed inspection.

The balcony door creaked as the wind blew, the strong ocean breeze whistling through the cracks. It wasn't fully latched. I quickly crossed the room, pushed it firmly shut, and turned the lock. Exterior doors had a way of becoming unlatched without the dead bolt, due to weather rot around the doorframes facing the sea.

Joshua's things were strewn about the space already: open luggage on the rumpled bed; sneakers kicked off haphazardly in the middle of the floor; bathing suit tossed over the wooden chair; laptop out on the matching oak desk, papers on the surface.

There were no signs of Amaya here. On my way downstairs, I checked the navy and yellow bedrooms, but didn't see any indication she'd moved into either of them. There was also no sign of her luggage on the main level, where Hollis stood before the front window, peering outside.

"Have you seen Amaya?" I asked.

"I haven't seen *anyone*. Guess they all drove over together. You good?"

I nodded, following her out the front door. But I couldn't shake the feeling that something was wrong.

It was the fact that Ian should be here, and his absence had thrown everything off balance. Nothing felt right, but then, it rarely did here.

CHAPTER 3

High Tide was most easily accessed via a series of paths between homes. Sprawling three-story vacation rentals sat side by side with older beach bungalows and converted trailers, overgrown grass and sand-packed gaps between the property lines. We had to cross only one paved road that locals called a highway but looked nothing like any highway I'd seen on the mainland. There wasn't even a light, or a crosswalk—just long gaps in the traffic when you could dart across the street, at will.

The restaurant was situated at the edge of the sound, jutting out over the water. The current was calmer here, a gentle lapping against the underside of the dock, but with an eerie haze that often hung over the sea at dawn and dusk. We'd spent many nights here over the years, and I recognized the hostess from every year past.

She must've recognized us too. As we stepped inside, her face changed immediately, deep grooves forming in her tan skin as her smile stretched wider. "I knew there were a few faces missing," she said in a gravelly voice. Then she looked behind us, as if expecting more.

I couldn't remember her name, but Hollis pulled it out of her memory instantly. "Hi, Joanie," she said.

Joanie grabbed two laminated menus and led us toward a long table in the corner, at the intersection of two walls of glass, sea and sky stretching outward in every direction.

There were two pitchers of beer in the center of the table, along with an assortment of fried appetizers, everyone eating like we were still in college. I took the empty seat beside Grace, facing the wall of windows, the blaze of an orange sunset reflecting off the sound.

Across the table, Oliver pulled out the chair beside him. "Hey, Hollis," he said as she sat. "Missed seeing you when we all got in."

Hollis started piling some of the coconut shrimp onto the plate in front of her, catching up with Oliver, while I scanned the rest of the faces at the table.

"Where's Amaya?" I asked.

Josh stopped chewing for a second, then swallowed. "She said she wasn't hungry."

"She's gone," I said, with a pointed look at Josh.

He shrugged, before grabbing a handful of nachos. "Cooling off, I guess."

"No, I mean, her bag is gone. Her car is gone."

The table fell momentarily silent, before Brody picked up a pitcher of beer, refilling his glass. "She'll be back, I'm sure," he said. Then he reached over to fill my glass as well.

"This has to be a record," Josh said, rolling his eyes. "What, she made it three hours this time?"

I wasn't the only one who gave him a look this time, though he didn't seem to notice.

I placed my phone on the table, frowning. Thinking I should find that number from her text earlier in the day and check in.

"I'll send her a message," Grace said, as if understanding the need to put the rest of us at ease.

Amaya had disappeared on us before. Ironic, considering she was the one who made sure we would all be here. Yet she had more trouble than any of us in staying put. She'd leave for a walk and say she lost track of time. She'd take her car for groceries and then check into the campground down the road for the night, before coming back the next day with breakfast. Like she could feel it too—the way any place could become a trap—and needed to prove to herself that she could escape.

Grace pressed her lips together, then raised her eyes from her phone. "She's fine. Says she just needs a little space."

"Is she coming back tonight?" I asked.

But Grace put her cell away, shrugged, then rested her hand on my arm. "Give her some time. You know how it can be." Grace and Amaya had formed a bond over the years in a way that others hadn't. From the way Grace spoke of Amaya, part of me wondered if Amaya wasn't a patient of hers too.

"What's the over-under on how long it takes her to come back?" Josh asked, like this was all a joke.

Right then my phone lit up with a text, but it was Russ's name on the display: *Made it okay?*

I texted back: *Yes, just settling in. Talk soon.*

"Seeing someone, I take it?" Brody asked, peering over my shoulder to see what I was typing.

I smiled at him, placing my phone back in my purse. I didn't want to share this part of my life with them. My past might have been irreversibly bound to them, but my future didn't have to be.

"Is it serious?" he asked, teasing, dimple forming as he leaned his elbow on the table and propped his chin in his hand, facing me.

"Not quite," I said, shaking my head, acknowledging the truth to myself even as I said it. I'd already told the first big lie to Russ—that I had to be on-site to cover for a colleague on a last-minute work trip—and it was only a matter of time before I told the second, and the third, burying myself in details I'd have to keep straight; a burden I wanted no part of.

This was self-sabotage, I knew, but I'd already set it in motion with the very first lie.

It was a shame. Things with Russ had been easy, until now. He generally didn't ask too many questions that required a lie or a pivot. He was four years older than me, and had a tendency to focus on the future. We'd met at our mutual favorite bar in the neighborhood, eyes catching immediately when he walked in; we liked the same things—from the appetizers on the menu to the songs playing overhead—and had a similar sense of humor. *Do you believe in fate?* he'd asked at the end of that first night—and I did, I do. And over the course of the last few months, I'd come to believe that, in a room full of people, I would be the one he chose to save. My misguided interpretation of love.

But he was too trusting, and now I knew it. It was only a matter of time.

"Ah, well," Grace said, gesturing to my full beer. "Have a drink, lovely."

I supposed no one was too surprised. Every year was pretty much the same.

Over the last decade, I'd had a series of failed relationships, in which I was either too attached or too aloof. It was an active process to fight for the middle—my hopes of an average life, an average existence—and I thought I might've hit it right with Russ. But now I was starting to think that there was no middle, that we were all just a set of extremes, balancing each other out.

I couldn't stop constantly reassessing, seeing myself from an aerial view. I knew too many hard truths about myself by now. I supposed that was the main problem with all of us.

"What about you, Brody? Did you set a date yet?" I asked, in an attempt to turn the focus away from me.

Brody lifted one shoulder in an exaggerated shrug. "Didn't work out," he said, pulling out his phone. "But I get this guy every other weekend." He turned the screen our way, and we leaned closer to see. Brody's son would be turning one at the end of this week, though the baby in the photo was tiny, swaddled in a white blanket, tucked up in Brody's arm.

"Adorable," I said, and it was. Both the baby and Brody, which was probably what he was going for. Even Hollis smiled warmly at him.

It was a comfort, at least, that no one else here seemed any better at maintaining long relationships than I was.

I drained the beer quickly, poured myself another. Found myself shaking off the initial resistance, sliding into it again—this place, the people. My second round quickly turned into a third, though I assumed others were further along. There was no point keeping count anymore. This was the way to get through day one.

At some point Oliver handed over his credit card to Joanie, and no one else complained or offered. There was no use pretending here.

I could see the rest of the night playing out, with a familiar comfort. Half of us would retreat to our rooms immediately, welcoming the sleep. The other half would sit out back around the fire pit, terrified of the quiet and the stillness. I hoped Amaya would be there, cooled off, flipping on the outside lights, watching for our return.

We walked home together in a cloud of alcohol and laughter that verged on hysteria. In an uncharacteristic misstep, Hollis tripped on a curb and Oliver caught her around the waist, and everyone started up again. I found myself leaning into Grace as we walked, felt Brody's proximity as he circled around us, making sure we all heard him tell the story of some bar fight he'd started, or ended—I couldn't tell. It was happening to all of us, the process of sloughing off our reservations. Stripping one another down again.

We stumbled up the porch steps in the dark. We hadn't bothered locking the door. There were only the isolated vacation homes that had been here forever, and the residents of the bungalows that had been here for even longer.

The inside felt alive and thrumming, waiting for us. We kicked off our shoes and filled up the downstairs with our laughter, some calls of good night, and Brody asking who was in for *one more by the fire*.

"Calling it," I said, feeling the pull of the bed. I was the first one up the stairs, eager for sleep. Ready to tick off the day, so I could get to the next, counting them down.

It took until I was in my bedroom—alone—to realize that Amaya had not yet returned. But then, my concern was dulled with alcohol. Besides, it would not be the first time she'd spent a night away. I removed my necklace, changed into pajamas.

The air felt humid, so I opened the balcony doors, letting in the night breeze. I remembered the water-logged phone I'd left outside, and went to retrieve it from the corner spot, a shadow on the deck railing. It was now cold to the touch, but at least felt dry.

Brody's laughter echoed from the patio as I closed myself inside again. I brought the damaged phone to the charger beside the dresser and plugged it in. Nothing happened, but maybe leaving it overnight would bring it back to life.

Then I curled up in the bed closest to the window with my own cell, scrolling through my messages. There was a note from my mom, asking if I could make it to my dad's birthday next month—her subtle way of checking in on me. And a text from my boss, Jillian. I'd sent her a note in a rush that I was heading out of town for a family emergency but would be working remotely, if a little off-hours. Even though she encouraged the rest of us to stay offline outside of work hours, she rarely did. She'd responded just a few moments before: *Take whatever time you need, and take care.*

Jillian was a great boss, flexible as long as I hit my deadlines, which I always did. I worked part-time for her company in corporate events, which generally allowed me to work from home with the exception of the events themselves. And the job played to my strengths. I confirmed and reconfirmed details, and then acted like it wasn't a big deal when a client requested a change of venue after a deposit was sent, or a last-minute menu add, or an edit to the already printed programs. It was high stress but low stakes. And then, when the event finally arrived, my job was to disappear into the background, become unnoticeable. I made sure everyone was where they were supposed to be, checked each item off a list, then slipped out of the room. Wiping my fingerprints, erasing my trail. As if I had never been there.

I adjusted my hours as needed, and I freelanced on my own

for smaller, local things. Like Russ, who taught math part-time at a local college as needed, but tutored for double that hourly pay on his own. The self-drive and hustle were just other things we had in common.

I scrolled to Russ's name, before deciding against calling him. He was too far away now. This was always the true danger here. The way these anniversaries became all-consuming, as if nothing else existed but us, and this place.

I heard a creak outside on my balcony, slid from bed, and stepped into the night again. "Amaya?" I whispered, thinking she'd want to avoid Josh when she returned. But the deck was empty.

Another creak, this time from above. Either Josh outside his bedroom, or someone visiting him.

I retreated inside, locked the balcony doors behind me, then wondered if I should leave them open, for her. I had this image of her sitting on the beach now, waiting for everyone to go to sleep, before climbing the steps, sneaking inside.

Amaya once told me—in the dark, in this very room—that sometimes, for no reason at all, she would become stuck. Like even the decision to move had become too much. Frozen by the responsibility of choice, in every moment of her life. She probably regretted telling me that.

But now I couldn't help picturing her stuck out there somewhere, unable to bring herself back. Maybe parked in the public access lot for the beach. Or outside the lobby of the nearest motel. Unsure what to do, or where to go.

I scrolled back through my texts, to the one from earlier today. To the unknown number I assumed was Amaya, asking if I had heard, and then sending the obituary. Bringing me here.

I stared at the open thread, my response the last message sent: *On my way*—showing delivered.

Now I sent another text: *Where are you??*

A buzz came from across the room, and I bolted upright in bed. It sounded like the vibration of a phone.

Maybe that damaged phone I'd plugged in, miraculously coming back to life after all.

But I sat very still, held my breath.

I looked back at the unknown number and pressed call.

I jolted as the phone vibrated again on the dresser. I could feel it thrum across every inch of my skin, a cold sweat, a rise of goose bumps. I had assumed this was Amaya's number, but that couldn't be her phone—I'd seen her at the house, just before finding it on the beach.

Which meant that someone else had texted me this morning. Someone else had wanted me here.

The buzzing continued, relentless. An engine droning around a curve in the road. A rumble of thunder in the distance. A portent.

Then, just like now, a warning that rattled deep in my bones.

THEN

HOUR 7

Amaya

The thunder was directly overhead, making each of them flinch. They could see one another shivering in the flashes of lightning, before they fell to shadows again. Some were huddled together, others were spread along the wide rock ledge.

But it wasn't the thunder that Amaya was worried about. It was the sound of the river, growing louder, closer. It was the water she could see lapping over the ledge, anytime the sky lit up.

It was no longer the same river they'd crawled out of. Its boundaries were expanding, the water consuming everything in its path.

Amaya knew what to do. She knew what she *had* to do then. It was a trait instilled in her from a young age, a belief that extended beyond herself. A responsibility.

The members of the Andrews family were overachievers, they were leaders, doers. Amaya had been bilingual since she could speak—her mother, an artist who had fled Cuba as a teen; her father, generations deep into North Carolina law—and she was well on her way to mastering a third. She was a triple threat: student-athlete-artist. She would attend Duke, just as her father and her grandfather had before. Great things were ahead.

But she understood too, more than the rest of her classmates, that risk was not a thing that could be calculated in math class or fully reconciled by history. That it was often tied to some element of loss. She had witnessed that dichotomy in her mother's expression as she told the stories of her past, triumph mixed with regret.

The Andrewses made their own fate, as her dad was fond of saying—but it was her mother who had truly embodied that motto, and she was a García. She pictured her mother now, stepping into a boat in the dark, keeping her face turned toward the open sea, heading into the unknown.

She knew what she had to do.

This trip had been Amaya's idea, as head of the Volunteer Club. She'd set it up, joining a Habitat for Humanity project where a string of tornadoes had ravaged a stretch of three entire towns in Tennessee. The mess they were now in was her responsibility.

The vans were gone. Both of them, washed away down the surging river. Washed away with—

Don't think it. Don't.

Her mother said Amaya was good at compartmentalizing, and she didn't realize that was a compliment until just that moment:

The bent metal, the shattered glass, the rush of water—in a box.

The two teachers and the classmates beyond saving—in a box.

The ones that were still missing—*don't name them, don't think of them*—in a box.

Amaya stared at the darkness, the rising water, the steep walls surrounding them, the people scattered on the rocks, shadows in the night. And it was like only she could see it. Something steadily coming for them, in the sound of the rushing river.

No one was looking for any of them. They'd left the highway miles before the accident, an ill-advised detour. Most likely, no one would notice their absence until the morning, at best. But Amaya was sure of one thing if they remained still, waiting:

They were trapped. And if they didn't move, they were going to die.

It was already too late for some of them.

Don't look at them. The ones pulled from the back of her van that they'd left huddled together, against the cliff wall.

There was nothing she could do for them now.

"Listen, we need to—" she began, but no one was looking at her or listening.

Only that one girl—Cassidy—who she'd never spoken to before. She could see the whites of her eyes shining in her direction, waiting. Like she knew exactly what Amaya had been about to say.

The promise of adulthood, the freedom to make the decisions—no one had told her the weight of it.

"We have to go," Amaya said. Softly at first. So that the only person who heard her was the one staring at her. It didn't matter that they weren't friends, that they knew nothing about one another except for their names. The night had stripped away everything else. A matter of hours, and relationships didn't matter. Pasts didn't matter. Only this, right now.

And now Cassidy was looking at her, wide-eyed.

Amaya stared back at her, like she was asking a question, or for permission, an acknowledgment that the decision was right.

Cassidy nodded.

"We have to move!" Amaya shouted now, hands cupped around her mouth, more sure of herself.

"How?" Brody asked, as the others pulled into a circle. They had already traced the perimeter. The cliff walls slick with rain on one side, the surging water on the other. And the river was too fast, too risky. They knew that now.

"Up," Amaya said. "We have to climb." There were ledges and grooves, at least as far as she could feel. They couldn't know more until they tried. And they had to try.

"We can't," Clara said, her words like a plea. "We can't just leave . . ." She looked behind her, but Amaya knew better. She'd looked once, and that was enough.

Amaya instead looked to Cassidy, hoping. Waiting.

Cassidy cleared her throat. "We have to try."

Ian was at Cassidy's side, had been that way since they arrived on the rocks, even though Amaya didn't think they'd known each other before tonight. It was like he was bound to her by some invisible force, or whatever had happened in the other van.

Ian was injured, his arm held close to his side. "Okay," he said, or she thought he said, his words swallowed up by another round of thunder.

Amaya knew there was power in numbers, and now she had three. Four, if she counted Brody, who hadn't answered either way, but she knew he would've argued if he didn't agree. And Brody would bring Hollis. Five.

Oliver, who had been standing behind her, was suddenly beside her. "Let's go, then," he said, as if it had been his plan all along. Joshua, standing on the outskirts of the group, said nothing, but he would come, too. She'd known him long enough to know he didn't make decisions, barely followed the path laid out before him unless he was guided along the way.

Grace stood behind Clara, arms around her shoulders, talking to her. "Grace," Amaya called, pulling her attention from Clara. "We're going," she said, decision made.

Clara's entire body was shaking. "No, we have to wait," she said.

"We can't wait," Amaya said. That time was gone.

"We have to wait with them." Clara gestured behind her.

"Clara," she said, eyes closed, "we'll send someone back for them. It's the only way."

"It's the only way," Grace echoed.

But Clara pulled away from Grace, disappearing into the shadows along the rocks. Amaya couldn't watch her, speaking with the dead. Grace hadn't moved. She looked over her shoulder at Clara, and then back at Amaya.

"Grace," Amaya said, "get her." Grace and Clara had been inseparable since middle school. They would stay or go as one.

Grace listened, slipping into the darkness. When she returned, she was dragging Clara with her, and then Brody had to help.

"Please," Clara begged, arms on Grace's, as if only she would understand.

But Grace pulled her closer. "Don't look back," she said, making the decision for her. And then she pushed her ahead.

"We have to get out *now*!" Amaya yelled. The words echoed through the group, a command, a force.

Amaya welcomed the rain, the thunder, focusing on that noise alone. And not the arguing, the crying. She put a foot on the first ledge, and pulled herself up. Oliver stepped up beside her, and quickly moved ahead. It wasn't as steep as she thought. Once they made it to the next level, there was enough room to lie down, to reach for the others, to help them along the way.

And then, with a sudden rush, Amaya heard the water rising, barreling toward them. Like some dam had been opened.

"Go!" she shouted, as she pulled Clara up. "Go, go, go!"

The next level was a rocky path, and they walked it like a tightrope in the dark, one hand on the arm in front of them, another on the rock wall. Amaya heard the river, coming even closer. *Look forward. Keep moving.*

She lost her footing only once in a frantic scramble, but Cassidy, who was behind her, had her under the shoulders before she could fall. "Keep going," Cassidy said, once she had her feet planted firmly again.

Amaya couldn't worry about the others, could only hope they were as lucky as she was, with Oliver in front and Cassidy behind her.

They came to the end of a path, with another rocky incline, slippery in the rain, and worked slowly, as a team. Joshua and Brody boosting all the rest, before getting pulled up themselves.

They kept ascending. In the dark, it was the only thing she was sure of. They were moving upward, putting more distance between them and the rising water. Somewhere tucked into the cliffside, they stumbled onto a trail. A path. A scramble of roots on their hands and knees.

And then: trees. Their hands on branches and trunks, pulling themselves up the incline. A frantic desperation. Finally: hope. She started to run, felt the others following. Branches catching on her face, her arms. Until suddenly the branches were gone, and she felt pavement under her feet. And they stood that way. Stood there together, waiting, in the pouring rain, lightning piercing the sky, thunder cracking overhead.

Until finally, a light appeared around the curve. They started screaming, arms waving in the air. A truck, brakes screeching, coming to a stop.

"Help! Help us!" Amaya yelled, the scream tightening her throat.

She ran toward the truck as the door swung open and a man jumped down, racing toward them, phone in his hand.

Amaya was shaking, with the cold, with adrenaline, with something unnamed, slowly clawing its way forward—

"See," she said, turning back to the others. *See*, she wanted to tell them. *Look where I have led you. Look what we did.*

We lived.

She waited for the relief to come, like elation. No one would meet her eyes.

"We made it," Oliver said, his body hunching. Then Grace began crying, loud, gasping sobs. Brody had Hollis under one arm, and reached out for Grace with the other. Cassidy kept a hand on Ian's shirt, soaked through, as if she thought he might still disappear.

As the man called 911, he counted them in the beam of the headlights. "Seven, eight, nine kids—"

"We have to go back," Clara sobbed. "There are—" But Joshua pulled her tighter, so tight, her cries were muffled into his shoulder.

"Shh," Josh said, close to her ear.

They'd all heard the violence of the river. The crash of the water flooding through the gorge, close at their heels. They knew there was no surviving it.

Amaya saw it all, a montage: the people they had left behind—injured, huddled along the base of the cliffs. The haunting look in their eyes. It was too late for them, she knew. She'd known it from the start.

It was then the boxes finally opened. There would be no going back—not ever. Anyone left behind was gone.

Amaya pictured her mother on a boat. Her bravery. And she tried to find the same feeling—defiance, strength. The inevitable choices that were required in desperate moments. Instead, Amaya saw their faces, yearbook shiny. She could smell Morgan's shampoo still, from where she rested her head on the seat beside hers; feel Ben's first kiss her freshman year, the way her heart had fluttered; hear Trinity screaming after them all as they walked away: *Don't leave us, don't you dare leave us—*

And Clara yelling over her shoulder: *We'll come right back!* The most generous of them, even with her lies.

Until the screams turned into something else, and then fell to nothing at all.

Standing in the road, under the rain, in the headlights of the truck, Amaya felt no relief. Only a crushing darkness.

MONDAY

CHAPTER 4

I was dreaming of it again. The darkness. The voices calling after us. The haunting echoes pulling us back, then and now. I imagined them tugging at Clara, impossible to silence. The nightmare that Ian had been trying to numb for the last decade.

The memory always came to me in the moments between sleep and wake, in a half dream, the sequence of events always the same: invariable, inescapable—a trap from which I would never be free.

The official story, which was told and believed, written up and then forgotten by all but the people impacted, was of a single incident. A terrible accident, with a small group of survivors. A horror from which, seven hours later, we finally clawed our way to safety.

The official report had a sharp delineation, a before and after. Victims and survivors in an instant. Luck and fate. We didn't *know* what had happened to the others, we claimed—whether they remained trapped in the vans, underwater; whether they freed themselves somewhere else, before succumbing to the elements.

That was the story we told the truck driver who found us, the police and rescue workers who came for us. And then it was the story we told our parents, the school officials, the lawyers. We did not tell the victims' families—we left that to Amaya's dad's law firm. And we did not talk to the press.

It was a tragedy, for sure, but it was not a *story*—not something with legs. It did not tell of either the layers of horror or the layers of survival. Not the layers of decisions that bound the nine of us together, and would continue to bind those of us who remained, for years to come.

It was so easy to agree to that pact. We kept each other's secrets, and we kept each other safe.

We were already part of it, whether we called it a pact or not. And maybe that was the comfort of being together each year at this time. Here, we looked at one another and knew we were surrounded by people who had made the same choice. Who rationalized it, and understood there was no other option. If we had remained, we would have perished alongside them. It was a collective guilt we bore together.

Who could fault us, really, for doing what it took to survive?

We could. Only we could.

• • •

The sound of a door slamming shut jarred me fully awake. It always took me a moment to reorient myself to the house, to this room with the aqua comforters and the dark wooden furniture. To process the muffled sound of a seagull's cry, the crash of a wave. A moment before my mind caught up and whispered: *You're back. You're here, at The Shallows. With them.*

The feeling slowly returned to my limbs. That phone was still in my hand, resting on my chest—how I must've finally succumbed to sleep in the predawn hours.

Orange light now filtered through the sheer curtains, casting a glow across the wood floor. I lifted the phone from my chest, stared at my dark reflection in the cracked screen, then pressed the power button, just to check.

Dead, again. Not a surprise—it had powered off anytime I disconnected it from the charger for long. I plugged it in, and it came to life again after a moment. There was no password prompt, but the home screen glitched every time I tried to open an app or the call log, the phone flashing green and then rebooting itself in the process.

Who knew how long it had been tossed around in the surf and sand.

But. This phone, which I had found abandoned and broken on the beach—it had been used to text me. To bring me here. And I had no idea who it belonged to.

A creak echoed from somewhere on the deck, and I sat up quickly, a slight headache forming behind my eyes. A quick rush of footsteps followed, and I bolted from the bed, leaving the phone behind. I pictured someone running away, someone needing help—

I threw open the doors to the deck, hand still gripping the sheer curtains that hung over the glass, my fingers catching in a tear in the fabric. But the only movement I saw was a person in the distance, feet kicking up loose gravel as they headed toward the beach. Hollis, in her workout gear, running with long, confident strides, now crossing the wooden path through the dunes.

I squinted against the sunrise, the bright reflection off the sea making my eyes water.

Another step came from the decking directly above me, and I craned my neck to the side, peering up. Joshua was leaning forward, his arms resting on the rail, watching her. Or maybe he was just watching the sunrise.

He didn't seem to notice me.

A phone rang—unfamiliar, and loud—and my heart jumped in response. But it was coming from above. "This is Josh," he answered immediately. A pause. "No, I'm out of office this week . . ." And then his voice trailed off as the door latched shut above. It seemed his call was complete. I imagined this was the way lawyers spoke, clipped and efficient, as if every word had a price.

I followed his lead, returning to my room, closing and locking the doors to the outside behind me. I stared at the phone on the dresser, unsettled.

There were only so many people who could've texted me

yesterday. I had assumed Amaya the most likely to realize I had changed my number and track me down, with her family and their connections in town. But by that logic, Josh could've done it too. He probably spoke to Amaya's family more often than she did.

It was a process of elimination, who this phone belonged to. I'd already seen Grace, Hollis, and Brody with their phones yesterday evening. And Josh didn't seem to be missing his either.

• • •

Downstairs, Grace was set up at the long dining room table, laptop open in front of her. She had wireless earbuds in, and was running her fingers through the ends of her dark hair as she nodded at someone on the other end of a video call.

I tried to bypass her field of vision on my way to the kitchen, but she held up a single finger, as if to warn me.

"Of course," she said into the laptop screen. "Yes, I have us down for Wednesday morning. We'll pick up then." She held her smile as she disconnected the video call. Then she shut the laptop, leaning back in the chair.

"Morning, lovely," she said, in that same voice, professional and warm, designed to lure something out of you. It was obvious she'd been up for a while, hair and makeup done and wearing pearl earrings to complement her emerald-green blouse.

"Work?" I asked.

"This was the best backdrop." She gestured to the whitewashed wall behind her, a simple clock with Roman numerals the only decor visible. "It's the only room where it didn't seem like I was on vacation. Hollis was still sleeping during my first appointment."

My gaze focused on the clock behind her—it was after nine a.m., much later than I typically slept at home. "She just headed out for a run," I said.

Grace shrugged, picking up the cell beside her, a decal of a star on the back of her case. "I've got a break now anyway," she said, placing her bare feet up on the chair beside her.

My parents had brought me to see someone like Grace in that first interminable summer after the accident. To be fair, I wasn't sure whether the person they set me up with was a therapist, exactly, or some life coach my mother was semi-aligned with. She greeted my mom by first name in the waiting room. Then she had me walk through a series of exercises, as a way to help *process*, she claimed, asking me to imagine that it had been someone else out there that night. Someone besides myself. As if what happened had been someone else's story, and I could see, from a remove, how to give them the grace and empathy I would give a stranger.

It didn't work. Mostly because I could only imagine her doing exactly what Grace did now. Shutting her office door at the end of a session, just as Grace shut the lid of her laptop. Closing the door on the events she was trying to guide me through, and trapping me there with them again—alone.

"Is everyone else sleeping?" I asked, keeping my voice low. Oliver's room was tucked across from the kitchen.

Her eyes followed my gaze. "Oliver and Brody went to the store a little while ago. Early risers."

"Oh," I said. I didn't know how I'd managed to sleep later than everyone else. I was generally a light sleeper, jarred awake by every noise from the apartment next door at home. But Brody had a baby now, and Oliver worked a high-pressure job.

I cleared my throat. "Amaya hasn't been back, you know," I said.

"She checked in with me this morning," Grace said, laying her cell on the surface of the table, as if I needed evidence. I twisted the phone to face me, saw the latest text from Amaya: *At the campgrounds.*

I looked at the time of her message. Two hours since she'd checked in, with no indication of whether she was coming back or what was keeping her away.

Grace dragged the phone back across the table. "What are you worried about, Cass?" she asked carefully, with a tip of her head. A strategy she must've employed with hundreds of patients.

Did she need me to say it? First, Clara. Now, Ian. His death had made this week feel essential again. "We come together for a reason this week," I said, just as carefully.

"*Amaya*," she said, much louder than necessary, before dropping her voice again. "She lives out there." The closest she'd come to voicing the thing we feared.

Her logic was sound. For reasons I could not understand, Amaya lived and worked in East Tennessee, the same area we'd all tried desperately to forget. She'd settled in Stone River Gorge, and then worked to establish a regional offshoot of the state emergency resource center, assessing need and coordinating volunteers. I'd seen the logo on the back of her car: *Build—Save—Grow*. Every year a new decal appeared on her back windshield—another cause she supported, another resource to be saved.

She must've driven past the site of our accident more than once. She must've heard the river in the background on her way to work. I understood what Grace was saying: Amaya faced it head-on, every day. If there was anyone we *shouldn't* be worried about, it was her.

"You know," she said, leaning closer, like she was getting ready to share a secret. "She even went to the memorial library dedication." Eyes widening. "Can you imagine thinking that was a good idea for her?"

I could not. Even after we had escaped the river, we were faced with countless traps, a series of events requiring us to revisit the trauma:

First the funerals. Then the one-year memorial, with the twelve bells for the twelve lives lost, and Clara's subsequent death later that night. If that all wasn't enough, our school decided they would dedicate a library to the lost. It had finally opened earlier this year, and we were all invited.

I got a chill, remembering that email, shiny gold script inviting me to the ribbon-cutting ceremony for the Long Branch Academy Class of 2013 Memorial Library.

I'd deleted it, and began the process of disentangling myself.

It was all too much, each time. Reliving our roles, revisiting our mistakes, wondering how we could've done it differently, who we could've saved this time.

"Look," Grace continued, "this whole thing is stressing her out." She moved her hands as if to signify: *this, us*—as if this week wasn't a source of stress for every one of us. "And I have *heard*"—she paused at the word—"that things haven't been great with her family. A fact Josh is probably all too aware of. So is it any surprise she doesn't want to stay in the same house as him?"

"You can't be sure—"

She waved me off. "You know how she is. She's unreliable, Cassidy." She spoke the word as if it were a diagnosis. "But this is not out of character."

"Can you send me her number?" I asked. I'd feel better if I could reach her, check in myself. Not just rely on Grace for information.

Another tilt of her head. "Don't you have it?"

How to say: *I deleted it. I deleted you all.*

"I got a new phone. Lost a bunch of my contacts when it transferred. Here, let me give you my new number." I rattled the digits off to her as she entered them into her phone. She looked at me quizzically, as if she could see right through me, then texted me Amaya's contact.

"If she doesn't want to be around us, she's not going to answer, you know," Grace mumbled. "If she needs space to process, then we should give her space, Cassidy."

I nodded, half listening as I saved the information in my phone. At least I had both Grace's and Amaya's numbers again.

The front door opened then, and Oliver barged through, carrying two trays of coffees. He spoke loudly into the room, but he didn't appear to be talking to us. "Right, that asshole always acts like he's been put in charge."

Brody trailed behind him, carrying a paper grocery bag from the local shop in town.

Oliver deposited the trays on the counter and started removing the cups, reading the names. He handed a cup to Grace, and then one to me.

I took a sip, and it was just how I liked it. Hazelnut, cream and sugar.

Thank you, I mouthed as he passed, catching his gaze before it slipped away, and he laughed at whatever someone was saying on the other end.

This was Oliver's skill: always able to remember the finer details. He made sure this rental was reserved at the same time each year, and didn't seem to expect much from the rest of us; he could negotiate a deal at the grocery store, while recalling everyone's coffee preferences from the prior year.

Oliver left the rest of the coffee cups in a line along the counter, names facing out. Only Hollis's was out of place, a cold berry smoothie in a plastic cup, condensation dripping down the outside. Oliver took stock of the room. Then, noticing her absence, changed his mind, sticking her cup in the fridge. "Yeah, yeah," Oliver spoke, "tell them no."

"Sleep okay?" Brody asked, dropping the grocery bag on the counter.

God, these really were the people who knew me best. Maybe not what exactly I did at work, or my daily routines, but how I took my coffee, the most likely state of my romantic relationship, the things that kept me up, or haunted me in my sleep.

I nodded. "Are there more groceries in the car?" I asked as Brody emptied the contents from the first bag directly into the fridge.

"Yeah," he said, "thanks."

Outside, Brody's trunk was open, and there were three more paper bags inside. I hitched one onto my hip before grabbing a second. Behind them, stuffed into the back of the trunk, Brody's EMT uniform was visible, as if he'd come straight from a shift.

There was a first aid kit behind it, along with a black toolbox, which reminded me that Brody was probably the only one of us prepared for an actual emergency. The only one who had trained and armed himself appropriately, who was capable of keeping someone else alive.

For as many times as I imagined a disaster striking, for as many times as I had to imagine who to save, for as much as I tried to plan for the worst, Brody was probably the only one of us who could do it.

"Thanks, Cass," he said now, brushing up behind me while my hands were full. "I think we're the only ones who actually took off this week. Even Hollis seems to be walking people through a workout remotely out back." He rolled his eyes, following me up the front steps.

"Sorry to say I've got a little work to do this week too." I pushed the door ajar with my hip.

"Still enjoying the event-planning life?"

"Yes," I said honestly. I had been drawn to the arts growing up, had always loved creating—but now I needed to ground myself with more substance, more facts. I enjoyed seeing assignments through from beginning to end, turning the abstract into the concrete.

Brody dropped the keys onto the island, then set the last bag down beside mine.

"Well," he said, "my job can't be done remotely. At least Oliver pays for everything here." He laughed. Oliver passed behind him but made no indication he'd heard. "Turns out kids are expensive," Brody added with a grin.

Our first year here, we had all taken off. Treated it like a retreat, or a vacation at least. But that too had shifted with time.

As we emptied the groceries, Joshua came down the steps, wearing the bathing suit I'd seen draped over his chair and a gray T-shirt. His dark hair was unstyled, held back by the wraparound sunglasses on top of his head.

"Have you been up in my room?" he asked before he'd reached the bottom of the steps.

"Nope," Brody said, and Oliver gestured to the earbud in his ear, ignoring his question.

"Not you," he said to Brody. "We all left for dinner together. I meant *you*." I could tell without looking up, just by the way he said it, that he was talking about me. It was the disdain, the accusation.

Hollis had stayed back too, but he wasn't accusing her. No, it was just me.

I set the orange juice I'd just pulled from the bag onto the counter, turning to face him.

"I had to latch the outer door, which you forgot to do. It sounded like someone was upstairs." I was oversharing, over-covering. But I'd done nothing wrong. I wasn't sure how he could tell someone had been up there; it was a mess. But if the door had become unlatched, papers could've blown off the desk.

"You didn't touch anything," he said. It wasn't a question but a confirmation.

I rolled my eyes. "I didn't touch anything but the door, Josh."

He brushed by me, finding the coffee container with his name, and inhaled deeply before his first sip. Maybe this would help his mood. Some of us were more caffeine-dependent in the morning than others.

Hollis walked in the back door then, finished with her workout, and without missing a beat, Oliver opened the fridge, handed her the drink. She smiled at him, her bangs slightly damp, clinging to the sweat on her face.

It occurred to me then that Oliver hadn't bothered to get something for Amaya, in case she had returned.

Meanwhile, there was a phone in my room that someone had texted me from, and no one seemed to be missing it.

"Hey," I said, because if Josh could be confrontational at nine a.m., then so could I. "Did someone text me yesterday morning? Before I got here?"

They looked to me, and then to one another, confused. Everyone shook their heads.

"What's going on, Cass?" Brody asked, stepping closer.

How to explain it. How to say it out loud. "Someone sent me a text with Ian's obituary," I said.

The room fell silent. The only noise came from the ticking of the clock over the dining room table.

"Who?" Brody added.

"I don't know, that's why I'm asking," I said.

"Let me see," Oliver said, finally off his call, reaching his hand out.

I pulled up the text thread on my phone and scrolled to the top, so he could see the phone number and the initial message: *DID YOU HEAR?*

Oliver frowned, looking closer. Everyone remained silent, like they were waiting for more.

"It wasn't one of you?" I asked, heartbeat racing.

"North Carolina number," Oliver said.

"I know," I said. It didn't seem like he was talking to me, but I had recognized the area code as where we were all from. I took the phone back from Oliver, before he could read any more.

"Don't engage," Josh said, sitting on a stool at the counter, turning his attention back to the coffee.

I supposed it could've been someone else who still lived in town. Someone who knew Ian, and me. But it had been so long since I'd lived there, and the obituary was three months old. I couldn't shake the feeling that everyone here knew something I didn't.

The pact was supposed to be an absolution, a promise that we were on the inside and would protect one another. It was supposed to mean: *Not us.* Except, for all I knew, there'd been a newer pact. A different promise.

I already knew we were all liars. The question came down to whether I believed them about this.

Did I trust their reactions? Did I really trust any of them? Not enough to tell them there was more to it. Not enough to say: *I have the phone*. Not enough to say, like Josh would, accusatory and to the point: *I know. I know it was one of you.*

CHAPTER 5

The unspoken rule of the anniversary week was to stay busy. There was an assortment of gear in varying states of usability stored in the small shed space under the main deck, a rusted lock hanging on the latch. Paddleboards and kayaks and a single life jacket; rackets and Frisbees and a half-deflated volleyball, along with a tangled net; folded-up beach chairs that got a lot of use and fishing poles that hadn't been touched in all the times I'd been here; two bikes with tires that had seen better days.

The morning had turned unseasonably warm, and Oliver decided it was a beach day. We were seizing the moment—you never knew what the rest of the week might bring. Even the weather was unpredictable.

I had three beach chairs hanging off my shoulders as we walked in a single line toward the sand. Oliver and Hollis carried one of the ocean kayaks over their heads, while Josh and Brody handled the second. Grace was running another virtual appointment after breakfast, but we didn't wait. We knew the rules: Keep moving. Keep going.

We set up the chairs just above where the sand was wet and packed from the retreating tide. They dropped the kayaks on either side of the area, like we were walling off our territory, even though there was no one else nearby. Down the stretch of beach, I could see a few other small groups, and a couple walking hand in hand, but they were silhouettes in the distance.

"Where is everyone?" I asked. I had expected more from a morning like this, people who had been waiting for a good beach day racing to the sand to soak up the sun, parched from the winter season.

Oliver squinted into the distance, like he was looking for something offshore. "Iffy forecast this week," he said. As if that would be enough to keep people home.

The sun hadn't reached its peak, but Josh stripped off his shirt and ran straight into the surf. He barely flinched before diving into the first cresting wave.

I kept my eyes trained on the sea, trailing him as he emerged on the other side of the breakers, shaking out his hair. He turned back immediately, letting the current force him in to shore. When he rejoined the circle, his skin was covered in goose bumps, and his dark hair was dripping down the side of his face, the scar on his cheekbone more pronounced.

"You look like you made a mistake," Brody said, leaning back in the striped chair farthest from the receding waterline.

Josh grinned tightly. "Wakes you up better than the subpar coffee."

"I'll take your word for it," Brody said. Like me, he didn't get in the water. Never did.

Josh grabbed the end of the nearest ocean kayak. "Any other takers?" he asked.

"Maybe later," Hollis said.

Josh shrugged, then headed back toward the surf. I watched as he paddled straight into the breakers, forced back twice before making it through.

The sound side was better for water activities—a calmer current, a buffer from the wind. Out here, the current was rough and the wind whipped the sand across the beach, stinging my ankles. There was no barrier reef. Here, we were subject to the full force of the Atlantic.

But the beach was more convenient to the house. And the ocean was the challenge.

"All right, who's in," Brody said, pulling a Frisbee from the sand, covering for the fact that he never touched the water.

Oliver stood first, then Hollis joined in. She avoided anything one-on-one with Brody, even when separated by an expanse of sand. It was predictable, if pained, because it only worked the one way. Brody treated her the same as he treated all of us—with an openness and vulnerability that drew people closer. "Nice, Holl," he called now, as she lunged for a catch.

Brody's phone lit up in the cupholder of his chair, a buzz that jolted me back to the night before. I reached a single finger to his armrest, flipped it against the other edge of the cupholder, so I could see the text lighting up the display. *Will you be there Sunday?* A woman's name, Vanessa, that I recognized from last year. *Vanessa's in labor.*

Probably his son's birthday party. A first birthday.

And then, as I was looking, another buzz. This time the number had no contact info. *Couldn't find anything.*

"I should've known," Grace said, from somewhere behind me. She was walking across the sand, hand clutching the bottom of her long cover-up to keep it raised over the sand. "No note?" she said with a small grin.

My heart rate slowed as I realized she was just annoyed that we'd left without telling her where we'd be. Maybe *annoyed* was the wrong term. She was smiling, as Grace often was, and she had a suit on under her cover-up, so she must've been able to see us from her balcony. We were hard to miss, as a group.

She took the seat beside me, pulling her cover-up skirt over her knees, feet digging into the sand, even cooler under the surface. Hollis bailed from the Frisbee game and joined us, slightly out of breath and glowing with exertion. "Okay," she said, hands resting on her sand-covered thighs. "I'm ready to cool down."

She took the second kayak and started dragging it toward the surf. "Wish me luck," she called, as the water crested her ankles. She turned away, then angled the kayak toward the horizon, and set out.

"I never understand how they make it look so easy," Grace said, watching Hollis navigate her kayak through the surf on her first attempt, a vision of balance. "I tried it once, flipped over at the first wave. I can barely balance on the sound side." She sighed, then took out a magazine, edges already fraying.

But I couldn't help keeping an eye on everyone. Hollis and Joshua, gliding effortlessly across the surface, rising and falling with the swells. Brody and Oliver on the sand, challenging each other with farther and farther throws. Grace lifted her gaze from the magazine as she turned the page. I felt her eyes on the side of my face. "They're fine," she said, as if she could read my fears. "Kayaks float. And they're together."

As if that was the trick. As if all we needed was a buddy system.

Maybe Grace had found the center I was searching for. The ability to acknowledge the danger, and then set it aside, focusing on something else. It was a trait I desired strongly.

"How are you so calm all the time?" I asked.

She laughed. "Well, we've been through the worst of it, right?"

I shook my head, confused that she could attribute her state of peace to that one horrific night. I couldn't fathom how. She'd told us she had found God out there, which I thought unlikely. It was back during our third or fourth reunion week, one of those nights when we kept opening more and more bottles, skirting dangerously close to the past—and even then I'd thought she was trying to convince herself of something.

Still, I envied her. The ability to believe, even if it was only in the lies she was telling herself.

"Do you ever think about her, Grace?" I asked. I knew I was breaking an unspoken rule, bringing up the past, but she had opened the door first. And this was Grace—she delved into the past on a daily basis, professionally. She could pretend I was a patient, or she could ignore the question, letting my voice be carried away on the wind, buried under the surf.

She paused, one hand on the edge of the magazine, like she'd been about to flip a page. "What do you mean?" she asked.

"Clara," I continued, wondering if she could feel it, some invisible thread, tugging at us. "And now Ian."

"It's not the same thing," she said sharply. Then she shook her head. "Of course I think about her. All the time. She was my best friend. You know, there's no friendship quite like the ones forged at that age. There have been studies."

I ignored the comment, because what did that mean, if the closest relationships I could hope for were with the people here with me, right now? And not the group I'd chosen for myself in adulthood, postcollege, who found my promptness charming, my propensity for lists an amusing quirk—and not the result of a trauma that had never been mentioned?

"Did you know Ian was that bad?" I pushed. "Did anyone talk to him?"

She reached a hand out for mine, her fingers cold, or my skin hot from the sun. "Don't do this, Cassidy. It's no one's fault. One of my patients is going through something similar, something he wasn't there to stop. So I'll tell you the same thing I told him." I was pretty sure there should've been some sort of confidentiality with her sessions, but that was another thing unspoken. The regular rules did not apply here; not this week, and not to us.

"It's natural to try to center yourself," she continued. "But that story isn't about you. We like to believe we could've changed it, if only we'd been there." She turned to face me, her eyes searching mine. "But, Cass, we couldn't. We weren't there."

"Okay," I said, cutting her off. I understood what she was saying: We weren't there for Clara. But we *had* been there with Ian. Maybe not when he died, but we had witnessed his descent, year after year. We let him drift. We didn't tell him to stop or to get help, or ask if there was something we could do. We sat back, and we watched. At some point he required something more than just our presence.

"God, would you look at her," Grace said, turning her focus to the water, as Hollis rode a wave back in to shore. "Seriously, Hollis, how do you look so good doing that?" Grace called as Hollis hopped out of the kayak.

The truth was that Hollis looked good doing everything. Her Instagram featured and charted the highs and lows of her training, with personal tips. She never posted pictures from this week, though. Last year there was a series of inspirational quotes and prescheduled photos that had nothing to do with the beach and gave no indication she was on a trip. *Never underestimate yourself*, the first one declared, while she held a barbell over her head, face a mix of exertion and triumph. *Only you can change your life*, claimed another, under a photo of Hollis stretching before the start of a race.

I wasn't sure if she fully believed her mantras, but judging from the amount of interactions on her posts, other people definitely did.

Hollis slowed as she approached, her smile faltering as she glanced over our heads. Grace noticed the presence of someone else before I did, her body twisting just as the shadow stretched over us.

I turned, squinting, and even as he smiled, it took me a moment to place him. "Hey, girl-I-met-yesterday," he said. It was the guy I'd spoken to on the beach the day before, with the fishing pole against his shoulder. Today there was no rod, just a metal detector in his hand, canvas bag slung over his back.

"Hi again," I said, feeling Grace moving her head back and forth between us.

He seemed much friendlier than I recalled from our prior interaction, when he was all, *hands up, the phone isn't mine, you deal with it.*

"I'm Will," he said. "Live on the other side of the street." He shot his hand in an arrow toward the dunes. I was guessing one of the older bungalows.

"Cassidy," I said. "This is Grace. And Hollis."

Grace raised her hand but didn't say anything. Hollis smiled tightly. Josh, who had ridden in after her, abandoned the kayak halfway up the sand to join us.

Our visitor had also drawn the interest of Brody and Oliver, who were slowly heading our way. There was another rule, determined the first year, when Brody brought someone home one night from High Tide. No outsiders.

"I've seen you all here before," he said. But I didn't remember him at all. Then again, our focus tended to be on one another. "Yearly reunion?" he asked.

No one answered. Finally, I cleared my throat. "Old friends."

Josh entered the circle, gestured to the metal detector in his hand. "You're not supposed to use those out here."

Will's smile stretched wider—knowing, cool. "You're not supposed to touch the dunes, or let a fire go unattended through the night either. And yet." He gestured back at all of us.

Definitely a house close by, then.

"Thanks for the feedback," Oliver said, hands on hips.

Will seemed to get the hint, gave me one final wave before stepping around us, continuing down the sand, in the opposite direction of the pier.

"New friend, Cass?" Brody asked, falling onto the chair beside me.

"I ran into him on the beach yesterday while I was out on a walk."

Josh was watching Will's retreat, but Brody was focused on me instead.

"I think your phone was buzzing, Brody," I said, eager to deflect his attention.

Brody reached his hand into the cupholder, scanned the texts, then replaced the phone without responding. His face gave away nothing. His reaction was unnerving, so at odds with his typical demeanor—everything on the surface, like it was impossible he could be keeping secrets.

Finally, when Will was almost to the edge of the beach, where a large outcrop of rock divided our section of beach from the dunes beyond, Josh turned to face the group. His mouth stretched into a wide grin. "Race you, Hollis," he said, then ran toward the surf without waiting.

Hollis cursed and took off sprinting, sand kicking over the rest of us as she laughed.

In no time, she was beside him, high stepping it through the breakers, diving into the foaming surf.

Grace groaned beside me. "I hate when they do this," she said.

They didn't race to any specific point. They raced until someone gave up. Until someone noticed that they were too far out, the swells blocking land. Or in danger of getting caught in a riptide.

The two of them were more reckless than the rest of us, as if they believed nothing could truly touch them. But this game of chicken that they pretended they were playing with one another, they were really playing with the sea.

Historically, Hollis had always won, but this time, Josh kept going, stroke by stroke, at her side.

There was a moment, far out, when I lost sight of who was who. Of whether they stopped to wave their arms for help or in triumph. Whether they were struggling or playing. I tried to focus on Grace's belief: *They're fine*. But I felt Brody tense as well, pushing himself to standing, staring out toward the horizon.

I followed his lead, then walked to the waterline, the cold of the ocean rushing over my toes, my ankles, goose bumps rising up my legs.

Brody stood behind me, feet just out of reach of the tide. "Do you see them?" he asked.

Just then I spotted a single head above the water. "One," I said, pointing to the form visible between swells. And then—"There's two." They were side by side and seemed to be moving in tandem, coming closer. It took them twice as long to come in, like they were fighting some current that was threatening to drag them back out.

There was nothing graceful about Hollis's return to shore. She was hanging on to Josh's neck, one leg lifted over the ground, a grimace on her face as a wave pushed them forward, both of them stumbling the last few yards in.

"What happened?" I called, stepping farther into the surf, the cold chill moving up my shins, my knees. I felt the rush of the water, pulling me in, and stepped back, on instinct.

"There's something out there," Josh said, peering over his shoulder. He coughed once, then ran a hand down his face.

"I felt something," Hollis said, clearly favoring her right leg. "On my ankle." She continued limping out of the water, shaking her foot out as she made her way closer.

"Seaweed?" I said, noticing strands of it curling up against the sand at the edge of the surf, before sliding back into the sea. Some had gotten caught on Hollis's legs.

She looked down, frowned at the water rushing back around her ankles. "No, I . . . felt like I was going under."

There was panic in her voice, so unlike the person I thought her to be. She crossed her arms over her bare stomach, shoulders hunched forward. Her entire body was trembling. She bent over to remove the last piece of seaweed clinging to her.

"You're bleeding," Brody said.

She lifted her foot, and I could see the pink trail from the side of her heel. "Oh," she said absently.

"Maybe something stung her," Oliver said, now beside us as well, towel in hand.

"Bit her, more like it," Grace said, guiding Hollis toward the nearest chair. "Here, come, sit."

Grace and Oliver helped her into the seat Brody had been using, and Brody crouched in the sand before her.

His hands paused only once, and only if you were looking for it, as he moved to examine her leg. They halted over her skin, a brief flinch, before readjusting, making contact, examining the wound. It made me wonder if they'd ever touched in the ten years since the accident. Her pale leg was covered in goose bumps, pink and blotchy in sections. Her toenails, bare of polish, were chilled a bruised blue underneath.

Josh remained staring off into the water. "Something's out there," he repeated.

I imagined claws, teeth. Tendrils stretching into the deep. Something coming back for us.

"Listen," Brody said, speaking to Hollis, eyes still on her leg. "It's not big, but it's kinda deep."

Grace was crouched beside him, brushing the sand off Hollis's heel, keeping the area clean.

"I felt something," Hollis said again, tipping her head forward to get a closer look.

"There's a first aid kit in the house," Oliver said. "In one of the downstairs cabinets." He looked to me—an order. Everyone else was occupied in one way or another.

"Be right back," I said, taking off through the sand.

When I reached the wooden steps, I bypassed the outdoor shower, even though I knew I was tracking sand through the kitchen under the soles of my feet.

I threw open the kitchen cabinets. There was a mini–fire extinguisher under the sink, along with cleaning supplies we never used. Other cabinets held the utensils and pots and pans. Next, the pantry, which contained boxes of pasta and flour and sugar that had probably expired. On the floor there was a fly swatter and bug spray, a vacuum and a broom.

I scanned the rest of the kitchen, opening the upper cabinets as I moved across the space. No kit.

But I knew I'd seen one—in the trunk of Brody's car, when I was helping bring in the groceries. And he'd left his keys sprawled on the counter as he'd put the food away.

I grabbed those keys now, striding toward the front of the house and out the door, to where his car was parked beside my own.

I clicked the button to pop the trunk, then pulled it all the way open, the inside light flicking on, exposing the mostly empty space. I pushed aside the uniform I'd noticed earlier, revealing a tangle of rope I hadn't seen before. Beside that: the toolbox and a first aid kit. I picked it up, ready to race back to the beach, but the kit rattled, weight shifting unnaturally.

I frowned, placing it back down, to make sure it had what we needed.

Inside the white case, the first thing I saw was a small, powerful flashlight—what I must've felt rattling inside. Then: a set of spare batteries, a container of waterproof matches. And underneath, a pack of emergency flares.

My stomach sank, breath stuck in my throat. These were all things that would've helped us, once upon a time. The things we'd needed, ten years earlier. Rather than bandages or painkillers, Brody's kit contained things that would help if he were ever stranded or lost.

I doubted he looked at a crowd and wondered who he could save first. But we weren't unalike, at the core.

I left the kit where I'd found it and shut the trunk. I left him to his secrets—it was the least I could do. We all had our own ways of coping.

• • •

Back inside, I headed for the downstairs powder room—no kit. There was only one more bathroom down here, attached to Oliver's bedroom.

He'd left the door closed, and the curtains of his room were pulled tightly shut, blocking all light, even though these windows had the most incredible view—over the dunes, blue sky and open air. I didn't bother with a light switch, heading straight for the bathroom.

Here, the lights buzzed an unnatural fluorescent when I flicked the switch. Oliver's toiletries were out on the tiled surface, all lined up perfectly. Razor, shaving cream, toothbrush. Everything in straight lines and right angles. Even this part of his life was efficient and orderly. Only his clothes crumpled in the corner gave away that someone had arrived home late last night, half-drunk and eager for bed.

I had already wasted enough time—I pulled open the bottom cabinet, and there, of course, in an official spot, hooked into the wall of the cabinet, was a large first aid kit.

I grabbed it and ran.

By the time I was back outside, kit tucked under my arm, they were already walking down the wooden path, in no obvious rush. Oliver had his arm under Hollis, so that she could put her weight on him as she walked gingerly, keeping her right foot—now wrapped in Josh's T-shirt in some makeshift bandage—off the ground.

"Sorry. Took me a while to find it," I said from the back deck.

"Good thing she wasn't bleeding out," Josh called.

No one smiled.

"I'm *fine*," Hollis called.

I met them at the base of the steps, on the patio.

"Really, it's fine," Hollis repeated, eyes locked on mine. "I just want to get it cleaned up."

Grace stepped into the alcove at the base of the deck with the wooden door, pipes shuddering as she turned on the faucet for the outdoor shower, where each of them took turns rinsing down their legs, the backs of their arms.

I opened the first aid kit, pulling out the disinfectant and handing it to Brody.

He looked to the bottle in his hand, then back at Hollis. "This is probably going to hurt," he said.

• • •

Even though Brody said, *I don't know, it could need stitches, hard to tell*, Hollis decided against urgent care. Urgent care required a drive over a bridge, required revisiting the event, voicing it to others.

We set her up on the living room couch, leg up, bandage on. It didn't look that bad, once we were back inside.

"What if it was something poisonous?" Grace asked, peering so deep into my eyes I could almost feel the fear, spreading.

"It was probably a shell caught in the seaweed or something," Hollis said, her voice low. But she cleared her throat, looking over to Josh, who was staring out the back windows, eyes unfocused.

A shell. A shell, and seaweed. Maybe a crab, the edge of a claw, a slice like a razor blade as it passed. The hook of a fishing line, drifting over from the pier. I thought of what Will had told me yesterday, about all the things churned up in the sea.

Even the river itself ultimately ended here. I pictured the glass windows from our vans, the bent and twisted metal. Everything made it to the ocean eventually.

CHAPTER 6

The clock kept moving.

Showers, lunch, each person splitting off to work after—or to watch Netflix on their laptops. Keeping to ourselves, to our thoughts. I wondered what Amaya was doing, down at the campgrounds. Whether she was meditating, listening to the sea; whether she was strolling the coastline, picking up shells; whether she was ready to come back to us.

The afternoon was more subdued in the house, like something had managed to sneak its way in. Maybe because of Hollis, usually so composed, clearly rattled. Or Brody, how his hands had flinched over Hollis's leg, something dark threatening to spill over from the past. Or Josh, looking out to the water, like he was trying to make sense of something inexplicable.

The image of Hollis and Josh hanging off each other as they emerged from the water. I wondered if we were all seeing it, trying to force it back down.

Good thing she wasn't bleeding out—

As if all our efforts to forget only made us remember instead. The more we fought it, the tighter it pulled, like a riptide.

I could feel it again, the direction of the river, a gentle tug toward the past. Could see the ghosts of them, shadows of the people I'd come to know that night.

By the time we regrouped, Oliver was on the phone, menu out

in his hand, ordering pizzas and wings. The decision to stay in for dinner wasn't something we discussed. Something we could blame on Hollis's ankle.

"It's not bad," she kept saying from her position on the living room couch, leg up, ice pack oozing water onto the faux-wood table beside her foot.

But I thought I heard a tremble in her voice. She could probably feel it too, something pulling at us—something poking at our borders. Something coming for us all.

• • •

I left the group quickly after dinner, claiming work, and no one questioned it.

Upstairs, I sent a text to the number Grace had given me for Amaya. Something short but pointed: *Let me know you're okay please.*

And then: *It's Cassidy.*

A dull worry had wedged its way in, and I felt the need to account for everyone. I knew she'd texted Grace, but I wanted to hear from her myself. Like I was counting heads in the surf.

I stared at the screen, willing her to reply. But the messages weren't showing as delivered yet. Knowing Amaya, if she wanted to be left alone, she'd probably just turn her phone off. Or she could've run out of power—the facilities were pretty rustic at the campgrounds, and I didn't think she'd packed for a long-term stay.

While I waited, I realized I *did* need to catch up on the day, making some progress on the work I'd promised Jillian.

Voices still carried from downstairs, but I'd changed into pajamas, settled on the bed.

Just as I opened my email, I saw a shadow under my door. Someone moving in the hall, shifting back and forth in front of the door, by the looks of it.

I slowly eased the laptop beside me on the bed, getting ready to stand, when someone faintly knocked.

"Yes?" I called, still cross-legged at the head of the bed.

The door opened slowly, and Brody poked his head in first, taking in the space. Just me, just the empty room. If he was expecting something different, he didn't say.

He slipped inside, closed the door behind him, leaning back against it. "Hey," he said.

"Hey," I echoed.

"What are you up to?" he asked, eyeing the laptop.

"I was working, but it can wait."

"I was hoping you were still up. I'm not good at being alone." He smiled, half-charming, half-self-deprecating.

As he stood there, a wave of laughter carried from somewhere downstairs.

"Sounds like a full house," I said.

He rolled his eyes, stepped closer, until he was standing at the foot of my bed. I held my breath, wondering what he was doing here. "They're playing cards," he said. "Someone found a pack on the kitchen counter." His mouth fell to a flat line, his expression dark. He shook his head. "You know, sometimes I have a dream that I show up, and no one else is here. That you're all out there, happy, living your lives."

My shoulders relaxed, and I felt myself nodding along with him. It was a relief to know I wasn't the only one. Maybe all it took to feel understood was us admitting it out loud. Maybe we just needed to release one another. "I almost didn't come," I said.

He raised an eyebrow. "Why did you?"

I closed my eyes, saw Ian's picture in the obituary—the version of him from so long ago. "Ian," I said. "I only just found out."

Brody stared at me for a beat too long, then took a seat on my queen-size bed, comfortably taking up space in my room.

"It's all fucking terrible. His poor family." He took a deep, fortifying breath. "The house feels off now, right?" he asked.

"Yes," I said, leaning forward.

His eyes flitted around the space. "I thought maybe it was just because I'd always had to share a room with Josh. And now I'm finally free."

"Well, you know where Josh is, at least," I said, my eyes drifting to Amaya's untouched bed.

His gaze followed my own, and he frowned. "She's at the campgrounds, right?"

I shrugged. "I guess. But I sent her a message, to check in. I just want to know she's okay." A pause. "Can you blame me?"

He ran his tongue ran across the ridge of his teeth, like he was considering something. "Well, you know how Amaya is . . ." He trailed off.

Grace had implied the same thing, that this wasn't out of character for her. But I didn't really understand. Amaya had become a shell of the person I'd first known. "I don't, really." Since we were admitting things, I might as well come clean.

He laughed. "Maybe I don't either. Maybe none of us really do." Then he looked to the gauzy curtains, the night sky visible beyond. "I bet it was her."

But I didn't know what he was talking about. I always felt a step behind, here. "Bet *what* was her?"

His eyes widened. "You know, the . . ." He moved his arms around, like he was trying to find the words. Then he lowered his voice. "The tell-all. Or podcast. Whatever the hell it's supposed to be."

I closed my eyes, shaking my head. "I don't . . . What are you talking about?"

His face changed, almost as if he were trying to take his words back, let the facade slide into place again. "You haven't been contacted?" he asked, keeping his voice low, like someone might be listening on the other side of the closed door.

"No," I said firmly. "Contacted by who?" I was desperately trying to catch up, figure out what this tell-all was, and who was doing it.

"Legal department? Fact-checkers? I don't know, I didn't respond, didn't ask for specifics." He tipped his head, eyes meeting mine. "You really don't know? I mean, you were on that email chain. Josh said to call if we needed advice."

That email chain. What could I say? *No, I wasn't getting them. I sent you all to junk. I pretended you didn't exist.* "I didn't see it," I said. "My email filters a lot . . ." My eyes drifted away, afraid he could read the lie in me.

But now I was seeing the last few days in an entirely different context. The undercurrent in the house, the tension, the things others were discussing when I walked into their space, before falling silent. This thing everyone was tiptoeing around, and why Oliver wanted to see my phone. *Don't engage*, Josh had said earlier.

"Well," Brody said, leaning closer, so the room felt smaller, warmer. "Someone's talking, Cass."

"About what?" I asked, voice just as low, afraid of the answer.

"Hell if I know. But whatever it is, it's enough to get someone interested in a horrible accident from a decade ago." He moved his jaw back and forth, until I heard a pop. "Anyway, Josh thinks it's Amaya. The settlement's running out."

I assumed he was talking about his settlement, as much as Amaya's. I had a bit left myself still, but I hadn't needed to use it for college.

After we gave our statements, after the bodies were recovered, after the funerals—there was an independent investigation. It was less about what happened at the river, and more about what led to the accident. Ten students and two teachers had perished on a school trip, and someone had to pay. When we crashed, no one knew where we were. We had no means to call for help. The investigation was swift, and the outcry fierce. Amaya's family firm represented us, as a group.

The school had decided to settle quickly with each of the families, instead of dragging things out in a publicized hearing. The dead got more than the living, which seemed fair, if impractical.

"But all of us got the same thing," I said. A motivation for her was a motivation for everyone. There was an improbable sum for the dead, paid out to their families annually, and an impressive one for the living. A solid seven figures for our troubles. It had felt like so much then, when we were eighteen. But it had been split nine ways, and given to each of us in a single lump sum. Maybe Oliver had invested his share and watched it grow, but others had to use it for school, for life. And then I leaned closer, hands braced on the bed between us. "Is that what everyone else thinks?" I asked. Now I understood why no one was surprised by Amaya's departure.

He lifted his hands, a *not guilty* move. "Well, no one wants to come right out and say it. But she went to the dedication for the library in January. Josh saw her. There must've been press there, right?"

My mind wandered. There'd been a fight, maybe Josh coming right out and accusing her: *I know it was you*. And whether he was right or not, she'd taken off.

Maybe it *was* her.

"I didn't know," I said, my mind moving too fast now. Wondering what would be worth knowing, ten years later. What would be worth someone revealing. Trying to decipher the market value of our secrets.

What are we doing here? I suddenly thought.

"You always were the most generous one," Brody said, pulling me back to the present. "With how you saw us. Saw me."

He smiled slightly. Fingers drumming on the surface of the comforter. He saw me looking, smiled again suggestively.

It's not that I hadn't thought of it before. Brody had the trifecta of charm and looks and talent that had manifested in high school and never quite faded. And there was something very specific about the pull of someone who had once been beyond reach. Someone who had never noticed me during the four years we spent together in school, who was now sitting on the corner of my bed, implication obvious.

It made me want to keep him here, in this limbo, before there were any repercussions.

My phone rang then, jarring us both, breaking through the private bubble of this room. I saw *Russ Johnson* on the display, and I felt a moment of relief. "I have to take this," I said.

He nodded, smiling tightly, before standing again.

Sorry, I mouthed. Even though it was for the best. If you believed in fate, then you had to go all in.

I waited until he'd backed out of the room and shut the door before answering. "Hey," I said.

"Hey there, just wanted to check in." Russ's voice was warm and familiar, and my hand went to my neck, a tether to reality, trying to hold tight to this other version of my life. But I'd left my necklace on the dresser, across the room.

"Figured I'd have better luck catching you at night," he said.

"All good at home?"

"Yep," he said. "Plants watered. Mail in." Steady, reliable Russ. I felt a pang, a homesickness, a preemptive sadness. I'd left him a key to my apartment, asked him to drop by throughout the week. More things I'd soon have to walk back, unwinding us. Retrieving the key, turning the lock.

I heard the drone of the television in the background, could picture him on his leather sofa, feet up on the ottoman. "What are you up to?" I asked, missing, already, the promise of an average existence, even if it was just a facade.

"Watching the game. Want to join me?"

"Wish I could," I said. "I've got to finish up some emails." I settled against the headboard, pulled the laptop back to my lap.

I was testing him. Waiting for him to ask something more. Something deeper.

"Good night then, Cassidy. Talk to you tomorrow?"

"Yes," I said, hanging up, feeling a faint disappointment.

I tossed the cell on the bed beside me, then pulled up my inbox again, saw that a new message had come through from Jillian, who must've still been working, all hours of the night, as usual.

But I couldn't shake Brody's comments. The fact that I'd been part of their email chain, and I'd missed the message. Maybe I'd missed the person who had originally reached out to them as well—the fact-checkers or the legal team. Maybe I could find answers.

I opened my junk mail folder, then watched as months of old emails poured in, from all the places I didn't want to hear from: retailers, political campaigns, clear phishing attempts. I kept scrolling, not seeing anything relevant.

But then I saw the most recent of the reply-all chain, from Josh. *You don't have to talk to them. I don't think they can move forward without us.*

So, they'd been trying to stop it, whatever it was. And from the fact that nothing had come of it, it looked like they'd succeeded.

I returned to the junk folder, moving backward in time, to see if there was anything else. And then I stopped scrolling.

A message from Ian Tayler.

I opened the email, thinking it was part of that group chain—but I was the only one in the address line.

My breath caught, and I leaned closer.

I can't reach you, Cassidy. Did they come to see you too? Please. You're the only one I trust. Call me.

A noise escaped my throat. The email was dated February 1. I checked the details of his obituary again: February 6. My god, Ian had reached out just days before his death. My stomach lurched. My heart sank. I'd been unreachable. Had marked the group email chain as junk. Ensuring I'd never see it.

He had reached out, just to me.

At the bottom, he'd left his number. It was a local area code, just like mine used to be—

My vision faltered; time slipped.

A jolt of familiarity. Of disbelief.

I scrambled for my cell, pulled up the unknown text thread that I'd shown to Oliver earlier.

North Carolina number, he'd said.

But more than that—it was *this* number, right here, in my email.

That phone. The phone I'd found on the beach. The number that had texted me, luring me here.

That phone belonged to Ian.

THEN

HOUR 6

Brody

Brody knew how it felt to drown. It was one of his earliest memories, from a summer day at a neighbor's pool: The bottom of the shallow end slowly slipping away beneath his feet. The sharp descent, and his feet desperate for purchase, arms reaching for something—anything—

He'd written about it in his creative writing elective during junior year even, thought putting it down on paper would help him process, move past it. He was surprised to learn he had to share it with the classmates at his table. And that only made him never look their way again, embarrassed by what he had revealed.

It was something even Hollis didn't know. And now she was staring at him, wide-eyed in the beam of Oliver's flashlight, trembling in the rain, so that his entire existence was her and rain and river.

He remembered that panic and desperation, his lungs rebelling against all logic in their most primitive need.

He remembered how the feeling lingered, even after he was safe. He remembered it every time his parents coaxed him into the indoor YMCA pool after, to make sure he learned to swim. To help him *get over it*. What it did instead was heighten and sharpen the memory. A trauma on top of a trauma.

So yes, technically, he could swim, but he wasn't going to do *that*. None of them should. Which was why he had voted, emphatically, *no*.

But he was the only one.

"Look," he said, though there was only that single flashlight. And Oliver was only pointing it, as needed, at individual faces, glowing like ghosts, so nobody could really look anyway. Brody still didn't know some of their names—but he knew their faces. Four years, and now he wished he'd paid more attention, so they would *listen*, which was what he was really asking. "Those cables are for holding luggage, not . . ." He gestured toward the river. It was insane. Ridiculous. The bungee cords had been pulled from the back of the second van, along with the bags they managed to recover on a search for anything else that might come in useful.

The idea was irrational and desperate. Where were the fucking adults here?

"But there are people missing," Hollis yelled.

Oliver swung the flashlight her way again, so that her expression was clear. The look on her face was one Brody had never seen in her, despite being together for nearly the entire school year. Something that made Brody feel this wasn't the same person he'd thought he'd known. The one he'd, improbably, been drawn to in a way that felt magnetic. The new girl with the ends of her hair dyed pink, and the black eyeliner that made her blue eyes look like ice. Quieter than anyone expected. But not anymore.

There were others who could still be out there; she was a stark reminder of that. They could be waiting for help. Or they could be *safe*. There could be a place that was better than here, just waiting for them to make their way, and then this would all be over. All it took was the faith to venture around the curve in the river. A curve they could not see past. A leap.

"Well, who's offering to swim out there?" Brody asked.

They were a group of volunteers, with no one actively stepping forward to volunteer. And so the vote wouldn't count, and they'd go back to waiting, which was the only thing that made any sense anyway.

"We'll draw straws."

Brody laughed, turning in the direction of the voice. Oliver. Oliver King was deciding they would *draw straws*.

"What straws, Oliver? What the fuck are we doing?" he asked. But the tall, skinny kid beside Oliver only nodded. Brody thought the two of them were friends; he vaguely recalled seeing them at the same table in the cafeteria.

"Cards," Amaya said, calmly, precisely, as the beam of the flashlight swung her way. "I brought a pack of cards. We'll draw cards. Lowest card goes." Brody knew Amaya—top of the class, always in charge. They weren't friends, but he *knew* her, in the same way he had assumed these people also knew him. But they were only listening to her.

She retreated into the dark, to the pile of luggage, and returned quickly with the red pack, corners soft from the moisture.

Everything felt like it was coming closer: the storm, the rising water, and something else—something he couldn't name, a coldness settling in his bones, setting everything on edge.

Amaya showed them the pack of cards, breathless, hand trembling—they were *all* trembling, even the beam of Oliver's flashlight now—as if preparing for a trick. She counted them out to herself, all the same suit, he noticed—the two through the jack of hearts—and Brody shook his head. "What about them?" He gestured to the three people huddled against the rocks. Three people not accounted for in the draw.

"They can't help," Amaya said. A girl named Trinity from his history class had a leg that was badly broken. Ben had a piece of clothing held tightly to his waist, which was bleeding at a disturbing rate. Another girl who he didn't know was lying flat, only semiconscious, injuries undetermined.

"Well, it didn't stop them from voting," Brody mumbled.

On that note, he felt he shouldn't have to draw either, considering he'd voted no. Amaya shuffled the cards in the dark, held them out in a fan, facedown, between them.

Everything was moving too fast—the rain, the river—and there was no time to take a breath, so little time to think things through.

Oliver shone the light directly in the center. Everyone's hands went to the cards, until there were only three left—waiting for Hollis, Brody, and Amaya.

Brody tried to lock his gaze with Hollis's. "I don't think we should do this," he said.

"Then don't," she said, as if he had a choice not to play. Before realizing she probably meant: Don't risk *her*. Volunteer in her place. *Save her.*

He pulled a card.

Hollis pulled hers after, and Amaya was left with the one still in her grasp.

Brody flipped his card over; he didn't need to see anyone else's.

The two of hearts was staring back at him. He crumpled it in his fist.

He said it one more time, phrased a little differently, its meaning perfectly clear this time. "I don't want to do this." And then, in case they didn't understand: "Please."

He was begging them now. These people who he'd thought looked up to him. These people who liked him, he thought. One, he would've sworn this morning, who loved him.

He didn't understand how this was happening to him. Everyone at school—in town, even—thought he was *great*. Enough to vote him homecoming king, to cheer his name at soccer games, to invite him into their homes. Everyone except Hollis's parents, which was why he had even come on this trip in the first place. All because of Hollis, and so he could be with her, alone.

But the look she gave him at the stop before the accident—it was like she had glimpsed whatever her parents were wary of. A click that finally caught. So that he felt only the insecurity of wondering what that thing was.

"You've got this," Oliver said, and Brody's laughter threatened to bubble up. Oliver King, giving *him* a pep talk? Then Oliver put the flashlight in Brody's palm, like he was passing a torch or a baton. "We just need to see what's around the corner. If anyone's there. If there's a way out." He paused. "It's not that far."

Brody shook his head, but the words were stuck in his throat, his chest. He felt like he might vomit. No, it couldn't be far, considering the length of the cables, which two of his classmates were currently attaching to the single tree trunk protruding from the edge of the cliff wall.

"We're good here," the girl called—he knew her from one of his classes. Cathy—Cassie. No, Cassidy.

Brody turned away.

He put his hands out as two people approached him with the cables—they were shadows; he couldn't see them clearly. "Stop." Finally, the words came. "I'm not fucking doing it," he said, making contact, pushing one of them away.

Someone grabbed his arm, and he wrenched it back. "I'm not getting in the fucking water!" He was shouting now, and he didn't care what they thought of him. He wouldn't do this. Couldn't willingly get into the river.

It was his basest instinct. But there was something baser at play, in the way no one else spoke. He felt something stirring, and he started backing away from the edge.

He shone the light at them, one by one, like a weapon. It was the only thing he had.

"Brody—"

He turned in the direction of the voice, and Hollis lifted an arm to her eyes, to block the light.

"Don't you fucking dare," he said now, voice low.

He knew, in that moment, he couldn't stop them if he wanted to. "Hollis," he added, voice wavering. His only hope.

But then the hands were on him, and something instinctive took over. He fought it, fought them. Called out, to anyone who would listen, "I can't swim!"

The hands stilled, finally, in a brief moment of humanity. He imagined they were considering his words. Had they seen him in a pool? At the lake? Could anyone claim definitively that Brody Ensworth was nothing more than a coward? A selfish liar?

"I'll do it." A voice came from behind him, while everything was still in flux.

He turned toward it and illuminated a tall, lean figure—Oliver's friend. Brody didn't know his name, was pretty sure it started with a *J*. But he didn't want to get it wrong. "Thank you," he said quietly.

But the other guy didn't respond to him. "He's going to be fucking useless out there, whether he can swim or not."

Brody stepped back, quiet. He watched instead. Watched as they wound the cables around the other guy's waist. Watched as they pulled at the cables, checking their security.

This was a terrible idea, but he wasn't going to bring any more attention on himself. He wanted to fade into the background. Disappear.

"Light?" the guy called, and Brody had to walk into their shadowed circle, place the flashlight in his hand instead.

"All right, then. Be right back," he said, with a flash of nervous laughter.

He took a single step off the rocks, into the river.

The water took him so fast.

Brody could track him by the flashlight in his hand, a beacon dancing in the rain. *See me. Find me. Help me.*

The cords snapped tight with a metal clang, hook straining against hook.

They watched, in silence, staring out into the darkness, where the light shimmered for a moment, and then disappeared.

"Where did he go?" Clara asked, stepping closer to the edge.

Someone else pulled her back. "Grace, where the fuck is he? Do you see him?"

All they could see was darkness. Rain, cliff walls, river.

Oliver grabbed on to the length of cable, checking to make sure it was still attached. "No," he said. A single word, drawing everyone's attention. He strode to the edge then, started yelling a name. "Jason!"

That was his name. Jason.

Brody looked to the ground, where Oliver had dropped the cable again, finally seeing what it was that had him yelling into the dark, a piercing, haunting scream.

The cables had lost all tension. Nothing—no one—was hooked on to the other end. Brody started pulling, dragging them back, as if he might be mistaken. A trick of adrenaline, of the dark, of the river. But the final hooks scratched against the rocks, still connected in a circle, where a body should be—where *Jason* should be—as if he had slipped from their hold. As if the force of the river had dragged him under, through. Gone.

Everything went numb then, and he couldn't breathe. Couldn't take in air to say anything, as his classmates screamed into the dark—as if Jason would just orient himself toward their voices, find his way back.

Brody felt it then, something seizing his lungs, like he'd been out there. Like he'd never crawled out of that van. Like he'd been left inside, after the impact; left, until the river started to rise, and he got swept away, encased in a metal tomb.

He put a hand out to brace himself as he sank onto the slick rocks.

Brody had read about dry drowning. It was a lingering trick of the water, a sneak attack that could come for you hours later, after you assumed you were safe. Maybe death had already played its hand, and he was walking on borrowed time. Like a slow-acting poison.

"That could've been me," he said faintly, the words stuck in his throat. The accusation he levied at them. Barely anyone heard it.

That could've been him. Lost at the end of a dangling rope. These people, calling his name, as the river crested his head, and his feet scrambled for purchase, and the current took him under.

It was unclear whether they were responding to him, when they started saying, *He knows how to swim. He's probably safe, around the curve.*

The lies these people could tell, to one another, to themselves.

They had almost forced him into it. And he'd let this kid he didn't even know (he hadn't even known his *name*) go in his place, because he was a coward.

But he was alive.

Hollis sat beside him, her body mirroring his. She placed an arm around him, and he realized she was crying, something helpless and raw. As if she hadn't been ready to send Brody into the river just moments earlier. As if she wouldn't have made him do it, just like all the rest of them. The weight of her arm—the very touch of her—sent a new chill through him. He felt his body hardening, shoulders tightening, something dark and angry fighting for the surface.

These people, he understood—when it came down to it, and there was no audience, no social clout—they did not care for him at all.

These were not his friends. If they managed to survive, he would not forget.

TUESDAY

CHAPTER 7

The house gave everyone away. Take a step, and the floorboards creaked. Open a door, and the hinges cried. Turn on the water, and the pipes groaned before a rush resounded through the walls. The Shallows was not a place for strangers. It was built for friends, for family. It was not a place that kept secrets.

I could hear Josh turn over in bed when I cracked open my bedroom door just before dawn. Inside one of the two shared bathrooms in the hall, Hollis's black bikini hung from the shower rod, and Grace's toiletry bag was ajar, with an orange prescription vial just visible inside.

I splashed water on my face and crept down the steps, hyperaware of every pop of the floorboard and of the five other people scattered throughout the house, presumably still asleep.

And then I waited, sitting on the taupe sectional couch in the living room, listening to the sounds of the house. I had to get into Ian's phone, but nothing would be open around here for another few hours. In the meantime, I wanted the opportunity to talk to anyone else, one-on-one. Anyone who might have more answers than Brody.

The wind was picking up, rattling the window frames, a shudder I could almost feel with each stronger gust. Like someone was shaking the doors, trying to get inside.

I felt sick. Like I'd swallowed too much water. Inhaled it into my lungs.

Like I had reached for Ian in the river—fingertips brushing his outstretched hand—and missed.

• • •

Ian had been the one person I trusted too. We had grown close in the months after the accident, over the subsequent season of memorial services.

There had been twelve.

There was only one funeral home in the town of Long Brook, a suburb on the outskirts of Greensboro, so the services had to be spaced out. There were too many deaths to prepare for and commemorate all at once.

At first everyone had attended—all the survivors—sitting scattered with their own friends, their own families. We were all there for the two teachers—Mr. Kates, Ms. Winslow—who had driven the vans. But little by little, memorial by memorial, our numbers had dwindled, just as they had that night.

I wondered if the others felt it—the guilt. Or if our discomfort was simply the weight of people's eyes on us. If the other survivors wondered whether the families looked at them, *alive*, and wished it had been the other way around.

Whatever the reason, by the time Ben's funeral came, it was only Ian and me.

My parents begged me to stop. They said that I was torturing myself, that I didn't even know these people.

It wasn't true—I had known them all. Had sat in the same classes for four years, heard their names called down the hall, listened to their chatter as we climbed into the van at the start of the trip.

But I understood what my parents were saying. They were used to my older brothers, who had made our house a hub of activity, with their teammates, their extended groups of friends. I had always kept a smaller circle: my group had been stagehands I holed up with backstage at the theater productions, where we wore black and whispered and joked about the rumors we overheard about the more outgoing crowd, as if no one noticed us standing there. I occupied a different social circle than my brothers had, but I was just as content. Happier, even. Free to pursue my passions, to disappear into my art, my writing, without the pressure of other commitments.

My closest friends, Colby and Ella, were twins, and they'd moved away the summer before. My senior year had turned unpredictably lonely and endless then—a series of motions, a daily routine, lunch most days in the library, where the librarian either didn't notice or kindly looked the other way while I read, or sketched, in silence. I just wanted it to be over, so I could move on to the next part of my life and all that it promised.

The service trip was supposed to be a delineation between the person I had been and the one I would become. But there were twelve of us who didn't survive, who would never have that chance. And so I kept going to their services, committing their names and their faces to memory.

I didn't know why Ian continued to come—whether it was the same guilt or because he didn't want to leave me there alone. This person I hadn't spoken to through all of high school, sitting at the other end of a row. Then sliding down until he was beside me instead, his warm hand reaching out for mine, fingers tightening, while the rest of the world went numb.

Eventually, we were spending entire days together. By summer, I'd come home from his house only when it was time for bed, and my parents grew increasingly concerned.

We skipped graduation together, sitting in his car instead, listening to too-loud music, and then driving around until it was dark, neither of us wanting to leave the confines of our bubble.

So I trusted him more than I trusted anyone else too—in the way that, as Grace claimed, there's nothing quite like the relationships forged during that time in our lives.

Enough to confide in him the things I wouldn't tell my therapist.

Enough to believe it was real love, instead of a codependency—though was that truly so bad, to need one another, to have one another, so completely? He was an outlet and a sealed box. It was my first real relationship, a kind of intimacy I'd been chasing ever since.

I'm not sure I would've left for college, if not for the fight we had, right before. Then the distance severed whatever was left.

I didn't see him again until the next spring, when we all gathered in the parking lot behind the school, the night after Clara's funeral. And I tried to remember the way it had been with him: the feel of his hand in mine; the way he leaned over me before dawn in my still-dark bedroom, like he was scared to go home.

But by then the memories were all mixed together: the cool touch of his arm, the cold of the river. His tentative smile, and his wide mouth open in a frozen scream.

I saw things more clearly now, with the benefit of time and distance and hindsight, in a way I couldn't back then: I was an addiction for him, something to fill a void, to quell his memory of the river, and in my absence, he had moved on to other things instead.

Back when we were together, there had been only the cigarettes he kept stashed in his tree house, or the occasional bottle swiped from his parents' cabinet. If he'd been using something more back then, I would've noticed.

I was sure of it. We *all* noticed, in the years that followed.

But ten years later, when it came down to it, there was still no one in the group I had trusted more. If you believed in fate—and I did, I *do*—then how could I not see what was happening—the text, the phone—as Ian, still reaching out, arm outstretched toward mine in the river? Trying to help me, to warn me?

I just didn't believe fate existed in a vacuum anymore. I believed you could prepare for it, and plan for the way it bent. I believed fate was an accumulation of decisions, not all of them yours.

So while I waited for the rest of the house to wake, I searched for and made a list of electronic repair shops nearby.

The message that had arrived, with Ian's obituary, had been sent from his phone. And I had no idea how it had gotten on the beach, washed up in the surf.

If his information had been in my contacts, I would've known the message had come from his phone from the start. Which made me consider the point of it—was the note sent to destabilize me, send me scrambling? Send us *all* scrambling?

But the thing that had me most unnerved was the fact that someone had been holding on to Ian's phone since his death.

It had been three months. Three months of waiting—for what?

And was it such a big leap to consider that whoever had this phone now had also been with him when he died?

The wind blew again, shaking the windows. Something under the house had come loose, knocking against the pillars below. Someone resettled in a bed upstairs, mattress coils groaning overhead.

I squeezed my eyes shut, pictured Ian alone somewhere, sending me that email. Typing my name with nicotine-stained fingertips, nails bitten down to the quick. Reaching toward me—

And finally, finally, I could see him as I always wanted to: alone, his mouth just above mine, his breath the only thing that existed in the world. I could smell a tinge of cigarettes, mixed with the leather of his favorite jacket. Feel the rough pad of his thumb running down the delicate skin of my neck.

You're the only one I trust.

Please.

• • •

Someone was talking—low and urgent. The sun had just started to rise, orange and pink filtering through the windows at the back of the house. I stood from where I'd been dozing on and off on the couch, followed the sound toward those windows, thinking it was coming from the back deck.

But the conversation was coming from Oliver's room instead. I paused at the entrance and leaned closer, just as the door swung open abruptly.

Oliver jerked back physically at my presence. "I'll call you later," he said into empty space, then removed the earbuds. "Can I help you?" he asked, dark eyebrows raised, but his face gave away nothing.

"Thought I heard someone outside," I said, gesturing to the glass windows, the red flag visible along the wooden path violently whipping back and forth. Our own warning system—high winds, dangerous surf.

Oliver cracked a grin. "Thought I heard someone too." He raised an eyebrow at me—this time friendly, joking.

"A little early for work, isn't it?" I asked. He smelled like soap and fresh shampoo, and was already dressed in khakis and a polo.

"Not when your clients are eight hours ahead, unfortunately." Then, eyes skimming up and down my body—at the fact I was already dressed for the day, like him: "Going somewhere?" he asked.

I nodded. "Yeah, figured I'd get out this morning before work." The closest repair store opened at ten, and it was in the next town up—too far to walk in any reasonable span of time, and Oliver's rental was blocking me in. "I was thinking of taking a drive," I said.

He tipped his head. "We can do a tour later this week." Which sounded like an answer, though I hadn't been asking his permission. He slipped by me, into the kitchen, to start preparing for breakfast.

If Amaya felt paralyzed by decision-making, Oliver was the opposite. Oliver had built a career on a willingness to take risks, on a series of split-second decisions. He could make them on the fly, as inconsequential as flipping a coin—and he had no problem making them for others as well.

Still, I knew better than to argue. I wanted to ask him about Ian, about whether he had received a text too—but he'd seen my message last night, and said nothing. I needed to tread carefully here.

"Oliver," I said. "What did the fact-checkers ask you?"

His hand paused on the open cabinet, and he turned slowly, taking me in. "I didn't engage. Like Josh advised."

Had I expected anything different? It had been a decade. A decade of burying the past. No one here would drag it out willingly.

"And that was it? They let it go?"

He shrugged. "Looks like Josh was right," he said. As if he was confident that nothing could move forward without one of us confirming the details. Then, after a beat, "Did you get another message?"

"No. Did you?"

He blinked. "We didn't get any texts, Cassidy," he said. The words weighted, eyes darting to the side briefly, before moving on.

But I was stuck on the way he'd said *We*—like there was a smaller group within our numbers. A tighter circle, of which I was still on the outside.

And suddenly I remembered Ian's email: *Did they come to see you too?*

Oliver stared out the back windows, pressed his hand to the sliding glass door just as it shuddered again from the wind. "Jesus," he said. "Guess we're going sound side today."

• • •

Sound side meant paddleboards and kitesurfing and Jet Ski rentals. It meant sailboats and fishing charters. The sound was on the west side of the island, sunset instead of sunrise, where fresh water from the mainland met the ocean. The water was brackish and shallow, less intimidating than the ocean, though the distance to the far shore—land that dipped over the horizon—still seemed insurmountable.

Hollis came down the stairs first, wood creaking under each uncertain step, shifting the tone of the room.

"How's it feeling today?" Oliver asked.

"Better. Just need to change the bandage."

I stayed in the kitchen, giving them space, watching. Watching their interactions, listening for anything I hadn't picked up on earlier.

Hollis had her leg up on the couch, leaning closer to see. Oliver stayed on the other side of the couch, smiled down at her. "Maybe no beach run today, but we'll have you on a Jet Ski for sure."

She smiled back, her face unreadable. "Wouldn't miss it," she said.

The sound of someone else coming downstairs broke them apart. Oliver turned back to the kitchen, as Hollis began scrolling through her social media.

Grace emerged from the stairwell, laptop under her arm. "Can I get the dining room for work this morning? Since Josh has co-opted any possible office space for himself?"

Oliver kept moving, pulling things out of the cabinets, making breakfast. "I'm reserving the space behind Coral's. Anyone can work there if they want."

Coral's was a hole-in-the-wall sandwich shop, served out of a window, across a shared gravel driveway from High Tide. It was highly frequented due to its proximity to the rental huts in a row beside it, and the public dock behind it. There were colorful picnic tables with chipping, splintered paint, which were first come, first served. And there was a rectangular area for rent, kept private via a step down between wooden beams, with hammocks strung between trees and long tables. Plus, it came with a key to the bathroom, which was the true value.

Grace dropped her laptop on the table, watching the clock. "I can't do video calls from outside, Oliver. It's unprofessional."

He rolled his eyes. "Well, I've got the space all day. Meet us there when you can."

"I have some calls this morning too. I'll head over later with Grace," I added, seizing the chance. I had a plan for today too.

Ian had sent me an email, five days before his death: *Did they come to see you too?* And three months later, his phone was used to send me a text with his obituary. No one else had received it. Once again, it was only meant for me.

The key was in my hands.

I was going to get into that phone.

CHAPTER 8

Grace and I promised to join the rest of them in the afternoon. I watched as they trekked down the road together, with hats and backpacks and towels over their shoulders. Hollis moved a little slower, trailing behind the three men.

Grace was set up in the dining room, and I couldn't leave until closer to ten, when the store opened, so I headed for the stairs, gesturing that I would be working up there.

Grace waved her fingers off-screen, never breaking eye contact with her monitor.

At the landing, I heard a familiar noise coming from the third floor—a hinge, a door, subject to the wind. Josh probably forgot to lock it again. I stood at the base of the steps, staring up.

In years past, at night, I would hear Ian talking in his sleep. A familiar nightmare.

Sometimes, even more occasionally, I would climb the steps to the third-floor bedroom and he'd be sitting on the edge of the bed, like he was waiting for me. It was different than the first summer, when we had been a comfort for each other. On those nights at The Shallows, it was an escape instead—from the memories, and ourselves.

I almost went up there now, except I remembered how suspicious Josh had been when he accused me of being in his room the last time. I imagined some high-tech laptop set up now, with a motion detector enabled, ready to catch me. So I left it alone—let the door blow open, and the salt water and sand blow in. Let him deal with the mess. He'd claimed the space for himself after all.

• • •

From my room, with the door cracked, I could hear Grace's voice echoing up the steps.

"Let's start from the beginning . . ." she was saying. And then, "Remember, you are not the worst thing you've ever done." I froze, spine straight, wondering if this was what she would tell the rest of us, what she must tell herself.

I eased the door shut, checked my canvas bag one last time, then hitched it across my back and quietly exited through the glass doors to the deck. Oliver's rental was still blocking me in; I probably could've maneuvered around him, pulling closer to the front steps, driving over the rocks and sea grass, but I didn't want to draw attention to the fact I had left.

I tiptoed down the wooden deck steps, until I was on the main level, just outside Oliver's bedroom, its shades still pulled tightly shut. I needed to get to the shed, which required me to pass by the large uncovered windows at the back of the house. Depending on the angle, Grace might have a clear shot of me, but I'd deal with that later, and only if asked. *Went for a walk. Got some fresh air at the beach.*

I chose the smaller of the bikes, so I wouldn't have to figure out how to adjust the seat, then walked it around the house, keeping close to the lattice under the deck. When I knew I was finally out of view of our windows, I hopped on, pedaling down the unpaved access road, toward the highway.

I loved being outdoors—it was part of the allure of that volunteer trip, even—and Russ had gotten me into biking the greenway trails on the weekends, but this bike frame seemed to list to the side; its handlebars didn't quite line up with the wheel.

Thankfully the highway wasn't busy at this time—there was no sidewalk in the section of road between towns—and the few cars gave me a wide berth as they passed.

It was a straight shot to the next town, marshland on one side, long paths to beach access on the other, and nothing else. It wasn't until the sign for the next town that the land widened again. There was a small grid of stores in a built-up area, restaurants over shops, and a fish market just before the sign for another pier.

I found the shop on the far corner—*We fix all electronics*—behind a darkened window, the door tucked around the side street. I leaned the bike against the blue siding, before pushing through the entrance.

A set of bells jangled over the entrance. I expected some sort of electronic beep, given the type of store. But I could see myself in several television displays in each corner, cameras set up to watch the interior lobby.

"Just a sec," came a voice from the back.

A woman appeared around the corner, in overalls and a tank top, a bandanna tying back her short blond hair, red-rimmed glasses resting over top. "What can I do for you?" she asked, hands pressed into the counter, leaning forward.

I brought my canvas sack to the counter, then fished out Ian's phone.

She grimaced immediately. "Took it for a swim, huh," she said.

"Not on purpose," I said, wincing for impact.

"No, I suppose not." She picked up the phone, pressed a button, then frowned.

"It works," I said. "I mean, it's not dead. It chimes. Sometimes I can get it to turn on, but it shorts out anytime I try to do anything."

She scratched a spot under her bandanna. "I can replace the screen, but I can't be sure what we're looking at till I open it up."

I nodded, encouraging her.

"Not gonna lie," she continued, "it might not be worth the cost. Might be best just to get a new one altogether."

"Please," I said, "I really need what's on here. Just, whatever you can do."

She looked at the clock over my head. "You want to wait, or come back?"

I looked toward the windows, which were darkened from the interior as well. I wasn't sure when I'd be able to make it back without drawing notice. "I'll wait," I said.

She gestured to two white plastic chairs along a bare wall. "Suit yourself," she said. Then she handed me a remote. "Just please, not those home reno shows, okay?"

The condition of the chairs and age of the remote did nothing to inspire confidence in an aptitude with technology here, but I turned on the television, which came to life on a local news station, with fishing conditions, tide reports, and weather updates promised every quarter hour.

"Low-pressure system just offshore today," the weatherman was saying. "Bringing in the *wind* today, that's for sure. Riptide warnings in full effect."

I turned the channel quickly, surfing through the available options—cartoon programs, old sitcom reruns—before landing on one of those home reno shows after all. I peered toward the counter, but she was in the back, so I kept the volume down, settled into the uncomfortable seat, and felt myself relax for the first time in days.

Sometime during the second—third?—thirty-minute show, the door swung open. I jolted alert, checking the time, as a delivery worker entered the lobby with several boxes.

The bell jangled overhead, but no one came out front.

"She working on something?" he asked me as he crossed the lobby.

"Yep."

"Libby!" he called, setting the stack of boxes on the counter. Then, at the sound of a chair scraping against the concrete floor, he gestured to the television. "You know, she hates that shit," he said with a grin.

I turned the television off just as Libby came out from the back, earbuds hanging around her neck, music still audible from across the room.

She signed for the packages, then spent the next five minutes engaging in what seemed to be local gossip, as if I weren't sitting there, waiting. I caught snippets about someone's boat; someone's fine; someone's breakup.

When he finally left, Libby placed my phone—Ian's phone—on the counter. "Good news, bad news," she said.

I stood, my pulse picking up as I crossed the room.

"The screen works now without shorting out the whole system," she said.

"Thank you," I said, but her hand still rested over the cell.

"Everything's asking for password prompts," she continued. Her face was impassive, large brown eyes assessing me. As if she understood that this phone did not belong to me.

"Okay," I said, fingers trembling as I took out my credit card. "How much do I owe you?"

She blinked slowly, unmoving. "Also, it doesn't hold any charge. I'd really suggest a new phone." Testing me. Warning me.

"Got it," I said, nodding. "Can I transfer the data to another device?"

"We're not set up for that," she said flatly, and from her expression, I knew I had pushed things a step too far.

For a moment I thought she wouldn't give me the phone. I worried that she'd confiscate it, turn it in to a real lost and found in the area, the police station, the fire department. I couldn't tell whether she thought I had stolen this phone, had taken it after some fight, or had thrown it into the sea myself, but she seemed suspicious of me. Or of whatever she'd seen inside.

Finally, she moved to the register and rang me up. The cost was indeed higher than I'd anticipated, maybe higher than the service was worth, as if she was daring me to push back.

But I smiled and turned over my credit card, before sliding Ian's phone quickly into my bag.

"Have a good one," I called as she handed me the receipt. I felt her standing there as I pushed through the door, watching me go.

• • •

My pulse was still racing when I stepped outside, so at first I thought I just wasn't focusing as I kicked up the stand on the bike and started pedaling for home. The bike swerved abruptly, and I had to put my foot down to keep from tipping over. I hopped off the bike, looking it over: the front wheel was bent inward, tire fully flat.

"Shit," I said to no one but myself. The tire wasn't just deflated—there was a fraying of the rubber, a split down the middle of the seam. It looked worse than a slow leak—something that had probably been exacerbated by my ride in.

I considered abandoning the bike—it couldn't be worth much, and I doubted Oliver would notice—and calling for an Uber. But car services were not prevalent or reliable out here either. I was running out of options.

"Hey there, neighbor-on-vacation." I turned at the voice, saw a man—Will—sitting on the back of a truck bed.

Well, at least I'd graduated from *girl I met yesterday*.

"What are you doing here?" I asked.

He hopped off the truck, gestured to the sign behind us, for the fish market. He had a cooler in his truck bed, along with his fishing gear. Today he wore jeans and a ball cap pulled low, his dark hair escaping out the bottom.

"Out for a ride?" he asked.

"I was," I said. "But ran into some tire trouble."

He whistled through his teeth, walking around the bike. "I'm amazed you made it as far as you did." He smiled, picking up the frame with one hand. "As luck would have it, I happen to be heading your way."

"Thank you," I said, as he loaded my bike into the back of his pickup, ignoring every warning I'd ever heard about trucks and strangers. This was maybe two degrees above hitchhiking. But it was broad daylight, and I knew his name and the general vicinity he lived in. This presumption of security was supposed to be the benefit of small towns.

I climbed into the passenger seat as he turned on the engine. "Surprised to see you out this way," he said, cutting his eyes to me. "By yourself, I mean."

I frowned, reconsidering him.

He laughed nervously. "Sorry, I just mean, you usually travel as a group."

That didn't make it any better. It sounded like he knew more about us than I'd thought. That he watched us.

"Do you notice this much about all the people staying around you?" I asked.

We were crossing the strip of road between towns, and now the barrenness felt eerie, ominous. Offshore, a shelf of gray clouds hovered in the distance.

"I try not to," he said. "But it's kind of impossible." He smiled, then continued. "You ever see your house from the outside at night? The whole place is lit up, on display. Trust me, *everyone* notices when you guys arrive."

"I didn't realize we made such a scene," I mumbled. We weren't a party house—there was nothing particularly festive about our gathering—but I guess we were distinct. Maybe others could feel it too, a different sort of energy, a somberness.

"I wouldn't say it's a scene. But it's hard not to notice when you show up." He cut his eyes to me once more. "We call it the ghost house."

I shook my head. "It's called The Shallows," I said.

"Call it whatever you want. Around here, it's the ghost house."

"It doesn't look that creepy," I said. Maybe the rickety steps, or the weatherworn siding, or the way it looked against a gray sky, eerie and haunting, gave it that name. But in the sunlight, it was beautiful, natural, a fitting part of the surrounding landscape.

"Yeah, but it's empty almost all the time," he said, jarring me. "A waste, don't you think, to sit unused through the summer?"

I felt myself losing my bearings—The Shallows was a prime location for summer beachgoers. I assumed it must be in great demand in the high season.

"I don't . . . I thought it was a rental," I said.

"Sure seems that way. Except the only people ever there, year after year, are you."

As if the house was always waiting, just for us.

As we crossed into town, my gaze drifted to the left, toward the sound. I knew they were somewhere back there—I could feel them, a pull, like a homing device. "I didn't realize," I said quietly.

Will turned the truck toward the beach, tires bumping over the unpaved road. "Pretty fucking weird that no one ever stays, except this one week a year. So of course I remember you. Everyone does. You're the only ones who stay at the ghost house. Can you blame us for being a little curious?"

I was shaken as he maneuvered around a deep pothole, tires crunching rock and sand. I could see the house from where we were—rising up against the gray sky, seagrass blowing inward. The gravity of it.

"I can just walk from your place," I said, as I realized he was about to drive me all the way there, where Grace would have a clear view out the window.

Will paused the truck but kept the engine running, eyebrows raised, as if waiting for me to acknowledge that this was, indeed, fucking weird.

I cleared my throat. "You're right," I added, "about us moving as a group. They don't know I'm out. I just needed some space, by myself, for a bit." I could only imagine the gossip this would inspire, if they already talked about us. *There's something not right going on. Something really fucking weird—*

"Suit yourself," he said, shifting the truck into reverse. He backed up about ten meters and pulled directly into a spot underneath a box-style ranch house, raised up on pilings.

God, he really did live close. From where I stood outside the truck, there was a clear view over a stretch of grassy marsh area, straight to our house on the beach. He could see every car, every balcony. I imagined it must be lit up at night, like he claimed. I could see it, the way we must look like ghosts, moving back and forth in front of the windows.

"If you ever need some space again," he said, as he helped me lower the bike from the back, "you don't have to go that far." He gestured to the setup he had under his house: a rustic, handmade bar; wooden stools on top of twisted metal legs; a spiraling metal staircase leading up to the deck. "I have an open-door policy here."

"Thanks," I said, and set off, pushing the bike down the unpaved road, toward the sea.

• • •

I dropped the bike back into storage and climbed the steps to the deck. And then I paused: Grace was clearly visible through the sliding glass doors, standing at the base of the steps and staring straight up, as if she'd just called my name, and was waiting for my response.

I knocked on the glass instead, watched as she jumped, then shook her head, smiling. She had to unlatch the doors to let me in. "Sorry," she said, sliding them open. "I locked them after everyone else left." She grinned sheepishly, then checked her watch. "Come on, they're probably eating without us by now."

She hooked an arm through mine, and I thought, not for the first time, that I would've gravitated toward Grace in any other circumstance. I liked to believe we'd be friends in our real lives, if not for the fact that being together would only serve as a stark reminder. But I always enjoyed her presence, when I was here. Even if it was just the calming cadence of her voice, words that traveled from her sessions through the halls. She was a weight that kept me grounded, kept me stable.

I let her guide me straight through the house and out the front door, while I retraced the steps I'd just taken. We passed Will's place, and I was surprised I hadn't noticed it before. We were always so focused on our group that the outside rarely registered. Most homes along the coast had a sign with a name, like ours. His was distinct in that it did not. But there was a rusted anchor beside his mailbox, the chain twining up the post.

Grace's hair whipped in front of her face. I felt remnants of sand in the air, swirling against my ankles.

She turned back, frowned at the sky, an eerie gray in the distance, far offshore. "That doesn't look good," she said.

I could see the change begin in her, the way the past was rising up. I slipped an arm into hers and pulled her forward. We both knew better than to look at a storm head-on.

CHAPTER 9

The sound-side water was a sharp contrast to the beach. The water appeared lower, like the tide had been pulled out, and there was no chop to the surface, just a fast-moving current you could see rippling with the wind. The sky was clear, no signs of any disturbance heading our way.

We saw their gear first—coverups and bags on top of the long table in the private area behind Coral's.

I didn't notice Brody until we'd stepped down into the trees. He was tucked into a rope hammock, one arm thrown over his eyes, phone facedown on his chest.

All of their things were left behind on the picnic table. If someone came to rob them, Brody's sleeping frame would be no deterrent.

"Boo," Grace said, leaning in close, laughing as Brody's arms flailed, legs coming down firmly on either side of the hammock.

"Shit," he said, pushing his hair back. He gave her a small smile, like he was trying to play at being amused.

Grace pulled her hair to the side and sat on the nearest picnic table bench. "What have you been doing?"

"Watching their stuff," he said, bloodshot eyes skimming the table surfaces, like he was performing his own delayed tally.

Grace laughed, head tipped back. "Good job," she said.

"There they are," I said. The others were just then approaching from the dock, heading toward the row of equipment-rental huts, all windswept hair and fast chatter and pink cheeks. Hollis had her foot wrapped up in a bandage, but she was walking normally in athletic slides, positioned between Josh and Oliver.

I saw the vendor closest tracking them, head swiveling as they passed. Another man sitting on the edge of the dock with a fishing line turned to watch them too.

Any other time, I would've thought it was because of Hollis, naturally drawing attention. But now I saw things through Will's perspective: people knew who we were, and they were curious. The way Will came up to us on the beach, saying he remembered us. The way Joanie knew which table we were heading to, and knew there should be more of us. *They're the ones*, I imagined them whispering to one another.

We were the ghosts, staying in a ghost house.

• • •

Oliver collected our orders to take up to the sandwich window. "Can someone see if Joanie will get us some pitchers?" he asked.

"I'll go," I offered, slinging the canvas bag over my shoulder. It's not that I didn't trust them. But I couldn't let Ian's phone out of my sight—not at the repair shop, and not now.

I circled around the lot and entered High Tide through the front. The dining area was relatively empty, the hours still hovering between lunch and dinner. Joanie and the bartender were leaning close behind the counter, talking, but they pulled apart when I stepped past the hostess stand.

"Hey there," she called. Now I was wondering what exactly she thought when she saw us. This was a painfully small town, and we were still early in the season. For nearly a decade, we'd been coming for this same week—and now we were down two.

"Hi, Joanie. Wondering if we can bring some pitchers out back?"

"Course," she said. "Mark can get you taken care of."

Mark looked about Joanie's age, with a salt-and-pepper goatee and a sharp widow's peak. Unlike Joanie, though, I'd never noticed him here before.

I hopped on the stool against the far wall by the register and placed our order.

Joanie unplugged her phone from behind the counter, texting someone on the other end. I imagined her typing out: *The crew from the ghost house is here again—*

"Hey, Joanie, any chance I can borrow that charger for a minute?"

"Course," she said again, barely looking up. She threaded the cable my way, across the bar top.

I fumbled in my bag for Ian's phone, then plugged it in, waiting.

I placed it on the bar top, then turned toward the television, hoping the phone would eventually power up. The television sound was off, but closed captioning was enabled, words appearing on the screen in block letters. It was the same local station the repair shop had been tuned to, and the weather report was beginning again.

Low-pressure system to move in tonight. High-water warnings in effect—

"Want to start a tab?" Mark asked. He didn't wear the deep blue shirt that the other staff all wore, and it seemed just as likely he was a friend of Joanie's as someone who actually worked here.

"No, this will be it," I said, sliding him my card. Someone else could get the next round, if they wanted one.

Ian's phone suddenly glowed to life, and I picked it up off the counter just as the home page appeared, as if by magic. There was no more crack running down the middle, or a green screen of death. I sent a silent thanks to Libby.

I tried the Mail app first, but like she'd warned, it asked for a password, his email name autofilled. I cringed—it was probably indeed obvious that I was not IanTayler9295.

Opening his social media apps produced the same general result—everything prompted for Face ID, then asked for a password. Even his calendar was tied to his email. At least the phone didn't reboot itself, but I was beginning to think it would've been just as productive to leave it in the sand, let it wash back into the sea.

Then I tapped the Photos app, and it opened. A grid of images scrolled across the screen, and I held my breath, preparing to see him.

But Ian was nowhere to be found.

I pulled the phone closer to my face, clicking on the first image. It was a photo of a house. Weathered gray cedar shake siding, rickety steps connecting each balcony, floor by floor. The structure rising up from behind the dunes and seagrass. The Shallows.

The next photo was a closer shot: an open door, a leg extended—someone stepping onto the back deck. Then, one floor up, a woman on the balcony. I zoomed in, trying to see clearly. She was out of focus, but I could tell by the gray sweatshirt, the dark hair: this was Amaya.

I could hear my heartbeat echoing in my skull.

There's someone on the beach, Amaya had told us, as she stood on the back deck. We had assumed she'd been referring to Hollis, but what if she hadn't been?

What if she saw someone watching, phone pointed our way?

She saw someone watching her, and she ran. And suddenly I wondered if she knew exactly what she was running from.

"Need help?" Brody asked, suddenly beside me at the bar.

I unplugged the phone quickly, dropping it back into my bag. Brody smiled down at me. "Figured you'd need another set of hands," he said.

The two pitchers were already set on the bar, condensation dripping down the side. There was a stack of plastic cups placed beside them, and the bill, slid closer my way. "Thanks," I said. "I was just paying."

He picked up the pitchers, backing away.

I smiled tightly at Brody. "I'll be right behind you," I said.

• • •

I'd disappeared into my room as soon as we were back that evening, hovering over the phone while it was connected to the charger.

The only other information I had access to was his contacts. I recognized his sisters' names, his parents. But most were people I hadn't known. They were a decade of new people, new experiences—colleagues, friends, maybe someone who meant even more. I paused at my own name—my old number, but my current email. At the bottom, there was an indication of a group name. I clicked it now, and a familiar list appeared: It was us. All of us in this house. The survivors. He'd called us, simply, *The Eight.*

While I'd deleted them all, he'd held us together—prepared, in case he needed to reach out.

Then, when that moment came, I wasn't there.

There were no other photos saved on Ian's phone—just a string of recent pictures of the house, all taken over the span of thirty minutes. I went through everything twice. Some photos were close up, and others were far away. I couldn't tell if the photographer had come closer, or whether they had just zoomed in from a spot on the beach. I could make out the outline of a person in most, but it wasn't always clear who was in frame.

What *was* clear, however, was that we were being watched.

• • •

I stayed up late that night, not wanting to miss anything. Only Grace went upstairs early, while the rest of us sat around the fire pit.

"Love you all," she said, which I thought, like most things, was something she had just decided, fairly haphazardly. "But some of us have to work in the morning."

"Oliver wakes up earlier than any of us," I said, keeping my eyes on his, lit by the fire between us, wisps of flame whipping around in the wind.

"Well, we can't all be the King," Josh said, smirking.

"Night, Grace," Hollis called, ducking lower in the Adirondack chair, tipping her chin inside the hooded sweatshirt she'd pulled on.

Grace passed Brody coming out through the sliding glass door, and he skirted to the side, giving her space.

"Look what I found," Brody said, backlit by the kitchen light, so it took a moment for my eyes to adjust. He had metal stakes in one hand, marshmallows in the other. "Like in the Boy Scouts?" he said, smiling.

"I hope they teach more survival skills than how to make s'mores," Hollis said, taking one of the stakes from his outstretched hand. Her comment changed the tenor of the gathering, Brody's smile faltering, silence falling. I wondered if it was intentional—with Hollis, it was sometimes hard to tell. Her exterior was hard to crack; she held all of us at a slight remove.

We roasted our marshmallows over the flame, like a group of friends bonding around the campfire, indulging in a late-night treat.

The wind funneled through the gate in a whistle, and the chocolate from the s'mores dripped over the edges, burning my hand. The door to the shed kept swinging open, smacking against the inside lattice, until Oliver pulled it tightly shut and snapped the lock in place.

It took another hour before anyone called it, like we were all trying to wait one another out.

"Should we get some water for this?" I asked, gesturing to the fire pit, remembering Will's comment about unattended fires. The implication that he knew—that he noticed. That everyone did.

Oliver paused on the bottom step, not answering. I went to the outdoor shower and filled a rusted bucket with water, the pipes groaning, then dumped it over the pit, fire sizzling, smoke caught up in the next breeze. We were suddenly bathed in darkness.

I understood, then, why we always left the fire burning. No one wanted to extinguish the light. I reached for the person beside me—Hollis—and made my way up the steps, toward the glow of the kitchen.

We each called our good nights, footsteps creaking up the stairs, hinges squeaking and doors latching shut.

I could see the lights turning off, one by one, from the balcony window, until mine was the only one left. Finally, I turned it off, then stood before the window, pulling aside the gauzy curtains, peering out toward the sea.

Then I quietly stepped outside, trying not to be afraid. I held tight to Grace's words—she had a way of putting things in perspective: *We've already been through the worst of it.* We had. And we had survived.

The moon and stars were hidden behind the weather system, and the waves were crashing violently, in a way that set my nerves on edge. I imagined Amaya standing here two days earlier, staring out at the ocean, the beach.

I wondered what she saw, looking back.

And then, just as I was watching, I noticed a faint light dancing along the beach.

I stepped to the side, to follow the movement, but it quickly drifted out of sight, to the left. In the opposite direction of the pier.

"Shit," I said, taking off down the steps, to the first level, and then to the patio with the still-sizzling fire pit. I jogged across the path until I came to the beach. I paused—the roar of the water, the sting of the wind, a rumble of something offshore . . . and then, *there*: a light, to the left.

There was only a rocky section of beach that way—not safe in the daytime, even less so at night. I took off toward it, thinking I was following something, only to realize the light was getting closer now, coming my way.

I froze, caught. And then the beam of light swept across the sand and landed on me. I brought up a hand to shield my eyes, as a familiar voice said, "Cassidy?"

I dropped my arm, let out a breath. "Oliver? What the hell are you doing out here?"

"I could ask you the same," he said.

"I saw a light on the beach."

"I saw something too." He looked over his shoulder, into the darkness. "I thought I saw someone out here. Came out to see . . ."

I looked around the beach, but couldn't see anything beyond the beam of his light. I could hear the waves crashing—closer now, like they were steadily encroaching.

He gestured down the beach with the light. "You know, on the other side of the rocks is the campground. Beyond that, another road."

I shook my head. I'd thought the rocks were the end of the beach. Not that there was another, just beyond.

"Amaya?" I asked.

"I don't know. Whoever it was, they left in a hurry."

A chill ran through me, and I hugged my arms across my stomach.

"What did you see?" he asked, voice low, like someone might be close by, listening.

"I think it was just you," I said. I didn't like how exposed we were out here. How much we couldn't see in return. "We're the only things visible right now."

He turned off the light, and we stood in silence together, listening. Another crash of a wave, the wind blowing over the dunes, and then a scurrying in the sand behind us. Oliver turned on the flashlight again, illuminating a space to the left, in the dunes. Two eyes stared back, like a deer in headlights, low to the ground, before the creature skittered away.

"Jesus," he said, dropping the beam to our feet.

I leaned closer, wrapped my hand around his wrist. "I think someone's been watching the house. I think someone's watching all of us."

He didn't answer, but I thought of the curtains pulled closed in his room. His insistence for us all to be out this afternoon. To be together. He must've had some reason to think the same.

"What do they want, Oliver?" Meaning: whoever was out there; whoever was contacting us.

Maybe it was the night, or the dark, or the fact I was still holding on to him, and being together always put us on the same team, the same side, with the same goal. Whatever the reason, he answered, as the beam illuminated the space between us.

"They wanted me to describe the knife."

THEN

HOUR 5

Oliver

The rain had started coming down in a heavy torrent, muting everything: their vision, their hearing, their perception of what was happening around them.

Oliver kept shining the flashlight at each person in turn, compulsively taking tally, keeping track of everyone. The van was gone, and there were no adults, no one in charge to tell them what they were supposed to do. No rules to follow. They were the only ones left.

So he kept shining the light—*click-click*—face by face. There were thirteen of them: nine survivors pulled from his van, and four who had managed to escape from the other before it sank—or at least that's all they knew of.

"Cut it out," Ian said, hand up to block the glare.

Oliver cut the flashlight for the count of ten seconds. Then he turned and illuminated the group at the base of the cliffs. Because of the light, he was in charge of checking on the injured. Trinity, with a broken leg. Morgan, with a head injury, he thought. And the thing he was most concerned about, the wound in Ben's stomach, and the way Cassidy had her hands placed over it.

She stared back at him, wide-eyed in the beam of his light. There was a flicker of terror in her face.

Click-click, he turned it off.

• • •

Oliver was afraid in the same dull, ever-present way he was afraid of most things: saying the wrong thing, making the wrong impression, choosing the wrong path. An anxiety that crept in whenever he was fully awake, that he noticed every morning, as he lay in bed and felt the familiar feeling wash over him. Otherwise, he could go hours forgetting it existed. It was background noise, a permanent condition, something for which he could find no obvious cause.

He had already survived the circumstances of his birth, which his parents often proudly recounted to others, like it was something Oliver had accomplished. When really it had all been outside his control: he had been born, he had been wrapped in a blanket and left under an overpass, and then he had been found. It was all very passive, none of which Oliver could claim credit for himself.

But he was a miracle, his parents were fond of saying: the miracle they had been hoping and waiting for.

He'd always felt like he had been waiting for something too. Only he wasn't sure what.

And now, at the edge of a river, at the base of a cliff, he could finally put a cause to that dull, ever-present fear. Standing in the dark, in the thunder, in the rain, he was afraid that he was about to lose it all. Everything he had managed to overcome. He was afraid that he had not taken advantage of his second chance. That he had spent it, always, waiting for something else to happen. And that this time, he would not be found.

Click-click: Hollis, staring at Brody.

Click-click: Brody, staring at the water.

Click-click: Joshua, staring at him.

He'd brought the flashlight on purpose, hooked to the belt loop of his shorts, to read in the dark van. (Which he did until Clara and Grace complained.)

But it was an accident that he had brought the knife. In any other circumstance, he probably would've gotten in a lot of trouble for having it in his possession.

They only discovered his father's switchblade in the outer pocket of his luggage as they were rummaging frantically for anything that might help them after the crash. The duffel bag belonged to his father, and so did the knife, which must've been left inside after his last camping trip.

The handle of the knife was red, and there was a crown engraved on one side—which his dad thought fitting, given their family name, and which had become the only way Oliver could convince people it belonged to him, after Amaya pulled it from the bag.

It was his. And therefore, he argued, he should be the one to hold on to it.

Jason had backed him up, even though he'd probably never seen it before—but he'd spent plenty of weekends at Oliver's house. He was a dependable witness, a dependable friend.

Oliver was not particularly outdoorsy. In truth, he was not particularly anything—no one would describe him as either athletically gifted or academically inclined—but he wasn't exactly the opposite either. He existed in what their small school would designate as the middle fifty percent.

But standing on the rocks with his classmates after they'd crawled out of the van, one by one, he discovered he was not particularly afraid either.

The dull, ever-present fear was there, of course. But not something sharper, deeper, that seemed to have taken over the others.

At least, he was okay until the knife went missing.

He kept looking for it—a red handle sticking out of someone's back pocket; the glint of the blade in the beam of his light.

They'd used it to cut the seat belts out of the van, in their shitty attempt to make a sling for Ian's shoulder, which was probably dislocated. And then they'd used it again, in their failed attempt to rig a tourniquet around Trinity's leg (she kept screaming; it seemed they were doing more harm than good), and now no one could remember who had the knife last.

He *knew* someone else had it now. He knew someone was lying.

So he wasn't just keeping an eye on the injured anymore; he was watching *everyone.*

One by one.

He started at the base of the cliffs, shining the beam in Morgan's face. He called her name, and her eyes fluttered open.

"Don't let her fall asleep," he said to Trinity.

"I'm trying," she said, through a grimace. Oliver worried she might also slip into shock, from the pain.

He cast a quick look over at Cassidy and Ben again. God, there was so much blood seeping through the balled-up clothes she had pressed to the wound. Oliver jogged to the luggage to find a new, clean shirt for her to use.

But someone had beaten him to it.

Ian was rifling through the luggage with his one good arm. He jumped back, as if Oliver had snuck up on him.

"Jesus," Ian said, then held out a white T-shirt. "Cassidy said she needed this."

"Thanks," Oliver said, bringing it back, leaving the light on Cassidy while she swapped out the makeshift bandaging.

Then Oliver returned to the rest of the group and started his tally again:

Click-click: Amaya, pacing back and forth, from end to end of their rocky clearing. Her mouth was moving, and Oliver couldn't tell if she was talking to herself or counting her steps.

Click-click: Clara and Grace, in a heated conversation. Clara was near hysterics, her voice at a fever pitch, and it seemed like Grace was trying to calm her down—

Hollis was suddenly in his face, closer than she'd ever been to him. She looked behind her once. "There have to be others," she said. He left the light shining on her panicked face.

"Where?" he said.

"The other van. They might've made it out." He could see her throat moving as she swallowed.

He had already started tallying the dead. Most of them had helped one another climb out of the back of Oliver's van, except for Mr. Kates, who they'd left exactly where he was, obviously beyond saving. Oliver had seen his body, seen it hunched over the wheel, his arms floating, but the rest of him unnaturally still, a haunting emptiness. The end, laid fully bare. But there were so many still unaccounted for from the other van. Oliver had seen it hurtling down the river, and he could only imagine the worst. He did not want to find them. He did not want to see them, or count them.

"I heard something out there," Hollis said, peering across the river, toward the far side. "A noise. People or . . ."

"An animal," Brody said, emerging from the darkness. "Did you see it too? The deer in the road?" A deer, leading to all this carnage.

Oliver swung the light his way. "I didn't see anything," he said. He had been sitting with Jason near the back of the second van, where they'd seemed to have the best luck, injury-wise. From the first van, only four people had escaped and made it to their group, Hollis included. They seemed relatively unharmed from the crash itself, beyond cuts and bruises and Ian's dislocated shoulder. But there were seven people from that van still unaccounted for . . .

"Listen, they were alive—" Hollis said, grabbing on to Oliver's wrist.

"Do you hear that?" It was Cassidy, his neighbor, and she was suddenly standing outside their group, but facing away. Her hands were covered in blood.

If Oliver listened closely, he could hear something too, the faintest sound of an alarm. A car in the distance, maybe. God, they had to be *so close*.

"What if that's some severe weather warning?" she said, eyes unnaturally wide.

Oliver felt a prickle of panic. He pictured a dam releasing, waters flooding through the ravine—

"The storm is only going to get worse," Hollis added, just as a bolt of lightning lit up the sky. The thunder followed in a near immediate clap, and Oliver felt himself ducking, felt his hands go to his ears, on instinct. "We have to go look for them *now.*"

The circle around him had grown, the light drawing them closer, moths to a flame.

"What are you all talking about?" Amaya asked, raising her voice to be heard.

"The rest of the people in the first van," Hollis said. "They could be out there. We should go look."

They all stared back at Hollis.

Oliver didn't know what had happened in the first van, but it made sense to him that the group who made it out would feel a responsibility to go check. Not just Hollis, but Cassidy and Ian, maybe even Joshua Doleman, who rarely seemed to have an opinion either way. Oliver already understood that so much came down to being on the right side of a count.

"It's too rough now," Brody said. "We'd never make it back."

Wasn't there some kind of saying about this kind of problem? The devil you knew? At least they knew what they had now, what they were up against.

"We wait," Brody continued. "There's no other way."

"We could send one person," Oliver said, and now Brody turned to stare at him, unflinching.

"Whoever makes it, *if* someone makes it, it's not like they'd be able to come back," Brody said.

"We have the cables," Jason added. "From the van. We could pull them back." Even now, the one person Oliver could count on to take his side.

"He's bleeding out," Clara said, her entire body trembling, her voice high and tight and desperate. "You see that, right?" She gestured behind her. They could. They could all see that. The wound in Ben's stomach was not the same as a broken leg or the busted nose or the cuts from the glass or the bruise Oliver could feel forming on his hip. "We need to get *help*," she said. Everyone knew that Clara had a crush on Ben Weaver. Or maybe *crush* was too mild a word: she sat next to him in class and at lunch; she knew his schedule; she laughed too loudly at his questionable jokes.

"Where is this help coming from, Clara?" Grace said, arms thrown out, like she was giving up, giving over. "Who's going to get it?"

"If we can go *look for the others*, then we can *get some fucking help* instead, don't you think?" Clara yelled.

"They're the same thing, Clara!" Hollis said, her voice rising to match Clara's. She gestured down the river. "Someone has to get in the river, either way! We find the others, or we find a way to get help. It's better than doing *nothing*."

Half of them were bordering on hysterics now; something was happening here, and he couldn't find the knife, and they were *trapped* in a deep ravine with a storm gaining force and the river growing louder, more menacing.

Someone had to make a decision. Someone had to take control. There was no more time for waiting.

Oliver heard the words coming from his mouth without even thinking of them first. "We'll take a vote," he said.

Brody laughed dismissively, but the others started nodding. In their silence was a permission.

"Hold on. Who put this guy in charge?" Brody asked, incredulous.

This guy. It occurred to Oliver then that Brody had no idea who he was. Had no idea who half these people were. "My name," he said sharply, "is Oliver King."

Oliver needed to do something. The knife was missing, but somebody had it. He had been given a second chance, but he would have to take the third. All life required a risk. A moment of vindication that only crystallized in hindsight. Even now, Oliver could feel that this was his.

He raised his voice. "We go look, yes or no," he said, turning the flashlight on the first person in the circle. Knowing, already, what she would say.

Click-click.

Hollis stared back with her icy-blue eyes, trembling in the rain. "Yes," she said.

WEDNESDAY

CHAPTER 10

The atmosphere at The Shallows felt like it was about to burst—both inside and out. The morning was a dark gray, and a low shelf of clouds swirled over a stormy ocean. There was too much humidity in the room, so I opened the outer doors, just to feel the cool, fresh air. But the air was just as thick outside, heavy with moisture.

Sometime today, in a town hundreds of miles away, a school chapel bell would chime twelve times, and we would not be there to hear it. Instead, a sea of students who had never known us would remain silent and still for the duration.

Maybe later today they would walk into their new Class of 2013 Memorial Library and remember what the *Memorial* stood for.

From my balcony, I could hear the surf, violent and close. I couldn't tell where the sea ended and the beach began. Behind me, the doors to my room blew inward with a bang, taking the white sheer curtains with them. I watched as the dark gray clouds slowly rolled closer.

It wouldn't be long now.

I took the rise of steps toward the third level, pausing halfway from a sense of vertigo, courtesy of the narrow footholds and the steep rise between boards, out of sync with the rest of the house. I held on to both handrails, straining to see over the dunes.

"Here it comes." A deep voice came from above, almost carried away on the wind. Like maybe he hadn't been speaking to me at all.

I looked up, tightening my grip on the rail.

Josh was directly above me, peering down from the third-floor overlook. Who knew how long he'd been standing there, in silence.

I turned back to the coast, but all I could see was a bird swooping down over the dunes, the dark rolling sea behind it.

"Do you see anyone out there?" I asked, thinking of the night before—the person Oliver had followed out there. The person, I believed, who had been watching this house.

"Just that boat," he said, finger extending toward the horizon. "Looks like it's heading back in." And then, after a pause, "I can see it rocking from here."

I felt my feet begin to sway in the wind as well, unsteady on the stairwell, like we'd become unmoored.

"Who would be out in this?" I asked, feeling the bite of wood slivers under my palms.

"Fishermen." He laughed, pointing again. "You see that?"

His finger traced the path of the bird, but now that I was looking closer, I could see the long red tail trailing behind it, the unnatural way it dove and rose again, in a spiraling arc. "Is that a kite?" I asked.

"There were more out there earlier," he said, like he had indeed been up there for a while, keeping watch. "But looks like they're finally calling it too."

The doors to my bedroom banged against the inner walls again, making me jump. "Jesus," I said, gripping the handrail tighter.

Josh laughed. "Yeah, that always makes me jump too."

I froze from his comment, then slowly began descending the steps to the landing outside my room. Everything Josh said seemed to be laden with extra meaning. From up on his perch, I realized, he could see over the entirety of the second-floor deck. The lights from our bedrooms shining outward, the sound of our voices carrying, the latching and swaying of doors.

Had he seen me last night, racing for the beach? Had he noticed

Oliver, doing the same? Or maybe I was just reading too much into offhand comments, finding hidden layers of meaning where there were none.

I wedged the outer doors to my bedroom shut, leaning into them as I turned the latch.

I could hear the rest of the house coming alive. Six people, each trying to carve out space. Grace, trying to get an early work call in from the dining room—she was right, we really should've used Ian's room as a private work area instead of letting Josh take it over—while the rest of us moved around her, grabbing breakfast, retreating. As if each of us could feel it: how close the atmosphere was to the breaking point.

Oliver's bedroom door had been shut when I made my way to the kitchen, but I imagined him standing at the large windows of his room, peering out between the curtains. He believed he had seen something last night, had tracked whoever or whatever it was back toward the rocky barrier. I didn't know who I was looking for, but I knew someone had been on the beach, watching us during our arrival.

And there was another person, other than Amaya, who might've seen them. Hollis had been out on the beach at the same time—she could've noticed them, without knowing what she was truly seeing.

• • •

From the second-floor landing, I heard Grace's voice carry up the steps, a calming lull. I tapped on the door to the yellow room, hoping Hollis hadn't attempted to go out in this. Finally, Hollis answered, dressed in a loose tank and yoga pants, like she'd been working out in her room. Her bangs were clipped back, giving her eyes an even wider look, deerlike and innocent. The only accessory was her diamond stud nose ring.

"You trying to stay out of the way too?" she asked, opening the door wider. A large bandage was fastened on the side of her heel, and she rubbed it with her other foot, like it itched.

I nodded, stepping inside. "I feel like I'm eavesdropping on someone's therapy session if I'm downstairs."

"Well, you are," she said with a laugh. "I can't tell if the house is shrinking or we're expanding. It used to feel so big."

"It's the weather," I said, not making eye contact. For me, a storm always felt like claustrophobia. Felt like slick ravine walls and a rising river and absolutely nowhere to go. The feeling had managed to seep inside this house. It was here with us now.

"My phone keeps buzzing with high-surf alerts and small-craft advisories," she said, with a glance toward the windows. Their curtains were held back with brass hooks screwed into the wall on both sides, a feature missing from my own bedroom. "It's like a giant warning: *Do not set foot on the beach*. We get it!"

I smiled tightly. "Not sure if everyone got the memo. People were flying kites out there this morning."

She grimaced, then turned her phone my way—showing me an article she'd pulled up: *Homes Lost to Sea.*

"Did you know last year several houses got swept away in another town up the coast? They had to shut the beach down here. Too much debris."

"Are you worried?" I asked. The Shallows had withstood decades of hurricanes and other storms. We were raised up, set back from the beach, a long wooden path connecting us to the sand.

"No." She cleared her throat. "Just, there are a lot of things in the water that can get pushed this way, from the currents." She smiled sheepishly, and I knew we were both thinking of how she'd emerged from the ocean, terrified. She must've been researching what might have been out there, catching on her leg. The thing she imagined pulling her back, pulling her under.

"Question for you, Holl. The first day, when we arrived, did you see anyone else on the beach with you?"

"I mean, sure," she said, tipping her head. "Not that I was really paying attention. But I saw you walking out there, if that's what you're asking . . ."

"Not then," I said, shaking my head. "Before that. When I first arrived, Amaya told us she saw someone on the beach. I think . . . someone might've been watching the house. I think she might've gotten spooked." I lowered my voice. "Especially with everything else going on."

Hollis sat cross-legged on the bed, back against the headboard, nowhere to go. Her face had shifted, like I'd trapped her there myself.

"I'm just curious what she saw," I added, trying not to worry her any more than she already was. I lowered myself onto the foot of the bed, mirroring her position. We probably looked like teens at a sleepover, though we never would've been at the same one, growing up.

Even now she was not one to lean forward and share secrets.

She fidgeted with the end of her ponytail, twisting it tightly and then releasing it. "Honestly, Cass, I wasn't paying attention. I was trying very hard not to pay attention, actually."

I remembered the image of her, meditating on the sand, eyes closed, posture perfect. "And yet"—I gave her a small smile—"you keep showing up here too."

"I didn't know we were allowed not to."

She grinned like it was a joke, but my stomach dropped as she said it. The thing I wondered for so long, until I decided, finally, that ten years past the accident had been long enough.

"But," she continued, "seeing as Amaya bailed and no one's dragging her back makes me think we really don't need to be here." She leaned closer. "Cass, I mean it."

We don't need to be here. There was power in numbers, and we were two. Judging from my conversation with Brody on Monday night, I thought he might make three.

"We should make a new pact," I said. "To be done with this—for good."

She laughed, loud and fast, hand to her mouth, eyes sparkling.

I let the warmth wash over me—the moments of comfort I'd

felt with these people, these near strangers, with whom I had become so deeply connected, by fate. Sometimes I would think of them throughout the year, my memory triggered by the sight of another girl with her hair dyed pink at the ends; a man in an EMS uniform; the scent of leather mixed with cigarettes.

I still periodically checked in—invisibly, silently, leaving no trace. Scrolling through Hollis's Instagram account or their employers' social media pages for event photos: performing a mental tally, confirming that everyone was doing okay. I had seen Brody in the background of a township Facebook post, paying tribute to their EMS team; Josh in the law firm Christmas party group photo; the announcement of Oliver's new position as hedge fund manager. I'd found Grace's patient reviews and discovered her schedule and availability through an appointment portal. I'd called the business line for Amaya's office, and listened to her familiar greeting on the other end—*Thanks for calling, this is Amaya speaking*—before hanging up.

It was easier to picture them doing well when we were all living our separate lives. I could imagine Brody with a baby on his lap, and Hollis encouraging a group of runners at the starting line, Grace helping ease someone else's trauma, and Joshua arguing a case in a courtroom. It was so easy to picture Oliver commanding a boardroom and Amaya making a true difference on the ground.

I preferred it that way, thinking of the versions of them I imagined moving forward, instead of the people we became when we were all back together.

What would a tell-all do to them? Other than forcing us to relive a trauma? Other than pulling us backward, into a past we'd already clawed our way out from?

"Well, on that note . . ." I said, standing from the bed, still smiling.

She leaned forward fast, grabbing my wrist—she was so much stronger than she looked, all lean muscle, perfect balance, precision and endurance. "Cass, hold on." She leaned even closer, so her icy-blue eyes were hooked on mine. "Did you say anything?"

I shook my head fast. "It wasn't me."

"No, I didn't mean . . ." She shook her head too. "I meant, did you answer them?"

"I didn't." It wasn't a lie. I had never said anything—to anyone—about that night. But no one had pressed me either. No one had shown up, asking for anything. *They wanted me to describe the knife*, Oliver had confided. I wondered what they wanted from Hollis. She had been the least tied to any of us—only to Brody, and look what had happened there. She was a transfer in her senior year, and she would've been gone the next. Did she really have any allegiance to the group, any roots to the town?

"Did you?" I asked.

She shook her head quickly. "No. *No.* It came through my Instagram. My business page. Looking to confirm, they said, how I found the rest of the group that night."

I stared back at her, the past rising up beside us. The wind whistled against the windows, and it was suddenly ten years earlier, in the dark, in the night. The sound of the river and the storm approaching, a flash of lightning in the distance, a resounding crack of thunder—

She released my wrist suddenly, and we were back in the yellow room. "I couldn't trace the user. Couldn't figure out who it was, behind a private account." She cleared her throat. "It's not a hard question, on its own. But it has to mean it's one of us talking, right?"

"I don't know," I said. "Ten years is a long time." There were small details that weren't important, that could've been mentioned offhand, without a second thought. Had Brody whispered something to a girl at a bar, doling out his stories like currency, drawing people closer? Had Amaya pointed out the spot of the accident to someone in town, in a push for more safety? Had she requested more lights, more patrols, because, *You don't know what it's like out there, at night—*

"Josh thinks it's Amaya," I said. "Brody too."

She frowned, a tiny line forming between her eyes. "Amaya? No. She couldn't. Her family would stop that . . . Right?"

Would they? Could anyone really stop one of us, if we had the will to speak up?

Grace had told me that Amaya had been having a hard time with her family. Josh must know that. Was this, then, the source of their conflict?

There was probably a record in her family's law offices. But the firm must've been bound by some sort of privacy laws or, at the very least, an allegiance to us. And anyway, we'd all always stuck to the same story, as far as I knew.

It wasn't even a conscious decision. The first lie begot the second. We fell in line, dominos in a row, in a method of self-preservation—an instinct. Josh said it first, when the police and that single ambulance finally arrived: *There are more of us. But we don't know what happened to them.*

It wasn't a lie. It was a slant. We didn't see, and so we didn't know. We could never be sure.

We agreed with his claim, because it was easier. Maybe we did it for Amaya, who had been bold enough to make the decision to move while we still could. Or maybe we did it for ourselves, who each agreed to leave the site of the crash—some more willing than others.

By the time the lawyer from the Andrewses' firm interviewed me for the suit against the school, I was used to the lines.

It was a friendly conversation, nothing like I'd come to expect from television. My parents and I in a conference room, with a camera, a lawyer—not Amaya's dad, but a younger man, with deep-set, kind eyes—asking me to walk him through the series of events.

We were stuck in traffic, I began. *We left the highway to find a bathroom.*

And did you?

No. Eventually, we just pulled over on the side of the road. The vans turned around.

And then what happened?

I blinked slowly. *We crashed.*

He nodded. *Did you see what happened?*

I shook my head. *It was all so fast—*

I understand, he'd said. *Just a little more, Cassidy. Who else were you with, after you escaped the van?*

Their names were a drumbeat in my head, and I listed them out—nine survivors, all of us together from the start. It was just us—always, only us. Then, like now, we did not speak of the dead.

Did you see what happened to any of the others?

I shook my head. My fingers had started to tremble, and my mother reached out and grabbed my hand, tethering me, grounding me.

Do we really need to do this? she'd asked, her voice cracking. *Hasn't she been through enough?*

It's best to do this when it's fresh, he said, before moving on to safer topics. *The school had a no-cell-phone policy?*

Yes, I said, clear and assured. Understanding what was most important to them. *We had no way to call for help.*

Just as he reached for the button to stop recording, he said, *Before we finish, is there anything else that happened that would be important to know?*

I held my breath. I felt the entire room holding its breath. I shook my head. *It was terrible,* I said. *We had to climb our way out. We had to . . .* If there was a moment to say something, it was this.

But after a stretch of silence, he saved me, filling the space. *Thank you, Cassidy. You did so good. We'll be in touch if we need anything else.*

But I didn't know for sure what the others had said in response to the same questions. What other information might be filed away, whispered behind closed doors.

I had no idea what it was like for Hollis in that room, or anyone else.

"I thought all of this was behind us," I said to her now.

Hollis nodded slowly. "Every once in a while," she said, "I get a message that makes me look over my shoulder. A user name that feels too close to one of theirs. Or a question phrased just a little off. Like *How fast can you run? How far can you swim?*" She shook her head. "But nothing like this. Nothing so specific."

"It has to be one of us," I answered, and she tipped her head faintly, lips pressed together.

The wind shuddered against the panes, and she locked her eyes on mine. "We're stuck here today, aren't we?"

Her balcony doors faced the side of the house, and with the curtains pulled open, I imagined anyone could see straight in, especially at night.

"I meant what I said, Hollis," I said, dropping my voice, leaning closer, so my vision focused down to just her. I thought she was holding her breath. "After this week, let's not come back."

Her eyes continued to search mine for another beat of silence, as if there were something else she might find under the surface of my words. Then she sighed, leaning back on the bed. "Sure," she said slyly. "Okay."

• • •

Grace was still on a call as I skirted by her and out the front door.

I couldn't stop thinking of what Hollis had told me about debris in the water, about things carried on a current from farther up the coast—things from other towns, other piers. And now I was picturing Will walking my way with a fishing pole slung against his shoulder the day of our arrival. I pictured someone hanging over the edge of the pier, phone in hand, before losing it to the deep.

Out on the front porch, the wind whipped my hair to the side, and I felt a gentle mist in the air—but I wasn't sure if it was blown in from the ocean or if the atmosphere had finally reached its saturation point.

Peering down the street, I saw that Will's bungalow looked quiet, secure. His truck was in the drive, and I imagined the weather was keeping him in as well. At least, I hoped he wasn't out on that fishing boat that Josh had seen, racing the storm back to shore.

As I walked his way, the sand blew from the tops of the dunes and swirled across the unpaved road. Nature, steadily encroaching. I was just at the mailbox with the anchor resting beside it, heading toward the spiraling steps, when the sound of laughter carried from inside.

I didn't want to interrupt a date, or any other visit. I really knew nothing about him—if he had roommates, or a girlfriend. Just that he'd given me a ride home when I'd been in need, said *Open-door policy*, and made me feel welcome.

I was standing there frozen, undecided, when the door swung open above me and footsteps resounded on the metal staircase, the iron clanging against the decking with each step. Two boots appeared first, then baggy jeans, a flannel shirt straining over his stomach. A man I didn't know paused on the steps, ducking below the wooden deck above him, a quirk to his mouth as he took me in.

"Hi there," he said. He had windburned cheeks, a wide-open smile, a softness to his vowels.

I took a step back, into the gravel drive. "Sorry, didn't mean to interrupt—"

"You here for Will?" And then, without waiting for my response, he raised his face upward and called, "Will!"

The door swung open again, and Will appeared on the deck above. He rested his arms on the railing, and I couldn't help but smile at his hair standing up at odd angles, against the wind.

He smiled back. "Hey there, new friend," he called.

I raised my hand in an awkward wave. "Cassidy," I said to the man on the steps. "Staying over there." I gestured in the general direction of Oliver's house, hoping he didn't ask for specifics.

"Well, I was just heading out," he said, jutting his thumb in the opposite direction, straight through the underside of Will's house, "that way." Beyond the bar area, there was a large rectangle of grass, and then another house, in similar style and structure to this one.

He picked up a square of metal sheeting that was leaning against the bar on his way, tucking it under his arm. “Thanks, Will,” he called, giving me one final wave over his shoulder.

Will watched him go, the sheet of metal bending and flexing with the wind, then turned his attention my way. “You all preparing?” he asked.

“I didn’t know we had to,” I said. It was a storm, but not a hurricane. There was no notice to evacuate, or even to pull out the storm shutters.

Will started descending the metal spiral staircase. “If the road’s in danger of flooding, the cops will shut it down. The ferries won’t run. With the number of people you have staying in that house, I’d make sure you’re stocked up at least.”

I looked over my shoulder, back toward the house—a series of cars lined up in a row.

We ran through supplies at an alarming rate. Towels required constant laundering, paper towels needed replacing, and water bottles overtook the recycling bin. A loaf of bread was gone by breakfast. A six-pack of Coke would last halfway through lunch. A twelve-pack of beer might not get much further.

We were always running out for something. There weren’t large grocery stores in town, but a variety of small convenience centers and stands to buy fresh fish, fresh fruit, homemade ice cream.

We should’ve planned better, making lists and stopping at a bulk store on the way in. But we had always played it by ear. We did not think long term. As if we were unsure, truly, how long we would be here.

Now I thought of the possibility of a flooded road. The sheet of metal the other man just took from Will’s house, large enough to cover a window.

I was still standing there as Will unlocked a shed tucked away to the side of the bar area, then started relocating the loose objects under the house.

"Want to give me a hand with this?" he asked. "Or are you just a casual observer?"

I smirked, then joined him. Under the deck, in the bar area, there were toolboxes, strips of metal, and several buckets filled with an assortment of metallic objects, things he must've uncovered with that metal detector on the beach. I could pick out multiple lengths of chain, the face of a pocket watch, and, if I was being honest, glinting pieces that did indeed look like they could've come from a shipwreck.

I deposited them inside the shed, which was much more organized than the one at our place. Wooden shelves lined the walls, light filtering through the gaps from outside. The items seemed to be grouped by size and function. A single bulb hung from the ceiling, though it remained off.

Outside, I ran my hand across the bar top, making sure there were no other loose objects to be secured. Up close, I could see the seams and joints of wood and various shades of metal, eclectically pieced together.

"You made this," I said.

"I did," he answered, picking up a folding chair and stacking it onto the next.

"Ah, so you're actually an artist," I said, feeling a connection to him.

He laughed. "It's just a hobby."

After depositing the chairs inside, Will started carrying a set of concrete blocks out.

"Grab that tarp, will you?" he asked.

The blue tarp had been folded into a perfect square and tucked into a built-in shelf behind the bar. After I shook it out, Will took the opposite corner, and we stretched it over what remained—larger tools, heavier wooden chairs—securing it with the cement blocks on either end. Then I listened as the rain finally began, in a steady *tap tap tap* against the tarp.

"Come on in," he said. "I'd make you a drink at the bar, but it's looking like an inside day."

I followed him up the spiral steps and emerged through a square hole in his decking. From above, the entrance to the steps looked more like a trapdoor—a feature I also couldn't imagine being quite up to code.

"Sorry to barge in like this," I said, and he laughed.

"This? Far from barging. My neighbor Kevin, on the other hand? No knock, no call, takes my open-door policy to an extreme. He also takes whatever he wants from outside." He smiled. "It's okay, he's my cousin."

I was drawn to Will in the same way I was drawn to Grace; the same way I had been drawn to Russ: quickly, and caught off guard. They all operated on the same wavelength, lacking boundaries, putting you at ease.

He held the storm door open for me, and I followed him in. I thought I knew what to expect inside—beach homes all seemed to exude a similar vibe. And at first, I was right: in front of me, the living room was spare, with minimalist decor and rustic-modern furnishings, as expected. But there was a door open to my right. Whether intended as an office or an unused bedroom, the walls and floor space were covered in twisted metallic decor: a homemade clock, metal stools and tables in various stages of completion, wire twisted into unrecognizable shapes.

There was a series of tools—pliers, scissors—and broken objects with jagged edges, but he pulled the door shut quickly, before I could get a better look.

"Okay," he said, scratching the scruff of his jaw, "*hobby* might've been an understatement. The off-season is long."

I laughed as he led me away from the room.

The rest of his place was almost entirely visible from the living room. A bar separated this room from the kitchen, and a hall extended straight past with several open doors—a bathroom, another bedroom—and another exit to the wraparound deck at the other end.

"How long have you been here?" I asked, leaning against the bar as he pulled two glasses down from the upper cabinets.

"In this house? About five years, maybe. But I grew up here. Left for the coast guard, came back after."

Long enough to know who should be here, and who shouldn't, for sure.

He pulled an unlabeled glass jug of orange juice from the fridge. "My cousin makes this fresh, so he's not all bad," he said. "I won't admit it, but it's the best in town."

I took a sip, and had to agree.

There was a long scratch across the back of his hand, swollen pink. "Occupational hazard," he said, when he noticed me looking.

"Did you find all of that on the beach?" I asked, gesturing to the room with the closed door behind me, like it was a living thing.

"Most, yeah," he said with a small grin. "Some stuff gets brought to me when other people find it too. Turns out this," he said, gesturing to the room again, "is not a secret."

"And yet," I joked, "you have no need for a phone."

"Doesn't really fit, I must say. Ever find the owner?"

I swallowed down my unease. This was what I came for, after all. "No. I'm wondering if it might've washed up from the pier. Did you see anyone out there that day?"

"No one looking for a phone. No one doing anything but fishing. Other than your friend, I mean."

I shook my head, twisting the cup back and forth. "No, not on the beach. I meant the pier."

He paused, then tipped his head. "I don't mean your blond friend channeling the Zen." He raised his arms to the side, palms up, like he was imitating her yoga pose. Then he dropped his hands back to the counter with a thud. "I meant the guy."

I stared back at him for a span of seconds, not breathing. Then

I pulled my phone from my back pocket. My hand trembled as I pulled up the message with Ian's obituary. I clicked the link again, zoomed in on his picture—though he hadn't looked like this in years. But suddenly I had this terrible hope that it had been Ian on the pier. That Ian, the purest of heart, had found a way out of this after all.

But Will frowned. "No, not him, the Asian one."

My back tightened, shoulders straightened. "Oliver was out there?"

Oliver had been the last to arrive at the house. We'd all been gathered in the Adirondack chairs on the lower patio, and he'd joked about how we'd managed to find our way inside this year. His was the last car. He'd pulled in behind me, blocking me in.

"Sure, yeah, earlier in the day," Will said, taking one last sip. "I saw him on the pier." He grinned. "That's how I knew you were all coming out again."

I gently placed my phone on the counter, faceup, Ian's face still visible. "When?" I said, voice low and scratchy. "What time, I mean."

He rubbed the side of his jaw. "Can't say, exactly. The hours kinda stretch out there, you know . . ." He trailed off.

Oliver. He had been here before we arrived. Had probably opened up the house, which was why we had been able to get in.

My eyes went to the nearest window, a low rectangle with a view out onto the road, and The Shallows in the distance.

"You're sure it was him," I said.

"Yeah, I'm sure. He's kind of hard to miss, with the way he was dressed, especially out on the pier. Like I said, it's how I knew you were coming."

Now I was running through the past few days, seeing them in a different light.

Last night, on the beach—had Oliver even been following anyone? Or had he been out there all on his own?

"That one," Will said, pointing at the phone—at Ian's smiling face. "He's not here, is he?"

I shook my head. Couldn't say the words. Didn't want to show him the rest of the article, admit that Ian would never be with us again.

"Didn't think so. I haven't seen that one since winter."

I stared at him, not understanding. "Haven't seen *what*?"

He tapped the display, pointer finger just under Ian's smile. "Him," he said. "Though he looks pretty different than this now, doesn't he."

"I thought you said the house was always empty." *Ian, alive. Ian, here.*

"It usually is, yeah. I told you, the only ones ever here are you."

"He was here," I said, needing him to confirm it. Needing to be sure. "In the winter?"

"He was here," he repeated.

I took a step back, trying to process. Ian, at The Shallows, all alone. I heard the rain picking up, dinging against the gutters outside. "Sorry, I have to get going before that gets any worse," I said.

"Yeah, listen," he said. "I know you're on vacation, but you really need to stay in tonight. The surge is no joke."

I nodded absently, barely processing his warning.

Will came around the bar, looking like he was going to come even closer, before stopping himself. "You look like you've seen a ghost," he said.

"Well," I said, trying to play it off. "I am staying in the ghost house, right?"

But I could tell he didn't buy it. His face darkened, easy smile flattening to a straight line. "I thought you said you were all old friends."

How to explain—for most of us, being together was less like seeing an old friend, and more like an old ex. There was both a comfort and discomfort to how deeply they knew you. Someone who knew how to play you to your highs and lows, equally. But someone, all the same, who had once been everything for you, even if only for a fleeting moment.

When I didn't respond, he took a step closer, lowered his voice. "You know, there are rumors. About what you all are doing here. A cult. Some tax shell conspiracy. Well, that last one was my cousin, but I don't think he knows what that means."

"And you?" I asked, voice just as soft. "What do you say?"

He looked off to the side, pursed his mouth for a second. "Cult seemed most likely to me, honestly. You keep to yourselves, move as a pack. But aren't those supposed to grow?" He turned back to me, waiting.

"No, no cult." I sighed, letting my eyes drift shut. "We went through something together," I said. "Survived an accident when we were kids. We get together every year now, to commemorate it. To pay tribute. To make sure the rest of us are okay. It's . . . not a happy thing, you know?" I cleared my throat. "Not everyone made it. But we helped each other through. We were the only survivors."

He took it in, then nodded once. "Ahh, you were the heroes, then."

"No," I told him as I pushed the storm door open, stepping out into the rain. "No heroes here."

CHAPTER 11

The rain was coming down at a steady clip, so I ran with my head down, gravel and sand crunching under each step. I didn't see the Jeep until it was already upon me, my hands coming down hard on the warm hood, bumper pressed against my body—

"Didn't you fucking see me here?" I yelled, staring through the windshield. The wipers moved back and forth, water streaking across the glass.

Brody lowered the passenger window. "Of course we saw you!" he called out into the rain. "That's why we stopped in the middle of the drive."

The surge of adrenaline was making my arms shake. I could feel the steady rumble of the engine underneath my palms. Brody was right. The Jeep was fully stopped; I was the one who had kept moving.

"I didn't see you—" I started, in half an apology.

"Get in!" Brody yelled over the hum of the engine.

I circled around the car to his window, then placed one wet hand on the edge of the lowered window. "It's fine, I can make it back."

Oliver was behind the wheel, dark eyes latched on mine from across the way. "Get in the car, Cassidy."

"We could use another set of hands," Brody added—a contrast, a balance.

"You're getting everything wet," Oliver added, though I hadn't been the one to lower the window.

Still, I got in the car.

Oliver's rental had that new-car smell and pristine floors, other than the mixture of grit and wet sand I had just tracked inside. There was a tag hanging from the rearview mirror with the rental company name, still crisp and unbent. I wouldn't have been surprised if he was the Jeep's first passenger.

"I'm not sure how you missed us," Brody said, as Oliver continued driving toward the main road.

"I was in a rush . . ." I began. Because I was in my own head. Because of the rain. Because of what Will had told me about seeing Oliver at the pier—

I caught Oliver's eyes in the rearview mirror, watching me back.

But it was Brody who spoke. "What the hell were you doing out in this?"

I didn't know whether they'd seen where I'd come from, or happened to stumble upon me in the road, just as I'd stumbled upon them.

"I was out for a walk. It wasn't raining when I left."

Brody twisted around in his seat, until he was facing me, dimple forming with an amused expression. "How could you not feel it coming?"

I lifted one shoulder in a shrug, went for the same self-deprecating expression Brody might've used. But I *could* feel something coming. The atmosphere, so tense it was bound to burst. It had been building not just today, but since we arrived. I was sure, now, that we had all felt it, from the start.

"Has anyone spoken to Amaya?" I asked, noticing an increased activity of cars and trailers leaving the campground.

"Grace has been texting her to come back," Brody said. "But she hasn't been able to reach her." The fact that Grace was concerned was enough to put me on edge as well.

We fell to silence then, nothing but the steady rain and the steady swish of the wipers, a cocoon of warmth and safety within. Then my phone rang, cutting through the silence—a call from Russ, unusual in the middle of the day. I pressed ignore; I'd call back later, telling him I'd been in a meeting or a venue walk-through.

"Holy shit," Brody said, leaning forward with his hands on the dashboard. "What's going on?"

I leaned between their seats, squinting as the wipers accelerated to double time. A line of red brake lights snaked into the distance. There was an electronic sign just within sight on the side of the road, orange text glowing through the rain: *ROAD CLOSED AHEAD*.

"They shut the highway," Oliver said, voice low. "Must be the high-water warnings," he continued. "The waves can flood over the dunes at high tide. It's probably just a precaution."

Though Will had said this was a possibility, I was still surprised it could happen so quickly.

"Turn on the radio," Brody said. The blaring alarm of an emergency broadcast filled the car, before a robotic voice relayed the notice. *High surf. Flash flooding. Strong winds. Remain inside and off the roads—*

I closed my eyes, but couldn't stop the image from appearing: the water, rising up and creeping closer, spilling over the barriers, flooding the pavement; people climbing out of car windows, calling for help; and wondering who I would save . . .

A car honked behind us, and Oliver threw up his hands. "Where would you like me to go, asshole?" he yelled.

Oliver turned on his blinker and veered immediately into the parking lot on our right, before we became trapped in a line of cars with nowhere to go. He took the back exit onto a narrow side street, navigating behind a series of strip mall units. Eventually, we pulled into the back entrance of the parking lot for Beach Provisions—a small mom-and-pop grocery and supply store.

Brody groaned, resting his head back. The lot was overflowing, and several cars were waiting for spots, blinkers on, claiming their places.

"Fuck it," Oliver said. He pulled up to the side of the store, braking abruptly. Then he put the Jeep into park and looked to each of us, like we might argue with him.

We did not.

"Ready?" he called. I imagined a silent count, remembered how we had once worked together, on the same side—"Go."

We threw open the doors, and ran.

• • •

Inside the store, it looked like the preparation for an impending apocalypse. There was one lone wide-eyed cashier staring down a line snaking straight through the middle aisle. The shelves were stripped almost bare, and there wasn't a free cart or basket in sight.

"Grab whatever you can," Oliver said.

"I'm gonna hold a spot in line," I said.

"Smart," Brody called, before taking off.

I couldn't tell whether the customers were mostly local or vacationers, except for the family in front of me. I recognized the little girl, currently perched on her mother's hip, peering back over her shoulder, straight at me, with wide blue eyes. This was the family I'd seen building a sand castle the day of our arrival.

"I told you we should've left yesterday," the mother said to the man beside her.

His arms were balancing an eclectic assortment of groceries, so his shrug was both muted and exaggerated. "I didn't see you trying to find a hotel on the mainland or change our flights."

"Because you wouldn't *agree*—"

Brody arrived with an expression of both exasperation and triumph, placing a jar of peanut butter in my grip. "Do not lose this. I think it's the last one in the store."

I swore an oath of safe-keeping, and then waited until they

returned with more goods. At first, we piled the larger packages on the floor in front of me, and I shuffled everything forward slowly with my feet. Halfway up to the register, I finally managed to snag a cart from someone leaving the store.

It felt like a game, a mission, a challenge—all of us, once again, on the same side. It was us versus nature, the scarcity, the others. When Brody came back with a loaf of bread, I threw my arms up in the air. When Oliver deposited the crate of bottled water in the cart, I cheered audibly. By the time we headed out (Oliver paying, all hands needed to load up the Jeep) we were actually laughing, from the relief. We ignored the looks from the other customers over our illegal parking—there were no repercussions, of course. I ran the cart back toward the front door as Oliver closed the trunk.

Brody waited for me in the rain, gripping the handle. He high-fived me as I passed, like we'd just won something.

• • •

It took the slow crawl of traffic to drag us back to reality—that we really could not go anywhere but back to The Shallows. My phone rang again—Russ's name lighting up the display—and this time, Brody twisted around in the seat and asked who was calling.

I turned my phone around on instinct, so he could see the name—as if he might have cause not to trust me. "It can wait," I said, letting the call go to voicemail. But I wasn't sure why he'd call twice in the middle of the day, instead of texting.

I was starting to worry, so I sent him a quick text: *In a meeting. Call you back in a few. Everything okay?*

"Does he know you're here?" Brody asked, meaning layered upon meaning. There was no explicit rule against telling others what we were doing. It's just not something I felt the need to offer up, generally. My parents knew—it's why my mom reached out that first day, checking in on me. I wasn't sure what Brody told his ex, but it must've been something significant to justify leaving her alone so close to her due date last year.

A buzz on my phone: *Yes, call me when you're free?*

I flipped my phone facedown in my lap. "No, he doesn't. I told him I was on a work trip," I said. "In New York."

Brody grabbed on to the back of the seat, only half his face visible, like he was preparing to tell me a secret. "I'm seeing my grandfather, he's been pretty sick."

After a beat, Oliver added, "I'm helping my parents move."

Brody laughed then, one loud burst, and it quickly caught. Strength in numbers, comfort in the pack.

"Whoa," Brody said, his body lurching back and forth as Oliver drove through a massive puddle. I felt the tires skidding, water flying, as the Jeep finally emerged through the other end.

"Sorry," Oliver said. "It floods fast."

My shoulders tightened, and I pictured the river. The churning dark of it, the unexpected rush. How fast that water rose, and kept rising. How the time we'd spent out there together in hindsight could feel both interminable and instantaneous. How seven hours could either make you or break you.

There were police lights ahead, a man with orange glowing batons directing traffic, like we were on an airport runway, being guided safely back.

"What's going on up there?" I asked.

"Looks like they're evacuating the people left at the campground over to the motel," Oliver said.

The sign for the campground was half buried in a dune at the edge of the road, and I couldn't tell whether it was for effect or not. The Dunes, it was called. Despite the name, people didn't camp or sleep on the dunes, so much as park campers or set up small pop-ups outside an SUV in the lot.

Now those campers were being pulled away by cars and pickup trucks, clogging up the road.

"Someone call Amaya," Oliver said. "Jesus Christ."

Brody already had his phone to his ear. "It's going straight to voicemail," he said.

"She's probably evacuating . . ." I said, hoping.

"She probably let her phone go dead," Oliver said sharply. But I could hear the concern under his critique.

The men with the glowing batons were redirecting the cars out of the campground, down our way, then blocking traffic again as they guided them into the lot on our right, to the Blue Whale. The motel was an aged, two-story gray-blue structure set back against the sound. Just as with the grocery store, the parking lot here was near the bursting point, cars parked up on the grass median dividing the road from the lot.

"Wait, pull over," I said. "In there."

Oliver obviously wasn't accustomed to taking orders from anyone else, so I continued. "The car. Right there. Is that Amaya's?"

Both of their heads whipped in that direction. It was hard to tell in the rain, but her car was a distinct dull rust color, and it stood out in a sea of black and white, silver and blue.

Oliver immediately put on the signal, waiting for our turn.

We snaked through the rows in the lot, moving with traffic, waiting as cars pulled out, or tried to wedge their way in, the campers jutting out too far to maneuver around in spots.

"This was a mistake," Brody said, but Oliver remained silent. I knew he wanted to see too.

Finally, we pulled up behind the rust-colored car.

The back window was covered in a row of decals—a series of causes, the logo of her foundation. "That's definitely hers," I said.

"She should be back with us," Brody said.

"What should we do?" Oliver said. "Go knocking on motel doors? Look at this place."

He had a point. Not only was there a line of cars snaking through the lot, but there was a line of people seeking refuge, stretching out the lobby door, huddling under hoods and umbrellas.

Still, I felt myself finally able to complete my mental tally.

What mattered was that we were all here, on this island, together. Each name accounted for. Maybe it was her that I'd seen on the beach the night before, watching us. Maybe Oliver had seen her there too and followed her back toward the campground. Maybe Josh was right.

Maybe I had been too untrusting of the rest of them.

Oliver waited at the exit of the lot, for his chance. A police officer stepped into the intersection, holding out his hands to block the flow of cars. The traffic opened up, and we were gone.

If even the storm wouldn't bring Amaya back to us, I couldn't imagine anything would.

• • •

A few moments later, we pulled into our drive in silence. It was the rain, whipping up in the wind. The house, looming before us. The way we were trapped in this place, together—something dangerous too close to the surface, hovering between us.

"Not gonna lie," Brody finally said, "this is looking pretty ominous."

"The house has seen a lot worse," Oliver said, as much to himself as to us. "It's just rain."

Just rain. As if he hadn't heard the same emergency broadcast warning as the rest of us. But I understood what he was trying to say: this was not a severe mountain thunderstorm, or a rising river suddenly unleashing its terrible power through a ravine.

But there was a terrible power to the ocean too—an endless expanse of currents gaining force.

From where Oliver parked out front, I could see the others through the living room windows. Every light in the house was on even though it was still day. But the storm clouds had cast a darkness over everything, and we all knew how claustrophobic it could get inside.

"On three?" Brody asked.

I raised my phone. "I'm gonna return this call first." I knew I wouldn't find any quiet inside, with all of us cooped up together.

Oliver threw open the door, and he and Brody raced for the trunk.

"I'll get the rest!" I called, but my voice was swallowed up as Oliver tucked another bag under his arm before slamming the trunk closed. Then it was just me in the Jeep, windows fogging from the inside, rain streaking down the glass.

I called Russ back, and held the phone tightly to my ear.

"Hey!" he answered immediately. "I've been trying to reach you."

"Sorry, I've been in a meeting, just stepped out for a second . . ."

There was a beat of silence on the other end, and I was wondering if he could hear the sound of the rain pummeling the hood of the Jeep, the wind blowing it sideways against the windows. I wondered if he could hear the lie in my voice—the distance between us, finally severing the connection we'd had.

"There's a nasty weather system moving up the coast," he said. "They keep talking about it on the news. Just wanted to make sure you were keeping an eye on it. You come back on Saturday?"

"Yes," I said.

"Any chance you'll be able to catch a flight home earlier? Looks like it'll be up that way right around then."

How to say: the storm is already here. I'm in it. There's no way out right now.

"Probably not," I said.

Another beat. "Just keep an eye. Okay?"

"I will. Is everything okay at home?" I asked, face pressed close to the phone.

He sighed, and it brought me back to the first time he'd stayed over at my place, the way he'd awoken the next morning, like he was resigning himself back to reality, before his eyes fluttered open.

"I just miss you, I guess. And then I saw the storm on the news and hadn't heard from you in a couple days . . ."

"I'm sorry. It's just been chaos here." I closed my eyes, cringing.

I hated to pretend, but there was too much to even begin to explain, and I'd already set the scene with my very first lie.

I noticed Brody running out for one last thing he must've needed from his own car—I remembered the supplies I'd seen stashed in his trunk earlier. "Can I call you tonight?" I asked.

"Sure. I'll talk to you then."

I hung up, then watched as Brody raced back up the steps and closed the front door behind him.

Sitting here, in the protection of the car, I realized no one could really see me. No one was looking for me.

I leaned forward, to check the tag hanging from the rearview mirror. It had the car company name, along with a serial number and a designated spot from the rental company.

I climbed into the passenger seat, trailing water across the armrest. I looked out the window toward the house again, then opened the glove compartment.

Inside, there was a folded-up pink paper, a carbon copy of the rental agreement. I carefully unfolded the page, saw Oliver's signature and credit card info at the bottom. I scanned the other details as quickly as possible, the print faint and hard to read in the dim of the car.

But there, in the reservation details: he had picked up the car on the sixth of May. The day *before* our scheduled arrival.

I folded the paper back up with shaking hands, left it exactly as I'd found it.

Then I slipped into the back seat and wiped down the console, erasing my trail, as if I had never been there.

Will had been telling the truth.

Had Oliver been here, down at the pier, watching as we arrived, one by one? Keeping his own list, his own tally?

It suddenly felt like this pact was less a promise to look out for one another, and more a pledge to look *out* for one another. I wondered if the purpose of this retreat, all along, was to keep one another from speaking honestly elsewhere. From drinking and reminiscing and saying the truth. It was a place where we would keep an eye on one another. Where we fell in line.

There was strength in numbers, as long as you remained on the inside.

As long as you reminded one another—*I know. I know what you did too.*

CHAPTER 12

Inside the house, everyone was hovering around the kitchen.

Our grocery haul, all laid out, amounted to about fifty percent alcohol, thirty percent paper products, twenty percent food.

"In our defense, there was barely anything left," Brody said as I stepped out of my wet shoes, then peeled off my socks.

"Think Joanie will let us spend the night at High Tide?" Josh asked.

"Everything's closed," Oliver said, with an authority that no one doubted or questioned.

But I was watching him carefully—wondering what he knew, and what he was up to. Why he would've arrived a day early, but pretended to get in last.

Oliver was the only person I had really known before the accident. Rather, he was probably the only person who knew me outside of school. Who'd have been able to say, *That's Cassidy Bent's house*, with the same authority he spoke with now.

He'd moved in down the street the summer before high school, and my parents had invited his family over before the start of school. While he seemed quiet, like me, he was also absolutely nothing like me. In my own family, I became invisible, overshadowed by my older brothers and their outgoing personalities, the way they consumed all the air in the room. In his, Oliver was the sun: he was an only child, the thing his family unit revolved around, attention always turning his way, people fully attuned to his needs. Even then, it was easy to envy him. Even then, even before Oliver was aware of it himself—he had always been the King.

Our households were not a good match. My family must have overwhelmed his, with our noise, our chaos, our way of needing to speak over one another in order to be heard.

"Did anyone get ahold of Amaya yet?" Josh asked.

"Everything's going straight to voicemail. My texts aren't showing as delivered," Grace said, staring out the window, straight into the heart of the approaching storm.

"We saw her car while we were out," Brody said, tossing the comment to the group as he tore the plastic off our sole crate of water.

The rest of the room fell silent—just the rustling of Brody crumbling up the discarded plastic.

"Where?" Grace asked, slipping onto a stool beside Josh. She dragged it closer to the counter, legs screeching against the wood floor.

"At that Blue Whale motel," Brody said.

"They were evacuating the campground, relocating everyone there," I added. I watched Oliver as I said it, but he had his back turned, loading drinks into the fridge.

Josh let out a noise, a *told you so* grunt, then took a bite of a granola bar.

Grace leaned against the counter, turning to face Josh. "What happened with her family?" she asked. "I heard they stopped speaking, after Christmas. I've been meaning to ask you."

Josh stopped chewing for a moment, then swallowed. "Where'd you hear that?"

Grace brought her hair over one shoulder. "You know how the town is. Word is she got in a pretty heated fight with her dad at the holiday party."

Josh wiped a hand across his mouth. "Yeah, that about sums it up."

"Seriously, Josh?" Brody said, standing on the other side of the counter. "That's all you're going to share with us?"

"Look, I don't really know what went down. Just, she was there, at the company party, and then, like you said . . ." He rubbed his hands together. "Next thing I see, her dad's escorting her off the premises."

"You didn't ask?" Grace asked, eyes wide.

Josh let out one single resounding laugh. "No, Grace, I did not ask my *boss* why he was asking his *daughter* to leave a company function." He smiled tightly, scar shining in the overhead light. "I do have some self-preservation instincts remaining."

I watched him closely. Josh was always good at the slant.

There are more of us. But we don't know what happened to them—

I couldn't stop thinking of the nine of us a decade earlier, locked away separately inside those conference rooms, sharing our stories. The things that might've been stored in back rooms and file cabinets.

They were a powerful firm, generations deep in the area. They'd told us not to worry about anything; they had resources, investigators, and a reputation. We were in good hands. We were *safe*, they promised. And they delivered. How lucky we had been, to have them on our side.

Now I was picturing Amaya, in some back room. Digging through files, unearthing our various secrets.

"But she was at the new library dedication?" I asked.

His eyes latched on to mine. "Yes. Our firm helped facilitate everything, between the school and the families. There were people there for everyone who died. Would've looked pretty bad if she didn't show."

"How was that?" I asked quietly. My imagination could make things worse than they were.

But Josh just kept staring at me, like I had asked him the most ridiculous question in the world. "Terrible," he said. As if he blamed us, too, for not coming. I imagined those twelve chimes of the bell, the way the toll had echoed inside Clara's heart, nine years earlier.

I wondered if he had to hear it that day, in the library. If Amaya did too.

And then all I heard was the rain blowing in sideways against the back windows, the whistle of the wind, straining against the doors.

Grace turned to the windows, narrowing her eyes slightly—nothing was visible beyond the gray. "She'll be back," she said.

Right then I wanted to believe it too. Amaya had been running from something, but she hadn't gone far. This house was the safest place to be. And yet, with the storm approaching, she hadn't come here—as if she understood something that I did not.

• • •

Hours later, the rain hadn't let up. We'd gone through what seemed like half the food from our grocery run, and we were making a serious dent in the supply of alcohol as well.

As the rumbling thunder grew closer, someone turned the music on. The surround sound speakers blared a deep bass throughout the downstairs, blocking out anything else.

From the outside, with our house lit up, I knew, it would seem like a party.

I looked around the room. Josh had his feet up on the couch, drink in hand, staring out the dark front windows. Hollis sat beside him, scrolling through her phone, moving her head to the beat. Brody was chatting up Grace in the kitchen, standing close and whispering—I wondered if it was about Amaya, about the things Josh wasn't saying, about her and her family.

Oliver, it seemed, had disappeared into his room.

I felt even more disconnected from the group than usual, without Ian here to bridge the gap.

It had always made things more manageable when I could picture him sleeping upstairs from me. When I'd wake in the morning and he'd already be out on the deck above, the scent of cigarette smoke wafting down. The times Hollis convinced us to join her on the beach, the way we both tried to copy her pose, impossibly contorting ourselves. Before Ian would collapse into the sand, eyes closed, face to the sun. Those rare moments of peace.

It was so different from my memories of the night, when I'd hear his nightmares carrying down the steps.

Please. You're the only one I trust—

And now I was picturing him here in this house, in the silence, without us. Wondering what it was he was doing here in the winter, all alone.

But we believed The Shallows was a safe place. It too was a survivor, surrounded on all sides by the endless deep.

Of course he would come here.

I tried to see a shadow of him moving through the kitchen, but there were too many of us in the downstairs, and the music drowned out anything else.

I watched the group of them again—tallying their names, remembering their places—and then I slipped up the steps. I didn't want anyone noticing me, following me.

The thumping of the bass softened in the second-floor hallway.

I looked toward the three bedrooms: yellow, navy, aqua. Would Ian have felt some protection here, in the places we came to be together? Would he find a comfort in the rickety, exposed steps out on the deck, leading up to the third level—a widow's walk, looking out onto the churning sea?

I headed up the next flight of steps, fingers dragging along the side walls, the open third-floor space finally coming into view. I tried to picture Ian there, head in hands as he sat on the edge of the bed, but Josh had all but wiped him from the space. It was Josh's clothes, tossed everywhere. His toiletry bag, half-emptied, contents spread on the surface of the dresser. His beach towel and a bathroom towel, hung from pieces of furniture. His open laptop, plugged in, screen dark.

There weren't many places left for something of Ian's to remain. Maybe the pillow, the sheets . . . If we were the only ones who used the house, I wondered if they'd been washed since he was here. The bed was low to the ground—no space for anything underneath either.

I checked the drawers to the dressers, one by one—empty, except for a spare quilt in the lower drawer. I did the same with the desk drawers, careful not to jar the laptop or the papers stacked in haphazard piles on top.

Inside the top drawer, there were several manila files, presumably belonging to Josh; a spare charging block, also Josh's; and a yellow lined notepad with curled edges underneath, blank and unused—which had probably been here from years before.

The only other space was a closet, tucked against the far wall. The entrance was lower than a normal door, due to the slanting ceilings. From the outside, it looked like a storage area more than a place to hang clothes.

When I turned the knob, the paint stuck, like it had been a long time since the door had been opened. As if the pieces had fused together, like something out of Will's spare room.

The first thing that struck me inside wasn't the chill or the dark. It was the scent. It smelled faintly of cigarettes and leather, like Ian's ghost was really here.

In the back corner, hanging from the rod, there was an object hidden in the shadows. I reached my hand in, felt the cool, softened leather. I closed my eyes, and knew exactly what it was: a brown leather jacket, with cracks at the elbows from age and wear, the scent of smoke clinging to the collar.

My hands shook as I pulled it off the hanger. I stretched my arms through the sleeves, tugging it over my shoulders, pulling the front closed.

Will was right—of course, Will was right. He was right about

Oliver, and he was right about Ian. He had been here. Right here, where I stood.

I reached my hands into the pockets, imagining him doing the same. My fingers brushed against a solid object in the right pocket—a lighter. And from the left pocket, I pulled out a sliver of paper. It was a receipt with faded print, a barely legible tally of numbers. But I recognized the logo on the top: *High Tide*. And the date, clearly visible below it: Feb-4.

Three months ago. Just before he died. Had someone called him here?

There was something visible through the other side—a note, or a signature. I turned it over, but the only thing written, in blue ink, was: *The Shallows!*

As if he was telling someone where he was staying.

A violent gust of wind shook the outer doors, and the room suddenly fell to darkness, to nothing.

I stood in the dark, waiting for my eyes to adjust. Only the light of a laptop power button, still churning on its battery, glowed in the room.

Looking down from the top of the steps, I saw there was no light coming from below either. I started descending, hands firmly pressed into the walls, careful not to miss a step. The music was off. The power had gone out.

A hum of conversation carried up the stairwell as I approached the second-floor landing.

And then: "Has anyone seen Cassidy?" Hollis, close to the stairs.

"Paging Cassidy Bent!" Josh called, from somewhere in the dark, sending a chill through my body.

"I'm here," I called back, hands tracing the wall on my way down.

"All accounted for," Grace said, like they'd been taking attendance.

I could see them only by the glow of their cell phone screens, until a flashlight flicked on in the kitchen. Oliver, shining the beam across us, one by one.

The room fell silent, and I wondered if we were all remembering the same thing. If we were all suddenly back at the river that night.

We waited in the dark now, listening to the storm. The rain and wind pelted the windows, the roof, the metal shutters. A crack of thunder, coming closer.

"Is it just us?" Hollis asked, voice high and tight.

I went to the front window, peered into the night. "I think it's everyone," I said. "No lights anywhere." Not even the porch lights from the neighbors or the always-on floodlights in the driveways or the soft glow of hall lamps behind curtained windows.

"It'll be back in the morning," Oliver assured us. But from the sound of the wind, I wasn't confident about that.

Brody had his face pressed to the window facing the sea. A bolt of lightning lit up the room in a quick flash, and he backed away.

I counted in my head—*one, two*—before the resounding boom followed.

"Here," Grace said, shining the flashlight from her phone into a kitchen cabinet. "I knew I'd seen candles somewhere." She pulled the set of tea lights down from the shelf, lining them up in a row. "Anyone have a light?" she asked.

I reached into the pocket of Ian's coat again, extending the lighter her way.

"Cassidy Bent," she answered, laughter in her voice. "Always the surprise."

I flicked the lighter, then watched as the flame caught to the wick, before moving down the row. In the dark, preoccupied by the storm, no one seemed to notice the jacket I wore. Or maybe they just didn't recognize it.

"We can bring these back to our rooms at least," Grace said.

"Please don't burn this place down," Oliver grumbled.

I took one of the candles and headed for the stairs. I felt Hollis following close behind, her own candle in hand.

Back inside the aqua room, I wrapped myself tighter in Ian's jacket, wishing for the comfort of him. Wondering, again, what he had been doing here. After the email from Amaya, after his email to me—

Please. You're the only one I trust.

I stood in the center of my room, with nothing but the glow of a candle on the dresser.

Did they come to see you too?

According to the receipt in his pocket, he'd gone to High Tide. Paid cash. And suddenly I thought: Was he looking for someone, or something, here? Or was he hiding—the safest place, surrounded on all sides by the endless deep, belonging just to us?

Would he have stood in my room, as I'd stood in his, imagining me here?

I turned on the flashlight of my phone, just as I heard others making it up the steps and down the hall. Doors closing, water running, gentle laughter coming from the room beside mine.

I opened the closet in my own room—but it was empty. I'd never unpacked, and neither had Amaya. There was nothing hanging from the bar, nothing even tucked away on the top shelf. Next, I did the same to the dresser drawers, but there was only a loose, dusty screw, rolling slowly back and forth.

There was nothing here that made me think Ian had been in my room. No place here to hide things either.

But the beds weren't low to the ground, like the one upstairs. I kneeled on the hardwood, shining my flashlight under the bed.

No boxes, no packages left behind for me. That had been wishful thinking, of course.

I arced the beam of the light one last time, and something caught my eye under the second bed, against the wall. A piece of paper.

I had to crawl under Amaya's bed to reach it, lying on my stomach, coughing from the dust lingering against the floorboard. But this piece of paper was miraculously free of dust. As if it had been only recently left behind.

I dragged it back against the floorboards, until I was sitting on the floor between our beds, resting my back against the wall. The paper was the size of a greeting card, folded in half, like it had once been propped up on top of a dresser or bed.

Holding the flashlight in one hand, I turned the paper over with the other. Three words, in neat block print:

GET OUT NOW

A buzzing started in my ears, louder than the rain slinging against the windows. The words echoed, until they were all I could hear.

Amaya's voice, whispering close, from across the room.

She had no way to reach me—she didn't have my new number—so she must've left this note instead—in the room that we always shared, meant just for me.

What was it, here, that she had become afraid of? So afraid that she wouldn't tell the others?

A creak sounded from out in the hall—I didn't know who it was. And I didn't know whom I could trust anymore. I didn't know, truly, what any of them were capable of.

I made my way slowly, carefully, toward the bedroom door. I placed my ear to the wood, listening hard as I held my breath.

And then, as quietly as I could, I turned the lock.

THEN

HOUR 4

Hollis

Hollis was lost.

She was all alone in the dark, but at least she wasn't trapped anymore.

She'd been stuck for what felt like an eternity—first in the van; then on a muddy riverbank, wedged between slick river rocks; and finally in a section of trees with no visible outlet, until she'd found a path, crawling over a felled stump, a tangle of roots. Pulling herself from one place to the next, with no idea which direction she was heading. Only that she had to keep moving.

Her lungs were still burning, her arms and legs were numb, and she thought, not for the first time, *I'm dead. I'm gone. None of this is real.*

She thought she heard something under the sound of the river behind her. A crunch of leaves. A scurrying of footsteps. She spun around and called out with desperation into the night, "Hello?"

Her throat was raw from adrenaline and tears and exertion, but she screamed as loud as she could: "Is anyone out there?"

But whatever she'd heard, it wasn't help.

She was still alone. Alone, though she didn't quite feel it.

At the stop before the crash, she'd felt this way too. The vans had idled on the road, engines running, headlights the only beacons in the night. But there were things moving in the woods around her, and she kept getting this feeling that she was being watched as she argued with Brody.

Hollis knew how others saw her, the things they said when she passed—*kind of odd; a little too quiet; sure, she's pretty, but what a waste.* Everyone in high school knew the things whispered about them, whether they'd admit to it or not. She just never knew that Brody thought them too, until that day. She'd won a scholarship, had been so excited when she told him, and he looked shocked. No, he seemed skeptical, even. As if he couldn't imagine her being capable of such things.

And so she'd said, in a moment of hurt and surprise: *I need a break.*

It didn't sink in at first. He'd tipped his head, jumped three steps ahead in the conversation, cutting her off: *Hold on. You're breaking up with me?* Except it came out as: *You're* breaking up with *me*?

She wasn't thinking that, not entirely, until he said it. Just like that. She marched away from him, back toward the road.

Don't be ridiculous. Get in the van, Hollis.

Which she'd been just about to do, until he said it, like that. And so she didn't. She switched directions and slid into the other van, while he watched incredulously. She'd leaned forward to Ms. Winslow and said, *Swapping seats*, then slid the door shut behind her, so that Brody couldn't follow her.

So definitive.

She understood, then, that Brody thought she was lucky to be with him. She understood that she had been undervalued, underestimated, underappreciated, and Brody could go fuck himself.

She couldn't see straight she was so angry, but she didn't want to crack. Didn't want to give anyone else the pleasure of seeing *Hollis March falling apart on a school trip.*

That's what she'd been thinking in the front seat of the first van, when it suddenly slammed on its brakes and veered, skidding, screeching, her hands braced for impact, careening off something, a weightless feeling, and then—

Impact. And then water. So much water.

Everything went numb. And then everything hurt, a jolt that worked its way from her skull to her legs.

It took too long to orient herself, to understand what was happening. To remember how to move.

She couldn't get free. Couldn't unhook herself from the seat belt for what felt like an eternity. Until finally the button disengaged, and then she felt herself caught in the tangle: arms, legs, bodies moving, desperate for an exit—hands reaching for a way out.

There were too many of them, and eventually, by instinct, she went the other way—down, deeper, until she felt broken glass—the front windshield?—and she couldn't tell whether it was under her or on top of her, but she kept moving. And then, just as she hooked her hands around the opening—an exit, freedom, *a chance*—she felt a hand on her ankle, gripping her, pulling her back.

But her lungs were burning and she couldn't help them. Her instincts took over, and she kicked, then kicked again, connecting with something solid, until the hold on her ankle dislodged, and finally, finally, she was through—

The first gasp of air over the surface, a desperate wheeze.

She'd let the current take her, until she felt a branch or a root, and grabbed on, held tight, climbed upward. And then she kept moving. The mud, the rocks, the trees. Until now she was here, in this in-between place. Hearing things. Feeling things.

Her head was ringing. She might've had a concussion.

With her feet sinking into the mud somewhere by the river, she kept feeling it: something brushing against her ankle, pulling her back.

This feeling that she wasn't *truly* alone.

She had to keep moving. She couldn't stand still. Every time she paused, she felt a tug. Pulling her back, killing her.

She had to get farther away. It didn't matter that it was dark and that she didn't know what direction she was heading in.

She stared at the dark river, alone. And she thought: *You are underestimated.*

A sound came from behind her, this time in the opposite direction of the river.

"Hello?" she called again.

She imagined the others escaping, the jumble and thrash of bodies.

No response but the sound of the river flowing, and a distant rumble of thunder.

And then: a change in the air, something carried on the wind. A whiff of something faintly chemical. Hollis whipped her head around, on high alert. A glow of red, in the distance, hovering faintly in the air—so faint she thought she imagined it. But she shifted to the side and saw it again: something glowing, or burning. A *signal. Help*.

She started moving toward it, as quickly as she could. She kept her eyes trained on that singular point, the light appearing and disappearing as she moved between the trees—a beacon for her to follow.

She kept moving, the river growing louder, taking her around another curve, another embankment.

And suddenly she stood on another riverbank, with her first clear view: a group of people on a cluster of rock, a red flare burning on the ground between them.

There they were, her salvation, on the other side of the river. Across a great expanse of darkness. The thing she'd just clawed her way out of, to freedom.

She had expected something else: someone here to rescue her. But they appeared to be looking for someone to save them as well.

She could see shadows moving on the other side, in front of the eerie red glow. She knew those people, knew that form, the way he walked with his shoulders slightly forward—

"Brody!" she screamed, but no one seemed to hear her over the river.

"Help!" she called again, but no one turned her way. And she had that feeling, again, that she wasn't really here. She stepped into the river, felt the current moving a little too fast, and quickly scrambled back onto the rocks.

"Hey!" she screamed, waving her arms. They'd lit a flare, and she had made it, she had found them. But it was too far for them to see her in the shadowed tree line. She had to get closer.

She kept moving, up the riverbank, in the opposite direction of the current, to a place where the borders narrowed, and where a large tree protruded over the water, its roots gnarled into the surrounding area, a graveyard under the surface.

She thought it again: *You are undervalued and underestimated.* She could make it. Maybe it was a concussion, or this fear that she wasn't truly *there*—but she was certain she would make it.

She shimmied out onto the felled trunk as far as she could, eyes still trained on the eerie red glow.

"Hello!" she called again, seeing the shadows moving back and forth, faster now.

Finally, she could hear someone screaming too. But not for her.

"Brody!" she screamed. But Brody was focused on someone else, and he didn't see her. They seemed to be arguing, shadows backlit by the eerie red. She recognized him, even in the dark. The way he moved, the way his hands came out in front of him. To push, or to pull.

Finally, at the edge of the rocks, someone noticed her. An arm, gesturing other people closer, calling into the night. "Is that Hollis?" A girl's voice.

Hollis laughed with relief. "I'm here!" she said, clinging to the trunk. She was alive, and she had made it, and she'd have to jump, she'd have to swim, but she could do it. She was stronger, more capable, than they thought. She'd done this much already.

When she jumped, there were several people linked together,

reaching out into the water, arms outstretched, ready for her. There was a moment when she thought they might miss her, but they didn't. She expected Brody, his arms swooping her up fast, holding her tight.

But it was Ian Tayler who had her around the waist. It was Cassidy Bent who grabbed on to her arms and didn't let go, and said, "Oh my god, you made it."

Until that moment, Hollis had no idea that others from her van had made it out. She'd thought that she was the lone survivor. It had been a frantic, desperate fight, a surge of limbs and adrenaline. *The hand on her ankle, pulling her back—*

But now there they were, pulling her closer: Ian, Cassidy, and hovering in the background, Joshua Doleman.

There could be more.

"I made it," she repeated, staring back at Cassidy, both their eyes wide with surprise.

She scanned the group for Brody; everything would be forgotten and forgiven between them now. But Brody hadn't looked up. He was hunched over the ground, and Grace was screaming for help. Hollis threaded her way through the group until she could see what had stolen Brody's focus.

She saw, then, what Brody was hunched over: a boy named Ben, lying on the ground.

Clara was leaning over him too, shouting, "What happened? Did you see what happened?"

"I didn't see anything," Hollis said, though Clara didn't seem to be speaking to her.

Ben, wide-eyed and confused in the eerie red glow, just shook his head, hands pulled back briefly from his stomach.

"Oh my god," Amaya said, falling to her knees, pressing her hands over his.

It was then, finally, that Brody registered her presence. He looked shell-shocked, somewhere else. Stuck in that in-between place. "Hollis?" he finally said.

"We need help!" Clara yelled. Everyone was moving then, jostling Hollis back and forth, as if they hadn't seen her there. Once again, Hollis felt alone. Trapped.

"Where the fuck is it?" Oliver asked, pushing closer, but she had no idea what he was talking about or what he was looking for.

In the final, sputtering sparks of the flare, Hollis saw a glint of metal on the ground, by her foot. A knife. Red in the glow. Red on red on red.

A shadow reached down for it, blocking the dying light.

And then it was dark.

THURSDAY

CHAPTER 13

The house felt alive the next morning. Without the air-conditioning, without the gentle hum of electricity, every noise from outside in the storm was heightened. The wind sighed, and it sounded like the house was breathing instead.

All through the night, the storm had pushed inland.

I'd slept in bits and spurts, visions of the river waking me to the sound of a deluge outside.

I knew it was after dawn, though the sky was still an interminable dark.

I paced back and forth across the length of my room, far wall to outer doors, where the rain was still beating against the deck.

The room was stifling, thick with heat and humidity and the leftover smoke from the wick of the candle, burned to the bottom. I heard the others starting to rise—just as I was sure they could hear me: the creak of my steps, relentlessly pacing.

The paper sat on the edge of my bed, words staring up at me any time I passed.

GET OUT NOW

But there was nowhere to go—a road closed, a campground evacuated, a motel overflowing. And there was another list taking shape in my head. A log of our names, disappearing, one by one, just as it had happened that night.

Our numbers had fallen between the time of the crash and the time we were found: Jason. Trinity. Morgan. *Ben*.

But now it felt like it had never stopped, that our numbers had continued to fall ever since. Clara, at the river. Ian, who had been in this house in the days before his death, only his jacket left behind. And now Amaya had taken off in a panic—but not before leaving a note for me to follow.

It was starting to feel like a pattern. Like we hadn't truly escaped that night, after clawing our way to freedom. That we were never meant to. Maybe the intermittent years were merely a reprieve, waiting for the moment when death finally caught up with the rest of us.

And the only way to outrun it was to move.

I snatched the paper off the bed and tucked it into my bag, beside Ian's phone. Then I slowly turned the lock of my bedroom door.

Grace was wrapped in a yellow towel, exiting the bathroom. Her hair was dry, in a bun on top of her head. "No hot water," she said, frowning.

She'd left a candle burning inside, the only light in the bathroom.

I took a quick shower in the near dark, goose bumps forming from the chill, fumbling for soap, and my towel. By the time I was out, I could hear the group gathered downstairs.

I wasn't sure who among them I could trust in this house anymore.

Maybe we were all here for the same reason. Not really *for* one another, but because we were scared to find out what would happen if we didn't come.

There was no way out of the pack, just like there was no way out of a pact. It was binding. Punishments justified. Too many secrets at risk.

We were stuck. And, for now, we were shut in with one another in this house. Trapped in the story we had told about that night.

• • •

I used the light on my phone as I descended the stairwell, dark from the lack of windows and electricity.

The first person I saw downstairs was Brody. He was sprawled on the couch, one arm slung over his head, one leg dangling off the edge—as if he'd slept here last night and had yet to rise from his position.

Hollis was moving around the kitchen, organizing the items on the counter, looking like she was trying to put together some kind of breakfast offering.

Oliver and Grace were set up at opposite ends of the long dining room table.

"Don't open the fridge," Oliver said, just as Hollis moved to do so.

She froze, hand on the edge, face scrunched up at Oliver.

"Things will go bad without the power," he added.

"I promise you, this will all be gone before it has the chance to go bad," she said, opening the fridge anyway.

Oliver had dark circles under his eyes, like he hadn't slept. Grace had her feet up on the chair beside her, scrolling her phone, like nothing was amiss. She'd taken down the bun, and her hair had settled into soft waves.

She peered up just long enough to take each of us in. "Anyone happen to pack a portable battery charger?" she asked.

My phone had nearly drained through the night as well—I was trying not to use it again until the power came back.

"I didn't," Oliver said.

I shook my head, just as Brody called out from the sofa, a surprising sign of life. "Grace, give it up."

"Well," she said, dropping her feet to the floor. "Guess I'll be canceling today's appointments."

I hitched my bag onto my shoulder, car keys in my hands.

"I'm going to make a coffee run," I said. "See if any of the stores have better luck with a generator."

Oliver's head swiveled my way. "Josh already went out." His eyes went to the front window. "He should be back soon."

Brody sighed, rolling over. "Probably looking for an open pharmacy," he said, couch springs squeaking as he pushed himself up to a half-sitting position.

Grace frowned at him. "What for?"

"You know," Brody said, moving his hand around, like he was searching for the word. "His pills. For sleep." And then, seeing the way we were all looking at him, he placed his arms on the back of the sofa, staring at each of us. "He usually has to take something to sleep, and judging by the fact he's wandering the house at all hours, he's definitely not right now."

"You sure about that?" Oliver asked, one dark eyebrow raised.

Brody pulled himself to fully sitting, ran a hand through his disheveled hair. "Yeah, Oliver. I'm sure. I've roomed with him every year past. He needs something to sleep. And he's all out."

He needs something to sleep.

I thought about that now—about what he saw as he drifted to sleep. About the things that might've haunted him.

"Well," I said, my keys in hand, "if I find anything open, I'll let you know."

My to-do list was simple this morning: find Amaya, and then find a way out.

• • •

Luckily, Oliver's car was no longer blocking me in. He'd taken Amaya's abandoned spot.

I passed Will's bungalow, the blue tarp still stretched over the gear in his yard, but the water had puddled in the grass, like his plot was slowly sinking below sea level.

Half the unpaved road was standing water, and I swerved to

avoid it where I could. My car was lower to the ground than the rental Jeep, more prone to the elements, with tires that could get stuck in water or mud, if I wasn't careful.

There was a moment, after I exited onto the paved main road, when I felt a pull. Something leading me to continue down the long highway and over the bridges, like a series of passageways to traverse that would then close behind me. I thought, for a brief moment, that I might keep going. Abandon my luggage, abandon the group, abandon Amaya. Listen to the voice that had whispered at me on a loop last night: *Get out now.*

I ran my hand across the necklace from Russ, clasped firmly around my neck, feeling a different pull—back toward my home, toward the life I had built for myself.

But an orange sign had been set up well before the highway closure of yesterday, before the motel even: *ROAD CLOSED AHEAD*. There was no way to leave, even if I wanted to.

There were no lights from the streetlamps or the shops—the entire town must've lost power. The lot for the Blue Whale motel was still overflowing with campers and cars, and it didn't appear to be running on a generator either. All of the doors faced the lot, two stories of rooms and windows stretching down two long rectangles, meeting at an angle in the middle. The front office was set at the junction, and the door was propped open, windows dark. Some of the room windows were also cracked open, protected from the rain by the breezeway overhang, beige curtains gently moving with the wind.

I passed Amaya's car again, relieved to see it was still here, in the same spot. There were no available spaces, so I channeled Oliver and pulled up straight to the curb near the entrance.

I ducked from the rain as I darted across the sidewalk, until I'd made it under the awning of the office. Inside wasn't quite as dark as I'd imagined, with a back wall of windows letting in the dull gray light. But the office was disorienting; it jutted out from an angle, back walls meeting sharply behind the desk.

A single man stood behind the counter, brown hair buzzed tight, except for the bangs that fell in a swoop over his eyes.

"No, I don't know when the power will be back," he said, not looking up from the notebook in front of him. He had a pencil behind his ear, long bony fingers tracing the lines on the open page. The room was stuffy even with the opened door, and up close, I could see the sheen of sweat across his forehead.

"I'm not staying here," I said.

He closed the notebook with deliberate emphasis, then shook his head. "We're all booked up," he said. "Overbooked, actually, as you can see." He tipped his angular chin to the bench beside the door I'd just entered through. A woman sat there with a backpack beside her and a young boy draped across her lap, thumb in his mouth, eyes closed.

The woman gave me a piercing look, as if I might wake her child—or attempt to jump her in line.

I spun back to the man at the counter. "I'm looking for a friend, actually," I said, leaning one arm against the counter, keeping my voice low.

"Sorry, can't help, the computers are down," he said.

But I saw the notebook on the counter, figured they had kept a backup.

"I haven't been able to reach her," I said. "I think her phone is dead." Let him think it was because of the weather, the lack of electricity, power draining on our phones. "But her car's out front."

"Look," he said. "I don't even know half the people staying in rooms. They started bunking up after we ran out of space. And there are plenty sleeping in campers out in the lot. If you want to leave a note, I can keep it on the desk, with their name, but I can't guarantee anything."

He pulled out a pad of paper with the logo for the motel on top, a blue whale over the motel name, water shooting out the blowhole, its mouth contorted into a smile. Then he placed the pencil over top, chew marks near the eraser.

I tapped my fingers against the notebook instead. "If you could just check, though, her name is Amaya Andrews."

He kept his hand palm down on the notebook, looking at me closely. His entire demeanor changed, no longer minimally accommodating. He straightened his back, pressed his lips together. "I'll tell you the same thing I just told your friend. For privacy reasons, for *safety* reasons, we do not share information about our guests."

I took a step back, jarred by the change in him. But more by the fact that someone else was looking for her.

Before I could ask anything more, he pointed toward the open glass door. "Also," he said, "you can't park there."

I felt the woman's gaze trailing me as I left the office.

Outside, the rain continued to ding against the gutters and the roofs of the cars and campers. I held my hand above my head uselessly as I jogged to my car.

Once inside, I backed away from the curb, then paused by the row of cars with Amaya's sedan. I scanned the lot, thinking of the likelihood of Amaya being inside one of those campers, then the logistics of knocking on doors, one by one, looking for her.

It was more likely, I thought, that she was inside one of those rooms. I noticed a lone child darting from one doorway, down the hall, into the next.

And then, in the open-air hall of the second floor, I caught sight of a man knocking on a door near the far stairwell. I watched as he stood there, ear pressed to the shut door, before moving on to the next. It seemed he was doing exactly what I was just considering.

I turned off the car engine, stepping back out into the rain. Then I watched as someone appeared in the doorway this time. I couldn't see clearly, with the man in the entrance blocking the view.

I took the steps at the edge of the building up to the second floor two at a time, my approach covered by the sound of the rain over the awnings.

On the landing, I finally got a clear look at him. He wore khaki shorts and a dark jacket, hood pushed back to reveal hair just as dark. One arm was braced against the doorframe as he handed his phone to the person on the other side of the doorway. That familiar bridge of his nose, the sharp scar against his cheekbone—Joshua Doleman was here.

Not on a coffee run either, as he'd claimed.

"Her name's Amaya," he was explaining, as the woman inside peered down at the screen of his phone. "I haven't been able to get ahold of her since the storm."

He gave her a smile that must've been convincing enough, because she called for someone else in the room to come take a look.

"I don't think so," the woman said, handing the phone to the man beside her.

They both appeared to be in their forties or fifties, and I heard the yapping of a dog behind them. "Shush," she said, turning around. And then, lowering her voice, "We're not supposed to have animals here, but what can you do?"

The man was zooming in and out on the photo, like he might recognize her. But all he said was, "Pretty," in a way that sent a shiver up my spine. "I'd remember her for sure." He smiled wide, gums exposed.

The woman rolled her eyes, then disappeared inside, scolding the dog.

The man seemed to register the presence of me lingering on the other side of the hall. He tipped his chin my way. "How about you, miss? You see this girl?"

He held the display of the phone my way, just as Josh slowly turned around.

The quick blink of Josh's eyes was the only thing that let me know he was surprised. My gaze went from Josh to the phone and back again. I could sense the tension rising in his shoulders, tightening his jaw.

"No," I said, swallowing air. "Sorry."

"Well," the man said, as Josh took the phone from his outstretched arm.

Josh tucked it away in his pocket, but it was too late. I'd already seen what was on it, and he knew it.

The picture on the phone was not just of Amaya. It was a picture of the two of them together, Josh's arm extended, like he'd been taking a selfie. Cheek against cheek, wide cheesy grins. Curls spilling down from Amaya's updo, the red sequins of her top visible in the frame.

"Good luck," the man called as he swung the door shut.

Then it was just Josh and me and the rain overhead.

"What the hell are *you* doing here?" he asked, as if he had nothing to hide.

"Looking for Amaya," I said. "Same as you, it seems."

I waited for him to explain. That picture was too intimate, too full of emotion. She looked beautiful draped under his arm, and his smile was wide and free, a side of him I'd never known.

"I've already knocked on every door in the motel," he said, arms crossed. "Not that everyone answered."

"Where is that from?" I asked, gesturing to the phone, tucked away.

He turned toward the steps, and I grabbed his sleeve. "Josh. What the hell?"

"This is really none of your business, Cassidy," he said, trying to put some venom behind it. "Now please, let go of my arm."

I released him, but stepped closer, into his personal space. "Well, seeing as we're the only two people out looking for her, I think that it is. Because you know what it looks like to me? And you know what it looks like to the guy working the front desk? It looks like you had a shitty breakup, and she was hiding from you, Josh. And now you're set on tracking her down."

He jerked back. "Jesus, no. I want to know she's okay. I want to know what the hell she's doing . . ."

"Right, because you two are obviously on such good terms." I remembered the way he'd cut into her that first day, the same way he typically cut into me. Belittling, cruel, in a manner meant to hurt, to find your flaws and exploit them. "You've been accusing her of talking. Of being the one behind the tell-all. I heard it from Brody."

"I wasn't lying yesterday, Cassidy," he said, voice low. "She's not talking to her family." He laughed, and it sounded pained. "She just also stopped speaking to me. No explanation necessary, apparently. So what does *that* look like to you?"

I didn't know. I didn't know how any of this looked. But he was avoiding the topic. "I didn't know you were together."

He threw his hands up, in a way that brought to mind rage, violence. "Yeah, well, it was brief. Okay? Just for a little while . . ."

"When?" I asked. Because the timeline mattered. Because someone had kicked something into motion, and he was right, it could've been her.

"She came home for Thanksgiving, and, you know, her dad tasked us with representing the firm at the dedication in January. She was *helping* . . ." He trailed off. "And then something happened with her dad at the Christmas party. I didn't see. We were trying to lay low, you know? And then she came to the library dedication, and when I tried to talk to her, she said it wasn't a good idea." He paused. "I thought she just meant, like, *right then*, but turns out that was her way of breaking it off. I only heard from her again when she sent the group email about this week. I left her a message about Ian, even. And nothing." He sniffed. "It was barely anything, really."

But from that picture, it didn't look like barely anything.

From the fact that he had kept it, even less so. Amaya had told me she had to hear about Ian from Josh. It seemed like there was too much emotion tied up between them, on both sides.

You can't just take whatever you want.

What should we do instead, Amaya? Should we draw for it?

"You didn't think this was a relevant thing to share when she disappeared?"

"Relevant? You think so?" And then his laugh turned low and

mean. "Oh please, give me a break. I know about you and Ian. Everyone does. That room has no doors, Cassidy."

I got a chill—that private bubble, the airless world we'd created, it had always felt safe, belonging just to us. Now I was imagining the shadow of someone in the stairwell, listening. At the entrance of the room. Outside on the deck, peering in.

"So tell me," he said. "Is *that* relevant now?"

This was what Josh did, twisting things around, using your own words against you—it probably made him very effective in a courtroom, where he could outmaneuver a stranger in a verbal battle.

But we were not supposed to be strangers here.

"God, you really do need to get some sleep, Josh. Stop taking it out on everyone else."

I brushed by him, but this time he grabbed my arm. "What did you say?"

I stared at my arm in his grip, then raised my face to his. "Brody said you must be out of your pills."

"No," he said, voice sliding closer, creeping up on me. "Someone *took* them. And I can't even get a refill called in based on the timing."

I thought of Ian's nightmares. Imagined Josh suffering the same, but silently—dulling it, escaping. I frowned, picturing the way he'd come downstairs that first day, accusing me of being in his room. The way the upstairs space looked like a tornado had passed through, toiletries and luggage in disarray—he must've been searching for his prescription.

"How can you be sure you didn't just forget them?" I asked.

"Because I *wouldn't*—"

"Hey!" We both spun in the direction of a man's voice, startling us. Josh dropped my arm suddenly, like he was entirely aware of what he'd been doing.

The man from the front office stood on the landing of the steps, and he had his phone out, like a threat. "I told you two to leave. Get the hell out of here, before I call the police."

Josh held his hands up, like he was proclaiming innocence.

"Sorry," I said, "we're just worried . . ."

He gestured to the steps. "Tell it to the cops, lady."

• • •

He watched us walk all the way down the steps, and then he watched us from the balcony as we crossed the lot to where my car lingered, beside Amaya's.

"You couldn't try to be a little less obvious?" Josh asked.

"Where are you parked?"

"Other side." He jutted his head toward the building, where there must've been overflow parking, tucked out of sight. Then Josh seemed to be scanning the lot, camper by camper.

"You checked every room?" I asked.

"The ones that would answer, anyway. I swear I could hear people on the other side of the door, pretending I wasn't there." His eyes didn't falter, like he might find Amaya darting between cars, in the rain.

"This doesn't feel right, Josh." I didn't think she would leave us, leave a note for me, and then camp out nearby as a storm approached. She wouldn't come over to the motel instead of back to the house when the campground was closed. She wouldn't ignore us. Not after a storm, when we needed to know she was safe. "If she wasn't planning to come back, she would've gone home by now, right?"

He didn't answer, but I saw his throat move as he swallowed. He slunk between my car and Amaya's, peering in her windows. Then he turned back to me. "Her locks don't work," he said, grimacing before pulling the driver's side door open.

It seemed to pain him to admit he knew that. I just wasn't sure if it was because they'd been seeing each other, or because he was watching her, following her.

He sat inside, and I followed—slipping into the passenger seat, escaping the rain for a moment.

It felt like the opposite of Oliver's rental. Worn fabric seats, a vent missing part of the cover, a feeling of being lived in.

"God, it's always such a mess," he said, but there was a softness to his voice, a kindness.

He flipped the visor down, looking for any sign of where she might be.

The cupholder was full of gas station and convenience store receipts. I unraveled them, checking for any sign of where she had been. "The last thing here is from a gas station on her way in on Sunday," I said.

Josh frowned, then twisted around to the back seat, looking for anything of hers on the floor.

I opened the glove compartment, but there was nothing there but the car manual, a series of maps, and one of those emergency glass-breaking tools. I had one myself, just like it.

I started to feel something else creeping in. A fear that she was running, but she hadn't been fast enough. The phone messages not being delivered, her calls going straight to voicemail . . .

"Josh, we should open the trunk," I said.

He didn't move at first, then slowly turned to face me. I could see it in his expression suddenly: the fear, the horror. He didn't break eye contact as he reached his hand down to the left, to the trunk release.

The trunk popped open, visible in the rearview mirror. Whatever was inside was getting rained on in the wait. But neither of us seemed ready to look.

I broke eye contact first, throwing open the door. Josh stepped outside at the same time.

He frowned, then pushed his wet hair back from his face, scar shining in the rain. He didn't move closer at first. Our eyes met, and he gave me the faintest shake of his head.

I approached the back of the car alone, feeling unsettled, like this was some prelude, a crackle in the air—like the moments before the accident that divided the before and after.

I raised the trunk farther. The space was empty. Blissfully, entirely empty. I gestured for Josh to look, and he let out a relieved sigh, an almost laugh, then ran his hand back through his hair.

"Jesus Christ, can we get the fuck out of here now?" he asked. I slammed the trunk closed, looking up at the motel rooms once more.

"Cassidy? Are we going?"

There was something to the word *we*, every time one of them said it. A door, held open. A welcome.

Every time, I took it.

CHAPTER 14

The island had been in the dark for more than half a day by the time we left the motel lot. The first sign of power returning came in the flicker of the streetlight—a surge through the cables—as I followed Josh's car back to our place. Then the glow of lamps in the homes lining the main road.

By the time I stepped out of my car at The Shallows, the low hum of an air-conditioning unit already felt like relief. If that wasn't enough of a giveaway, there was a cheer coming from somewhere out back.

"Josh, hold on," I said, following him up the front steps. "I know you're worried too. Just as much as I am." I'd seen it in his expression sitting in Amaya's car, when I asked him to open the trunk. An unspoken fear that neither of us wanted to address head-on.

"I don't know. Disappearing, going off-grid, it's not really that out of character for her. She ghosted me pretty good." But he didn't move, didn't step closer or meet my eyes. He stared off into the distance as the rain continued, a little lighter than before. "Maybe it's a simple thing, Cassidy," he said, his voice barely above a whisper. "Maybe you just underestimate how much she hates me." Then he looked at me, one side of his lip curling. "I'm sure that wouldn't surprise you."

And then he opened the front door, leaving me trailing three steps behind.

Inside, there was a new feeling, a buzzing in the air, like something had burst. Every light was on, along with the overhead fans. The back sliding door was open, letting in a mist from the rain.

Only Grace seemed to notice our arrival, turning from where she stood at the back windows.

"Any luck?" she asked.

"No," Josh answered. He didn't pause, barely glanced around the living room space before heading toward the steps. "Going to charge everything."

Grace raised her eyebrows at me. "He does seem crankier than usual," she said conspiratorially.

"Where is everyone?" I asked.

"Found some umbrellas when the rain started letting up. They just went down to the beach to celebrate the storm moving on," she said.

"That sounds like a terrible idea," I said, and Grace cracked a grin.

Hollis came down the steps then, wearing athletic shorts and a windbreaker. "Better than being stuck inside, right?" She smiled tightly, and I wondered how close everyone here was to their breaking points.

Every year, we returned like we were expecting some new breakthrough. But year after year, the only thing that ever cracked was us.

I joined Grace at the back window, watching as Hollis strode quickly down the wooden path.

Grace frowned. "It's probably half-underwater out there still." I pictured quicksand, riptides, debris churned up and left behind in the storm's wake.

A round of cheering carried toward the house, just as Hollis disappeared from sight—as if the rest of them were celebrating her arrival on the beach. Like a taunt against nature: *We're still here . . .*

I stepped back from the window, like I was taking a hint from Josh. "I have a ton of work to catch up on," I said.

"Same here," Grace said, though when I turned for the steps, she was still standing at those back windows, watching the place where Hollis had just disappeared from sight.

• • •

I needed to charge my phone, which had drained so low it was in danger of powering off.

Above me I could hear Josh moving around—footsteps, drawers opening and closing—like he was still searching. As if the pill bottle might've rolled into an unchecked corner or fallen behind a dresser.

How he could spend this long searching for his medicine, and only half a morning looking for Amaya, I didn't understand.

I wanted to tell him: *She left a note.*

I was sure she was running from something other than Josh. Josh was more passive in his aggression, more words than action. And he worked for her family—had started interning during summers home from college, sliding into their world, just as Amaya distanced herself from it. He had changed the trajectory of his life for the better, and she had watched him do it. If Amaya truly believed he was dangerous, that *she* was in danger from him, she would've said something to them, at the very least.

As soon as my phone had gained some charge, I started making calls:

I called the campground—still closed, line not serviced.

I called her office—*She's out for the week, is there something I can help you with instead?*

Then the Blue Whale motel, hoping there was an automated system that would let me call individual rooms from the main line (there was not).

I tried calling Amaya directly, even, leaving her a message and explaining my concern when the line went straight to voicemail, the phone still completely off-grid.

I couldn't stop picturing all the things that could've happened to her. That moment before we'd peered into the trunk, that horrific crackle of possibility—

"Hey," Hollis said, practically sliding down the hall, raincoat slung over her shoulder, water dripping from the ends of her hair. She was breathless, glowing. "Oliver found out High Tide is opening." She smiled. "I'm so ready to get out of here." Then she moved on, wet feet padding against the hardwood floor. "Josh, did you hear? We're going out for lunch!"

• • •

Thirty minutes, a series of fast showers and quick changes, and we were moving down the block as a group, a singular force under umbrellas and a steady mist of drizzle.

It seemed the entire town had the same idea. There was a line stretching out the door, with groups waiting to be seated. Joanie greeted everyone by name, so I assumed the majority were locals, feeling the same as us. Stuck, yes, but no longer stuck inside.

"Thank god we came as early as we did," Grace said, eyes wide as we crammed into a corner table, which seemed to be the last one available. We had to borrow an extra chair and squeeze together at a table meant for four or five.

It was early afternoon, but there were groups sitting and standing around the bar, where the single bartender—Mark, again—seemed to have given up on keeping track of things, refilling glasses while people left cash behind on the bar top, in an honor system.

Though the room was loud and boisterous, our table remained eerily quiet. Heads bent over phones, like we were stuck in our heads, content to let the surrounding noise cover for us.

Eventually, our order was taken by a girl who didn't look old enough to work. The table beside us seemed to know her by name. I assumed she was someone's daughter, brought in for extra coverage.

Brody abruptly dropped his phone to the table. He ran both

hands through his hair, and took a deep breath, looking around the packed room. "Okay, I cannot in good conscience order beer from the preteen," he said. "Be right back." He rose from the table, hands in the pockets of his jeans, wedging his way forward.

I watched as he leaned around someone at the bar. I recognized Will, sitting on a stool, speaking with a few men who were standing behind him: his cousin Kevin, cheeks ruddy, and another man, tall and broad and loud, moving animatedly as he was relaying some story.

Brody slapped his hand on the bar, shouting out his order, just as that man backed into him.

I saw the change take over Brody immediately. The slow-motion swivel of his head, the harsh set of his jaw. How his arm came around so fast, I thought he would hit the man, instead of just grabbing on to him, jostling him. I could read his lips well enough, each syllable enunciated—*Watch it*.

"Oh shit," Josh said, sitting back in his chair, arms crossed. Grace leaned forward, mouth slightly open. Everyone was watching. We were supposed to be on the same side, supposed to protect one another. But there were limits to what anyone would actually do.

I pushed back from the table, wove my way through the crowd to where Brody was standing his ground, mean smile on his face, like he was daring someone to do something. Like he was asking for a fight.

"Brody," I said, grabbing on to his elbow.

He tensed before looking over at me, frowning.

"I would like to eat before we get thrown out," I added. In my job, I'd had more than my share of experience in deescalating scenes at a bar. I knew well how quickly a moment could turn physical. If I was lucky, I could divert the incident.

Brody didn't crack a grin, but he did let me lead him away, the circle of men closing behind him, watching us go, until we were outside.

He slammed the door behind him, unnecessarily. I cringed, worried the glass would shatter, but it held.

"Jesus, Brody, what the fuck?"

He paced back and forth in the drizzle. A couple gave him a wide berth, heading for the entrance.

"She's suing me for sole custody," he said.

"What?"

He motioned to the door, like he was talking about someone inside. "Vanessa. Accused me of being an absent, negligent parent." He'd gestured with quote marks, as if those were the official charges levied at him.

"What the fuck?" I asked, though I had no idea whether he was, indeed, absent or negligent. "Did she just text you that?"

I saw the way he'd thrown his phone down, but had assumed he was just low on patience, desperate for a drink—all of us, ready to snap.

"What?" He stopped pacing and shook his head. "Oh, no. That was my lawyer. Costing me a fucking arm and a leg, I might add. And he's turning up shit." He sniffed, then extended his arms. "I really do not need this right now."

Finally, his eyes latched on to mine.

"You shouldn't have come," I said. He should've been home, getting ready for his son's birthday. He should've stayed at work. We all should've been anywhere other than here.

"I *have* to be here," he said. As if this were his responsibility to bear alone. A call to answer. A compulsion to satisfy. Then he tipped his head back and groaned. "I really do want that beer now," he said, grimacing.

"Give it a few. I'm betting they'll forget about it in a minute or two. I'll go handle it."

He smiled, and I saw that same charming Brody I knew from high school. The same charming Brody who had stepped into my bedroom, earlier in the week, seeking my company—or more, I was pretty sure. "You're one of the good ones, Cass," he said.

I hated the way I warmed at his compliment. "Five minutes," I said. "It was a pretty large group."

• • •

Back at the bar, it seemed that most everyone had indeed moved on. I slipped through the crowd, largely unnoticed. But a hand came down on my shoulder just as I had started placing my order with Mark.

"You need to reel your boy in." It was the man with whom Brody had almost come to blows. He was blond, with a broad chin, and I couldn't tell whether he was twenty-five or forty-five. He was also unsteady on his feet, in the middle of a Thursday, bracing himself against my shoulder.

"That's what I'm doing," I said, turning back to the bar. "And another of whatever he's having," I added to Mark.

That seemed to do the trick. He tipped his current beer bottle my way, then scooted onto an open stool.

I stepped out of the way to wait for my order, hoping not to engage again. Will suddenly appeared between us, a welcome buffer.

He made a noise with the side of his mouth—a click of derision—then leaned closer, to speak directly into my ear. "That was not the guy I'd pick to mess with here."

I rolled my eyes. "Yeah, well, it wasn't my choice either."

How quickly I became liable for anything that happened within our group. All I'd done was break it up, lead Brody out, buy the wronged party a drink. And yet here was Will, spreading the blame.

I handed Mark my card, and Will laughed. "That's gonna take a while."

"Well, I've got nowhere else to be," I said. We were all trapped here together, and I started to get anxious if I thought about the reality: we were buffered in by blocked roads and the violent sea. All of us at the whim of nature, and each other.

Will's cousin was just behind him, now talking with the guy on the next stool. They must've all been together.

"Everything okay?" Will asked. "At the house, I mean?" His eyes were unfocused, like this was definitely not his first drink of the day either.

"Yeah, made it through fine."

"Power back up?" he asked.

"Seems that way."

He nodded. "Sometimes you need to hit the breaker a couple times, back and forth."

How much he seemed to know. How much he seemed to see: Oliver on the pier the first day; Ian arriving in the winter. He seemed to notice much more than I thought a neighbor down the road normally would.

He leaned against the bar, took a deep breath. "Good news." He jutted his thumb at his cousin. "Those guys work cleanup. They'll probably be opening the road by morning."

I felt my shoulders relaxing. "That is indeed good news."

Then he cleared his throat, and I could feel something shifting. Some warning. An instinct. "Hey," he said, nonchalant, slightly glassy expression. "Was this it?"

He pulled out his phone, pulled up a headline. It was obvious he'd been searching, with the little information I'd given him. *We survived something* was all I'd really told him. But he'd managed to unearth something, all the same.

School Trip Accident Leaves North Carolina Town Grieving

I averted my gaze, waiting for Mark to return with my card.

"No," I said, on instinct, wanting to unwind everything. He knew too much: where we were from; when it had happened. I felt myself shutting down, defenses up. *No outsiders.* That was the rule for a reason. Leave the past to the past. Give a hint, and they want it all. He'd probably already told the group around him about what he'd uncovered, and now he was going for more. Maybe he'd known about the accident from the start and had sought me out instead, pulling me in with his demeanor, winning some bet with his friends.

I was not a good judge of what people wanted of me.

Mark arrived blissfully quickly with my credit card, and I smiled tightly at Will as I left with our drinks.

"See you round?" he called.

I nodded as I passed, but he wouldn't. I did not make the same mistakes twice.

• • •

A late lunch stretched past dinner—no one wanted to leave, to return to The Shallows, all alone.

But ultimately we had no more excuse to stay, and the young waitress eventually told us they had other patrons waiting on the table.

We trudged back home, feet sinking into the soft earth of the unpaved access road, water still pooled in the grooves. The house was lit up against the gray sky, like a gothic painting looming in the distance.

Oliver abruptly stopped walking. "Did you see that?" he asked.

I followed his gaze toward the house. "See what?"

"I thought I saw . . ." He watched silently for a moment, eyes trained on the structure. Eventually he shook his head. "Probably a bird or something."

But he seemed distracted the rest of the way back, keeping his eyes fixed on the house. And now I was imagining something too. A person in the window. A ghost.

I wasn't sure what Oliver was expecting when he walked in, but he seemed to be moving carefully throughout the space, as if he didn't trust his own assessment that we were truly alone.

Grace went straight to her laptop left on the dining room table. "Back to reality," she said. "At least for those of us who have work."

"Some of us *can't* work remotely, Grace," Brody said, flopping on the couch, exactly as I'd found him this morning.

Hollis joined Oliver in the kitchen, filled a glass from the sink, and guzzled it down. "God, I'm parched."

Josh sat across from Grace in the dining room, scrolling through his phone, frowning. I was guessing he had a backlog of work messages from the last day of being mostly off-grid.

"Oliver," Grace said, pressing some keys on her laptop. "I don't think the Wi-Fi is back up."

"Maybe we should try to reset the breakers," I said, remembering Will's piece of advice.

I didn't know how Will knew what to suggest, or whether he was just referring to the power situation on our street in general.

Oliver frowned. "I think we can start with rebooting the modem," he said from the kitchen. He pointed to the corner shelving unit in the space dividing the kitchen and the dining room. "It's up there."

I dragged one of the dining room chairs over to the corner, eager to make myself useful.

Even then, I had to reach up to feel around for the modem. I reached toward the flashing red lights, then pulled the box forward, bringing the wire with it. I pulled at the wire, trying to find where it threaded to the wall. But there was something positioned just behind it, tangled with the cable. A second wire, leading to the same power block.

I wasn't sure whether this was also part of the internet system, so I pulled both forward, disconnecting them from the source.

It wasn't until I stepped down from the chair that I saw what I'd uncovered.

I turned slowly, holding them both out in my hands. "What is this?" I asked. "Oliver, what *is* this?"

But I didn't need him to answer. I knew exactly what it was. I just needed someone else to acknowledge it.

"Is that a camera?" Hollis asked, eyes widening.

I turned it over, saw the logo engraved on the bottom: *Watching-Home*.

"There are *cameras in this house*?" Brody said, standing from the couch.

Oliver's eyes darted from my hand to the upper corners of the house, like he was seeking something out.

"Are there *more*?" Josh said, standing back abruptly.

"Let me see that—" Grace reached for the camera in my hand, but I held it tight.

I opened my mouth to speak, to ask, to accuse. But something in Oliver's demeanor had changed.

"Wait," he said. Then he put his finger to his lips.

As if someone might still be listening. Or watching.

CHAPTER 15

We were silent for the beat of one, two, three seconds.

Josh grabbed the camera, looking at the specifications. "This system operates on Wi-Fi. If the Wi-Fi's down, nothing can transmit. Even if there are more still plugged in."

Grace snapped first. "What the hell, Oliver? Is this like standard vacation-rental operating procedure?"

"No," he said, hands held up in a proclamation of innocence. "It's not, I didn't—"

"Oh," I said, cutting him off, "but this isn't a rental, is it."

He frowned, then took the camera from Josh, wrapping the cord around his hand, turning it over to examine the specifics. "I didn't put this here. I swear. I had no idea."

"Bullshit," I said. "I know this house sits empty the rest of the year. That we're the only ones ever here." I pointed to the camera. "If that's here, it's just for us."

He looked up sharply, quickly, but he didn't erupt. Not like Brody might, or Josh. No, he was even and contained, in a way that was somehow even more unsettling. You could not get an emotional rise from him.

"*What?*" Hollis asked.

Finally, Oliver tipped his head to the side, in concession. "So this house sits empty. So I don't rent it out anymore. So what? I can do what I want with it. It's mine. I bought it off my parents years ago."

"You came out a day early, though," I said carefully. "You were here early, but then you left, and arrived at the house last."

You had to be careful with your accusations here. You could state a fact, but not a guess. There were too many things we didn't want to answer for.

So I did not say what I thought, which was: *You wanted us to think you weren't here. You made us believe you were the last to arrive.*

We didn't like to push too hard. Didn't like to point fingers and accuse, because of all the things we weren't sure of about one another. We knew enough: we knew that we would each leave others to die in order to save ourselves. And we thought that this spoke to something deeper, darker, within us.

It was just the beginning of countless possibilities, but it applied to each and every one of us.

"Why do you know this, Cassidy?" Oliver asked.

I jerked back, feeling the weight of his words. The fact that he was leveling a careful, subtle accusation of his own. And he wasn't wrong. I'd gone through his things. I'd been watching.

Still, I had facts. "The rental car agreement," I said. Not wanting to add a guess: *You were seen on the pier. I'd been asking around.*

He looked around the room, at the fact that the rest of the group was waiting, that right now, he had to answer for his actions, his half-truths. "I could only get a flight in the day before. And I don't like being here alone, so I spent the first night at an inn, came back when I thought you'd be arriving—"

"Then why did you buy this place?" Hollis asked. I could feel us circling him, peeling away the lies, and I was afraid. Afraid of what I'd find at the core.

"Because it's ours," he said, the first sign of emotion rising. "Because it's important that we have this place. And that it's here whenever we need it." He swallowed, waiting for the room to assess him. To deliver their verdict.

"But this." He held up the camera. "This isn't me. Why would I need this? I'm *right here.*"

"You swear," Grace said, pointing to the camera. "You swear that wasn't you."

His face softened, eyes holding her gaze. "I swear, Grace."

She stared back at him, and then nodded. That was how Grace operated. You had to be all in. You didn't agree, you swore. You didn't become friends, you pledged an allegiance. And then she trusted you. It was as simple as that. As if she believed she could read the true character of a person by the level of their commitment.

But this blind allegiance, these endless pledges—this was how we remained stuck in the past, getting absolutely nowhere. We never pressed. We were scared to dig.

"Did you know Ian was here?" I said, shattering the fragility of the moment.

The attention of the room turned toward me. Turned on me.

"What are you talking about, Cass?" Brody asked, though I hadn't stopped looking directly at Oliver. His demeanor changed, the soft expression he'd given Grace suddenly shifting. A defensiveness. A mask he was desperately trying to slide back into place.

Now I took in the rest of the room—confusion, shock, disbelief. I seized on it.

"Ian was here, in February," I said. "I found his jacket in the upper-floor closet, with a receipt in his pocket . . . So, Oliver, did you?" *Did you know, did you hurt him, what did you do?*

Oliver stared back, for a long, painful moment. "You seem so sure I'm the bad guy here, Cassidy. But what were *you* doing up in that room? Why were you even *looking*?"

The problem with all of us was the way our motives were tangled. Our fears, our suspicions. And how quickly an accusation could be turned around on any one of us.

But all my emotions were too close to the surface, and I couldn't stop myself now. Everything was coming out. It was the way Ian's laughter—real, and unguarded—could fill up the downstairs of this house. The way I could feel his presence when he entered a room, and how he always seemed to notice me, just the same. How I used to tell him everything. The memory of his face, hovered above mine. His mouth, open in a frozen scream.

I squeezed my eyes shut. "He tried to get ahold of me, and I missed it. Just a few days before he overdosed." My hand shook as I brought it to my mouth. "I wasn't there for him." The truth. He needed me, and I hadn't answered. I'd missed him, and now he was dead.

Something cracked—a tic in Oliver's jaw. His eyes drifted closed, and he placed his hands on the table, and I thought, *My god, what have you done?*

"I missed him too." Oliver raised his eyes to mine, and they were no longer defensive, but full of devastation. "He reached out to me too. To come here. And I didn't make it in time."

"You came here?" I asked.

"He asked me to." We had pledged to always be there for one another. After Clara, we promised to always come—

"Jesus," Josh cut in. "Why didn't you say anything? We're supposed to reach out if we need help—"

"No one would've been able to help!" he shouted, an unexpected outburst. He took a deep breath, then sat in the nearest chair at the table, like he was giving up. "I couldn't help him either. But it wasn't me. Please believe that." He was searching our eyes, as he had searched Grace's. But I wasn't sure what he was asking for.

None of us spoke, waiting for him to say more.

Oliver stared out the back window. "He sent me an email, to my work address—I guess he looked it up, to make sure I got it. . . . He said he needed my help. That he was heading here—he said it was an emergency, and I told him the code. Thought that was the end of it, but then he emailed again, asked me to meet him here." He shook his head. "No, he *told* me to. *Come to The Shallows. It's an emergency*. That's what he said."

He took a deep breath, even as I realized I was holding mine. This was the Oliver I had first met, before high school. Unsure and quiet. His voice was barely over a whisper. "When I got here, he was gone."

I didn't grasp the depth of his confession, the way he was pleading with us to understand. The way he was inching toward something instead.

"I was too late to help him," he said.

The room was eerily silent, as we tried to process what he was saying.

"Here?" Brody asked, looking around the room. "He overdosed *here*?"

Oliver dropped his head into his hands and nodded.

"Oh my god," Grace said.

I couldn't breathe, couldn't quite take it all in. *Ian, here. Ian, gone.*

I pictured him alone, in this empty house. Deciding, after all this time, it had finally been enough. "You found him dead?" I finally asked, voice just barely over a whisper.

"Yes," he said, head still down, like he didn't want to say it.

"What did you do?" Josh asked. The lawyer, always the lawyer.

"I couldn't . . . he couldn't be dead here. Not with the email, and . . . god, there are people who would happily see my demise, you have no idea."

"Oliver, I have no idea what you're saying right now," Brody said.

"He moved him," I said, voice stoic, the room gone cold. "You found Ian here, and you moved him." I could barely get the words out. But my accusation hit the mark.

I stepped back, hand to the couch, to steady myself. I couldn't breathe.

Of course Oliver couldn't stand to be here. Didn't want to be here alone, with the ghost of Ian haunting him. Didn't want us cooped up in this place. Always getting us out, out, out.

"You would've done the same," Oliver said, directing it at all of us, I supposed. An accusation for an accusation. And who could say? It's what we believed about one another, at the core.

"Where . . ." I said, though I wasn't sure I wanted the answer. I hadn't known the details of his death. They hadn't been specified in his obituary. I had just assumed he'd been at home.

"I carried him to his car—it was the middle of the night. He had gotten so skinny, so light, you know?" As if we hadn't all noticed that Ian had been gradually disappearing, for years. "Drove him back to the mainland, this rest area where I knew people would sleep sometimes . . ." Oliver said.

"No," I cut in sharply. "Where did you *find* him."

His throat moved, like he was working his way up to it. Remembering. "Downstairs," he said. "My room."

I sucked in a breath, imagining Ian there. Lying in bed, lifeless. The shell of him, this person I had once loved. Who I had cared for, for much longer.

But I shook my head. Would he have taken Oliver's room, if he had the house all to himself? I couldn't picture it. He'd loved that upstairs space, and I'd found his jacket in there . . .

"Oliver, are you sure it was Ian who sent you that email?"

"What do you mean?" Grace said.

"I mean, someone used Ian's phone to get me here. Texted me from his number, and then I found the phone, washed up on the beach."

Someone sucked in a gasp. Silence hung in the air as the realization sank in.

Each and every one of us had been lured here.

"What?" Hollis finally said, incredulous.

"I found out after. That number that I showed you that had texted me? It was Ian's. And his phone was on the beach."

It was getting dark, and I could feel the fear in the room. Like we were trapped on the edge of a river, around a flare, slowly dying.

The lights in the house did nothing to ease my rising panic. It felt like we were a beacon in the night—not to be saved, but to be trapped.

"I thought it was a suicide," Oliver said, throat moving. And what he had left unspoken: that he had made sure Oliver would be the one to find him. Such a heavy burden to bear.

"Can you check which email address he wrote you from, Oliver?" Grace asked, but he was already shaking his head.

"I deleted it," Oliver said. "Wiped it. Didn't want evidence tying us together . . ."

"The camera. Is there any way to see who can access it?" Hollis asked.

Josh shook his head. "No, I mean, the only thing we'd be able to check is if someone is on the same Wi-Fi who shouldn't be . . ."

"Then who the fuck has been watching us?" Brody asked, coiled to snap.

"Oliver," Grace said, as calmly as possible, though I could hear the tremble in her voice. "Who has access to this house?"

He shook his head, like he was trying to think it through. "The cleaning company. Probably the old rental management place we used to use. I haven't changed the key code in years, there didn't really seem like a point. It's not like there's anything of value . . ."

"But still," Josh said, "most likely someone close." He was levelheaded, problem-solving. The side of himself he must've utilized in a trial.

Someone close.

Right then I got a chill, thinking of Will, of the fact that he was nearby when I'd found Ian's phone, and he was right there when my bike had a flat. The bike that had been fine until I'd disappeared into the store. And how he was fishing for information on the drive home, gently easing it out of me.

How he seemed to know more about us than I thought possible, pulling that article up at the bar, asking me about it.

"I feel like someone's been in the house," Hollis said. "Looking through things . . ." She cut her eyes to Grace briefly. "I thought it had been you, going through my luggage."

Grace didn't object to the accusation, just shook her head firmly. "It wasn't me."

Josh's gaze drifted to the stairwell. I remembered the door left open upstairs, the sound of footsteps out on the deck at night that I'd assumed were his—but it could've been anyone.

"Someone's been watching us," I said.

"The campgrounds," Brody said. "Anyone could be staying there. Would be close enough to come over the rocks . . ."

Oliver's eyes met mine, and I imagined we were remembering the same thing. The light dancing on the beach at night that had drawn us outside. Heading back to the campground. The same place Amaya had been staying . . .

"Amaya saw someone," I said. "She told us, the first day. That someone was on the beach."

I saw Josh flinch—I wondered if he was remembering too, how he'd brushed her off, mocking her by saying *It's a beach, people do tend to use it* . . . Belittling her.

"She was all alone out there," Josh said, voice low and gravelly. I pictured Amaya at the campgrounds, thinking she had escaped something—suddenly finding herself in danger instead.

Everything was coming out now. We had always been so careful and quiet. Not willing to accuse, lest we be accused in return. There was a balance, and there were too many ways we could tip.

"It could also *be* her," Brody said. "She said she was at the campgrounds . . . Maybe she was staying close to keep an eye on us . . ."

"I don't think so," I said. "I think she saw something—or someone—and ran."

"Well, if she did, she didn't care enough to warn the rest of us. So excuse me if I think she's the one behind this," Brody said.

But I didn't think Josh believed that anymore.

I pulled the letter from my bag. Block print, folded like a card. "She left this in our room."

GET OUT NOW

I watched them each, slowly taking it in.

"You didn't think this was important to share?" Hollis asked, grabbing the paper. Her blue eyes widened, hollow shadows visible underneath.

"I only just found it. The wind must have swept it under the bed. And I didn't know who she was running from."

"And she only cared about you?" Brody asked, like the idea was so ridiculous. "She didn't say anything when she texted later that day?"

Oliver laughed, low and surprising. "Oh. You thought she was running from one of us?"

I didn't answer. I had, of course I had.

But look at all the secrets we had kept. Ian, dead in this house. Oliver, who found him, and was the last person to communicate with him. Josh's secret relationship with Amaya, and whatever made her leave him. And those were just the ones we'd forced out. I knew, deep down, there were more.

They passed the note around, person to person, as if someone might see something in it that the others did not.

Finally, it ended in Josh's hand. He stared at it, frowning. Then he smacked the paper down on the table, making us jump. "I'm not sure this is her handwriting," he said. "Are you?"

We knew a lot about one another in some regards, but so little, in other ways. Had she ever written me a note before? Had she written one to Josh?

"How should we know?" Brody asked, but Josh was looking at me now.

The realization slowly dawned: that maybe this note hadn't been left by Amaya but *for* her instead.

GET OUT NOW

I heard an echo of her voice from that night, long ago—something visceral, cutting across time. *We have to get out now!*

Someone was close by. Someone was watching.

Did they come to see you too?

The whisper in my ear, no longer in Amaya's gentle voice.

Instead it was a threat. A threat that had sent her running.

"I'm getting out of here," I said, turning for the stairs.

Oliver grabbed my arm as I passed. "We'll go in the morning," he said, like he was in charge.

"I'm going now," I said.

"It's not safe out there right now. And the road is closed. There's nowhere to go."

"I don't care," I said. How could they stay, when everything within me was begging me to run?

"We have to stay together," Oliver said, voice rising. This whole week, trying to keep us as a group, move us as a pack. Like there was safety in numbers. Yes, he had understood the danger from the start. "We survived," he added, "because we stayed together."

I shook my head. How could he forget? Revise our history, excise the people who had not made it out? The ones we *left*?

"So come with me," I said. I could not stay here, in this place where Ian had died. I could not stay, when Amaya was also gone, and there was a note in our room, and a camera set up to watch us. How could any of them? I looked from person to person, waiting. I remembered that night, Amaya telling us: *We have to move. We have to go.* The pull of her words. The force of them. A decision I'd already believed, deep in my core, but needed someone else to make for me.

And yet, tonight, one by one, they looked away. When I climbed the stairs, I was alone.

• • •

I organized my gear as quickly as possible. I put that necklace on, a tie to home, a promise to my future. And then, on instinct, I called

Russ. I wanted someone to know where I was. I wanted to confess. What did I have to lose?

"Cassidy, hey," he said, like this was a happy surprise.

"I lied," I said, voice shaking, desperate. "I'm sorry, I'm not in New York. I'm in the Outer Banks."

There was a beat of silence, while the words processed. "You're where?" he asked, as if he needed me to confirm it.

"In the Outer Banks. I've been coming here for years. It's a long story. But it's a promise I've kept to a group I've known for the last decade." A pause. "I'm sorry I didn't tell you. I didn't know how to explain . . . But I have to get out of here."

Another long pause, while I considered my options. I dropped my luggage on top of the bed.

"Cassidy? I don't understand. What's going on?"

"I don't know. I don't know, but something's not right, someone's been watching . . ."

I was losing the track, losing my focus. I started throwing my things into the bag, not thinking. Ian's phone. Ian's jacket. "It doesn't matter."

The line crackled, like I was losing the connection. "I don't understand what you're saying, Cassidy. But wherever you are, I can come to you. I can start driving now."

I closed my eyes—isn't this what I'd always wanted, always hoped for? Someone to choose me. To choose to save me.

"No, it's okay. The roads are a mess. You won't make it . . . I just wanted you to know the truth. I'm going to come home. I'm getting out of here as soon as the roads are clear."

The toiletries went in next, and then the chargers, disconnected from the outlets.

Another crackle of the line, like I was too far away—in another world, another dimension. "You're scaring me, Cassidy."

"I'll explain when I'm home. I promise." And then I hung up, connection severed.

I finished tossing everything inside. I did what I should've done from the start, when Amaya left. When Ian's phone turned up in my hand.

I grabbed my keys, hooked my bag on my back, and opened the door.

Grace stood just across the entrance to my room, eyes wide. There was a bag in her hand, another on her back. "Please," she said, looking back down the hall once. "Get me the fuck out of here."

"Gladly," I said. Grace had no car of her own here. The last few years, she'd flown into the nearest airport, which was still over an hour away—needing to take an expensive cab ride the rest of the way.

Grace stopped at the entrance to the yellow room before heading downstairs. "Hollis," she called, but Hollis was perched on her bed, staring out the window. "Hollis, come on, we're going."

Grace spoke to Hollis the same way she used to handle Clara, guiding her, directing her, the more dominant personality.

"I don't want to drive in this," Hollis said.

"Then come with us," Grace said. "Leave the car. Figure it out later."

But Hollis was not easily swayed. "I'll go tomorrow, with the rest of them."

We left her there, then passed the guys, still downstairs gathered around the dining room table with the camera between them, like they were convening in secret.

They stopped whatever they were discussing as we passed, watching us.

"Don't do this," Brody said, as we headed for the exit. "It's not safe."

I stopped at the door. "You should all get out. Right now."

• • •

It took only until we reached the end of our unpaved road for me to start second-guessing myself. If we couldn't get out of town, we'd be trapped with no other options. But having Grace beside me urged me forward. She too understood the danger. She too had decided to go.

We drove past the sign warning of an upcoming road closure. Eventually, I could see the barriers ahead. I pulled up almost flush with the blockade, as if I had to get as far as I possibly could.

There were two orange-and-white-striped blockades, weighted down with sandbags. And a sign attached to both, clearly indicating *ROAD CLOSED*, just in case that wasn't clear enough. A plow was parked off to the side of the road, at the edge of the dunes.

A fine mist hung in the air, visible in the headlights. A tunnel of darkness snaked between the dunes, past the place we could see.

"Will said they had cleared the road, mostly," I said.

"Well," Grace said, taking a deep breath. "One way to find out."

She stepped out of the car, and I followed wordlessly. The barriers were not difficult to move, especially with the two of us. We opened up the right lane, a darkness yawning.

Back in the car, I turned on the high beams, and slowly crossed the divide. We didn't stop once—not even to replace the barrier.

We knew how to escape:

You left when you could. And you didn't look back.

• • •

Neither of us spoke as we traversed the closed section of highway that would bring us to the next town, closer to the bridges connecting us to the mainland, not sure what we would find or whether we'd become stuck somewhere in between. There was a thick grit under the tires, like we were driving across a layer of the encroaching beach that had spread over the road. But I could just make out the tire tracks of the plow that must've come through earlier, so I tried to keep the same path, the comfort of dark highway pavement visible in the tread marks.

Eventually, we came to another set of barriers, and Grace and I repeated the process of unblocking the lane.

We were free. We had made it.

Grace started laughing as we pulled into the next town. "Never thought I'd be so happy to see that roadside fish shack. And yet."

"And yet," I agreed, driving past the darkened storefront windows.

Just before the first bridge, another set of lights appeared in the rearview mirror. Grace spun around in the seat. "Do you think one of them followed us?" she asked.

"I think they would've let us know," I said.

Grace checked her phone, frowning.

The car remained behind us as we crossed the bridge. I kept checking the mirror, but it wasn't like there were many options for driving here. If someone was heading out, they'd have to follow us just about the whole way.

I tried to relax by counting the series of bridges, one by one, tracing our path back home. After the final bridge, there was a long expanse of road, with marshlands on either side. I pulled abruptly into the first gas station on the mainland, then watched as the car behind us continued on. I noticed Grace following the car with her gaze too.

I tried to shake off the paranoia—we were out. We were free. I topped off the tank, before slipping back into the car beside Grace.

"Where do you want to go?" I asked. She'd flown in from Atlanta, but the airport was in the other direction from where I was heading, and I was sure the storm had thrown the schedule into chaos; there'd be no flights for her tonight.

"Let's just get as far as we can," she said.

• • •

Grace offered to split the driving, so we switched seats after another hour, the darkness and monotony of the scenery a dangerous lull. It was getting late, and the road was mostly unlit and unoccupied, except for the rare car that would suddenly appear in our mirrors, and then disappear.

I must've dozed off in the passenger seat, because I jolted awake to a sudden light and the sound of a door latching shut.

I was alone in the car, but the keys were still in the ignition, engine running. I oriented myself slowly—an empty parking lot, a convenience store—and realized we were just at another gas station.

We were alone in the lot, except for one other car parked against the side of the building, probably belonging to a person working inside.

Grace was visible inside the small store, speaking to the man behind the register as he rang up her purchase. She checked her phone as she walked my way, then smiled when she opened the door and saw I was awake.

"There's a good place to stay about five miles up the road. Want to stop?"

It was almost midnight, and we were far enough inland that I couldn't hear the sea or smell the salt in the air.

No one knew where we were. I checked my phone, but no one had tried to contact me. It was a different type of isolated, a different type of safe.

"Yes," I said. "Good plan."

THEN

HOUR 3

Grace

Grace had the knife.

Something wasn't right, and she was the only one who seemed to sense that.

Her classmates who had escaped from the first van had just made their way to her group, but there were only three of them: Ian, Josh, and Cassidy. So many were still missing from that van. So many who could be—were probably—dead now. And no one seemed to be asking *why*.

From the second van, where Grace had been, nearly everyone had survived the crash—the vehicle driving over the edge, falling into the water, and then abruptly coming to rest, wedged into a corner of rock in a bend of the river. Everyone except for one person: the driver, Mr. Kates.

She kept trying to make sense of it all: Her van had crashed, and Mr. Kates was dead. Or—and this was what she was worried about—was it the other way around? Had something happened to him first? Her favorite teacher, the one adult she believed truly understood her?

He wasn't that much older than she was—five years; she'd asked—and he seemed to be in that same nebulous, in-between space. The way he laughed at their jokes, and wore jeans with his blazer and the same sneakers as half the kids in class; the way he ran his hand self-consciously through his curly hair when he wasn't sure of an answer, like he was still within reach. He understood how they communicated; how they saw the world.

When he spoke, she was enthralled.

She would be lying if she claimed he wasn't the reason she'd come on this trip.

She had started to wonder if she wasn't the only one.

The week before, Ben had raised his hand and asked why they kept reading *all this dark shit*—in a way that seemed phrased to incite a reaction. He was always testing, pushing against authority. Smart, but an asshole—a dangerous combination—and he loved an audience. His parents were on the school board, and everyone knew it. If there was a line, he had yet to find it.

But Mr. Kates had barely looked his way, his voice sliding across the room, a balm to her soul. *Because there's a darkness in everyone*. His eyes had skimmed the classroom, until they landed on Grace. Like he could see straight into her.

It was the same thing she'd written in her journal, and instead of ignoring it, or chalking it up to *being a teenage girl*, he'd circled it, and written: *More*. He was always leaving little notes of encouragement in the margins: *yes* and *good* and *go deeper*, and she did.

Grace always saw into the darkest parts of people. She felt like a magnet, like the darkness was seeking her out. Like she could see straight into the heart of others, the unspoken things they were thinking, or wondering, and something within her pulled it closer. Something within her encouraged them, promised them, *I won't tell*.

Even Clara, who had seemed like the light.

It was like Grace was a black hole, and the closer people got, the more distorted they became. She had started to think maybe she was drawn to it, instead of the other way around. This thing she could sense in others, matching some yearning of her own.

She'd written it all in her journal, like it was a confessional, instead of a class exercise to be judged and graded. And now here he was, with a door held open for her.

But when she lingered after class that day, as she always did, he'd asked Ben to stay behind instead. *We need to discuss this*, he'd said, with Ben's semester paper on his desk.

The school was very strict about the honor code. It was a one-shot policy. This was the last semester of their senior year, and Mr. Kates was running his hand back through his hair, like he wasn't quite sure of what to do.

And now, not only was Ben *not* expelled, he had come on this trip—why was he even *on* this trip, if not because of this? He'd sat near the front of the van, and Mr. Kates was the only person who didn't make it out alive. There was so much blood, the water swirling red with it in the gleam of the headlights under the surface.

It didn't seem right. How could no one else see this? But apparently only Grace saw into the darkest parts of people. Only Grace seemed aware of what they could do.

The others kept talking about a deer, but she hadn't seen it, and it was so dark—who among them was really watching the road?

What she *did* see was Ben arguing with Mr. Kates in the woods at the stop before the crash. The two of them were the same size; outside of school, away from the structured order of things, there was a leveling of positions. They were just two men, eighteen and twenty-three, on opposing sides of a manufactured divide. But instead of a fight, Grace heard a plea. It sounded like Ben was begging. *Look, I'll redo it. I swear, I'll do whatever—*

And Mr. Kates saying, *You can take it up with the administration when we're back.*

Ben grabbed his teacher's shoulder as he turned away and said, very clearly, *I don't think you want to do this. Everyone sees the way you look at Grace Langly. I'm sure the administration would be interested in that too.* His voice echoed through the night, in threat.

Grace felt something stirring. A terrible thrill, the dip in a roller coaster, the weightless moment at the highest arc of a swing. Then there was a noise to her left, a crack of a branch, an animal in the woods, and both men turned to look that way. But the only thing they saw was Grace, who stood there, staring back.

Ben smiled wide, a Cheshire cat grin, and Mr. Kates said something very low, and then Clara was calling her name back at the road.

When they returned to the van, Ben sat directly behind the driver's seat, so that their eyes had to meet in the rearview mirror. Grace was in the back, with Clara. She didn't know, really, what happened up there, once Brody climbed in and slammed the door shut.

Where's Hollis? Mr. Kates had asked.

Other van, Brody said, and Clara had widened her eyes at Grace, in secret understanding.

Grace had always wondered what drew Brody and that new girl together. She and Clara had discussed it often.

But all of that now felt like a lifetime ago. The crash had happened moments after; they existed, now, in another time.

Everything was darkness now. It surrounded her, surrounded all of them.

She couldn't let go of the possibility . . . The more time that passed, the more it seemed like the only logical explanation. And she had set it all in motion, with her presence.

Mr. Kates was dead. He was dead. She'd seen the blood in the water—the darkest thing she'd ever seen—and she felt something disconnect within her, the sobs overtaking her body.

She had watched as the others had crawled out of her van, one by one, then helped carry Trinity and Morgan, who were unable to move on their own. Then she had watched them pull the luggage from the van, as the water around it got deeper and deeper, until it gained a weightlessness, wedged between the rocks and a felled tree, floating, as the river continued to move around it.

All the while, Grace watched. She heard herself calling out for her teacher, uselessly, expecting something different to happen. Expecting a miracle. As if, for once, the light would find her instead.

She watched as Cassidy and Josh and Ian joined their group—but no one else made it from the other van. She watched as Brody pleaded with them about it, voice rising in panic, shaking with emotion: *Where are the rest of them? Where's the van now?*

No one wanted to acknowledge the truth.

She watched, numbly, as Amaya pulled a knife from one of the bags, and Oliver claimed it as his own. She wondered why it was here, what it *meant* that it was here, on this trip with them. All the dark things people could do with it.

She watched as Jason borrowed the knife from Oliver, then used it to cut the seat belts, to help make a sling for Ian.

He placed it down, just for a second, when he was attempting a tourniquet around Trinity's leg, just long enough for Grace to grab it—

"Hey." Oliver was standing in front of her now, flashlight shining in her eyes. "Have you seen my knife?"

She shook her head, even as she felt the bite of it in the pocket of her jeans, pressed against her skin.

Clara was looking at her closely, and Grace wondered if Clara had seen her take it.

She ignored Clara's questioning look now. "Come on," she told her. Amaya was asking for help organizing the rest of the supplies. Anything they could find that might help.

But every time she closed her eyes, she saw Mr. Kates, his eyes shining in the woods. And then Ben, with that wide, chilling grin, teeth glowing in the moonlight.

Now she was trapped. They were all trapped. And Mr. Kates was dead.

Everything they had was spread out in front of them: A length of luggage cables. A stash of candy and protein bars and chips. A pack of cards. And from the space under the floorboard of the trunk: a wrench and a single roadside flare—

"Save that," Amaya said. "For when someone can actually see us."

They zipped things back into bags, to protect them from the rising water and the mist hanging in the air. She couldn't tell whether it was coming from the river or the sky.

"Grace?" She heard that familiar, cocky voice now, just behind her. "Come help me check the rest of the van one last time?"

"We've got this," Amaya said, not looking up. "Go ahead."

Grace followed him wordlessly, feeling a vibration in her heart, in her soul. First a fear, then a rage, clawing its way outward. It was like he wanted her to see which of them had prevailed: *Look, look at him now. Look what happens in the end.*

She wanted to scream, but she forced the urge down, forced herself to remain perfectly still. Instead, she pictured the knife. Pictured it in her hand, darkness seeking dark.

The back door of the van had been left ajar, and the front bumper was pressed downward, wedged against the trunk of the fallen tree, but the van still moved with the current, an ebb and flow, a rise and fall. Mr. Kates was still strapped into the front seat, now fully submerged.

So no, she would not touch that water.

Ben went ahead, wading into the back of the van, climbing over the last bench row.

Everyone sees the way you look at Grace Langly—

The threat, implicit. He could ruin his career. He could ruin his life.

What had Mr. Kates said that she hadn't heard? And Ben, sitting just behind him in the van—what had he *done*?

So when she heard the creak of the log while he was still inside the van, she said nothing.

And at the crack of the trunk, the slow-motion snapping of rotted wood, she'd said nothing still, all while he'd held up a pair of headphones like something from a treasure hunt.

So when the log finally gave way, and the van dipped precariously, she'd stepped back instead.

"Holy shit, Ben, get out!" Clara yelled, clawing past Grace to reach the vehicle. "Get out now!" The van was going to dislodge, and Ben was going to go with it, and he was too far into the van; she could count the seconds until it was too late. "Grace, help!"

But Grace only stood there, feeling the bite of the blade in her pocket, pulling her closer. Ben dove over the last of the seats, as Clara reached an arm in. As Clara, and then Cassidy and Amaya, reached in and grabbed him, in the seconds before the log gave way, and the van was gone.

Headlights. Any light. Mr. Kates. All gone. She drew the knife slowly from her pocket, clenched it in her fist.

"Are you okay?" Clara asked. Grace was not okay, but Clara hadn't been talking to her.

"Yeah," Ben said, almost out of breath. "Yeah, I think . . . Yeah."

Grace was frozen. She was putty. She was weightless and ungrounded and she'd almost watched him die.

"Holy shit," he said. "That was close."

Clara took Grace's hand in the dark. Looked into her eyes, darkness seeking dark, as she pressed against the softest pressure point of Grace's wrist, until her fingers unspooled, and Clara took the knife from her hand. She said nothing. She didn't have to.

She looked wide-eyed between Grace and Ben—whom Clara had always liked, for reasons Grace could never comprehend—as if weighing her allegiance.

"What the hell happened to the van?" Brody asked. The darkness made everyone take on a more grotesque form, disembodied voices in the night.

"It washed away, down the river," Ben said, still out of breath. "Almost took me with it."

"What did you *do*?" Grace said, voice low and haunting, drawing everyone's attention.

"*Nothing*," Ben said, looking at the empty space behind him. "It just . . . gave way."

"No," Grace said. "Before. What did you do to Mr. Kates?"

"What?"

"You did something to him, and then we crashed."

Ben backed up, hands up. "What the—Grace, there was a deer in the road. Ian, you saw it, right?"

"Yeah," Ian said slowly, but he sounded less certain, not at all convincing. And Grace was suddenly sure there hadn't been a deer at all.

"Why are you here, Ben? Why are you even *here*?"

"Why are *you* here?" he asked in response. "I'd say it was because of some ridiculous, fucked-up fantasy, but what do I know about what goes on after school hours?"

"Oh, please. You guys want to know why Ben Weaver is here?" Grace asked, voice rising, turning to the rest of the gathering group. "Because he was going to get thrown out of school. He cheated, and Mr. Kates knew it—I heard you arguing in the woods, right before we crashed. I heard you."

"So what?" he said, his voice rising to match, in the way that people did, when they had nothing else to fall back on.

"So, he's dead, and we're stuck down here, and our friends . . ." She gestured somewhere into the darkness, into the river. "Are *gone*. Because of you." She was the first one to say it, first one to admit it. And it fortified her. "I know you, Ben Weaver. I know what you did."

And for the first time since the accident, all she could hear was her own breathing and the rush of the river. Something was happening. The silence stretched, and something was happening.

Ben laughed, a light, nervous sound. It was the shadows in the night. The way none of them could see one another. "Did you hit your head, Grace? Or did you finally, fully crack?"

"Don't talk to her like that," Clara said. But Grace did feel that way, like something had finally cracked open. A dam, a siege, a terrible clarity. She could see the darkness pulsating. She closed her eyes and saw Mr. Kates again, that very last time he looked at her, that sad, sad expression, like he knew what was coming.

God, didn't Mr. Kates know? You didn't trigger someone like

Ben. Even she had sensed that. There was something truly dangerous under his surface—the things he was willing to do.

"He's gone," Grace said, a sob escaping. "They're *all* gone."

She couldn't see Ben anymore. She couldn't see any of them, and she was afraid of what was happening in the places she couldn't see.

She heard someone else choke on a cry, but she wasn't sure who. She had been the only one to say it, to acknowledge it: The rest of that van, other than Ian and Josh and Cassidy—they hadn't made it. Not Ms. Winslow. Not Collin or Jenna or Bryce, kids she'd gone to school with since the elementary years. Not Hollis, with her big blue eyes, her pink-tipped hair, a vision of light under Brody's arm—

"Grace, stop it, I didn't *do* anything," Ben said, but it came out like a plea, just like she'd heard in the woods. Like he was desperate, grasping.

"Yeah, well now the van is gone too," Josh said, another layer of accusation.

Oliver turned on the flashlight, as if he could sense it too, a pulsating dark that he was trying to dispel. He moved the beam from person to person. A tally. This was all of them, then. And they could count the dead by their absence. They were all that was left: the only survivors.

"Now what?" Clara asked.

Oliver pointed the flashlight up the steep rock wall. In the narrow beam of light, it seemed to stretch forever. They began moving, but there was a different energy, a different quiet.

The darkness felt like a tangible thing.

Grace went to their supplies at the base of the cliff wall, to the pile she'd organized herself.

"Oliver, can I use your flashlight?" she asked. There was too much darkness, and she couldn't see anything.

But Oliver didn't seem willing to relinquish his hold on the light. Instead, he crouched beside her, shining the beam where she indicated.

She held up the single roadside flare for him to see. *One-hour use*, it said, in bold letters.

"We should ask the others . . ." he said quietly.

"Read me the directions," she said, cutting him off.

He shined the light on the back of the package, reading out loud.

Her hands shook as she followed his guidance—the strike of the edge igniting, the light so bright it burned her eyes, spots lingering in her vision for long after.

Grace held the flare away from her body, the red smoke swirling, rising.

At least there was a light.

She wanted to be found.

Everything was out of her control.

Everything, she realized in that stark moment of clarity, had always been out of her control.

And she thought: she would be punished, or she would be rewarded.

She would live, or she would die.

Everything was out of her hands now, but she felt the darkness spreading.

FRIDAY

CHAPTER 16

My stomach kept dipping, my head spinning, like I'd been dreaming of the winding road. The sickening swerve of the van. The crash. The fall.

I jolted awake, struggling to orient myself to the present time and place. The bed seemed to be moving, as if I were still adrift in a current.

I was no longer in the aqua room at The Shallows, but an unfamiliar, nondescript rectangle. The dimly lit hotel room had two full-size beds with scratchy sheets, and a churning air-conditioning unit that sounded like something had come loose inside. And yet, I realized it was maybe the best sleep I'd had all week. Even Grace, closer to the rattling unit, was still sleeping, though sunlight was streaking through the gap in the heavy curtains, inching closer to her face.

We'd seen the sign for the hotel right off the highway exit, with several fast-food options connected via parking lot access.

I fumbled for my phone charging beside me—this early, it was automatically set to do not disturb. I had six missed calls from Russ, and a string of texts of escalating concern. I snuck into the bathroom and tried calling him back, but it went straight to voicemail. I knew he had a full day of classes on Fridays, so I sent a quick text: *Stopped at a hotel on my way home. Sorry, was driving and then sleeping. See you soon.*

Both Grace and I had collapsed as soon as we got into our room, from exhaustion, remnants of adrenaline, lingering fear. I'd checked on Ian's phone, buried deep in my luggage, as if it may have disappeared between there and here—but it was still safe in my possession.

Neither of us had called the others. It was like we were operating under the same unspoken dilemma: unsure who among them we could fully trust.

And so we were here, tucked safely away, momentarily off-grid. But I was increasingly worried about Amaya. Her phone still wasn't receiving messages. The fact that someone was watching the house, and she had been all alone, rattled me. She may have taken refuge at the motel through the storm, but the fact that she hadn't checked in when she must've known we'd be concerned was out of character. She cared too deeply to leave us like this.

Everyone I wanted to speak to was frustratingly unreachable.

I took a quick shower. When I got out, Grace still hadn't stirred, so I slipped out of the room to find the complimentary coffee promised at check-in. Grace had paid for the double room, and I had promised to take her wherever she decided to go today.

The lobby was eerily quiet for a Friday morning around rush hour. Just a silent news program playing over the coffee bar, and the sound of the receptionist typing away at the computer.

I was filling the second cup for Grace when I felt the presence of someone standing just behind me, impatiently shuffling back and forth. I moved over to give the other person access to the coffee dispensers, and cut my eyes briefly to the side. It was a stranger: a man in a dark blue polo straining over his stomach; he had work boots and a crisp baseball cap and a gentle accent as he said, "Mornin,' miss."

I smiled and tried to make myself relax: lower the shoulders, breathe from the gut. Part of me had expected Oliver or Joshua or Brody. I even thought of Will, the memory of headlights in the rearview mirror following us out of town. I found the paranoia difficult to shake, even on this side of the last bridge.

I repeated to myself: *We made it. We're safe.*

In the elevator, I focused my to-do list down to its most essential items for today: drop Grace wherever she needed to be; head home. Anything else could come later.

With the two cups of coffee balanced in one hand, I slid the key into the hotel door, then came face-to-face with Grace, who was partly inside the closet by the entrance.

"Hi!" she said, too cheerful. "Oh, is that for me?"

But I was distracted by the fact that she was hovering over my luggage, open on the stand in the closet. "Are you looking for something?" I asked.

"Yes," she said, one side of her mouth pulled into a coy grin. "Face wash. I think I left mine in the rush last night."

"In the bathroom," I said, but she didn't back away from the closet, didn't move to take the coffee from my hand.

Instead, she cleared her throat and reached an arm into my bag. "Is this it?" she asked, pulling out Ian's phone, as if it had just been lying there, when it had actually been buried under a layer of clothing.

The fact that she had it now made me think she'd been looking specifically for it.

I swallowed, nodding, desperately wanting it back in my possession.

"And you just found it? On the beach?" She turned it over in her hands, looking at the new screen, the scratched backing.

"Yeah," I said. I placed the cups on the nearest shelf, hands itching for the phone.

She frowned. "I've been thinking about that. About why someone might've had it . . . Like, if it somehow got left behind . . . or." She shrugged, though her eyes were latched onto mine.

Left behind. Meaning, when Oliver moved his body. A shudder rolled through me, a violent wave of nausea, picturing Ian, in that house, in Oliver's room. Dead.

And now Grace seemed to be asking whether I thought the

phone accidentally got left behind in the house three months earlier for someone else to find, or whether someone took it with them after Ian's death, and then brought it back. Either way, someone must've known exactly what they had.

"Oliver?" I asked. He was a risk-taker, in business, and in life. Had won big only by making big moves. Was this nothing more than another risk worth taking for him?

Grace tipped her head. "I don't know," she said slowly. "I just knew I had to get out of that house. Could you access anything on it?"

"No," I said. "It doesn't really work anymore." I cleared my throat. "Just receives and sends calls and texts. Everything else I tried to open needed a password."

She sighed. "I wish I knew what Ian was doing there." She turned the phone over again, then pressed the power button, like she was checking my claim for herself.

My shoulders tightened, eyes burning with tears. "Like I said, it doesn't really work." I took the phone from her hand, relieved that she didn't resist.

"What are you going to do with it?" she asked.

"I don't know yet."

She widened her eyes, and she seemed even closer. "Be careful, Cassidy. If anyone finds out you have this, the first question they're going to ask is *why*."

Her gaze held mine, until I had to look away first. She'd just walked me through how improbable it all sounded. *Just found it on the beach. Three months after he died.*

I didn't like the way she was questioning me, like she was suspicious. This was the subtle way we accused one another, never outright, always in subtext. *Be careful, Cassidy.*

I suddenly didn't want to be in this hotel anymore, in the middle of nowhere, when no one knew I was here. Just like the paranoia of discovering that camera, and the realization that someone had been watching us.

I zipped up my luggage and waited for Grace to back away. "Have you thought about where you want me to drop you off?" I asked.

Finally, she stepped backward, toward the entrance of our bathroom. "Actually, I was thinking, we're only two hours from home."

Home, she said, like it was mine as much as hers. The small town of Long Brook, claiming us both.

"Would it be on your way to drop me at my parents' place? I can figure out what to do from there."

"Sure," I said, though a buzzing had immediately started in my ears.

I didn't go back there anymore. Not since my parents moved my freshman year of college. Long Brook wasn't far out of the way, though—less than two hours from where I now lived, just south of Charlotte.

"I'll be ready to go in ten," she said, then closed the bathroom door.

To the sound of the running water, I plugged Ian's phone into my charger. Wondering why all of his earlier texts and calls were wiped. Wondering if this was part of Oliver's plan, deleting the evidence of his involvement, wherever it might be—photos, texts, call log. I wondered how many secrets Oliver was keeping.

As soon as the shower turned off, I tucked the phone back into my bag, double-checking the outlets for any cables left behind.

"Are you ready?" she asked a minute later, gathering up her things.

"All set," I said.

• • •

From the parking lot, I could hear the sound of cars on the highway. The air was so much thicker inland, a humidity that got caught in the trees, a heat absorbed into the pavement.

In the morning sun, the light shimmered off the surface of the road, like water. A mirage where we were complicit, and driving straight for it.

On this empty stretch of highway, it felt like you could see forever.

• • •

Grace spent half the drive looking out the window, forehead resting on the passenger window, and the other half checking her phone.

"Have you heard from any of the others?" I asked, when I noticed her checking it one more time.

"No. But if they're all driving, I guess we probably won't . . ."

Still, she seemed concerned enough to keep checking. But she was approaching the situation like I might: carefully and quietly.

"Grace," I said cautiously. "Do you think someone else knows? About the others?"

Even as I said it, I hoped she would pretend I was asking something else. Let her ignore the question. Let us go back to a decade of avoidance and lies. We had been so lucky—not only that we had survived, but that the river had washed away our collective crimes. It had destroyed any evidence of our actions, any timeline of events. There was nothing to suspect. No reason to think a sign of injury was anything but from the crash itself, shattered glass and twisted metal. No way to know where—or for how long—others might've survived. The force of that water superseded all that had come before.

She lifted her head from the window, slowly pivoted my way. "What," she said in a voice I barely recognized. "Do you think they scratched the details into the rocks? Think they had time to leave a note? Maybe a quick: *Ben was here*?"

My eyes widened, shocked by her tone. Shocked, because it was how Josh might've said it instead, crass and callous.

"No," I said, "but I think there's a reason everybody lied about it then." Or rather, Josh lied, and we agreed, in our silence. We were complicit from that very first moment. "What do you think would happen if the truth came out now? After all this time?"

"We're not sociopaths, Cass. We did what we had to do to

survive, no one would fault us for that. What was the other option? What good would it have done to stay?" She lowered her voice. "Or to say we had to leave them. Do you think their families would rather think *that*? That they *almost* made it?" She sounded like she'd told herself this story before. Like she'd had plenty of practice justifying it to herself. Or to someone else. "It's the kinder thing, in the long run, for them to think it was quick."

"Do you really think," I began, "that we did it out of *kindness*?"

She shifted in her seat, took a slow and calming breath. Centering herself, grounding herself. "It's been ten years, Cassidy. A decade. We're all different people now."

"Exactly, it's been a decade. So what's the point? Someone knows something they *think* matters, Grace. Or they wouldn't be contacting us ten years later. They wouldn't be"—I waved my arm around uselessly—"leaving *cameras* in the house where we're staying."

What could be worthy of a tell-all, if there was nothing new to tell? Who were the producers? What was the angle? Why else would they be interested in something that happened ten years earlier? We went off the road, and a bunch of innocent young people died. It was a tragedy you didn't want to look at too closely, if you didn't have to. No, they knew there was something here. Something deeper, darker, more damning.

"But even if anyone suspects something, don't you see?" she said. "They need us to confirm. Without us, there's nothing to go on. Nothing."

"Unless it's one of us. And then, they're already talking."

I thought of Amaya and Josh, at the library dedication ceremony. The press that must've been there. The families of the dead, coming face-to-face with the survivors. A terrible collision. Secrets spilling over, seeping out.

She twisted so she was facing me. "You need to forgive yourself. I mean it. Listen, Clara got stuck. I should've seen it, should've noticed sooner . . . She got stuck on this, and now she's gone, with the rest of them." She placed a hand on my arm. "If I can do it, so can you." I heard the echo of her words from a session, carrying up the steps: *You are not the worst thing you've ever done.*

I swallowed nothing, picturing Clara on the precipice. Standing in the dark, at the edge, unsteady on her feet. Eyes closed, hearing those screams, calling her back. Calling us all back—

"Something happened out there," I said.

Grace remained silent, but I felt her attention now, the way I'd always hoped to command a room. Finally, I had her.

"Ben was fine, and then he wasn't," I continued. I saw him then, in the dark. Lying on the rocks, hands pressed to his stomach, the shock in his eyes.

"He was alive when we left. We're not killers, Cassidy," she said.

But that was not true. That was not entirely true.

Grace had cast blame, set something in motion, and someone had acted on it.

And that was the secret: there *was* a killer among us, we were pretty sure. Not just killing by neglect, by leaving, by refusing to look back. And not just by recklessly drawing cards and sending someone into the river before that. But intentionally, with a knife in their hand. It was one of us. There was no way around it: it had to be one of us.

It was a dangerous thing, to go looking. To ask, to unwind it, to try to figure it out. We weren't supposed to reopen the past.

We had been complicit in leaving the others behind. We had been complicit in sending Jason into the water, to his death. We had become complicit in the cover-up of a crime the moment we decided not to speak up. And now we were all bound by it.

This was our pact, really, when it came down to it, what showing up every year really meant: I promise not to dig. I promise not to go back.

How quickly an accusation could turn against you if you faltered. We knew how it worked—you wanted to be on the side with the numbers.

But I never knew, exactly, why we had stayed silent: Was it because we were ashamed we left them, or because we'd voted to send someone into the river, or because of Ben?

I waited. But she looked straight ahead, the vision of calm.

"No one could find the knife after," I said.

And in the moments and days and weeks that followed, at funeral after funeral, I kept circling back, approaching my memories from every direction, trying to understand. I'd wake in the middle of the night, still tasting river water, still seeing their eyes glowing in Oliver's flashlight. It was a nightmare that had followed me out, and I couldn't escape.

"So what, Cassidy? I lost everything I brought on that trip too. It's probably somewhere in the river, with the rest of it."

"What is it that you think they're after, Grace? They asked Oliver to describe the knife, did you know that?"

"Yeah, well, it's *gone*, Cassidy, and no one knows what happened. It might've turned out exactly the same no matter what we did or didn't do," she reiterated, as if I were too close to cracking, and needed the next line to deliver. A warning. A subtle reminder.

"It's going to come out," I said. Couldn't she feel it, simmering underneath? Ten years, and the night was still coming for us all. *Clara, Ian.* We had never fully escaped, and we couldn't contain it any longer.

"No," she said, very calmly, very Grace. "I don't think it will." As if she was willfully disbelieving. She leaned forward. "You're gonna miss the turn, Cass."

"Jesus." I veered quickly, crossing over a lane, cutting off a silver SUV as they leaned on the horn.

How many times had I purposely driven past, purposely averted my eyes from the sign for the Long Brook exit, my instinct always to keep my distance.

How many times had I imagined those chapel bells chiming—one for each of the lives who had been lost that night. I could hear the ghost of that echo as I crossed the town line. Imagined Clara standing in the courtyard on the one-year anniversary, the vibration resonating in her bones; something she couldn't shake after. For the rest of us, a danger we were careful to avoid, taking ourselves far, far away, to the coast, over a series of bridges, where the sound of the waves could drown out the sound of the bells.

The town now took on the quality of a dream, hazy around the edges—recognizable, but not quite the same. Everything was just slightly askew from my memory. The familiar location of a box store, now with a different name. A burst of wildflowers in the median, where there had been only dirt and untamed grass before.

"Take a left at the next light," Grace said, peering out the window. "My parents moved." As if I had ever been invited to her other house. As if we'd been friends.

"They're in a retirement community," she continued. "All cookie-cutter and quiet. Everything looks the same. There's no evidence of my existence." She laughed once, but I recognized the flatness of her tone.

"Mine moved away years ago," I said. "My oldest brother got married, had a kid. They're up in Connecticut, all together."

"That'll do it," she said. "Hollis's family is gone too. But otherwise, most everyone has stayed, haven't they?"

"I wouldn't know," I said. But that wasn't entirely true. We'd all kept tabs on one another. Checking in, checking up. A tally of names, of lives—a responsibility.

Grace guided me into a neighborhood of identical ranch homes with perfectly manicured yards. Each unit had a single-car garage and a mailbox out front, and there was a series of oddly placed speed bumps that slowed our progress to a crawl. It seemed impossible to tell anything apart, but she leaned forward, scanning the streets, directing me when to turn. Then finally, she jabbed her finger into the window. "This one, right here. Just park in the road."

The only defining features to this home were the woven flower wreath on the front door, encircling a cursive letter *L*, and the large matching potted plants framing the porch entrance.

"My mom sure loves daisies," she said, with half a smirk. She opened the passenger door and stared at the house, as I popped the trunk.

"Can I use the bathroom before heading out?" I asked.

"Sure," she said. She peered up and down the street before grabbing her luggage. The street was eerily quiet, though there were cars in the majority of driveways.

"Are they home?" I asked, following her up the paved walkway, skirting between the potted daisies.

"No, the irony of them living in this retirement community is that they're not actually retired yet."

She checked under the brown welcome mat—daisies surrounding the word *Home*—and behind the wreath hanging on the door. Then she ran her hands along the chairs on the porch, lifting the cushions one by one, until she finally held up a single key, in triumph.

"This town," I said, shaking my head.

This town, we had been told all our lives, was *so safe*. And we were *so lucky* to grow up here. We'd heard our parents extol these facts, the mayor reiterate them, our teachers confirm. Even after twelve tragic, untimely deaths, there was a feeling that as long as we remained here, within these borders, we would be protected. It was only when we were outside them that things went so terribly wrong.

As if, out there, the world was unpredictable, and we became unpredictable, in turn.

Grace slid the key into the lock. As soon as she pushed it open, the sound of an alarm beeped its warning. She went straight down the white tiled floor to the keypad, then typed in a code. The beeping continued, and Grace frowned.

"Should we call them?" I asked, feeling a chill. Unsure of who Grace truly was, in this unfamiliar place.

But she tried a second code quickly, and the system declared *Disarmed*.

"There," she said.

She turned on the hall light, illuminating a mirrored entry, giving the impression of a funhouse. I smiled at the mirror version of Grace.

The house was lacking wall decor, lacking photos on the mantel, lacking any personal touches on the shelves. The couch and furniture might've come with the house, all part of the cookie-cutter package. "It looks like they're still moving in," I said.

"They've been here for over a year, believe it or not," she said. She walked down the hall and pushed open a door at the far end, revealing a bathroom. "There you go," she said.

She was right—in this house, there was no evidence of her existence, which had to be jarring for her. I could only imagine, as a therapist, what she would make of this.

When I returned from the bathroom, Grace was staring out the front window, behind the tilted blinds. She was standing so still, I imagined something out there: a car, parked behind mine; a person, creeping closer.

"You don't think someone followed us?" I asked, standing just behind her, nervous to check.

"No, but we're definitely being watched." She beckoned me closer, then laughed. On the other side of the street, an older couple walking a tiny poodle was examining my car carefully.

"I should get going," I said, shoulders relaxing. "Take care, Grace."

She pulled me tight then, like we always did at the end, overcome with relief. She smelled like the minty shampoo from the hotel, but before we parted, I always pictured the same thing: that moment, huddled together on the road, in the headlights of the truck, when we were finally found.

• • •

Outside, the couple made no move to hide the fact that they were examining me as I approached.

"Hello!" I said, too cheerful. "Just visiting the Langlys."

"They're not home," the woman said, frowning.

"No, I know. I'm a friend of their daughter's."

"Well, she doesn't live here. What's your name?"

"Cassidy," I said.

"Cassidy what?"

"Cassidy Bent," I said.

I saw her lips moving, repeating it to herself, as if it were meaningless. The names remembered around here were the ones we never mentioned, who never made it out. The names I imagined now on the plaques in the new library. Twelve chimes for the dead.

I slipped away, taking the speed bumps too quickly. Imagined myself slipping from her memory, just as fast.

CHAPTER 17

I knew exactly why I had continued to avoid the town of Long Brook. The danger here was the same as a danger anywhere you had left behind. It was too easy to remember the person you were before. To find yourself slipping back into it again. The spaces you once moved through, like a ghost. Figments of the past, rising to greet you. Dip in a toe, and you may soon be consumed.

Here was the street I'd grown up on, with older brick homes surrounded by mature trees, limbs arching down, haunting and willowlike. I passed the Kings' house first, where Oliver's parents, I believed, still lived, a permanent grounding as their son went on to other heights. And then, halfway down the street, was the place I'd once called home. The brick was now painted over in a brilliant white, the dark front door a pale blue, the brown shutters a light gray surrounding updated, modern windows.

Everything changed. And yet, being here after all this time, it felt that I had not.

• • •

I had to pass through downtown on my way out, and I felt another type of gravity kicking in, drawing me to the one place I'd found solace, that summer after our accident.

Ian's home was in a similarly aged neighborhood to mine, but the houses were smaller, cozier, with trees that seemed to tower over them instead. That summer, I used to take the most direct path—by bike, on a nature trail connecting the backs of our neighborhoods. But in a car you had to loop around past the town center first—restaurants and dentist offices and, with a large sign beckoning you closer, the law firm of Andrews & Andrews. It was an establishment almost as old as the town itself, housed in one of the brick-front standalone buildings, ivy creeping up and over the roof.

Ian's street was walkable from downtown, which made it a prime place to live. Once upon a time, Clara and Grace had lived here too. Pulling onto their block, I could see why Grace's family moved—it seemed like several of the homes were in the process of massive renovations, exteriors pushing the boundaries of the lots, trees that had been lost in the process. It must have been the ideal moment for them to downsize.

I idled in front of the Taylers' home. The curtains were pulled back, so I could see straight into the dark living room. Unlike in the retirement community, no one seemed to be keeping track of who should be here, and who shouldn't. There was a lawn crew a few doors down, and the steady drone of a mower dulled the sound of my steps as I walked up the drive.

I rang the bell, just to check, but it didn't look like anyone was home. Then I circled around back, to their large backyard. At the edge of their property, a tree house had been built into a large oak. I could still picture Ian lying on his back, cigarette between his fingers, scent wafting downward as I climbed the steps to the platform.

Now, as I climbed those same wooden rungs, I saw that even this had changed. Inside, there was a collection of pine cones and sticks lining the borders, colored chalk in a bucket, names written in boxy print. I wondered, for a moment, whether his family had moved, and someone new had taken over. But then I remembered that his sisters were older, just as my brothers were, and his obituary had mentioned that he was an uncle several times over.

I lay flat in the spot he preferred, staring up at the slanted roof, imagining my body outlined in chalk. An imprint. A memory. Up above, in the groove where the roof met the wall, I knew, was a hollow carved out of a rotten segment, where he used to stash a small box just large enough for his lighter and a pack of cigarettes. Things kept out of sight of his parents, though it wasn't exactly a secret, and by then they were just glad he had made it home from the trip. If they noticed me here too, they never said.

I stood and reached my hand into that space now, brushing damp plastic, something kept safe from the elements from long ago. The bag was covered in something dark and slippery, and I didn't want to guess whether it was mud or rot or mold. Inside was that same wooden box latched shut; I felt a lighter moving around inside as I tipped it back and forth. I pulled it from the bag just as movement caught my eye below.

"I see you up there."

I jolted, then stuffed the box into my purse. The woman's voice had come from just outside the tree house; there was nowhere to go, nowhere to hide. I stepped into view of the window.

Below me, Ian's mom stood with one hand wrapped around a ladder rung. Her expression shifted, and she pulled herself closer. "Cassidy?"

"Hi," I said, sitting on the edge, preparing to lower myself down. "I'm sorry. I knocked, and . . ."

I was rambling as I descended the rungs, but she was smiling when I finally turned around, feet planted in the grass. Sometime in the last decade, she had transformed into a grandmother—smaller framed, with deeper smile lines and silver-streaked hair pulled back in a bun. "Cassidy Bent, my god, look at you."

"Hi," I said. I had no idea how she recognized me so quickly, so easily. Maybe I only thought I had been invisible, then. Maybe it was just how I'd felt in high school.

"Oh my goodness," she said. I let myself be taken into her arms, warmth radiating off her. And I began, suddenly, unexpectedly, to cry.

"I'm so sorry," I cried. "I only just heard." I could feel my sobs pulsating through my body, my knees in danger of giving out. Everything, finally, inescapably and tragically real.

"Oh," she said, arms tightening. "Come, now. Won't you come in? You've come all this way."

I leaned into her as we crossed the yard together, grass tickling my ankles, Ian's box loose in my bag.

What I remembered most of Ian's house from our summer together was a warmth, a homeliness that made it a place I wanted to be. A place where your presence was always noticed, and acknowledged.

It would've been so easy to imagine that Ian was still here now, if not for the living room display. The room was covered with photos of Ian, though he wasn't their only child. A memorial, a shrine.

"I almost didn't believe it," I said, staring at the photos. "I called his phone, and it still worked."

"Oh," she said, hand to her cheek. "Well, he had a family plan with his roommates. I guess they never got around to removing him. Boys, you know how they are."

She gripped my hand, and hers felt so cold, roughened, and I wished, once more, that I had been here. That I had been here before, when he reached out. That I'd seen his email, and come. So that he didn't have to move on to Oliver. To whatever had driven him to The Shallows, all alone.

Then I noticed pictures on the wall of small children—grandchildren.

She saw me looking. "He was such a great uncle," she said. "Those kids adored him."

"I can't believe you remembered me. It's been ten years." Ten years since the accident, ten years since I'd given myself so openly to another, bound together in tragedy and grief.

"You meant so much to him. I know you drifted apart, but you got each other through that first hard time." She tapped her chin a few times. "He told me, you know. That he was alive because of you. So of course I remember you. You brought him home."

As if that extra time had been a gift, even with him now gone.

"Also, look at you," she said. "How could someone forget that face?" She smiled, lines stretching out from her eyes.

I laughed. "I always loved it here."

"Would you like something of his? I've been offering things to those who've stopped by. You would know, better than me, what holds meaning. Come on upstairs."

"Oh, I don't want to take anything—" I already had his leather jacket, his scent clinging to the collar. The strongest memory I could imagine. And now I also had the box from the tree house in my bag, which was also for her benefit, and the small children who now played up there.

"Please," she said. "It makes me happy, thinking of pieces of him having a second life."

I followed her up the carpeted steps, to the first room on the right.

Ian's room, unlike Grace's, had been left almost the same as when he'd last lived here. The twin bed pushed up against the wall, with no headboard. The wooden desk on the other side of the room.

"If there are pictures left, they'll be in there," she said.

I opened the top drawer now, which was covered with an assorted collection of scraps of paper. I picked one up, saw a string of letters and numbers.

His mom chuckled behind me. "He could never remember passwords. Even when he wrote them down, he'd lose them constantly. Had to change them all the time. No idea what these were for, but I can't bring myself to throw anything away that belonged to him."

I wondered if any of these would open the email on his phone; I imagined they were all from long ago. I opened the next drawer, trying to remember what to expect. But I had never sat at his desk, gone through his things. We were never that type of friends.

"I would've set something aside, if I'd known what. Everyone else has already been through."

"What do you mean, everyone else?"

"Well, Josh Doleman. He was here for the service of course. Did you know they used to be friends?"

I shook my head.

"Long, long ago, used to play in that tree house out back, before they grew up. I thought it was fate that they survived together." She sniffed. "And Grace Langly was here."

"I didn't know that," I said, feeling unsettled again by all the things I hadn't known. I didn't think Ian and Grace had been that close, but she had grown up down the street. Her parents lived close by; she must've heard, come home.

"Yes, second time I'd seen her, after a long time. You know, she was here for the library dedication too."

My shoulders tightened. "I did not." We must've all gotten the invitation. But I had not imagined any of them had gone willingly.

"Hard to know whether to go to those things. But I live here, figured it would've been worse if I didn't show. I told Ian not to go, though. I told him I'd represent him. I was a little surprised to see Grace there, considering."

"Considering what?"

"Well, she doesn't come home anymore . . . doesn't talk to her parents. Or maybe it's the other way around."

I frowned. "I just dropped her at their house."

She stared at me. "Well, maybe I'm wrong. Maybe they've reconciled." But I'd shaken her, shaken something.

His mother nodded at the framed photo I'd just exposed in the bottom drawer. "You should take that," she said.

I picked it up, held it closer. It was a framed photo of all of us, that first year, at The Shallows. Sitting on the steps, crammed together. Looking at it now, I could remember the feel of Ian's hand tentatively on my back, Amaya pressing tightly on the other side, body tense. My knees wedged behind Josh's back, who leaned slightly forward, annoyed, as always, by my presence.

She placed a hand on my shoulder. "Cassidy, I know." I looked over my shoulder, stared into her eyes, the same as Ian's. "I know it must've been so horrible. He was never the same." She swallowed. "I guess none of you were." I felt my heart in my throat. My own family tiptoed around the topic, pulling back, veering away, as if I could continue on as I had always been, so long as it was never discussed.

I sat on the edge of his bed, looking at the younger version of us, two years beyond the tragedy. I had been twenty; my final exams had just finished. And while my classmates were out celebrating, I'd driven straight to The Shallows, instead. I hadn't seen any of them since the night after Clara's funeral, but we pressed in tight, strength in numbers, power in unison.

The Eight, that's what he'd called us in his phone.

"I'll be downstairs whenever you're ready," Mrs. Tayler said, the carpeted floor creaking as she descended the steps.

I didn't know if she meant for me to take the frame, or just the picture, so I turned it over and unhooked the backing, to slide the photo out.

On the back, a second picture had been attached with Scotch tape. Clara, alone, a vision of light. Up close and smiling, head tipped back in laughter, sunlight reflecting off her necklace, sunburn visible on her shoulders. The tree house was in the background; this had been taken in Ian's backyard. I didn't have to check the date to know it had been taken before the crash—another summer, a happier time. Back when Ian and Clara and Grace were childhood friends, living on the same street.

I left her image taped where it was, then tucked the photos into my bag. He'd kept us together like that, from when there were nine of us instead. It felt right to keep it that way.

Downstairs, his mother was waiting in the living room.

"Thanks for this," I said. "I wish I'd been here. I'm sorry."

She shook her head. "I understood why you didn't come back. Why so many of you still can't. It's probably for the best. He really spiraled after Clara's death."

My spine straightened, after just seeing that haunting, smiling face. "I didn't know that."

She gazed out the back window, a faraway look. "The paranoia. It was the first time we realized we had to get him help."

I'd thought it was the accident, those seven hours, the choices we'd made. Not that it was Clara's death the next year that had messed with his head the most. "I missed it." I had missed so much, trying to move on, away from them.

By the next year, at our first trip to the Outer Banks, Ian and I would sometimes find each other again, but it was never the same. I'd climb the steps to his room, after hearing him calling out in a nightmare—or waking from my own. We grounded each other, reminded each other that we were still here.

Her eyes slid back to mine, and now they were seeking, asking. "After Clara, he became convinced that he was going to be next. Like there was something after you all."

The room was buzzing. Clara's picture on the back of the other photo. Ian's paranoia. It was all I could do to hold my breath, hold her gaze.

She clenched her hands together, chasing the thought. "But of course there wasn't. He struggled for almost a decade, but I would also see him so happy sometimes."

I nodded, swallowing nothing.

Then she stepped closer, hand on my arm. "I'm sorry it ended so suddenly between the two of you. I thought you were really good for each other. Balancing each other out."

"We did." I stepped back, needing space, needing air. I pictured Ian at the other end of a chapel pew, sliding closer; Ian, behind the driver's seat, belting out the wrong lyrics to a song; Ian, on a lounge chair in my backyard, eyes closed and face tipped toward the sun. "I can't believe how long ago . . ." I said, voice raspy. "I'd better get going."

Once upon a time we had been so close. My entire world had been wrapped up in his, and his in mine. It wasn't a balance; it was all-consuming. And I'd felt hollowed-out and adrift when he pulled back. When he finally saw me.

Everything changed after that first summer. We'd had a fight—a disagreement—and I'd left for college soon after. He pulled away, or maybe I did. Either way, the calls, the texts, everything slowed—and then stopped altogether.

I didn't see him again until the next year, after Clara's funeral. He didn't confide in me about his fears. I didn't notice the paranoia his mother spoke of. He retreated inward instead.

In all the years since, he hadn't come to me with anything real. Not until the email, just before his death.

Please, you're the only one I trust—

There was a killer in our group, and what would they *do* if the truth was about to come out? What would they do if they believed that Ian was going to talk?

What would they do, now, if nothing had stopped with Ian's death, the information spiraling forward with a life of its own, wanting to free itself? A current, a force, pushing toward shore?

And then I thought—was Clara going to crack, nine years earlier? Was she getting ready to say the truth? Did Ian know it too?

I was shaken standing outside the house, Ian's warning ringing in my ears. *I'm going to be next.*

• • •

The new school library was impossible to miss. It was a modern structure made of glass, in the midst of a place that had otherwise leaned into its gothic history—all brick and ivy.

At the chime of a nondenominational chapel bell, a sea of students filed out, heading for their cars and busses. I entered the library via a door held open by a girl who didn't even look my way.

Inside, there was so much light. The building was a large semicircle, glass windows reaching up to the arching ceiling, overlooking the trees out back. There were several rough paths through those trees that students would sometimes sneak away down during class.

Now I couldn't help but feel they'd be exposed. There was no way to slip from view here.

A series of pillars stretched up to the dome, each bearing a bronze plaque, reflecting the light through the windows.

I approached the first, read the name: Ben Weaver.

Goose bumps ran up my arms, the back of my neck. I paced to the next: Collin Underwood.

My eyes scanned the room. Twelve pillars, twelve bronze plaques, for the twelve lost souls, like a clock. A circle of windows, a thousand ways out.

At the top of the windows, in dulled, muted bronze, the engraving read: *Class of 2013 Memorial Library*.

The people who still lived here had to face this every day. I couldn't imagine Josh, working less than a mile from here. The chimes of the chapel within earshot every day.

I couldn't imagine Amaya being here, looking at those names—the people we couldn't save, the people we had left. Seeing the bereaved families watching them back now.

I tried to picture Grace, standing here, just like I was now, surrounded by ghosts.

God, how could they stand it? I imagined Grace as they read out those names, telling herself *You are not the worst thing you've ever done*. Josh, staring out the window, willing himself somewhere else. Amaya, beside her father, stuck in the moment, unable to jar herself free.

The eyes that must've been on them. A penance. A price.

"You can't be here."

I spun, faced a woman who must've worked here. I couldn't remember if she was here at the same time as us. I didn't recognize her, if so.

"We've been very clear," she continued. "No press."

No press. As if others had been prying.

"I'm not press," I said, eyes meeting hers.

She opened her mouth, like she was going to tell me I still had to go, but I put up a hand. I couldn't stand to be here any longer either.

"I'm going," I said.

Sorry, I thought, as I backed away. The only atonement I could offer. *I'm so sorry.*

• • •

I filled up my tank on the way home. Removed the photo from my purse, flipped it back and forth. The eight of us on one side. Clara on the other.

And then I slid Ian's box from my purse. It was old and wooden, and just large enough to hold a pack of cigarettes and a lighter, if that. I wondered if that's what I'd still find, after all this time. Or whether he'd moved on to other, more dangerous things he'd needed to keep hidden now.

I opened the box, but there was no lighter inside. No pipe or pills or powders or anything else. I blinked twice, processing. There was only one item: red handle, an embossed crown. Rust streaking the once-silver edging.

Oliver's knife—the knife that no one could find, after that night—sat at the bottom of this box.

The one Ian must've kept, and kept hidden, all this time.

CHAPTER 18

I didn't know what to do, other than to keep moving. The knife was in my possession. The knife that had moved from person to person that night, before disappearing. The knife that no one would admit to having.

I couldn't get rid of it, couldn't hold on to it. Didn't know what it meant, or why he had it.

That entire summer when we were together, he had never mentioned it. It hadn't been in this box—I would've known. I'd seen inside plenty of times, and there was no knife. So it was a secret he had also kept from me. My heart pounded, as I tried to imagine why.

The night at the river, I'd been with Ian, helping Hollis make her way to us, when Ben got hurt. Ian hadn't been the one to hurt Ben. I was sure of it: *It hadn't been him.*

For that whole summer, we'd clung to each other; I'd believed we had told each other everything. I knew I had. But he knew something more. He'd protected someone. For nearly a decade, he'd kept someone else's secret safe. And he might've gone to his grave with it.

• • •

I didn't want to go home now, to my empty apartment, where nothing but my memories waited for me. Not with this knife—and whatever it *meant*—suddenly in my possession.

There was a long list of things I owed, to a long list of people. But right then I couldn't stop thinking about Russ.

Russ lived in a townhome on the outskirts of a sprawling campus, a narrow rental within walking distance of my favorite haunts. It was after dinner by the time I arrived, and I assumed he'd be home, but my knocks were greeted by silence on the other side.

I tried calling him, but his cell went straight to voicemail. I guessed he had a faculty activity at the school, the way he often did. But the string of his missed calls concerned me. Made me think he'd been worried enough to come looking for me. Made me imagine nighttime driving and an accident and someone else using his cell to call me—

But this was just how my catastrophic imagination worked. Always seeing the danger, wondering who I needed to save, in any given moment, in every given moment.

His next-door neighbor, a woman about my mom's age, exited her apartment then, and gave me an appraising look. As if my behavior was making me come off as desperate. As if I should've known better.

"Have you seen Russ?" I asked. I presumed she'd recognize me. I'd passed her coming and going dozens of times.

But her gaze skittered over me, and I caught a chill, remembering how often I'd fallen invisible in the past. I'd thought it was just the time of my life, the place. I'd made a name for myself here. I'd made a life.

"I think he's gone," she said, without pausing. I couldn't tell whether she was trying to get rid of me or just stating the obvious.

I sent him one last text—*Almost home. Call me.*—before heading out.

The sky was darkening as I pulled into the lot of my complex. The overhead lights and the sound of crickets gave off the feeling that you were much farther from the city than you really were. I dragged my luggage behind me, as flustered as I'd been when I'd left five days earlier.

My unit was a two-bedroom located on the top floor, because I couldn't sleep with people walking overhead. And I loved the balcony out back, without wondering if someone was above me, peering down.

The three plants beside my front door looked brittle and dried out, leaves curling in sections. I pressed my finger to the soil, and it was dry.

At least the mail hadn't been left in the metal box.

I slid my key into the lock and turned, but the door to my apartment was already unlocked. I thought, for a moment, that maybe Russ had rushed over here, to beat me back, bring in my mail and attempt to salvage the plants. It was obvious he hadn't been keeping up with them.

The light down the hall was on, casting a glow against the balcony sliding doors. They had been left open, curtains blowing inward. Someone—something—was moving in the back of my apartment, behind my bedroom door, which was only slightly ajar.

"Russ?" I called, from just inside the front entrance.

The movement stopped. I took a step cautiously back, hand on the knob, fumbling for my phone.

"I'm calling the police!" I shouted as I groped inside my bag, thinking of the knife instead, suddenly within reach.

"Please don't, Cassidy."

I paused, but stayed at the entrance. I waited for the intruder to appear.

Three steps, the familiar creak of my bedroom door, and there he was.

Joshua Doleman, uninvited and unwelcome, stood in the entrance to my bedroom.

"How the fuck did you get in here?" I shouted, heart racing as I tightened my grip on the handle.

He raised both hands, in an attempt to calm me, or persuade me he was unarmed. Neither worked.

"It was open," he said.

"Bullshit," I said. I should've known, Josh would be the most likely to track me down, to have the resources to know where I was, to sneak in when I wasn't aware.

He took a tentative step closer, ran his hand back through his dark hair. "I was just going to wait for you, I swear. I called you, but it turns out you changed your number." There was an accusation in his voice, but he was the one currently standing in *my apartment.*

"So excuse me for being a little concerned, given the circumstances," he continued. "I tried the handle and it was unlocked, so I came to check . . ."

"You've been *checking* my bedroom?"

He closed his eyes, shook his head. "Please, can we just talk for a second?"

I had not loosened my grip on the handle. "Outside," I said. "The balcony. I see you've already *checked out there* anyway."

I refused to be trapped with him inside this apartment, with his body between myself and the exit. The balcony overlooked a courtyard. It was Friday night. People would hear.

He tipped his head, then started walking down the hall—*my hall*—past the kitchen, into the living room.

I followed him, unsettled by his familiarity with my apartment, wondering just how long he'd been here. The place was a mess; he'd obviously been through the front rooms first. Cushions out of place, drawers not fully closed, as if he'd been searching for something. My mail was spread out on the coffee table, scattered, like it had been rifled through.

"Jesus," I said.

"I was going to clean up . . ."

"Oh my god, seriously, Josh? When did you get here? *How* did you get here?" I asked, as he slid the balcony door fully open.

He paused, looking back over his shoulder, eyes narrowed. "We all left last night, Cassidy. After you and Grace didn't come back. It seemed like the right thing to do."

Meanwhile, I'd stayed at a hotel, then dropped Grace, visited

Ian's family, and stopped at the school, before returning here. Josh practically had a day's lead on me.

"You came straight here?" I asked, stepping out onto the balcony with him.

"No, no. I went home, and . . ." He frowned, lowering himself into one of the wrought iron chairs. There was only a wooden rail separating us from a three-story fall. My stomach plummeted as I took the other seat. I had thought him more words than action, but now he was *here* in my house. I wanted more space—from him, and from the edge. I pushed the chair back, closer to the door. The quickest way to the exit—

"Something came for me, in the mail." He took an envelope out of his jacket, turned it over in his hands. The top had been torn open, but the contents looked to still be in place. "It was just waiting for me, at home. And I thought . . . I can't be the only one."

"So you drove to my place?" I asked, incredulous. "And *checked*?"

"You're the closest one now."

I stared at him, until he finally met my gaze.

"You've kept tabs on me, Josh?"

"It's not hard to find someone's address, Cassidy. It's not like you were hiding." And then, after a pause, "Were you?"

I ignored the question and gestured to the envelope in his lap. "And? What is it?"

"It's about that night. It's about . . ." He shook his head, as if he was avoiding the thought.

All I could picture was the knife in my bag, pressed up against my leg. I imagined it in Josh's hand that night, instead. I imagined him at Ian's, searching for it after he died, just as he was searching my place now too. I tightened my grip on the bag.

"Well? Did you get what you came for, Josh?"

He laughed, one bark that echoed out into the night. "There's nothing here," he said, as if the absence implied something else.

"Josh, I don't know what you're doing here, what you're hoping to find."

"The letter. It was postmarked from the Outer Banks, earlier this week."

He waited for me to understand the implication. "You think it's from one of us?"

He stared back at me, as if my questions would tell him all he needed to know. He must be skilled at reading people, at getting them to admit things, at twisting an argument.

"I don't understand. What is it?" I asked, gesturing to the letter. There was black ink on the outside, his name, written in boxy print. Like the handwriting on the note I'd found in my room. *GET OUT NOW.*

Even hundreds of miles away, it still sent a chill through me.

He ran his hand back through his hair again. "It's details from that night. From the accident. It's about me. I think . . . I think this is what they're going to share. Or publish. Whoever it is. My part of it, at least."

I felt a cool gust of wind, goose bumps rising on my arms. "The tell-all?"

He nodded once, jaw clenched, mouth a flat line.

The chair legs squeaked as he shifted my way, leaning on the armrest, his face suddenly so close. "There are only so many people who could've known this, Cassidy." His voice was low and rapid, his gaze fixed firmly on mine, as if he was trying to read something in me. "And you didn't get anything in the mail."

"What, you think *I'm* the one talking?"

He shrugged, a crack in his harsh exterior, calling back to his youth, the person he used to be. "You don't respond to emails. You changed your number. You can see how this looks, right?" He raised his hands, as if he were displaying the pieces of evidence in a trial. A compelling closing argument.

Panic and indignation rose within me, momentarily displacing the fear.

"It wasn't me," I said. "All I know is *you* work for the people who interviewed us. Maybe someone there is responsible instead."

"Not possible," he said, leaning back in his chair, shutting down the line of questioning.

"How do you know?"

"Because it's in their best interest that none of this gets out, Cassidy. Do you know what it would look like for them? They didn't only represent us. They also represented the dead. What do you think it would look like if the daughter of a partner was potentially involved? They'd be implicated in a cover-up. Trust me, they don't want this getting out, any more than the rest of us."

The sound of laughter echoed from below, shadows moving in the lights that lined the sidewalk.

"The law firm," I said. "Amaya's family. They know. They know what happened out there, don't they?" It was the first time I was sure.

He didn't confirm, but he didn't deny either.

"Who told them?" I imagined all of us as teens, in the conference room with the lawyer, one by one.

He still didn't answer, and for a moment I thought it was because he didn't know. Until I realized that Josh only didn't answer when he didn't want to admit something. "It was you?"

"No," he said quickly. "No, it wasn't." He placed his foot against the railing, tipped his chair back, then let it drop. "But not for lack of trying. Did you ever wonder how I got that job, Cassidy?"

I hadn't, really. I'd been surprised, of course. He went from barely graduating to finishing law school and being offered a full-time position with Amaya's family's company. But we'd all changed.

"I saw an opportunity, and I took it. For once, I saw it coming."

Josh's meaning, suddenly apparent. What he had done to change his life. The opportunity unveiling itself.

Blackmail. Such a stark, cliché word.

"You threatened them?"

"No, see, I didn't have to say anything at all. It was obvious they already knew. I showed up and they offered me an internship, a scholarship, a position. Like they knew exactly what I was there for. I thought it must've been Amaya, but . . . now I'm not so sure."

"Who, then?"

He tapped his foot against the floor. "Clara. She went back to them, before she died."

Clara, who died on the one-year anniversary.

"This winter," I said, "Amaya must've found out they knew." I said it as a fact, though it was a question. But Josh must've come to the same conclusion. It made sense, the timing, the rift.

If Amaya found out that, all along, her father had known the truth about that night and had kept it a secret, for *her*, it was a debt she could never repay. The way her family must've looked at her. The things they must've thought.

"She must've thought you told them, since you were working there," I said. She probably put it together, how Josh rose to his position.

He rubbed the side of his face, fingers absently pausing on his scar.

"Josh, Amaya's family . . . Would they do something, if they thought the details would get out?" Who else could make Amaya disappear? Who else could scare her into running like that?

"No," he said quickly. "I can assure you, no."

"How can you be so sure?"

"Because when I went to them, they gave me a job with zero hesitation. Because when Brody got arrested last year in a bar fight, they made it go away. Because, every year, they ask Amaya to come back, and every year she doesn't, and they still donate money to her foundation."

But that all sounded like they were keeping us in line, more than anything. Promises with their generosity. Threats with their reach. He was too close to see it.

Clara told them, and she was dead.

Ian had the knife, and now he was dead.

And now Amaya was missing . . .

He stood abruptly, legs of the chair crying against the decking. He leaned over the rail, staring over the edge, and I got a sense of vertigo, that he was looking somewhere else, another time, another place.

"Let's go," I said, wanting him away from the edge. He stayed there for another beat, two, before turning and following me back inside.

He paused inside my apartment, taking everything in.

"It had to be Ian, Cassidy. It had to be him."

"Josh, he wouldn't."

Except, maybe he would. How much we each had changed from the people we'd once been. And addiction, it made different people of us. Maybe he needed the money. It had run out for many of them already.

"Why do you think no one has contacted you?" he continued.

I shook my head, not wanting to believe it.

"I know how close you were," he continued.

He was right: It only made sense if it was Ian. Maybe he wanted to protect me.

"But he's dead, and it's still happening." Like whatever he started had taken on a life of its own.

"I don't think we can stop it now," he said, as if he'd already resigned himself.

We stood in silence for a long moment, until finally, I spoke.

"I found something, at Ian's," I said, in my own confession.

He turned quickly. "What did you find?"

I stared back at him. I didn't need to say it. He knew. He'd been looking.

He moved his jaw, back and forth, a slow clicking. "I saw him pick it up that night," he said. "I didn't know he still had it, but yeah, I looked. I knew I wouldn't be the only one looking."

Ian had kept all the secrets. But now I held some too.

"Are you going to tell?" I asked.

Something twitched in his jaw, a sign of emotion, a tell.

"I've owed you for a very long time, Cassidy," he said, and suddenly, we were back. All it ever took was a sentence fragment, a pulse of memory. The night, the dark, the water. Hands connecting in the terror.

I didn't answer. It was the first time he'd ever acknowledged it. And maybe that was why he'd hated me for so long. It was an irredeemable debt.

"I consider us even," he said.

I nodded once, a new pact. A promise.

He tapped the edge of the envelope against the kitchen countertop.

"Are you going to read it to me?" I asked.

He shook his head, looked away. "I can't." Then he took a deep breath, pushed his shoulders back. "I'm on my way to find Amaya," he said.

"Where?"

"To the Stone River Gorge." *I'm going back.* "To her place, to wait for her. I want to make sure she's okay."

I felt myself softening. "You're not such an asshole after all, Josh Doleman."

Another twitch of his mouth, another crack in the facade. "Do us both a favor and don't pretend. We both know that's not true."

I grabbed a piece of paper from the nearest drawer, wrote down my cell number. "Let me know when you get there. When you find her. Just, let me know, okay?"

Josh seemed to be thinking it through, then dropped the envelope on the table. "Keep it," he said.

"Why?"

"It's nothing you don't know," he said.

I swallowed nothing, imagining the horrors within. And then not needing to imagine them at all.

"So it's the truth?" I asked.

"It's true enough. It's the type of truth that only comes from someone on the inside. They did their research on the rest." He stopped at my door. "It's not just about what happened. It's about me. If that tell-all happens, everyone's going to know what I did."

"You didn't do anything, Josh," I said.

"I know that, Cassidy Bent. Trust me, I know."

THEN

HOUR 2

Joshua

Joshua Doleman was sleeping when it happened, which was completely on trend with his life to date. He had been sleeping when the bus stopped at his house on the very first day of high school freshman year, his mother barreling him out of bed and pushing him out the door—so that he showed up to school with nothing but the clothes he'd woken up in, setting the tone for the four years to come.

He'd been sleeping when his name was called in the auditorium his junior year for some high score on a national test he barely remembered taking. And he had been sleeping in the back of the classroom when the college counselors went over the requirements for graduation, which was how he'd ended up with an email the week earlier, warning him that he did not have the required volunteer hours needed to receive his diploma.

And now he was here—flying, *falling*. Suddenly unsure whether he was dreaming or not.

His body hit the seat in front of him, and then the ceiling. Two consecutive thuds, and he couldn't take a breath—the air knocked from his lungs. And then, suddenly, he could, in a flash of pain that resonated down his spine. He heard a ringing in his ears, or was that a scream?

How he survived, he would never be sure. Some instinct, displacing the fear? Compensating for the lack of knowledge, his careless lack of seat belt—a half dream, where his body knew what to do. A cat, its body twisting to land, by pure instinct, on all fours.

It didn't matter that the van was upside down, that he was scrambling along the underside of the roof, that there was water coming in from below, seeping in from every possible gap. He didn't know how long he'd been feeling along the edges around him as the waters rose, pushing at the corners, desperate for an exit.

He did know that the water pouring in meant there had to be an opening he might be able to escape through, but the force of the rushing water kept pushing him back. The panic kicked in when he felt along the cracks of the glass window, kicking, but unable to get enough leverage in the rising water. Like a dream, when everything was in slow motion.

And then, miraculously, the glass was shattering. But the force of the water was sending shards of glass inward, all around him, in the water now. He felt it in the bite of his palm as he reached out. And then a sharp cut on his cheek. He gasped on instinct, taking in too much water. It was too dark, and he couldn't find the way.

He was panicking, and he couldn't orient himself, and he wondered if it would be so bad, really, to sleep forever—

A hand had him under the arm then. There was another person in the dark, pulling him. And he let himself go, let himself ride the current, his lungs starting to burn.

And suddenly his head was above the water, and he was hooked to some girl, the girl who had been beside him in the van, tucked into the corner of the back seat—Cassidy Bent—and she was screaming something at him. "Josh! Grab the . . . Don't let go!" But half her words were swallowed up in the river water. He was choking on it, spinning in a circle. A whirlpool, where he couldn't orient himself.

He wasn't sure what he was supposed to grab, and in the presence of too many decisions, he did what he always did, which was nothing at all. But Cassidy had him under the arm still, and she'd wrapped herself around a branch, or a log, and Josh felt the water rushing by him, around him. Cassidy pulled him closer, and suddenly they were in mud, on earth, on solid ground. Joshua was heaving on all fours.

Behind them, the van had come to rest against something beneath the water, the headlights still on, shining just over the surface, wheels protruding from the river.

Josh had collapsed onto his side, but she was still yelling at him.

"We have to go back!" she said, before coughing violently.

Josh looked toward the light—the van was caught in an eddy, a tree trunk blocking its forward progress.

"Josh, wake up!"

He heard the metal groaning, two opposing forces. He knew how this would go. Basic physics, a math equation written on the board, an answer in his head that he never bothered sharing.

It wouldn't hold for long, and then they'd all be gone.

"Come on!" she yelled, but he didn't move. He didn't do anything at all. Sometimes Josh felt like there was a disconnect between his mind and his body. That it took him too long to realize he needed to move. He was better when he wasn't thinking, when he wasn't overwhelmed with options and possibilities. When he was asleep, and the van was in motion, and somehow he just knew what to do.

Cassidy left him there and trudged back up the riverbank, toward the van. He knew how this would go too. She would go in and wash away with all the rest, and he would be it, the only survivor. Least likely to be here, least likely to graduate, least likely to amount to anything at all. But it would be him.

He went as close as he dared, to the edge, gripping on to a tree root extending from the river. He watched as she walked along the edge, peering into the river.

And then she disappeared under its surface. Josh stared at the spot she'd just been. He stared and counted the beats of his heart resounding in his head, but still he didn't move.

And then she resurfaced again, on the other side of the log, flowing down the river again. There was another head beside hers, gasping for air. Ian Tayler, who used to play video games in his basement, in another lifetime.

Cassidy was screaming at Josh again. "Help us!" They were floating by, and Josh was hanging on to that same fucking tree root. And it was Cassidy herself who had to reach out and grab him instead. Her hand hooked around his waist, so that he had to grab her in response, lest he get pulled down with them.

She clawed at him, and he felt the pressure of the river pulling them all. He was sure she was going to kill them all, for nothing. For Ian Tayler, of all people.

But then Ian had hold of the roots behind him, and they were free of the current.

There was no moment of relief, no time to process. Ian turned back to the dark river and yelled, "What about the rest of them?"

Cassidy and Ian were staring at each other when the van suddenly dislodged from the eddy. There was no going after it. The van disappeared from sight before it rounded the bend, lights first, and then tires, sinking under the water. And the last thing Josh could see in the headlights was Ian's face, his mouth open in a frozen scream. And Cassidy, mask of horror and disgust, turning to face Josh.

He could read enough into it: *Such a useless piece of shit—*

This was not supposed to be his story.

He braced for the brunt of her anger, for her rage, but she just ignored him. She pulled Ian, who was shaking and possibly in shock, farther back from the water.

And then they sat there, in silence. As if they would hear someone else coming back. As if the others from the van would meet them there. He had no idea how long they stayed like that, immobile at the edge of the river, waiting.

Finally they did hear something. But it wasn't from that direction. It was from behind them.

Cassidy was on her feet. "The other van," she was saying.

Ian stood, though he seemed unsteady, unfocused, like Josh.

They walked single file, but Josh couldn't get his bearings. He placed his feet where Ian's had been before him. But he couldn't figure out how they had come to be in a river, at night. How they were now trekking through a gathering of trees and rocks and mud. How there appeared to be a dark, dark cavern surrounding them, and only the faint glow of the moon behind the dark, dark cloud cover.

"Where are we?" he finally asked. "What's happening?"

At first no one answered, just their steps crunching roots and mud. "There was an accident," Cassidy finally said.

"I can see that," Josh said, picking up his pace. "But where the hell are we?"

"We went off the highway in the traffic jam, looking for a rest area," she said. Then she stopped abruptly, turned to face him. "You don't remember? Did you hit your head in the crash?"

He had slept through all of it. Vaguely registered lights turning on in the van, doors sliding open and shut. But that could've been as much a dream as flying through the air, as walking through the muddy riverbank. He'd been curled up against a window, feet extended as far as he could, nudging against Cassidy's bag that she'd put up as a divider, a deterrent for his long legs, stretching across the bench seat.

"There was something in the road," Ian said, though his gaze was still faraway, lost. "I saw it."

Cassidy turned back, kept walking. "There, look," she said. She sucked in a gasp, or a laugh. "I think they're okay." She started moving faster. The other van had somehow come to rest right side up, like it had driven down an incline, as opposed to catapulting through the dark night.

But someone was crying, loud gasping sobs. And Josh didn't think everything was okay, as they made their way closer.

He purposely slowed his steps. He sensed Ian doing the same.

"What did you see?" Josh asked Ian quietly.

"It came out of nowhere." Ian's gaze was faraway, up toward the top of the ravine, the place where the dark rocks faded into the sky. "A deer."

And then he heard it: Grace Langly was screaming for their teacher. It was the first thing he saw, on the other side of the river. Mr. Kates, slumped over the steering wheel. The terrible luck of where he'd been sitting. The violence of it all.

Whatever adrenaline had propelled him to this moment had finally begun wearing off, and he felt the swelling around the cut on his face; the bruising on his wrists, from where he'd desperately pounded at glass and metal. He noticed the way Ian was holding his arm, like it had been dislocated.

He remembered those terrible moments of panic, before he'd been pulled from the van.

Before he had been saved.

He had been closest to the exit at the back window. That's all there was to it. That's all there really was, between life and death.

For the first time in a long time, he was wide awake.

SATURDAY

CHAPTER 19

I was back at the river. Choking on storm water, on river water, as I hauled Josh to shore. Desperately racing back for Ian. Reaching for him, again and again, feeling the cold of his hand as he slipped away from my fingertips this time—

The phone on my bedside table was vibrating, and I bolted upright in bed. It was later than I thought, and I was startled by the midmorning daylight, trying to tear myself away from that night.

My first thought, as I pulled the phone to my face, was: *Amaya.*

But my eyes focused on a text from Russ: *I'm sorry, had a family emergency, had to drive to their place.*

And another: *Are you home?*

I texted back, *I'm home*, then watched, waiting for it to show as delivered. Everything felt on a delay, as if I were stuck in a current, in quicksand, the geography shifting beneath my feet. As if the distance of this week had officially been too much. Like I wouldn't ever be able to make it back to the person I used to be.

The only other person who had checked in yesterday was Jillian, sending a text to ask if I was okay. A subtle reminder, or maybe a genuine worry, that I had not done the things I had promised this week. It was unlike me. Unlike the person she knew me to be, at least.

No one else had reached out. Not Josh, to let me know whether he arrived at Amaya's. Not Grace, checking in to see if I'd made it the rest of the way home.

I wondered if anyone else had received a letter.

I wondered if they understood, like Josh had.

I pushed myself out of bed, stomach twisting—I'd finished a bottle of wine last night. Needed the first glass to make it through the letter to Josh the first time. Needed the rest to make it through again and again.

I could recite it by heart now, the words resounding in my head. Even the first time I read it, I knew what was coming, like a whispered echo.

Josh was right that this information could have come only from me or from Ian. We were the only ones there. Hollis had escaped the sinking van on her own, and later made her way back to the rest of us once Grace lit that flare. The only people who knew what had happened with Josh and Ian were the three of us.

The only people who knew I had pulled Josh from the van were the two of us.

Someone other than Josh had been through my apartment.

I'd kept the journals at the bottom of my fireproof safe for as long as I could remember. Underneath my passport, my birth certificate, my social security card. Hidden safely under the legal settlement and my bank paperwork. As if I were offering all this up first, should someone come looking.

But all of this was undisturbed, and still the bottom of the safe was empty. My passport, my birth certificate, my signed settlement—all accounted for. But where there had once been a flattened layer of journals was now just an exposed metal base, dust gathered in the corners.

The only things missing were the books.

The proof.

Why did no one contact me? Why did no one reach out, as they had to Oliver, to Josh, to Hollis? It was a question that had nagged Josh, and bothered me.

And now I understood.

They didn't have to reach out to me, because they already had everything they needed.

A familiar type of fear gripped me—a fear that this was all my responsibility, and I was too slow, too late to stop it. To save them.

When was the last time I'd seen the missing journals? Before a trip to Europe last summer, when I'd needed that passport?

The key was still here, tucked safely away in my nightstand drawer, under the book I'd been reading. I didn't think Josh would have replaced it so carefully, seeing how the rest of the apartment had been disturbed. I would've seen the journals on him before he left, if he was the one who took them.

No, this wasn't Josh.

I splashed water on my face, orienting myself, and desperately circled through the rest of my apartment again. Checking places already checked, against all logic and reason, as if I might've misplaced the journals in my memory.

I checked the boxes in the closet, the space under my bed, the upper kitchen cabinets, as if, in my subconscious, I had moved them and forgotten.

But the journals were gone.

Everything was my fault. My responsibility. I felt the pounding in my chest, the sinking of my stomach, the same feeling when I'd shared them with Ian, for the first time, back in that summer when we were together. Giving voice to something that had only lived inside me, the expectation and thrill of putting it out into the world.

The look on his face was a fraction of how he'd looked at the river that night. Confusion. Surprise. Horror.

We all had our own ways of coping. He should've known that—I was *sure* he understood that. But in the end, he really didn't approve of mine.

• • •

In the months after the accident, I'd written it all out, in a desperate attempt to understand.

I'd been in Brody Ensworth's creative writing elective the year before. I'd sat behind Joshua Doleman on the bus for three straight years. I'd lived down the street from Oliver King. Hollis March was partnered with me as a guide when she entered school; we ate lunch together until she got swept up into Brody's world. And I'd been part of this Volunteer Club with Amaya for the entirety of our high school career, had heard her talk about her family as if it defined her as well. I felt like I knew them all.

It was my therapist who asked me to do this, to try imagining someone else out there that night, instead of me. So I might give them the grace and empathy I should give myself.

But something had happened out there, some darkness I couldn't shake. The words poured out of me in a fever dream. I had always loved to write, but this wasn't the same. It wasn't an outlet, but a compulsion—an obsession. I couldn't get the words down fast enough, as if they would slip from my grasp if I didn't get them down immediately. I needed to turn my fragmented memories into something concrete and real.

Ian was the one person I trusted, so I showed the journals to him near the end of the summer, when I was finished, hoping he could help me fill in the blanks. That, with his help, I could piece the rest of the night together. So that we could both understand.

But I'd misjudged the depths of his understanding and acceptance.

You can't. You can't write it down, Cassidy. My god, what the hell are you thinking? Why do you know all of this about everyone?

He looked at me then like he was seeing me for the first time. And maybe he was. He hadn't noticed me in four years of school. So many of them hadn't.

I promised him I'd get rid of them, but I knew instantly that something had been severed between us. I'd forgotten that he had a history with so many of them from before. That Ian had grown up on a street with some of these people, had been close in a way I was not. That he had other allegiances, other reasons to keep them safe.

Destroy them, he'd said. *Promise me.*

I said I would. Back then I wanted to do anything he asked. But I kept them instead, for the same reason, I now understood, that he must've kept that knife. Proof that it happened. Proof, should we need it. A level of protection; an accusation, ready in response. A way out.

The journals had never been far from my sight. They'd come to college, stuffed in the top of my closet; they'd continued to my first apartment that I shared with a roommate from school; and they'd followed me here. A comfort, in their proximity. I hadn't read them in nearly a decade, and so the words in Josh's letter lingered in the air, familiar and not.

But now I saw that Ian was right. I should've destroyed them. Out of my hands, they had taken on a life of their own—a force I couldn't stop.

What if someone thought I had given them freely, as Josh implied? How many others would recognize me in the background of every scene? That the threads of information followed only my path that night?

My hands shook as I found Josh's number and tried calling him—no answer.

The only other people I could think to call were Amaya's parents, but their home was unlisted. The only public number was the listing for Andrews & Andrews. It was a Saturday; I assumed they'd be closed. Still, I imagined they must've had someone checking their answering machine.

I left a message, curt and to the point. "Hi, this message is for Mr. Andrews. This is Cassidy Bent. I'm worried about Amaya. She was with us this week, but she left, and no one has heard from her since. I can't get ahold of her. Please, let me know if you've heard anything."

All these people I felt were my responsibility. A list of names, to keep track of. To ensure they were okay. There were so many people I couldn't help any longer:

Jason, Trinity, Morgan, Ben.

Clara.

Ian.

I wished I understood what Ian was doing at The Shallows, before he died. I wished I could see who he contacted, or who had contacted him. Whether it was through text or email or personal letter. Whether it was through Instagram, like for Hollis. Or email, for Oliver. It seemed like the method most likely to rattle each person.

I should've taken the slips of paper from his room and tried them all, so I could get into his email. I plugged his phone into the charger, so I could check again, methodically, folder by folder. Everything was enabled for Face ID or asked for a password.

I opened a list of apps, hoping there was something labeled *passwords*—maybe he'd moved on to a method like this, instead of stuffing scraps of paper into his desk.

But I found only an assortment of games and social media apps. Even his Notes were empty.

The folder labeled *Home* contained his banking app and a string of food delivery services. But at the very bottom was an app that tugged at something in my memory. Made me look twice.

WatchingHome.

It was the same name as the label on the camera I'd found at The Shallows.

I sat on the edge of my bed, staring at it.

The camera.

Maybe no one had been using it to watch us this week.

Maybe that camera belonged to Ian.

I opened the app now, holding my breath, except he must've had Face ID enabled here too. I didn't know the password. I tried his birthday, since his mom said he was always forgetting passwords, needing to write them down—

And then I raced for my luggage, still out in the hall, near the front door. Now I laid it flat, unzipped the top, and rifled for his familiar jacket, which I'd packed under a layer of my things.

I reached my hand into his pocket and pulled out the receipt from High Tide. It was meaningless; he had no reason to keep it. Just a note he'd written on the other side . . .

The Shallows!

Except, maybe not a note. With shaking hands, I tried it now, in the password prompt, all one word: *TheShallows!*

And suddenly, miraculously, I was in.

My heartbeat resounded inside my head, and the phone was trembling in my hands.

There were several notifications asking for renewal information and for credit card payment. A note popped up warning that the membership had expired.

I ignored the warnings, and instead scrolled to the label marked *Recordings*, hoping there was still something here, despite his lapsed membership.

Several folders popped up. The recordings were labeled by date, organized by most recent. The most recent saved recording was the end of February. He must've paid for only that single month.

I held my breath and pressed play.

The image was like a distorted fishbowl, from the hidden camera angle over the corner shelving unit. There was a widescreen view stretching across the living room and dining room, with the dark stairwell in the distance.

The first sound on the recording—the creak of the front door opening—shattered my nerves.

At 9:10 a.m., a man and a woman carrying various cleaning supplies through the entrance started moving around the living room. I let out a breath. The cleaning company, as Oliver had mentioned. The recording captured them as they crossed back and forth through the room often. They left two hours later.

There were no other triggered recordings until several weeks earlier, on February 5.

The front door creaking open again, this time in the dark. It was the middle of the night, and none of the lights were on, inside or out.

"Hello?" a voice called.

A light suddenly flipped on, and Oliver stood in the entryway, blinking as his eyes adjusted. "Ian?" he called.

My hand went to my mouth. Oliver went to the stairs first, the first place I would've looked—up to his room on the third floor.

It felt like I was walking the steps with Oliver—except I knew what he was about to discover. And yet, I couldn't look away. Some dark path I couldn't free myself from. Eventually, Oliver returned downstairs, and I heard cabinets opening and closing in the kitchen, the sound of running water as he filled up a cup.

He must've thought Ian was not in the house.

And then he came back into camera view. He pulled out a dining room chair, frowning. He'd spotted Ian's backpack, and now he turned it over in his hands, called his name again into the house.

Oliver then carried the bag out of frame, toward the back of the house.

I could only imagine he was heading toward his bedroom. I could only imagine what he saw.

It wasn't in the frame—I didn't see what happened, didn't see the reaction, but I heard it. Heard Oliver calling out his name, just as I would've called it. The horror of it.

It was a sound I had heard only once before from him—screaming Jason's name into the void, after he'd been swept away by the river. A tragedy Oliver must've realized he had set in motion with the vote to send someone into the water, and then with the decision to draw straws. He'd risked then, and he'd lost. The worst had already happened—and he'd survived it.

I closed my eyes, the call of Ian's name rattling my heart. Had Oliver tried to revive him? Or had he decided he was too far gone?

I didn't want to know. These were secrets Oliver could keep.

Eventually he came out of the room and sat on the living room couch with his head in his hands. He stayed like that for so long I believed the feed had frozen.

And then he stood abruptly, hooked Ian's bag onto his shoulder, and disappeared from view. The light turned off, and the recording stopped.

I didn't know what happened to Ian's phone then. Whether Oliver had taken it, or it was left inside the house. Whether someone had been there earlier. And I was scared, for once, to know the truth.

Wasn't that the truth with all of us, though? We didn't *really* want to know. Not anymore. We didn't want to know who had hurt Ben, with a knife. We didn't want to think about the way we had circled Brody, almost forcing him into the water. How we heard Trinity yelling after us as we walked away. We didn't want to know what happened to any of them after we left—and I suddenly didn't want to know what happened to Ian.

He'd been paranoid, his mother said, after Clara's death. What if that wasn't an effect of his addiction, but the cause?

I owed it to him. Of course, I owed it to him to bear witness. I owed them all so much. I had to watch. Who else was left to do it?

On the WatchingHome app, I navigated to the day before—the first day of any recording. The first thing I saw was Ian's face, so close, like a funhouse mirror. Large brown eyes and hair cropped short and his teeth caught on his lower lip. He was adjusting the camera, brown eyes staring directly into the lens as he stood on a chair.

I could tell from his expression that something was off. He exuded a nervous energy, gaze a little wild—a little too intense. He flinched as his eyes seemed to latch on to mine, his pupils wide. I held my breath, imagining he was seeing me, across time—*I'm here*—before realizing he must've just caught sight of his own reflection.

He was so close. So close I felt I could reach out an arm for him, one last time.

Then he stepped off the chair, ran his hand through his short hair, the tremble of his hand visible as he did. I pulled the phone closer to my face, like I was losing him. Like the current was taking him away. Like I'd reached for him one last time, and missed.

He checked his phone, looked back up at the camera, like he was making sure everything was working correctly. Then he went to the front window, peering out.

I could hear his voice, thought he must've been talking on a phone I couldn't see. I turned up the volume, leaned closer—but it seemed he was talking to himself. His words were indecipherable, but the cadence unsettling. Haunting.

Ian was spiraling, and no one was there to help him. I hadn't made it. Oliver hadn't made it. There was no one there to stop his descent. No one there, even, to witness it.

Ian came in and out of frame often, but nothing was happening. Nothing but his own descent, the pacing increasing, pausing only as he peered out windows in something that verged on obsession, or paranoia.

I scrolled forward, watching as he paced from the front window and then back to the kitchen, as if he was waiting for someone.

Finally, as he was standing at the front window, something seemed to jar him. He turned abruptly, staring toward the back of the house.

I rewound, watched again, listened closer.

A knock on the back door.

As if whoever he had been expecting came around the back, instead of the front.

Ian cast a quick glance toward the camera, before crossing out of frame, to the back of the house.

There were two voices, but I could only hear Ian's clearly. I had turned the volume all the way up, and could tell how he was trying to project, while the other person was not.

"Yes, I have it. Yes, this is where we meet."

My god, Ian, what did you have? What were you giving away?

Ian entered the frame, as if he was trying to lure the other person into view. As if this was his plan all along—to catch them.

A way out. A way to protect us. To save us.

"Why were you at the back door? Where's your car?" he asked.

"I'm staying at the campground." A man's voice, soft but determined. Something familiar in the cadence. I cycled through their faces: Oliver, Brody, Josh. Will? Nothing clicked into place.

The campground. Where Oliver believed he'd seen someone heading on the beach that night. Someone Amaya might've seen, days earlier. And someone who might've seen Amaya there, after she left us . . .

"Can I see your phone? I mean, it sounds like you're recording me." The voice had shifted, a little nervous, a little confrontational. I couldn't be the only one noticing Ian's unstable demeanor.

"I'm not," Ian said, but I watched as he placed it on the kitchen counter, arm extended out of frame. It was gone, possession passing like Oliver's knife the night of our accident.

There was a long stretch of silence, where the other man must've been looking at Ian's phone. Finally he said, "Can I get a drink?"

Ian disappeared from frame, voices faded and harder to hear.

Finally, Ian reentered the frame, like he was trying, desperately, to move the conversation toward the front of the house. Catch it on the camera. His plan, all along.

"You said you would help," the other man said. "You said you had it."

How quickly this was turning. Ian was not going to help. I could see that from the start. He was trying, against all odds, to save us. And he was in no shape to do it alone.

"Listen, they're not bad people," he said. "You don't understand." The same way I would've claimed it, believed it even. Because we made a pact, and to admit otherwise would force you to go back, look again, to unearth the truth.

"They are *very* bad people," the other voice said, louder now.

"You know how I know that? My sister told me. Before she died, she told me that."

The word buzzed in my head. *Sister.* How many people could have told him that? Grace, Hollis, *Clara.*

There's only one person Ian would've felt compelled to help, other than us. The only other survivor, who was no longer here. Clara. Her picture taped to the back of ours. He would've done this for Clara.

"You don't understand," Ian was saying, voice rising. "You weren't there."

"Clara was, though. And she told me. She told me you had all done terrible things—herself included. She didn't want to talk about it. After she died, I kept an eye on you all—"

"You've been *watching* us?"

A pause. "Checking in," he said. "Just seeing what you were up to. There's so much information available online . . ."

I got a chill as he spoke, thinking he was keeping tabs on us, just as I had been doing over the years. Scrolling social media feeds, reading job announcements, searching our names and locations.

"I felt like I knew you all. But Clara protected you, and so would I. And then I got the invitation for that ridiculous memorial library dedication. I showed up, and you know what I noticed? There's not one mention of Clara. *Nothing.* She's not one of you, and she's not one of them." His voice, for the first time, grew louder. "How does she not count as a victim? How are we not part of the victim compensation settlement? I went to the lawyers while I was in town, to try and get Clara included, and they shot me down immediately. Total bullshit. I'm not gonna lie, Ian, I could really use that money right about now . . ."

"I know," Ian said. "Trust me, it's been a hard time for all of us. We could all use some help."

The other man laughed, something mean, angry. "At the dedication, they had some pictures out, of that first-year anniversary.

That fucking memorial, where they rang the bells. She had insisted on going. The day she died, remember?"

Silence.

"You know what I saw in those pictures?"

Still, he didn't respond, as if he already knew.

"So many of you were also there. You and Grace and Josh Doleman. Brody and Hollis. Amaya Andrews. Oliver King."

The hair on the back of my neck stood on end. My parents had moved by then, and I had stayed far, far away. But they had each been there, or they had returned. As if there had been a pact, even before I was a member.

"You know what *I* think?"

Again, Ian didn't respond.

"I think Clara was trying to tell the truth. And now she's dead."

"It's been nine years," Ian was saying, a defense, a desperation. "Please, stop this—it's *torment*." I could feel it in Ian's voice, the way he was being tormented by this man. And this was his only way out. He was stuck in a spiral, and there was no one there, no one who would pull him out this time—

"Yeah, imagine that," the man continued. "Nine years, and she's all but forgotten. Another thing in the past you're all sweeping under the rug."

"No, we didn't."

But I heard his mother's warning, Ian's paranoia: *I'm going to be next*—

"Clara told me you were the one person who knew what happened that night."

"No, I don't."

"She told me you were the one with proof. That you had evidence. That it was all written down somewhere, and you told her. She needed you, Ian. She needed you on her side. And now I do."

I felt something coming. Something closing in. A rumble of thunder. A warning, a portent.

"I don't have it anymore," he said, though I knew that was a lie. He'd hidden the knife, to keep it safe. The safest place he knew. "And I'm not the one who wrote it all down. I saw it once, but that was a really long time ago—"

"Who? Who had it?"

"Cassidy, but they're *gone* now—I swear it."

Oh, Ian, no.

My name, a thread to follow. He'd sent this man my way, and he got what he needed after all.

"So then what are we even doing here?"

Silence, as the realization settled in. Ian was never going to deliver. He was not there for him. He was there, once more, for us.

"Let's go out for a walk, Ian." I heard the back door open and close, and the video faded to black. There was no motion ever triggered again. Whatever happened after they left, Ian had never made it back to the living room.

There was no proof.

He was never in frame. Never. But that voice . . .

I clutched the necklace hanging around my neck, felt the cold metal in the center of the palm of my hand. The interlocking circles, the letter *C*.

There's a moment, when your mind rebels against what it knows to be true. A van hurtling through space in the night; water rushing higher and higher, chasing you, consuming everything. When it comes up with a thousand other possibilities instead.

I took Ian's picture of us, from that first year at The Shallows, and I turned it over. Clara, smiling into the sun, light catching off her necklace—

And still, I didn't want to believe. The letter *C*.

The man who said, *I saw this and thought of you*, and hadn't been thinking of me at all.

All along, he'd been thinking of his sister. Clara.

CHAPTER 20

I felt sick—the same type of nausea that came with sudden motion, with disorientation. I stood up, and the room tilted. I took a step, and the floor rolled. My stomach rebelled, and I found myself on the floor of the bathroom, knees pressed into the cool tile, desperate for relief.

Not Russ, who I'd let into my home, my life, my bed.

Not Russ, who had showed up at The Shallows to meet Ian, who wanted something from him—who'd been promised something that Ian didn't deliver.

Who must've then tried to frame Oliver for Ian's death—writing to him from Ian's phone, asking to meet him there.

Who was trying to ruin us.

There was no other way around it. He was trying to destroy us, one by one.

Russ hadn't tried to FaceTime all week. I'd been relieved, thinking he wouldn't find out that I was lying about where I'd gone. But all along, he knew where I was. He knew *exactly* what I was doing.

He'd had Ian's phone. He'd taken Ian's phone the day he died.

I flashed back to Sunday morning, when I was sitting in his kitchen, obviously with no plans of leaving. And then I'd received that text, when I thought he wasn't looking. When he was busy sending it instead.

He needed me to go. He needed me to go to The Shallows, because he was heading there too.

Still, I needed to be sure.

I searched his name—Russ Johnson—and the college; nothing came up. But then, he'd said he was filling in as needed. It's possible he wouldn't be on their website. I took a deep breath and searched Clara's name instead, then clicked on her obituary, scrolling the details.

Clara Poranto, 19. Survived by her parents, Louis and Jane Poranto; and her brother, Russell J. Poranto—

I couldn't breathe, couldn't slow my racing pulse. I hadn't known Clara's brother—hadn't been to Clara's funeral, hadn't grown up on their street, or overlapped with him at school. But it seemed he knew me—knew me well enough, either through Ian or by keeping tabs, to understand that I would keep him a secret from the others.

But now I pulled up the photos on my phone, scrolled back to a night out at our favorite bar, the same place we'd first met.

I sent it to the one person who I was sure would know. Russ was four years older than we were, but Grace should still know. Grace must've gone to Clara's funeral; they'd been so close. I sent a text: *Do you know who this is?*

And then I stared at my phone, watched as she typed, stopped, typed again. *Yes. That's Clara's brother. Why are you with him??*

I couldn't respond. Why was I with him? Because he'd shown up at my favorite bar, and his eyes caught mine across the room; he asked me if I believed in fate, and I did. Of course I did.

I felt the memory of Grace leaning close to see my necklace, holding it closer, letting the interlocking circles slide between her fingers—like maybe she was searching for the letter *C*. Did she think it was a coincidence? Did she suspect something was off, even then?

I didn't respond, still unsure who to trust. I felt my entire world shifting, like it had when Ian walked away. When I'd misjudged how deep he was in.

When I'd believed he accepted all the parts of me—that, in the end, he'd choose me, save me.

And then I'd fallen so quickly, so readily, for Russ.

Who was this person I thought I knew? I'd believed everything he'd told me. His last name, even. I thought he was too trusting, when really it was me. We were still in the early months of a relationship, before we had the opportunity to meet families, discuss holidays—before we had to get too deep.

I had preferred it that way—someone who focused on the future, instead of the past. I wanted to keep my true past private too. And he'd capitalized on that, used that so callously.

His neighbor said she thought he was *gone*.

As if she'd barely known him too.

As if he'd just slipped into a life briefly. He had a job he could do anywhere, and he'd chosen a place with month-by-month rentals, across the street from my favorite bar. A wave of shame rolled through me now, imagining him watching me, before I met him. Following me, deciding on his angle. Deciding to *notice* me, in a world that had so often failed to do so.

All because Ian had sent him my way for the journals.

I watched the video of Ian's last day again, picturing Russ on the other side of the kitchen island, just out of sight. He talked to Ian like he knew him—and of course he did; they'd grown up down the street from each other.

The person Amaya saw on the beach; the figment we followed back toward the campgrounds; the shadow Oliver saw in the window—they were all Russ. He knew everything about that place. He knew everything about us. Tormenting not only Ian but us. Going through our things, taking Josh's sleeping pills . . . leaving a note for Amaya to get out. He was targeting us, one by one. Sowing discord and paranoia between us all.

Now I imagined him in my apartment, opening my laptop while I was asleep, going through my nightstand while I was in the shower.

In response, I'd given him a key. And I'd just told him *exactly* where to find me.

Was he on his way? Was he *here*?

I had to get out. But where was safe? There was no one to go to. There was a pact, and I had broken it. I had broken it very, very badly.

Ian understood that.

Maybe he had always been trying to protect me. Begging me to destroy them, for my own good.

Clara broke the pact, and she was dead.

Ian had told his mother: *I'm going to be next*. But it had taken nine years. Nine years, for Russ to come for him. To feel the sting of his sister's erasure at the dedication; to be denied his fair compensation; to see a picture that made him believe that something had happened to her, instead. Ian was the first point of contact—the name Clara had given him. And he was the one most likely to crack.

But I had broken our pledge the worst. There was no fixing it. I'd seen how fast they could turn on you. Pushing to send Brody into the water. Blaming Ben for the crash.

If they had figured out the real truth, I was in danger.

I peered out the bedroom window, which overlooked a corner of the lot. I couldn't see if Russ's car was there. There were no windows facing the walkway or landing—everything was oriented toward the back courtyard.

Now I stood on the side of the door, wondering if he was already here. If he was walking up the steps. If I'd open the door and become trapped.

Of course, I was already trapped. He had a key. I was three stories up.

I turned off all the lights in my apartment, imagining him out there. Imagining a knock on the door.

I tried once more to call Josh, but he wasn't answering. And then, as I was watching my phone, a text message arrived. My heart leaped into my throat, seeing the name.

Amaya Andrews.

Finally, *finally*, she was reaching out. Maybe her parents got my message, told her to call us. To let us know she was okay.

I opened the message, read the words on the screen. Three words, that haunting echo. Chilling in their simplicity: *I'm going back*.

• • •

It was three hours to the border, when you'd cross into Tennessee after the tunnel cut through the mountains, like humanity had given up on trying to make our way over and around. Not much farther to Stone River Gorge.

I had avoided it for a decade.

My memory of the crash was dizzying, foggy. A before, to an after. A flashback under a layer of fog, stripped down to its most essential elements.

Josh, sleeping beside me. Ian, head resting on the seat in front of me—

I grabbed my bag, grabbed Ian's phone too, as if I was afraid to leave him behind again. Strength in numbers.

Ian had been trying to save us. Picking up where he'd fallen was the least I could do now. I had to go. There was no other way. This was my responsibility.

Heart pounding, I crept out of my apartment, easing the door shut, so sure that Russ would be right outside, heading this way. But the concrete breezeway was empty. The only person I saw on the way to my car was a man walking his dog. As I darted past, his face faltered, like he could see something off in my demeanor.

I locked my car doors and pulled out quickly. Up the street, I stopped to fill the tank of gas, then started driving.

But the closer I got, the more a new thought emerged: *Confess.* I wondered if it echoed inside all of us. This urge to tell someone else the truth.

Was this the way out? One way or another, was this the only way?

I was shocked by the impulse, after all this time. Maybe it was just this drive. There was something visceral about it, in the way night was falling, just as it had then. It was the same time of year, almost to the day, separated by a decade.

In my journals, I hadn't written about the drive—only the aftermath. After the crash, after the fall. I had tried to track each person, working through the motivations, trying to make sense of it all. I'd written frantically, afraid the memories would leave me, that I'd lose my grip on them, instead of the way they seemed to pull tighter, clarifying with time.

A pull I could feel, drawing me back.

There were the brake lights in the distance, a trail, a ghost. I was Ms. Winslow, or Mr. Kates, riding the brakes, hearing the groans of the students in the back.

Ten years earlier, we first hit the traffic inside a tunnel, and there was a sense of claustrophobia, an omen, a portent. Lights flickering, horns blaring, a steady tension rising.

By the time we made it into eastern Tennessee, we were desperate for a break, for a bathroom.

We'd taken an exit, looking for a rest area. We wove our way up, up, up. Switchback after switchback, but there was nowhere to stop, nowhere to turn around.

Ten years, and I knew exactly where to go, feeling the gravity of it across time and space, latching on to me, pulling tight.

Unlike when I'd just visited my old town, here everything was exactly as I remembered it. If anything, it only gained clarity, only sharpened the memory. The haze lifted, so that I could hear the ghosts of my classmates singing the lines to the latest pop song together, one catching my eye, as if welcoming me to join. But I couldn't; the twists of the road distorted everything.

Now I knew the trick—eyes on a fixed spot in the distance. Track the yellow line in the headlights. Orient yourself to the here and now.

Ten years ago, I'd been sitting in the back of a van, wholly at the whim of the driver, the terrain, the disorienting night.

I pulled onto the shoulder now, set off just before the sign for Stone River Gorge. I didn't know where to go next. I entered Amaya's address into my GPS—I'd had her address from years of keeping tabs—and was directed to a house less than a mile away.

Her house was down a fork in another direction, following the curve of the river.

I pulled into the drive, careful to put my high beams on in the dark, to see where the edges were, the gravel rock, the open air.

Josh's car was already in the driveway. The garage was closed, though; the house was dark.

Outside, I heard the sound of the river—something not quite as harrowing as in my memory. But then, there'd been the storm, the current as violent and as unpredictable as us.

I couldn't understand how she could live here. A daily punishment, a perpetual reminder. A horror interlude every time she peered out the back windows.

I stood at the entrance of the drive, staring off down the road, at the curve I'd just come in on, the thicket of trees.

We were not in the place where we'd gone off the road—that was higher up the series of switchbacks. Instead, I believed we were closer to the place where we were ultimately found.

The truck screeching to an abrupt stop. Josh, pulling Clara tight, telling her to be quiet. A man stepping down from the driver's side, calling for help. Counting us, one by one, in the glow of his headlights.

All along, I'd had it wrong. This wasn't a place of punishment, but of triumph. Somewhere, behind her house, against all odds, we'd climbed. We'd clawed our way out. We'd saved ourselves, and each other.

Of course I would come for her now.

There was a flash of light in a window at the edge of her house.

The only light I could see. Like a signal, or a warning. Like Oliver in the night, shining the light at each of us, one by one. Making sure we were still there.

I noticed the front door was open, a darkness within, beckoning. When I stepped inside, I could see straight through the house, just like at The Shallows. The back door was open, wind funneling from outside, straight to the front. I turned at the sound of rustling, but it was just papers on a side table, caught in a gust.

I ran my hand along the wall, searching for a light switch, the terror rising. But once more I was caught—and stuck—in darkness.

CHAPTER 21

"Amaya?" I called into the dark house, my voice sounding unfamiliar, haunting. "Josh?"

I used the flashlight on my phone to illuminate the room. There was no sign of anyone here. I crossed the living space, toward the hall, heading closer to the place where I'd seen the light flashing in the window.

"Hello?" I called again. I found a lamp in the living room, turned it on, and a dim yellow glow lit up the room.

The door to the bedroom down the hall was also open. I shone my torch around, taking in the unmade bed, Amaya's luggage on the floor.

A light flashed just beside the window, a blue glow reflecting in the glass. I crossed the room to get a closer look—it was Amaya's phone, lighting up with notifications. It flashed again, and I noticed a missed call from Oliver, texts from Brody, from Hollis.

Hold on

I'm on my way

I'm coming

Her message, just like Clara's, must've gone out to all of us.

This time, we would all come for her.

"Amaya?" I called, louder this time. I started moving faster, no longer worried about trespassing, about invading her space.

I exited out the back door, the sound of wind chimes like rain falling on a tin roof growing louder.

"Josh!" I called, but my voice was swallowed up by the sound of the wind and the river.

I stepped deeper into the yard, flashlight illuminating the trees ahead of me. Eventually I came to a path: a series of rock steps built into the side of the ravine, leading down, down, down. I called their names again, listened to my voice echo back.

At the back of the property, there was also a shed, glass windows where I thought I caught a sign of movement. But then the glare of headlights shone on the glass instead. Another car, turning into the driveway.

I crossed back through the house.

From just inside the entryway, the first person I saw was Grace, stepping out of the passenger side, staring back at me.

"Grace!" I called.

I took a step outside.

"Cassidy?" she called in return. As if she was confused to see me here.

And then Brody exited the driver's side. "Where's Amaya?" he asked, striding across the drive.

"I don't know. She's not in the house."

Brody opened his trunk, pulled out the high-powered flashlight he stored for emergencies, and lit up the front yard in a way that I could not.

Another car pulled in right behind them, as if they'd come in a caravan. Oliver and Hollis, and that was all of us.

Of course we all came.

"Josh is here?" Oliver asked.

"He came last night," I said. "He was trying to find her. Before. But I can't find him either."

Brody frowned, then stepped inside the house. In the halo of his flashlight, I could see the source of the noise—the papers I'd assumed had scattered across the room.

But it was a deck of cards. I felt the moment Brody registered it. A pause in his movement, in the beam of the light arcing across the space.

I heard the echo of Ian's plea: *Please, stop this—it's torment—*

Russ had been pushing at all of us. Amaya, with the note in our room; Brody, with the deck of cards; Josh, missing his medication, sending him into his own insomnia-triggered spiral. And me, with Clara's necklace. Every memory, everything I believed, taking on a twisted, disturbing meaning instead.

I wondered if Russ had sent a letter to each of them, detailing their own moments of horror—things he must've learned from my journals. I wondered what moment Brody's must've detailed. I closed my eyes, could imagine it well enough: the cards; the way we'd almost dragged him into the river. The way, I was sure, he would never forgive us.

A chill ran through the room—I imagined it running through all of us.

Wind chimes resounded with the breeze, drawing our attention to the back of the house. And there, a silhouette stood in the doorway. Skinny and small, curly hair. Brody shone the light on her, arm out to block the glare.

She was alive, big brown eyes, hollows underneath, slightly unsteady and unfocused.

"Amaya?" I said.

Her gaze sought mine. "I'm sorry," she said. "I'm so sorry." Her words picked up speed. "I tried to come back, but it was too late . . . he was *there*."

I started moving toward her, drawn like a magnet, relief flooding through my veins. "It's okay, I'm just so glad you're okay—"

But her expression had hardened, and she turned her head very slowly, toward something we hadn't noticed just yet.

Then she jolted forward, like she'd tripped, or been pushed.

Russ came in behind her, Brody's light catching on the object in his hand. "Whoa, whoa, what the hell," Brody said, already stepping back.

I heard Oliver curse beside me. Time stilled.

Of course, he had a gun. You could do whatever you wanted when you had a weapon.

My hand instinctively went to my bag, to the knife. I sought it out, making contact, and slowly pulled it out.

Russ looked so different to me than he had a week ago. Now I could see only the common features to Clara. The color of his sandy blond hair, the smile that could light up a room.

He froze when his eyes met mine.

My stomach hollowed out. This man, who I believed would choose me, save me—instead would rather see me suffer.

He opened his mouth, and for a moment I thought he might apologize, try to explain things, tell me something I could believe. But instead he said, "This is how I know someone hurt my sister. You all came."

We'd been lured here—a test, a trap.

"Did you act as a group? Was that it? Part of this pact?" he asked, voice rising. As if he believed we had converged on Clara as a group, forced her over the edge, into the river—

But we were still down a number. "Where's Josh?" I asked.

Amaya made her eyes go wider, just as Russ frowned. "He was less than forthcoming."

A shudder rolled through my body, and I thought I was going to be sick again.

Russ made a face, like he didn't understand my reaction. "He's fine," he said. "I'm not a monster."

Not a monster. As if he wasn't tormenting each of us, one by one. As if he hadn't betrayed me in the worst way possible.

But all I could say, voice scratching against my throat, was "You're holding a gun." How could he claim he *wasn't* a monster right now?

"Amaya," he said, ignoring me, "you can go get him now."

She disappeared out the back door, like she was compelled to obey him. And maybe she was. He had a gun pointed in our direction, vaguely drifting from person to person. It didn't take much more than that implicit threat to our safety.

"Come right back," he called, gesturing the gun toward us a little more assertively.

We waited in silence, hearing the wind chimes, the river, the sound of footsteps in the grass.

Finally, Josh emerged into the room, blinking slowly. He looked like he had when I'd pulled him out of the river. Shocked, slow to react. Hunched over, as if he wasn't sure entirely where he was hurt. "What are you doing here?" he asked.

"They're here to decide on some things," Russ said.

I felt another chill.

"I know what you did." My voice wavered, just as my grip tightened on the knife. "You killed Ian," I said.

I felt everyone's attention turn my way.

"I . . . what?" He shook his head. "I didn't *touch* Ian." And then he gestured at the people beside him. "I didn't hurt Amaya. Didn't hurt Josh."

"You locked me in a fucking shed," Josh said. And he did look hurt, from the way he was holding on to his arm, and the series of scratches along his wrists, his hands. As if he'd been trying to fight his way out of there too. I closed my eyes, imagined him inside the van, fighting and fighting—

"Yeah, well, I didn't leave anyone behind to die, did I?" Russ said.

Hollis flinched, and Oliver looked down. It had never been spoken aloud like that. Never directed at us, in accusation.

"You and Ian, it's on tape," I said. Sometimes, you had to lie. You had to bluff. "He set up a camera in that house, to expose you."

Was this it? The one way out?

But Russ only smiled, a knowing, cruel grin. "I did not hurt him. And if you had it on camera, like you claimed, you would see that. You think I wanted him to die?" He shook his head. "He was a fucking mess, I know that. He was in a bad place, and it only got worse. I told him to take a minute, get a grip on himself . . . but when I came back, I found him out back, exactly where I'd left him. He had fucking overdosed."

"You tried to frame Oliver." At the very *least*, he had done that.

A bark of laughter. "No, I definitely didn't do that either. I brought Ian inside, contacted Oliver—it was his house. I thought Oliver would call it in when he found him. My god, Oliver, really? What is wrong with you all? Oliver knew Ian was supposed to be there, it was in his email. I thought he'd call for *help*."

I heard the echo of what he'd told Ian: *They're all very bad people.*

Even then, maybe he underestimated just how callous and terrible we were, that Oliver would move Ian's body. That he would tell no one. That each of us, in our way, would bury the past so willingly and efficiently.

We'd had a decade of practice. Burying the truth somewhere deep, and never, never looking back. You did it the same way you escaped.

"You lied to me," I said, with more force than I'd managed before. Because wasn't that the worst of it? I'd trusted him, and he'd used me, used all of us.

"I did what I had to do," he said, as if he was appealing to something deep inside all of us.

"No, you didn't have to *do* that."

His gaze turned hard, unfamiliar. "Ian said you wrote the journals. That you trusted him—that he was the *only* one you trusted. That you had been together." A twitch of his lips, as if I could see the pieces lining up. A pattern he would follow. "If you didn't have them still, I figured you could at least tell me what was in them. I needed you to trust me, Cassidy."

The sting of betrayal, the rush of shame. What must Russ have learned about me? What must he have seen? How transparent I must've been. Such an easy mark.

But I thought of what I saw on the camera, the way he had been tormenting Ian, and thought he was motivated by something else. "No, you just wanted to hurt us in the worst way possible."

He blinked slowly, not quite denying it. Maybe he wasn't sure himself. "I just want the truth," he said. "That's all I ever wanted. And finally, I found it." He smiled then, something harsh and knowing. "Want to tell them how I know so much about them, Cassidy?"

I shook my head. Couldn't look at them. "I made it up," I said. I looked at each of them, terrified. I remembered how quickly they'd turned on Ben. How quickly they'd turned on Brody. You want to be on the right side of the numbers. You want to be inside the pact.

"It was just an exercise my therapist suggested," I said desperately. "A way to cope."

"What the fuck, Cassidy? Journals?" Brody said, just as Josh mumbled, "I knew it. I knew it was you."

"No," I said. "No, I didn't mean to. It was something I wrote, for myself." I pointed at Russ, ignoring the gun pointing back. "I had *no* idea who he was. He pretended to be someone he's not, sneaking into my life. Sneaking *through* my life . . . He stole them."

"You wrote it *down*?" Grace asked. "What, exactly, did you *say*, Cassidy?"

I looked at each of them, desperately wanting them to understand. Hollis averted her eyes; everything was shifting. "Please, I just wanted to understand. I needed to try to make sense of what happened that night."

Amaya was staring back at me, stoically. And I wondered if she knew more than she'd ever said too.

"She knows everything about you," Russ said to the others. "Every one of you. But you know what I noticed? In your journals, there's nothing at all about you, Cassidy."

I paused, felt the silence falling around the room.

"I'm there," I said.

I was in the shadows, in the background.

"Cassidy," Oliver said, quietly, tentatively. "What did you *do*?"

"Yes, Cassidy, what *did* you do," Russ repeated. And then, slowly, he asked, "What's that in your hand?" The piece of evidence he'd been looking for, from the start.

"Ian had it," I said, feeling the weight of it in my palm. The power of it.

I felt Grace reaching for it, darkness seeking dark, but I tightened my grip. This was the only proof left, and Ian had kept it safe.

"So now I'll give you all a choice," Russ said. "Tell me who killed Ben, and I'll destroy Cassidy's fine work. We'll never speak of it again." He gestured to the floor. "You can draw cards, for all I care. But one of you is going to pay. For Clara."

But we were a vault, a pact of silence, even now.

"Russ, listen to me, nobody did anything to Clara," Grace said, speaking to him for the first time. I had expected her therapist voice, something calming and rational. But she sounded panicked, desperate.

"Yes, Grace, someone did. Clara was going to tell, and then she died. So many of you were there with her that day. I saw the picture from the one-year anniversary at the memorial. So I'm just trying to find out, which one of you had the most to lose, that you were willing to hurt my sister before she told?" He stared at us, one by one. And then, "Or was it all of you?"

I waited, again, as the silence stretched. Remembered the moment when Ian and I pulled Hollis from the water. When we turned around and saw Ben on the ground, hands pressed to his stomach, in surprise—

"Brody," Grace said, and at first I thought she was calling on him to answer. But his name was a complete sentence. The answer itself. A name given so quickly and readily, as if she'd been waiting all this time.

My head whipped to her, just as Brody said, "No."

"He was so upset. He was so angry at Ben . . ."

"Grace," Amaya said, "what the hell are you doing?"

"Stop this," Brody said, but his voice was wavering. I pictured him as he was that night, drawing the lowest card, a circle of bodies closing in on him, while he scrambled desperately for an exit.

Russ smiled wide, nothing like the man I thought I knew. "But *you* told them that Ben was responsible for the crash, Grace," he said. "So I'd say it was at least partly your fault."

She flinched, clearly surprised. She probably hadn't yet received the letter that was waiting for her. Had no idea the extent of what Russ knew.

"Yes," she conceded, eyes cutting to me. As if she understood now that I was the only one to blame. "And like I said, Brody was very upset."

"Grace, I said stop!" Brody yelled. Like he had that night, as we closed in on him.

"Ian said you were wrong, Grace," Russ interjected. "He said that Ben didn't cause the accident. That there was no reason for him to be killed."

I couldn't imagine the things Russ and Ian might've talked about, before meeting at The Shallows. The things they might've discussed out back, on the patio, when they left the range of the camera. I couldn't imagine what things Ian might've told Russ. The confessions he made.

"Ian didn't know everything," Grace said unconvincingly. She'd been caught off guard, was scrambling to keep up now.

"Maybe not. But he seemed pretty clear on that point. Pretty sure of it. All this death, and for what? Some stupid crush on your teacher?"

All these secrets Grace thought she was keeping. But she raised her voice instead, in defense. "You don't understand. Brody thought Hollis was dead in the other van, and he and Ben got in a fight."

"Grace!" Brody shouted, as if he had any hope of stopping her now.

Hollis turned to stare at Brody, like she was finally understanding something about that night. While she'd been finding her way to safety, he thought she was dead. He thought she was dead until she came upon him, standing over Ben's body—until he finally registered her presence. Turning around, surprised, like he was seeing a ghost.

"We got in a fight, yes," Brody said, "but I didn't hurt him. I didn't. I never had the knife."

I remembered the way he leaned over Ben's body, his blank expression.

"I swear," he continued, "I only pushed him, and the next thing I know, he was bleeding out on the ground. It was so dark. I don't know how it happened, only that it wasn't me."

The last person I saw with the knife that night was Clara, after they got Ben out of the van as it drifted away. But she had adored Ben Weaver.

What had Clara known? Was she, then, the one who knew the truth?

I looked, suddenly, to Grace, eyes locking, darkness seeking dark.

Brody and I must've come to the realization at the same time. Grace was the only person willing to throw out a name.

She had killed Ben. Not just in her lack of action, but with that knife in her hand.

She'd broken the pact, to protect herself.

"What did you do?" I said. In an echo of what she said that night, to Ben.

What did you do, that night. What did you do, when Clara was going to come forward. What did you do, that made your parents cut you out of their lives. What did you do what did you do what did you do—

Russ seemed to understand at the same time. His gaze turned to Grace.

"What did you do to my sister, Grace?" Russ asked.

But she just tilted her head, like she was looking deep into his heart, his soul.

"I didn't *do* anything to her. She did it to herself," Grace answered.

"She was going to the police. She was going to the lawyers," Russ said.

"Yes, yes, she couldn't take it. I know, I was there. We saved her, and for what? For what?" Grace asked, arms out, beseeching us.

"You were with her that night," Russ said. "I know she wouldn't have done that."

Things were spiraling out of control, they were moving too fast, just like they had that night, with no time to think things through.

"But see, that's where you're wrong," Grace said. "I was with her, yes. Which is how I know what happened. I watched her do it."

A chill worked its way from the base of my skull down my spine.

"I made it out there," she said, "just in time. Just like you all ran here. Except that time, I was the only one." An accusation, to deflect from the reality.

"What did you do?" Russ asked, a layer of horror creeping into his voice.

"I didn't know what to say. Didn't know the right things, the right way to convince her . . . to help her. She said she'd gone to the law firm, and instead of helping her, they asked her what she needed."

Amaya sucked in a breath, eyes fixed on Grace.

"She was so upset," Grace continued. "That nothing was happening, that nothing would change. That they would just bury the truth. She didn't *understand.*"

Russ took a step closer, gun trained clearly on Grace. "I'm going to ask you one more time. What did you do to my sister, Grace?"

I saw her throat move as she swallowed, but she held his gaze. Held strong to the moment. Maybe, this time, she would know the right things to say. The right things to do. "Nothing, Russ. I did absolutely nothing."

We stood in silence, shocked. Appalled.

She peered around the circle of us, staring at her in open horror. "Oh, you're all *just* as guilty. None of you stopped her either."

"We weren't there!" Oliver said.

"I know," Grace said, venom in her voice. "I noticed." She narrowed her eyes then. "And so did Clara."

Clara, Ian. We hadn't made it in time for either of them. Had missed the calls for help. Had thought only of ourselves.

"You know the worst of it?" Grace asked, turning things on us instead, doubling down. "Clara *asked* me to do something that night. She had the knife, you know. And when Ben and Brody were fighting, she begged me to do something. She gave it back to me. Said, *Do something, Grace*. It was an accident. I was just trying to get it to stop!"

Grace had killed Ben, and then she followed Clara to the river gorge. She didn't stop her. She watched her die.

"And you never said anything?" Hollis asked.

"Say what, exactly?" Grace shook her head. "My parents knew I had been out that night. They didn't even *ask* me, just told me I should go back to school immediately. If they didn't believe me, what chance did I have?"

"You're telling me the law firm *knew*?" Russ asked, incredulous. "Why the hell would they want to protect *you*?"

I looked to Josh, who had his eyes fixed on Amaya instead.

Amaya, who hadn't budged, but seemed to have become a different person, standing there. She must've understood the truth.

They wanted to protect Amaya.

"Clara was always so kind," Grace said. "Even when she confessed, she was kind. Said that there was a group of us, fighting, before Ben ended up on the ground, bleeding from a knife wound. Me, yes. But also Brody, Amaya . . . and she didn't know what happened."

Amaya sucked in a breath. All eyes turned to her.

"It was an accident, Russ," she said, words spilling out quickly. "I promise. I tried to pull him away from Brody. I jerked him back, and he fell into Grace. But I know how it looks. It looks like I'm an accessory."

And her family had to protect her.

Somehow, I had always worried I was on the outside. That there was another pact within our group. But it went deeper than I imagined: a secret cover-up; a possible cold-blooded murder.

I still didn't know if I believed Ben's death was an accident. I wasn't sure if Clara believed that either.

I could picture, just as easily, Grace following Clara to the river. Arguing, like I'd seen them do that night. Pushing her. The sway of her voice, the force behind her—

I imagined Russ could picture it just as readily.

Russ stepped forward, gestured with his weapon. "Outside," he said.

Grace stared at the rest of us, as if we would stop this. As if we *could*.

Would we watch? Would we watch Russ take his revenge and then go on with our lives? Six of us, finally freed?

"Now," he said.

She put her hands up, confused, eyes wide with shock.

"You wanted the truth, and I gave it to you," she said, as if she were speaking to someone who thought and operated just like her.

Her eyes cut to each of us as she passed, as if we would come to her defense. As if she hadn't thrown Brody's name out there. As if she hadn't been willing to let him take the fall in her place. She'd have done the same to any of us.

I followed them outside, felt the others doing the same. "Russ, stop," I said. This had to stop.

He turned around, shrugged.

"Okay, fair enough," he said. "Call the police. Tell them." *Confess.*

Grace stared back at him, a twitch at the corner of her mouth.

"All this death, because of *you*. So call the police." Russ waited again, the wind chimes rattling. "Tell them what happened because of you!"

Russ swung the gun out to the side, in a wild gesture. And in that moment, I watched as Grace took off, into the distance. Escape—the basest instinct.

She took off toward the path, the group of us scattering after her into the night.

I tried to keep my eyes on her, on Russ. I followed them into the night, into the trees. Saw him catch up with her just ahead, where the steps stretched down into the canyon.

I ran with my arms brushing against branches, the river growing louder. The sound of our escape that night, except this time we were racing toward it.

I slowed as I entered the clearing: they stood at the edge, together. Two shadows, intertwined, so I couldn't tell who was who. Only that they were struggling.

I pictured Brody and Amaya and Grace and Ben in the dark, the chaos, the split-second decisions everyone made. The way nothing was fully clear in hindsight.

"Everyone's dead because of you, Grace," Russ shouted. "You think you don't deserve this?"

But were we really so different? Didn't we believe, at the core, that we were all killers? It was the thing we had in common, that bound us together, in ways big and small. Brody fighting with Ben, until Amaya, and then Grace, put an end to it. Hollis, who had been so desperate to look for the others, at the expense of those who had survived. Oliver, whose series of decisions ultimately led to Jason's senseless death. Joshua, frozen and useless on the riverbank as the rest of his van was swept away. Amaya may have been the one to tell us to leave, but we had each agreed to it. We were all complicit, and we had made that pact because of it.

"It's not her fault," I yelled, over the sound of the wind, the water.

My presence threw something—or someone—off balance. Grace pushed him backward, or Russ lost his footing—I imagined Clara reeling back, arms desperate—and Russ reached an arm out for Grace as the gun went off, to take her with him.

The knife fell from my grip as I lunged for them—like reaching into the river, everything slow motion in the water, begging to connect with another hand. *Please—*

I had someone's hand, in the dark. Felt Grace's body fall on top of mine, both of us slumping to the earth. A scream echoed from below.

Grace pressed her hand to her side, staring up into the night sky. "Oh," she said, as I rolled her onto the rocky earth.

I pressed my hand over hers. "Hold on," I said.

Her panicked eyes sought mine in the night, and I thought she could see straight into the heart of me. All the things I'd done; all the things I'd failed to do.

Really, everything was my fault. Of course all of this was because of me.

THEN

HOUR 1

Cassidy

The trip had been a series of tiny disasters from the start. From the moment my dad had dropped me off, and I'd wondered where to put my bag. Mr. Kates was walking around with a clipboard, tallying off our names, one by one.

He'd done a final count, looking around, and then called, "Paging Cassidy Bent!"

I waited for the count of three; I was right there, in the middle of the group. His eyes skimmed right over me. I'd been in his class all year, sat right beside Grace Langly, watching as she scribbled furiously in her journal during every free write.

"I'm right here," I finally called, making Mr. Kates look twice. It was the same feeling I'd get in my house sometimes, like I moved through spaces unnoticed, invisible.

"Hey, hi," he said, trying to mask his surprise. "You're in the first van."

Joshua Doleman laughed, slung his bag onto his back, then climbed into the van and claimed the back seat as his own.

By the time I filed in, a girl from my history class pushing me backward, so she could take the spot beside her friend, the only open seat I noticed was the one beside Josh, and that barely counted. I had to ask him to move his legs, then carve out a tiny space for myself, wedging a backpack between us to keep the soles of his sneakers from pushing up against my thighs.

I'd spent the majority of the drive like that, trying to make myself small, trying to find a comfortable position.

The claustrophobia set in during the tunnel, the bright headlights like a mirage, shimmering off the walls. The rumble of car engines and this feeling we were still in motion, somehow.

I thought it would get better when we finally made it through, but then there was the dark mountain exit, the winding switchbacks, a depth of darkness, the jarring, snaking motion.

I felt that creeping hot wave of carsickness I hadn't experienced since I was a child. It was the way I was being jostled over the back tire, in the tiny sliver of space not occupied by Joshua Doleman's sleeping body.

Ms. Winslow must've known this was a mistake, but now we were stuck, and there was nowhere to turn around, and so we kept going higher, curves pulling tighter, and the people in front of me kept saying, *I really, really think we should turn around.* And behind me, the headlights of the other van shone straight into the window, disorienting.

"I'm going to be sick," I said, but Josh didn't move, didn't stir. I leaned forward, head on the seat in front of me. "I'm going to be sick," I repeated. And this time, Ian Tayler, who I'd never spoken to before in my life, raised his head from the back of the seat and passed the message forward.

I heard the flashers turning on, a steady blinking, like a warning, and I put my head between my knees, willing myself not to be sick in this van. Eventually we pulled over onto a wide section of shoulder, abutting the forest.

"Five-minute break," Ms. Winslow called. "Stay close."

The van door slid open and half of us climbed out, scattering into the woods.

I ran straight through, as deep as I could get, away from anyone who might notice, before falling onto my knees and losing the entirety of the fast-food dinner I'd grabbed at the last stop, before the traffic jam.

This was not the way I wanted to be remembered. *Cassidy Bent? Who? You remember, the girl who puked her guts up on the side of the road, I had to sit next to her after . . .*

I wiped the back of my hand across my mouth, but still felt too hot, claustrophobic. Humidity hung in the air, fog was lingering in the trees. It felt like the sky was about to burst open. There was a faint rumble in the distance. I placed my cheek down on the colder earth, felt a leaf, damp and cool, against my neck. I took several slow breaths, then turned over, facing up.

And then I heard the crack of a twig. I froze, on high alert. I shifted in that direction to see Grace Langly standing perfectly still, staring at something in the distance. I followed her gaze to where Ben was standing with Mr. Kates. I'd seen the way Grace hung around after his class, recognized her infatuation. But there was something wrong about the way Ben was challenging his teacher, a shift in power.

I tried to back away, but they must've heard me, everyone turning to look. A deer was just to my right—how long had it been standing there? It was so close, close enough that it should've spooked by now. Like something was wrong with it . . .

And then Clara was calling Grace's name, and the deer took off through the trees. I waited for them to leave. Waited for a count of ten before starting to follow them back toward the vans.

But when I stood, I became disoriented. My knees were still wobbly, head spinning slightly. I needed water.

And then I heard it: whispers, escalating voices. I followed the sound, trying to guide my way back, but it was just Brody and Hollis, arguing. The vans were in the background, headlights along the road.

I watched them tracking back toward the vans—a tangible distance between them. I was fascinated by the way Hollis seemed to have seen something new in Brody Ensworth out here. All the things that were only possible when we left the enclosure of school, our long-rehearsed roles, expected places.

I followed them, trailing at a distance, and then the deer crossed in front of my path again, as if I had been invisible even to it.

I paused, staring back, waiting for it to see me, to notice me.

That's when I heard the sound of the van doors sliding shut. The rumbling engines coming to life, as the vans headed down, down, down the road.

Run.

I took off at a sprint. They were leaving, they were *leaving me—*

I cut through the woods, branches snapping around me, tripping, hands braced for impact. Skidding along, begging, *See me, find me, save me.*

I beat them to the next turn, adrenaline coursing through my veins, sliding out into the street first, hands held up, *Here I am, here I am, please see me—*

And then, finally, they did. I saw Mr. Kates through the windshield, the moment his eyes latched on to mine, wild and desperate. I saw the moment his face shifted to horror, the squeal of brakes, the wheel cutting at the same time.

The sound of metal on metal, the first van making contact, hurtling overhead, into the night. The second van pushed through the guardrail, disappearing out of sight.

The horror. The emptiness of the air. Before the sound of a crash—a splash—below.

I ran to the edge, where a metal guardrail had just been, but was now crumpled and twisted.

Run. The voice in my head, the basest instinct.

I fell, I slid, palms and arms against rock and root. I followed them down, down, down. The water was so much colder than I imagined. It stole my breath. I felt the rush of the current, pulling me away.

I saw the headlights bobbing in the water, saw the place I was supposed to be.

I dove straight in.

SUNDAY MIDNIGHT

CHAPTER 22

"Cassidy!" I heard someone calling.

How quickly they could turn on you. How quickly I had always imagined they would, if they knew the truth. I'd seen it happen to Ben.

But also: how quickly they would come to you, if you needed them.

I'd always been afraid of being too invisible. But the real danger was when you finally became wholly visible. When you were finally, finally seen.

I'd always believed Ian knew the truth—the one person who saw something in the road, before the crash. Who said, in his kindness, that it was a deer. And maybe he really had thought it at first, until he had to revisit the moment, as we all did, and his memory clarified, sharpened. He saw something out there, but I had saved him, and he didn't want to say what it was that he saw.

But it was me. I knew—he had seen me.

"Paging Cassidy Bent!"

I recognized the voice. Joshua Doleman, of all people.

"Here! We're here!" I said.

I held on to Grace as we waited for help, felt her breath coming slow and labored.

Brody's flashlight finally swung onto us, illuminating the scene.

"Oh my god," Josh said.

I didn't need to say it—I was sure they could see the horror in my eyes. There was so much blood.

Brody dropped to his knees on the other side of Grace, issuing commands—to me, to her. "Hold on," he said. Even then. "Hold on, Grace."

I finally registered Hollis's voice in the background, on the phone begging for help. "We're at the Stone River Gorge . . . we're at . . . Amaya, where are we?"

Amaya took the phone then, while Hollis came to our side.

"Grace," she said, repeating her name. A question, an answer.

"Where is he?" Oliver asked, spinning in a circle, as if he could defend us if only he could see it coming now.

"He's gone," I said. I'd heard the scream. There are some things you hear, and you remember, forever.

"Don't tell," Grace whispered. "Please don't tell."

• • •

In the end, we made a new pact.

Because you could not pull one thread without unraveling all the rest. Because we all, a decade later, had too much at stake.

But if you believed in fate, and I did—even after everything, I did—then at some point you had to believe you found each other for a reason. That each person contributed to another's rescue. An arm, catching you as you slipped on the climb; a hand, reaching out into the river; the light of a flare, guiding you back.

We were, to one another, both a reminder of the worst night of our lives and evidence of the greatest thing we had ever done.

We did not take either of those things lightly.

• • •

When the police arrived on the scene—one woman with a gunshot wound, one man fallen over the edge, search crews out there now, but we all knew it was too late—we stuck to our lines. We were good at this.

It was mostly truth: Amaya told us how Russ had stalked us on our vacation. He'd been at the motel—but had used the campgrounds as a cut-through to watch us. And she saw him, couldn't figure out how such a coincidence would happen: *Russ? Is that you?*

Trapping herself.

How he used the threat of violence against the rest of us to keep her quiet. And then lured the rest of us back here with a text for help from Amaya's phone.

The easiest thing to say was that he was obsessed with us, and angry, so angry, his grief twisting him, emerging as something else. His sister neither survivor nor victim. There was no name on a plaque, no improbable payout for her loss, no person still alive.

I remained out back, while they brought Grace to the ambulance, assuring us she was going to be okay. I retraced my steps, back and forth, but I couldn't find the knife.

When I turned back for the house, Oliver was standing there, watching me, hands deep in his pockets.

"It's gone," he said, an echo of what I'd said about Russ. I imagined him tossing it into the river. Imagined it churned up in the silt, trapped in an eddy against the rocks—something that might be found days from now; weeks; years. Just an old knife, with a rusted edge, a faded crown on the handle.

All evidence, wiped clean by the river.

There was only one more thing on my list: the journals. I had to hope Russ wouldn't leave them far from his reach—the same instinct that had led me to keep them close, for a decade.

I found his car in Amaya's garage, while the police were still interviewing the last of us out front. Found the journals, small and tattered, in a sealed plastic bag inside his trunk. I felt a pull, to open them, read them, after all this time. To see if our story was the same as how I remembered it—remembered them.

But I owed it to them to destroy the evidence, to do what I promised: leave the past to the past, and never look back.

• • •

I joined the others on the front drive, as we watched the lights of the emergency vehicles disappearing down the mountain road.

Brody sat beside me on the pavement. The others moved closer—Josh and Oliver, sitting on the curb, Amaya and Hollis, standing nearby, watching the ambulance lights, glowing like a flare over the trees, somewhere in the distance.

Josh rubbed the side of his chin, a streak of mud sliding along his skin. "I don't know what to think, about Grace. About how Clara died."

I felt he was asking a question, but I didn't respond.

Did she do it? I could never be sure.

Did I believe her? That was a different question.

We knew deeper things, darker things, better things about one another now. We had been changed—we had changed ourselves.

Amaya, spending her life atoning for her role in Ben's death and for bringing us all on that trip. For not being able to save the rest.

Brody, making a career of saving the lives of strangers.

Grace, like them, had dedicated herself to helping others. An atonement, I chose to believe, for not knowing how to save Clara.

There are things you have to do to survive, and there are things you have to believe too—and this was one of them.

"Did she push Russ?" Hollis asked.

"I don't know," I said. "It was so dark, I could only reach one."

Now I reached out for Brody's hand in the dark—the closest person to me—and closed my fingers around his, felt the blood pulsing through both of us.

You picked a side. You chose. You let someone go, to let someone else live.

I owed them. Because they were all, after what happened, my responsibility. Everyone they became was ultimately because of me.

Who do you save in the moment, when you have the chance? The answer was simple, and obvious, and always, always the same: whoever you can.

ACKNOWLEDGMENTS

Thank you to the wonderful group of people who helped guide this story from the initial spark of an idea to the finished book:

I am so grateful for the brilliant guidance and insight from my editor, Marysue Rucci, and agent, Jennifer Joel, on each and every draft. Thank you also to the entire team at Marysue Rucci Books and Scribner, including Nan Graham, Stu Smith, Brian Belfiglio, Katie Monaghan, Clare Maurer, Brianna Yamashita, Andy Tang, Jaya Miceli, Laura Wise, and many others who have had a hand in bringing this book into the world. It's such a pleasure getting to work with you all.

Thank you to fantastic friends and critique partners, Elle Cosimano, Ashley Elston, and Megan Shepherd, for all the feedback, brainstorming sessions, and encouragement along the way.

As always, thank you to my family, who found that phone on the beach, and then brought it back to life—setting the idea for this mystery into motion. This story would not have existed without you.

Lastly, to all the readers—thank you.

ABOUT THE AUTHOR

Megan Miranda is the *New York Times* bestselling author of *All the Missing Girls*; *The Perfect Stranger*; *The Last House Guest*, a Reese Witherspoon Book Club pick; *The Girl from Widow Hills*; *Such a Quiet Place*; and *The Last to Vanish*. She has also written several books for young adults. She grew up in New Jersey, graduated from MIT, and lives in North Carolina with her husband and two children. Follow @MeganLMiranda on Twitter and Instagram, @AuthorMeganMiranda on Facebook, and visit MeganMiranda.com.